The Waves

The Waves

VIRGINIA
WOOLF

Annotated and with an introduction
by Molly Hite

Mark Hussey, General Editor

A Harvest Book • Harcourt, Inc.
Orlando Austin New York San Diego Toronto London

www.HarcourtBooks.com

Library of Congress Cataloging-in-Publication Data
Woolf, Virginia, 1882–1941.
The waves/Virginia Woolf; annotated and with an introduction by Molly Hite;
Mark Hussey, general editor.—Annotated ed., 1st ed.
p.   cm.—(A Harvest Book)
Includes bibliographical references.
1. Identity (Psychology)—Fiction.   2. Friendship—Fiction.   3. Psychological fiction.
I. Hite, Molly, 1947–   II. Mark Hussey, 1956–   III. Title.
PR6045.O72W3   2006
823'.912—dc22   2005037770
ISBN-13: 978-0-15-603157-8   ISBN-10: 0-15-603157-4

Text set in Garamond MT
Designed by Cathy Riggs

Printed in the United States of America

First edition
DOM 10 9 8 7 6 5

CONTENTS

The Waves

VIRGINIA WOOLF

VIRGINIA WOOLF was born into what she once described as "a very communicative, literate, letter writing, visiting, articulate, late nineteenth century world." Her parents, Leslie and Julia Stephen, both previously widowed, began their marriage in 1878 with four young children: Laura (1870–1945), the daughter of Leslie Stephen and his first wife, Harriet Thackeray (1840–1875); and George (1868–1934), Gerald (1870–1937), and Stella Duckworth (1869–1897), the children of Julia Prinsep (1846–1895) and Herbert Duckworth (1833–1870). In the first five years of their marriage, the Stephens had four more children. Their third child, Virginia, was born in 1882, the year her father began work on the monumental *Dictionary of National Biography* that would earn him a knighthood in 1902. Virginia, her sister, Vanessa (1879–1961), and brothers, Thoby (1880–1906) and Adrian (1883–1948), all were born in the tall house at 22 Hyde Park Gate in London where the eight children lived with numerous servants, their eminent and irascible father, and their beautiful mother, who, in Woolf's words, was "in the very centre of that great Cathedral space that was childhood."

Woolf's parents knew many of the intellectual luminaries of the late Victorian era well, counting among their close friends novelists such as George Meredith, Thomas Hardy, and Henry James. Woolf's great-aunt Julia Margaret Cameron was a pioneering photographer who made portraits of the poets Alfred

Tennyson and Robert Browning, of the naturalist Charles Darwin, and of the philosopher and historian Thomas Carlyle, among many others. Beginning in the year Woolf was born, the entire Stephen family moved to Talland House in St. Ives, Cornwall, for the summer. There the younger children would spend their days playing cricket in the garden, frolicking on the beach, or taking walks along the coast, from where they could look out across the bay to the Godrevy lighthouse.

The early years of Woolf's life were marred by traumatic events. When she was thirteen, her mother, exhausted by a punishing schedule of charitable visits among the sick and poor, died from a bout of influenza. Woolf's half sister Stella took over the household responsibilities and bore the brunt of their self-pitying father's sorrow until she escaped into marriage in 1897 with Jack Hills, a young man who had been a favorite of Julia's. Within three months, Stella (who was pregnant) was dead, most likely from peritonitis. In this year, which she called "the first really *lived* year of my life," Woolf began a diary. Over the next twelve years, she would record in its pages her voracious reading, her impressions of people and places, feelings about her siblings, and events in the daily life of the large household.[1]

In addition to the premature deaths of her mother and half sister, there were other miseries in Woolf's childhood. In autobiographical writings and letters, Woolf referred to the sexual abuse she suffered at the hands of her two older half brothers, George and Gerald Duckworth. George, in one instance, explained his behavior to a family doctor as his effort to comfort his half sister for the fatal illness of their father. Sir Leslie died

---

[1]Woolf's early diary is published as *A Passionate Apprentice: The Early Journals, 1897–1909*, edited by Mitchell A. Leaska. A 1909 notebook discovered in 2002 has been published as *Carlyle's House and Other Sketches*, edited by David Bradshaw (London: Hesperus, 2003).

from cancer in 1904, and shortly thereafter the four Stephen children—Vanessa, Virginia, Thoby, and Adrian—moved together to the then-unfashionable London neighborhood of Bloomsbury. When Thoby Stephen began to bring his Cambridge University friends to the house on Thursday evenings, what would later become famous as the "Bloomsbury Group" began to form.

In an article marking the centenary of her father's birth, Woolf recalled his "allowing a girl of fifteen the free run of a large and quite unexpurgated library"—an unusual opportunity for a Victorian young woman, and evidence of the high regard Sir Leslie had for his daughter's intellectual talents. In her diary, she recorded the many different kinds of books her father recommended to her—biographies and memoirs, philosophy, history, and poetry. Although he believed that women should be "as well educated as men," Woolf's mother held that "to serve is the fulfilment of women's highest nature." The young Stephen children were first taught at home by their mother and father, with little success. Woolf herself received no formal education beyond some classes in Greek and Latin in the Ladies' Department of King's College in London, beginning in the fall of 1897. In 1899 she began lessons in Greek with Clara Pater, sister of the renowned Victorian critic Walter Pater, and in 1902 she was tutored in the classics by Janet Case (who also later involved her in work for women's suffrage). Such homeschooling was a source of some bitterness later in her life, as she recognized the advantages that derived from the expensive educations her brothers and half brothers received at private schools and university. Yet she also realized that her father's encouragement of her obviously keen intellect had given her an eclectic foundation. In the early years of Bloomsbury, she reveled in the opportunity to discuss ideas with her brother Thoby and his friends, among whom were Lytton Strachey, Clive Bell, and

E. M. Forster. From them, she heard, too, about an intense young man named Leonard Woolf, whom she had met briefly when visiting Thoby at Cambridge, and also in 1904 when he came to dinner at Gordon Square just before leaving for Ceylon (now called Sri Lanka), where he was to administer a far-flung outpost of the British Empire.

Virginia Woolf's first publications were unsigned reviews and essays in an Anglo-Catholic newspaper called the *Guardian,* beginning in December 1904. In the fall of 1906, she and Vanessa went with a family friend, Violet Dickinson, to meet their brothers in Greece. The trip was spoiled by Vanessa's falling ill, and when she returned to London, Virginia found both her brother Thoby—who had returned earlier—and her sister seriously ill. After a misdiagnosis by his doctors, Thoby died from typhoid fever on November 20, leaving Virginia to maintain a cheerful front while her sister and Violet Dickinson recovered from their own illnesses. Two days after Thoby's death, Vanessa agreed to marry his close friend Clive Bell.

While living in Bloomsbury, Woolf had begun to write a novel that would go through many drafts before it was published in 1915 as *The Voyage Out.* In these early years of independence, her social circle widened. She became close to the art critic Roger Fry, organizer of the First Post-Impressionist Exhibition in London in 1910, and also entered the orbit of the famed literary hostess Lady Ottoline Morrell (cruelly caricatured as Hermione Roddice in D. H. Lawrence's 1920 novel *Women in Love*). Her political consciousness also began to emerge. In 1910 she volunteered for the movement for women's suffrage. She also participated that February in a daring hoax that embarrassed the British Navy and led to questions being asked in the House of Commons: She and her brother Adrian, together with some other Cambridge friends, gained access to a secret warship by dressing up and posing as the Emperor of Abyssinia and his retinue. The "Dreadnought Hoax" was front-page news, complete with photographs of the phony Ethiopians with flowing robes, blackened faces, and false beards.

To the British establishment, one of the most embarrassing aspects of the Dreadnought affair was that a woman had taken part in the hoax. Vanessa Bell was concerned at what might have happened to her sister had she been discovered on the ship. She was also increasingly worried about Virginia's erratic health, and by the early summer 1910 had discussed with Dr. George Savage, one of the family's doctors, the debilitating headaches her sister suffered; Dr. Savage prescribed several weeks in a nursing home. Another element in Vanessa's concern was that Virginia was twenty-eight and still unmarried. Clive Bell and Virginia had, in fact, engaged in a hurtful flirtation soon after the birth of Vanessa's first child in 1908. Although she had been proposed to twice in 1909 and once in 1911, Virginia had not taken these offers very seriously.

Dropping by Vanessa's house on a July evening in 1911, Virginia met Leonard Woolf, recently back on leave from Ceylon. Soon after this, Leonard became a lodger at the house Virginia shared with Adrian, the economist John Maynard Keynes, and the painter Duncan Grant. Leonard decided to resign from the Colonial Service, hoping that Virginia would agree to marry him. After some considerable hesitation, she did, and they married in August 1912.

By the end of that year, Woolf was again suffering from the tremendous headaches that afflicted her throughout her life, and in 1913 she was again sent to a nursing home for what was then called a "rest cure." In September of that year, she took an overdose of a sleeping drug and was under care until the following spring. In early 1915 she suffered a severe breakdown and was ill throughout most of the year in which her first novel was published.

Despite this difficult beginning, Virginia and Leonard Woolf's marriage eventually settled into a pattern of immense productivity and mutual support. Leonard worked for a time for the Women's Cooperative Guild, and became increasingly involved with advising the Labour Party and writing on international politics, as well as editing several periodicals. Virginia began to establish herself as an important novelist and influential critic. In 1917 the Woolfs set up their own publishing house, the Hogarth Press, in their home in Richmond. Their first publication was *Two Stories*—Leonard's "Three Jews" and Virginia's experimental "The Mark on the Wall." They had decided to make their livings by writing, and in 1919, a few months before Woolf's second novel, *Night and Day,* was published, they bought a cottage in the village of Rodmell in Sussex. After moving back into London from Richmond in 1923, Woolf would spend summers at Monk's House, returning to the social whirl of the city in the fall.

"The Mark on the Wall" was one of a number of what Woolf called "sketches" that she began to write around the time she and Leonard bought their printing press. *Night and Day* was the last of her books to be published in England by another press. In 1919 Hogarth published her short story *Kew Gardens,* with two woodcuts by Vanessa Bell, and two years later came *Monday or Tuesday,* the only collection of her short fiction published in Woolf's lifetime. Her next novel was *Jacob's Room* (1922), a slim elegy to the generation of 1914, and to her beloved brother Thoby, whose life of great promise had also been cut short so suddenly. Woolf had written to her friend Margaret Llewelyn Davies in 1916 that the Great War, as it was then called, was a "preposterous masculine fiction" that made her "steadily more feminist," and in her fiction and nonfiction she began to articulate and illuminate the connections between the patriarchal status quo, the relatively subordinate position of

women, and war making. Thinking about a novel she was calling "The Hours," Woolf wrote in her diary in 1923 that she
wanted to criticize "the social system." Her inclusion in the
novel of a shell-shocked war veteran named Septimus Warren
Smith would confuse many of the early reviewers of her fourth
novel, *Mrs. Dalloway* (1925), but others recognized that Woolf
was breaking new ground in the way she rendered consciousness and her understanding of human subjectivity.

By the time she wrote *Mrs. Dalloway,* Woolf was also a sought-
after essayist and reviewer who, like many of her celebrated
contemporaries, was staking out her own particular piece of
modernist territory. The Hogarth Press published radical young
writers like Katherine Mansfield, T. S. Eliot, and Gertrude Stein.
Approached by Harriet Shaw Weaver with part of the manuscript of James Joyce's *Ulysses* in 1918, the Woolfs turned it down.
Their own small press could not cope with the long and complex manuscript, nor could Leonard Woolf find a commercial
printer willing to risk prosecution for obscenity by producing it.
In 1924 the Hogarth Press became the official English publisher
of the works of Sigmund Freud, translated by Lytton Strachey's
brother James. Woolf's own literary criticism was collected in a
volume published in 1925, *The Common Reader*—a title signaling
her distrust of academics and love of broad, eclectic reading.

The staggering range of Woolf's reading is reflected in the
more than five hundred essays and reviews she published during her lifetime. Her critical writing is concerned not only with
the canonical works of English literature from Chaucer to her
contemporaries, but also ranges widely through lives of the obscure, memoirs, diaries, letters, and biographies. Models of the
form, her essays comprise a body of work that has only recently
begun to attract the kind of recognition her fiction has received.

In 1922 Woolf met "the lovely and gifted aristocrat" Vita
Sackville-West, already a well-known poet and novelist. Their

close friendship slowly turned into a love affair, glowing most intensely from about 1925 to 1928, before modulating into friendship once more in the 1930s. The period of their intimacy was extremely creative for both writers, Woolf publishing essays such as "Mr. Bennett and Mrs. Brown" and "Letter to a Young Poet," as well as three very different novels: *To the Lighthouse* (1927), which evoked her own childhood and had at its center the figure of a modernist woman artist, Lily Briscoe; *Orlando* (1928), a fantastic biography inspired by Vita's own remarkable family history; and *The Waves* (1931), a mystical and profoundly meditative work that pushed Woolf's concept of novel form to its limit. Woolf also published a second *Common Reader* in 1932, and the "biography" of *Flush,* Elizabeth Barrett Browning's dog (1933). She went with Sackville-West to Cambridge in the fall of 1928 to deliver the second of the two lectures on which her great feminist essay *A Room of One's Own* (1929) is based.

As the political situation in Europe in the 1930s moved inexorably to its crisis in 1939, Woolf began to collect newspaper clippings about the relations between the sexes in England, France, Germany, and Italy. The scrapbooks she made became the matrix from which developed the perspectives of her penultimate novel, *The Years* (1937), and the arguments of her pacifist-feminist polemic *Three Guineas* (1938). In 1937 Vanessa's eldest son, Julian Bell, was killed serving as an ambulance driver in the Spanish Civil War. Woolf later wrote to Vanessa that she had written *Three Guineas* partly as an argument with Julian. Her work on *The Years* was grindingly slow and difficult. Ironically, given Woolf's reputation as a highbrow, it became a bestseller in the United States, even being published in an Armed Services edition. While she labored over the novel in 1934, the news came of the death of Roger Fry, one of her oldest and closest friends and the former lover of her sister, Vanessa. Reluctantly,

given her distaste for the conventions of biography, Woolf
agreed to write his life, which was published in 1940.

In 1939, to relieve the strain of writing Fry's biography,
Woolf began to write a memoir, "A Sketch of the Past," which
remained unpublished until 1976, when the manuscripts were
edited by Jeanne Schulkind for a collection of Woolf's autobiographical writings, *Moments of Being*. Withdrawing with Leonard
to Monk's House in Sussex, where they could see the German
airplanes flying low overhead on their way to bomb London,
Woolf continued to write for peace and correspond with anti-
war activists in Europe and the United States. She began to
write her last novel, *Between the Acts,* in the spring of 1938, but
by early 1941 was dissatisfied with it. Before completing her
final revisions, Woolf ended her own life, walking into the River
Ouse on the morning of March 28, 1941. To her sister, Vanessa,
she wrote, "I can hardly think clearly any more. If I could I
would tell you what you and the children have meant to me. I
think you know." In her last note to Leonard, she told him he
had given her "complete happiness," and asked him to destroy
all her papers.

BY THE END of the twentieth century, Virginia Woolf had become an iconic figure, a touchstone for the feminism that re-
vived in the 1960s as well as for the conservative backlash of
the 1980s. Hailed by many as a radical writer of genius, she has
also been dismissed as a narrowly focused snob. Her image
adorns T-shirts, postcards, and even a beer advertisement, while
phrases from her writings occur in all kinds of contexts, from
peace-march slogans to highbrow book reviews. That Woolf is
one of those figures upon whom the myriad competing narratives of twentieth- and twenty-first-century Western culture in-
scribe themselves is testified to by the enormous number of

biographical works about her published in the decades since her nephew Quentin Bell broke the ground in 1972 with his two-volume biography of his aunt.

Argument continues about the work and life of Virginia Woolf: about her experience of incest, her madness, her class attitudes, her sexuality, the difficulty of her prose, her politics, her feminism, and her legacy. Perhaps, though, these words from her essay "How Should One Read a Book?" are our best guide: "The only advice, indeed, that one person can give another about reading is to take no advice, to follow your own instincts, to use your own reason, to come to your own conclusions."

—MARK HUSSEY, GENERAL EDITOR

CHRONOLOGY

Information is arranged in this order: 1. Virginia Woolf's family and her works; 2. Cultural and political events; 3. Significant publications and works of art.

1878   Marriage of Woolf's parents, Leslie Stephen (1832–1904) and Julia Prinsep Duckworth (née Jackson) (1846–1895). Leslie Stephen publishes *Samuel Johnson*, first volume in the English Men of Letters series.
England at war in Afghanistan.

1879   Vanessa Stephen (Bell) born (d. 1961). Edward Burne-Jones paints Julia Stephen as the Virgin Mary in *The Annunciation*. Leslie Stephen, *Hours in a Library*, 3rd series.
Somerville and Lady Margaret Hall Colleges for women founded at Oxford University.
Anglo-Zulu war in South Africa.

1880   Thoby Stephen born (d. 1906).
William Gladstone becomes prime minister for second time. First Boer War begins (1880–81). Deaths of Gustave Flaubert (b. 1821) and George Eliot (b. 1819). Lytton Strachey born (d. 1932).
Fyodor Dostoyevsky, *The Brothers Karamazov*.

1881   Leslie Stephen buys lease of Talland House, St. Ives, Cornwall.

Cambridge University Tripos exams opened to women. Henrik Ibsen, *Ghosts;* Henry James, *The Portrait of a Lady, Washington Square;* Christina Rossetti, *A Pageant and Other Poems;* D. G. Rossetti, *Ballads and Sonnets;* Oscar Wilde, *Poems.*

1882   Adeline Virginia Stephen (Virginia Woolf) born January 25. Leslie Stephen begins work as editor of the *Dictionary of National Biography* (*DNB*); publishes *The Science of Ethics.* The Stephen family spends its first summer at Talland House.

Married Women's Property Act enables women to buy, sell, and own property and keep their own earnings. Triple Alliance between Germany, Italy, and Austria. Phoenix Park murders of British officials in Dublin, Ireland. James Joyce born (d. 1941). Death of Charles Darwin (b. 1809).

1883   Adrian Leslie Stephen born (d. 1948). Julia Stephen's *Notes from Sick Rooms* published.

Olive Schreiner, *The Story of an African Farm;* Robert Louis Stevenson, *Treasure Island.*

1884   Leslie Stephen delivers the Clark Lectures at Cambridge University.

Third Reform Act extends the franchise in England. Friedrich Engels, *The Origin of the Family, Private Property and the State;* John Ruskin, *The Storm-Cloud of the Nineteenth Century;* Mark Twain, *The Adventures of Huckleberry Finn.*

1885 First volume of Leslie Stephen's *Dictionary of National Biography* published.

Redistribution Act further extends the franchise in England. Ezra Pound born (d. 1972); D. H. Lawrence born (d. 1930).

George Meredith, *Diana of the Crossways;* Émile Zola, *Germinal.*

1887 Queen Victoria's Golden Jubilee.

Arthur Conan Doyle, *A Study in Scarlet;* H. Rider Haggard, *She;* Thomas Hardy, *The Woodlanders.*

1891 Leslie Stephen gives up the *DNB* editorship. Laura Stephen (1870–1945) is placed in an asylum.

William Gladstone elected prime minister of England a fourth time.

Thomas Hardy, *Tess of the D'Urbervilles;* Oscar Wilde, *The Picture of Dorian Gray.*

1895 Death of Julia Stephen.

Armenian Massacres in Turkey. Discovery of X-rays by William Röntgen; Guglielmo Marconi discovers radio; invention of the cinematograph. Trials of Oscar Wilde.

Thomas Hardy, *Jude the Obscure;* H. G. Wells, *The Time Machine;* Oscar Wilde, *The Importance of Being Earnest.*

1896 Vanessa Stephen begins drawing classes three afternoons a week.

Death of William Morris (b. 1834); F. Scott Fitzgerald born (d. 1940).

Anton Chekhov, *The Seagull.*

1897   Woolf attends Greek and history classes at King's College, London, and begins to keep a regular diary. Vanessa, Virginia, and Thoby watch Queen Victoria's Diamond Jubilee procession. Stella Duckworth (b. 1869) marries Jack Hills in April, but dies in July. Gerald Duckworth (1870–1937) establishes a publishing house.
   · Paul Gauguin, *Where Do We Come From? What Are We? Where Are We Going?;* Bram Stoker, *Dracula.*

1898   Spanish-American War (1898–99). Marie Curie discovers radium. Death of Stéphane Mallarmé (b. 1842).
   H. G. Wells, *The War of the Worlds;* Oscar Wilde, *The Ballad of Reading Gaol.*

1899   Woolf begins Latin and Greek lessons with Clara Pater. Thoby Stephen goes up to Trinity College, Cambridge University, entering with Lytton Strachey, Leonard Woolf (1880–1969), and Clive Bell (1881–1964).
   The Second Boer War begins (1899–1902) in South Africa. Ernest Hemingway born (d. 1961).

1900   Woolf and Vanessa attend the Trinity College Ball at Cambridge University.
   Deaths of Friedrich Nietzsche (b. 1844), John Ruskin (b. 1819), and Oscar Wilde (b. 1854).
   Sigmund Freud, *The Interpretation of Dreams.*

1901   Vanessa enters Royal Academy Schools.
   Queen Victoria dies January 22. Edward VII becomes king. Marconi sends messages by wireless telegraphy from Cornwall to Newfoundland.

1902   Woolf begins classics lessons with Janet Case. Adrian Stephen enters Trinity College, Cambridge University. Leslie Stephen is knighted.

Joseph Conrad, *Heart of Darkness;* Henry James, *The Wings of the Dove;* William James, *The Varieties of Religious Experience.*

1903   The Wright Brothers fly a biplane 852 feet. Women's Social and Political Union founded in England by Emmeline Pankhurst.

1904   Sir Leslie Stephen dies. George Duckworth (1868–1934) marries Lady Margaret Herbert. The Stephen children—Vanessa, Virginia, Thoby, and Adrian—move to 46 Gordon Square, in the Bloomsbury district of London. Woolf contributes to F. W. Maitland's biography of her father. Leonard Woolf comes to dine before sailing for Ceylon. Woolf travels in Italy and France. Her first publication is an unsigned review in the *Guardian,* a church weekly.

"Empire Day" inaugurated in London and in Britain's colonies.

Anton Chekhov, *The Cherry Orchard;* Henry James, *The Golden Bowl.*

1905   Woolf begins teaching weekly adult education classes at Morley College. Thoby invites Cambridge friends to their home for "Thursday Evenings"—the beginnings of the Bloomsbury Group. Woolf travels with Adrian to Portugal and Spain. The Stephens visit Cornwall for the first time since their mother's death.

Revolution in Russia.

Albert Einstein, *Special Theory of Relativity;* E. M. Forster, *Where Angels Fear to Tread;* Sigmund Freud, *Essays in the Theory of Sexuality;* Edith Wharton, *The House of Mirth;* Oscar Wilde, *De Profundis.*

1906   The Stephens travel to Greece. Vanessa and Thoby fall ill. Thoby dies November 20; on November 22, Vanessa agrees to marry Clive Bell.
Deaths of Paul Cézanne (b. 1839) and Henrik Ibsen (b. 1828). Samuel Beckett born (d. 1989).

1907   Woolf moves with her brother Adrian to Fitzroy Square. Vanessa marries Clive Bell.
First Cubist exhibition in Paris. W. H. Auden born (d. 1973).
Joseph Conrad, *The Secret Agent;* E. M. Forster, *The Longest Journey;* Edmund Gosse, *Father and Son;* Pablo Picasso, *Demoiselles d'Avignon.*

1908   Birth of Vanessa Bell's first child, Julian. Woolf travels to Italy with Vanessa and Clive Bell.
Herbert Asquith becomes prime minister.
E. M. Forster, *A Room with a View;* Gertrude Stein, *Three Lives.*

1909   Woolf receives a legacy of £2,500 on the death of her Quaker aunt, Caroline Emelia Stephen. Lytton Strachey proposes marriage to Woolf, but they both quickly realize this would be a mistake. Woolf meets Lady Ottoline Morrell for the first time. She travels to the Wagner festival in Bayreuth.
Chancellor of the Exchequer David Lloyd George (1863–1945) introduces a "People's Budget," taxing

wealth to pay for social reforms. A constitutional crisis
ensues when the House of Lords rejects it. Death of
George Meredith (b. 1828).

Filippo Marinetti, "The Founding and Manifesto of Fu-
turism"; Henri Matisse, *Dance.*

1910   Woolf participates in the Dreadnought Hoax. She volunteers for the cause of women's suffrage. Birth of
Vanessa Bell's second child, Quentin (d. 1996).

First Post-Impressionist Exhibition ("Manet and the
Post-Impressionists") organized by Roger Fry (1866–
1934) at the Grafton Galleries in London. Edward VII
dies May 6. George V becomes king. Death of Leo Tol-
stoy (b. 1828).

E. M. Forster, *Howards End;* Igor Stravinsky, *The Fire-
bird.*

1911   Woolf rents Little Talland House in Sussex. Leonard
Woolf returns from Ceylon; in November, he, Adrian
Stephen, John Maynard Keynes (1883–1946), Woolf,
and Duncan Grant (1885–1978) share a house together
at Brunswick Square in London.

Ernest Rutherford makes first model of atomic structure.
Rupert Brooke, *Poems;* Joseph Conrad, *Under Western
Eyes;* D. H. Lawrence, *The White Peacock;* Katherine
Mansfield, *In a German Pension;* Ezra Pound, *Canzoni;*
Edith Wharton, *Ethan Frome.*

1912   Woolf leases Asheham House in Sussex. Marries
Leonard on August 10; they move to Clifford's Inn,
London.

Captain Robert Scott's expedition reaches the South
Pole, but he and his companions die on the return

journey. The *Titanic* sinks. Second Post-Impression-
ist Exhibition, for which Leonard Woolf serves as
secretary.
Marcel Duchamp, *Nude Descending a Staircase;* Wassily
Kandinsky, *Concerning the Spiritual in Art;* Thomas
Mann, *Death in Venice;* George Bernard Shaw, *Pygmalion.*

1913   *The Voyage Out* manuscript delivered to Gerald Duckworth. Woolf enters a nursing home in July; in September, she attempts suicide.
Roger Fry founds the Omega Workshops.
Sigmund Freud, *Totem and Taboo;* D. H. Lawrence, *Sons
and Lovers;* Marcel Proust, *Du côté de chez Swann;* Igor
Stravinsky, *Le Sacre du printemps.*

1914   Leonard Woolf, *The Wise Virgins;* he reviews Freud's
The Psychopathology of Everyday Life.
World War I ("The Great War") begins in August.
Home Rule Bill for Ireland passed.
Clive Bell, *Art;* James Joyce, *Dubliners;* Wyndham Lewis
et al., "Vorticist Manifesto" (in *Blast*); Gertrude Stein,
Tender Buttons.

1915   *The Voyage Out,* Woolf's first novel, published by Duck-
worth. In April the Woolfs move to Hogarth House in
Richmond. Woolf begins again to keep a regular diary.
First Zeppelin attack on London. Death of Rupert
Brooke (b. 1887).
Joseph Conrad, *Victory;* Ford Madox Ford, *The Good Sol-
dier;* D. H. Lawrence, *The Rainbow;* Dorothy Richardson,
Pointed Roofs.

1916   Woolf discovers Charleston, where her sister, Vanessa (no longer living with her husband, Clive), moves in October with her sons, Julian and Quentin, and Duncan Grant (with whom she is in love) and David Garnett (with whom Duncan is in love).

Easter Rising in Dublin. Death of Henry James (b. 1843).

Albert Einstein, *General Theory of Relativity;* James Joyce, *A Portrait of the Artist as a Young Man;* Dorothy Richardson, *Backwater.*

1917   The Hogarth Press established by Leonard and Virginia Woolf in Richmond. Their first publication is their own *Two Stories,* with woodcuts by Dora Carrington (1893–1932).

Russian Bolshevik Revolution destroys the rule of the czar. The United States enters the European war.

T. S. Eliot, *Prufrock and Other Observations;* Sigmund Freud, *Introduction to Psychoanalysis;* Carl Jung, *The Unconscious;* Dorothy Richardson, *Honeycomb;* W. B. Yeats, *The Wild Swans at Coole.*

1918   Woolf meets T. S. Eliot (1888–1965). Harriet Shaw Weaver comes to tea with the manuscript of James Joyce's *Ulysses.* Vanessa Bell and Duncan Grant's daughter, Angelica Garnett, born; her paternity is kept secret from all but a very few intimates.

Armistice signed November 11; Parliamentary Reform Act gives votes in Britain to women of thirty and older and to all men.

G. M. Hopkins, *Poems;* James Joyce, *Exiles;* Katherine Mansfield, *Prelude* (Hogarth Press); Marcel Proust, *À l'ombre des jeunes filles en fleurs;* Lytton Strachey, *Eminent Victorians;* Rebecca West, *The Return of the Soldier.*

1919 The Woolfs buy Monk's House in Sussex. Woolf's second novel, *Night and Day,* is published by Duckworth. Her essay "Modern Novels" (republished in 1925 as "Modern Fiction") appears in the *Times Literary Supplement; Kew Gardens* published by Hogarth Press.

Bauhaus founded by Walter Gropius in Weimar. Sex Disqualification (Removal) Act opens many professions and public offices to women. Election of first woman member of Parliament, Nancy Astor. Treaty of Versailles imposes harsh conditions on postwar Germany, opposed by John Maynard Keynes, who writes *The Economic Consequences of the Peace.* League of Nations created. T. S. Eliot, "Tradition and the Individual Talent," *Poems;* Dorothy Richardson, *The Tunnel, Interim;* Robert Wiene, *The Cabinet of Dr. Caligari* (film).

1920 The Memoir Club, comprising thirteen original members of the Bloomsbury Group, meets for the first time. *The Voyage Out* and *Night and Day* are published in the United States by George H. Doran.

Mohandas Gandhi initiates mass passive resistance against British rule in India.

T. S. Eliot, *The Sacred Wood;* Sigmund Freud, *Beyond the Pleasure Principle;* Roger Fry, *Vision and Design;* D. H. Lawrence, *Women in Love;* Katherine Mansfield, *Bliss and Other Stories;* Ezra Pound, *Hugh Selwyn Mauberley;* Marcel Proust, *Le Côté de Guermantes I;* Edith Wharton, *The Age of Innocence.*

1921 Woolf's short story collection *Monday or Tuesday* published by Hogarth Press, which will from this time publish all her books in England. The book is also published in the United States by Harcourt Brace, which from now on is her American publisher.

Aldous Huxley, *Crome Yellow;* Pablo Picasso, *Three Musicians;* Luigi Pirandello, *Six Characters in Search of an Author;* Marcel Proust, *Le Côté de Guermantes II, Sodome et Gomorrhe I;* Dorothy Richardson, *Deadlock;* Lytton Strachey, *Queen Victoria.*

1922 *Jacob's Room* published. Woolf meets Vita Sackville-West (1892–1962) for the first time.

Bonar Law elected prime minister. Mussolini comes to power in Italy. Irish Free State established. British Broadcasting Company (BBC) formed. Discovery of Tutankhamen's tomb in Egypt. Death of Marcel Proust (b. 1871).

T. S. Eliot, *The Waste Land;* James Joyce, *Ulysses;* Katherine Mansfield, *The Garden Party;* Marcel Proust, *Sodome et Gomorrhe II;* Ludwig Wittgenstein, *Tractatus Logico-Philosophicus.*

1923 The Woolfs travel to Spain, stopping in Paris on the way home. Hogarth Press publishes *The Waste Land.*

Stanley Baldwin succeeds Bonar Law as prime minister. Death of Katherine Mansfield (b. 1888).

Mina Loy, *Lunar Baedeker;* Marcel Proust, *La Prisonnière;* Dorothy Richardson, *Revolving Lights;* Rainer Maria Rilke, *Duino Elegies.*

1924 The Woolfs move to Tavistock Square. Woolf lectures on "Character in Fiction" to the Heretics Society at Cambridge University.

The Labour Party takes office for the first time under

the leadership of Ramsay MacDonald but is voted out within the year. Death of Joseph Conrad (b. 1857).

E. M. Forster, *A Passage to India;* Thomas Mann, *The Magic Mountain.*

1925   *Mrs. Dalloway* and *The Common Reader* published. Woolf stays with Vita Sackville-West at her house, Long Barn, for the first time.

Nancy Cunard, *Parallax;* F. Scott Fitzgerald, *The Great Gatsby;* Ernest Hemingway, *In Our Time;* Adolf Hitler, *Mein Kampf;* Franz Kafka, *The Trial;* Alain Locke, ed., *The New Negro;* Marcel Proust, *Albertine disparue;* Dorothy Richardson, *The Trap;* Gertrude Stein, *The Making of Americans.*

1926   Woolf lectures on "How Should One Read a Book?" at Hayes Court School. "Cinema" published in *Arts* (New York), "Impassioned Prose" in *Times Literary Supplement,* and "On Being Ill" in *New Criterion.* Meets Gertrude Stein (1874–1946).

The General Strike in support of mine workers in England lasts nearly two weeks.

Ernest Hemingway, *The Sun Also Rises;* Langston Hughes, *The Weary Blues;* Franz Kafka, *The Castle;* A. A. Milne, *Winnie-the-Pooh.*

1927   *To the Lighthouse,* "The Art of Fiction," "Poetry, Fiction and the Future," and "Street Haunting" published. The Woolfs travel with Vita Sackville-West and her husband, Harold Nicolson, to Yorkshire to see the total eclipse of the sun. They buy their first car.

Charles Lindbergh flies the Atlantic solo.

E. M. Forster, *Aspects of the Novel;* Ernest Hemingway, *Men without Women;* Franz Kafka, *Amerika;* Marcel

Proust, *Le Temps retrouvé;* Gertrude Stein, *Four Saints in Three Acts.*

1928   *Orlando: A Biography* published. In October, Woolf delivers two lectures at Cambridge on which she will base *A Room of One's Own.* Femina-Vie Heureuse prize awarded to *To the Lighthouse.*
The Equal Franchise Act gives the vote to all women over twenty-one. Sound films introduced. Death of Thomas Hardy (b. 1840).
Djuna Barnes, *Ladies Almanack;* Radclyffe Hall, *The Well of Loneliness;* D. H. Lawrence, *Lady Chatterley's Lover;* Evelyn Waugh, *Decline and Fall;* W. B. Yeats, *The Tower.*

1929   *A Room of One's Own* published. "Women and Fiction" in *The Forum* (New York).
Labour Party returned to power under Prime Minister MacDonald. Discovery of penicillin. Museum of Modern Art opens in New York. Wall Street crash.
William Faulkner, *The Sound and the Fury;* Ernest Hemingway, *A Farewell to Arms;* Nella Larsen, *Passing.*

1930   Woolf meets the pioneering composer, writer, and suffragette Ethel Smyth (1858–1944), with whom she forms a close friendship.
Death of D. H. Lawrence (b. 1885).
W. H. Auden, *Poems;* T. S. Eliot, *Ash Wednesday;* William Faulkner, *As I Lay Dying;* Sigmund Freud, *Civilisation and Its Discontents.*

1931   *The Waves* is published. First of six articles by Woolf about London published in *Good Housekeeping;* "Introductory Letter" to *Life As We Have Known It.* Lectures to London branch of National Society for Women's Service on "Professions for Women." Meets John Lehmann (1907–1987), who will become a partner in the Hogarth Press.

Growing financial crisis throughout Europe and beginning of the Great Depression.

1932   *The Common Reader, Second Series* and "Letter to a Young Poet" published. Woolf invited to give the 1933 Clark Lectures at Cambridge, which she declines.

Death of Lytton Strachey (b. 1880).

Aldous Huxley, *Brave New World.*

1933   *Flush: A Biography,* published. The Woolfs travel by car to Italy.

Adolf Hitler becomes chancellor of Germany, establishing the totalitarian dictatorship of his National Socialist (Nazi) Party.

T. S. Eliot, *The Use of Poetry and the Use of Criticism;* George Orwell, *Down and Out in Paris and London;* Gertrude Stein, *The Autobiography of Alice B. Toklas;* Nathanael West, *Miss Lonelyhearts;* W. B. Yeats, *The Collected Poems.*

1934   Woolf meets W. B. Yeats at Ottoline Morrell's house. Writes "Walter Sickert: A Conversation."

George Duckworth dies. Roger Fry dies.

Samuel Beckett, *More Pricks Than Kicks;* Nancy Cunard, ed., *Negro: An Anthology;* F. Scott Fitzgerald, *Tender Is the Night;* Wyndham Lewis, *Men Without Art;* Henry Miller, *Tropic of Cancer;* Ezra Pound, *ABC of Reading;* Evelyn Waugh, *A Handful of Dust.*

1935   The Woolfs travel to Germany, where they accidentally get caught up in a parade for Göring. They return to England via Italy and France.

1936   Woolf reads "Am I a Snob?" to the Memoir Club, and publishes "Why Art Today Follows Politics" in the *Daily Worker*.
Death of George V, who is succeeded by Edward VIII, who then abdicates to marry Wallis Simpson. George VI becomes king. Spanish Civil War (1936–38) begins when General Franco, assisted by Germany and Italy, attacks the Republican government. BBC television begins.
Djuna Barnes, *Nightwood;* Charlie Chaplin, *Modern Times* (film); Aldous Huxley, *Eyeless in Gaza;* J. M. Keynes, *The General Theory of Employment, Interest and Money;* Rose Macaulay, *Personal Pleasures;* Margaret Mitchell, *Gone with the Wind.*

1937   *The Years* published. Woolf's nephew Julian Bell killed in the Spanish Civil War.
Neville Chamberlain becomes prime minister.
Zora Neale Hurston, *Their Eyes Were Watching God;* David Jones, *In Parenthesis;* Pablo Picasso, *Guernica;* John Steinbeck, *Of Mice and Men;* J. R. R. Tolkien, *The Hobbit.*

1938   *Three Guineas* published.
Germany annexes Austria. Chamberlain negotiates the Munich Agreement ("Peace in our time"), ceding Czech territory to Hitler.
Samuel Beckett, *Murphy;* Elizabeth Bowen, *The Death of the Heart;* Jean-Paul Sartre, *La Nausée.*

1939   The Woolfs visit Sigmund Freud, living in exile in
London having fled the Nazis. They move to Mecklenburgh Square.

Germany occupies Czechoslovakia; Italy occupies Alba-
nia; Russia makes a nonaggression pact with Germany.
Germany invades Poland and war is declared by Britain
and France on Germany, September 3. Deaths of W. B.
Yeats (b. 1865), Sigmund Freud (b. 1856), and Ford
Madox Ford (b. 1873).

James Joyce, *Finnegans Wake;* John Steinbeck, *The Grapes
of Wrath;* Nathanael West, *The Day of the Locust.*

1940   *Roger Fry: A Biography* published. "Thoughts on Peace
in an Air Raid" in the *New Republic.* Woolf lectures on
"The Leaning Tower" to the Workers Educational Association in Brighton.

The Battle of Britain leads to German night bombings
of English cities. The Woolfs' house at Mecklenburgh
Square is severely damaged, as is their former house
at Tavistock Square. Hogarth Press is moved out of
London.

Ernest Hemingway, *For Whom the Bell Tolls;* Christina
Stead, *The Man Who Loved Children.*

1941   Woolf drowns herself, March 28, in the River Ouse in
Sussex. *Between the Acts* published in July.

Death of James Joyce (b. 1882).

Rebecca West, *Black Lamb and Grey Falcon.*

INTRODUCTION
BY MOLLY HITE

LEONARD WOOLF read the finished manuscript of *The Waves* in July of 1931. In a diary entry for July 19, Virginia Woolf reported his verdict: "'It is a masterpiece,' said L., coming out to my lodge this morning. 'And the best of your books.' This note I make; adding that he also thinks the first 100 pages extremely difficult and is doubtful how far any common reader will follow" (*Diary* 4: 36).

Her husband's judgment of *The Waves* accurately predicted the critical and popular response for the next several decades — and predicted, too, the difficulty the novel would present to contemporary and future audiences. To the surprise and delight of both Woolfs, "the common reader," the newly literate individual whose literary taste Virginia Woolf fostered in many of her critical essays (Cuddy-Keane 59–69), was as receptive to her unconventional "masterpiece" as were more elite readers of the London *Times*. As sales grew brisk she reported, "The unknown provincial reviewers say with almost one accord, here is Mrs. Woolf doing her best work; it can't be popular; but we respect her for so doing; and find *The Waves* positively exciting." She added, with unusual exuberance, "I am in danger, indeed, of becoming our leading novelist, & not with the highbrows only" (October 17, 1931, *Diary* 4: 49).

But as Leonard warned, most readers found the novel difficult as well, and not only in its first hundred pages. The strangeness of its shape and the intimate yet stylized presentation of its characters struck many readers as unnecessarily obscure, even precious, or else, as Mark Hussey later would put it, "a serious failure on the terms of [Woolf's] own aesthetic" because of besetting problems with a "disjunction between language and reality" (Hussey, *Singing of the Real World* xx). Even those readers who shared Leonard's judgment often echoed E. M. Forster, who in a memorial lecture pronounced it "her greatest book," but added, "though *To the Lighthouse* is my favorite" (Forster 17).

In the decades after Woolf's death, its reputation declined. In the 1970s and early 1980s, when feminist critics restored Virginia Woolf to the status of indisputably major modernist writer, they at first concentrated on polemical essays like *A Room of One's Own* and *Three Guineas* or novels like *To the Lighthouse* and *Mrs. Dalloway,* which seemed to present female protagonists triumphing over various societal and personal obstacles. *The Waves* did not offer such exemplary female characters or themes: Indeed, it gave its female characters stereotypical female pursuits, while its male characters were writers and also active in the public sphere. As a consequence, some of the most important early studies of feminist formal innovation ignored it altogether, despite its structural and stylistic experimentation (DuPlessis 1985, Marcus 1987). Only when feminist readings began incorporating psychoanalytic and poststructuralist theoretical approaches, in the 1980s and '90s, did feminist critics revive *The Waves,* generally reading its radical revisions of narrative practice as challenges to norms of gendered or national identity and behavior (Minow-Pinkney, Caughie, Laurence, DuPlessis 1989, Marcus 1992). Critical emphasis on how to construe the novel as a whole, however, often leads to ignoring most of the details: the complex development of the italicized interludes and the often conflicting observations by the various characters. This "difficult" novel seems hard to discuss without in some way homogenizing it, making it add up so quickly that what is most attractive and provocative in it is absorbed into sweeping statements about its overall project and achievement.

And this novel is attractive and provocative in a number of ways, most significantly because it presents competing opinions about what life is and how one should live it, while offering little authorial guidance on what positions readers should favor. In *The Waves,* Woolf provided fewer *tonal cues*—guides within the text helping readers discern the attitude they should take toward events and statements—than in any other of her novels, a problem discussed in the closing section of this introduction. The difficulty of *The Waves* is not a matter of language. The sentences are generally shorter and more declarative than in *Mrs. Dalloway* or *To the Lighthouse.* The word choices are no more unfamiliar or specialized than in any of Woolf's novels, and although there are an unusual number of allusions, readers can follow what is happening without knowing that Rhoda's cry, "Oh! to whom?" comes from Shelley's poem "The Question," or that Percival has a long literary and operatic history as a questing knight, as well as an intimate connection to Woolf's dead older brother, Thoby Stephen. Most surprising for readers familiar with the subtleties of Woolf's free indirect discourse in *Jacob's Room, Mrs. Dalloway,* and *To the Lighthouse,* in *The Waves* there is no doubt about whose point of view is presented at a given point, although at various moments readers may initially have trouble discerning where characters are or what they are doing.

What is difficult about *The Waves* is its violation of certain narrative assumptions that are so ingrained we may not realize they *are* assumptions. One of the assumptions, rarely discussed in the context of this novel, is that a work of fiction presents characters in a hierarchy. In most works of fiction, a few characters are major, while the others are minor. *The Waves,* however, has six protagonists, three women and three men. Despite differences in roles and in the amount of space given to each, they are presented as having equal value to the novel as a whole. Usual habits of reading resist keeping so many characters in the forefront of awareness. Sorting out major characters from minor is part of the business of finding our way into novels. Once we know who is major, we can pay attention to that character's speech, thoughts, and feelings: These, we know, will be important and are more likely to articulate the larger concerns of the work as a whole. Lily Briscoe, Mrs. Ramsay, and Mr. Ramsay are major characters in *To the Lighthouse;* although the narrative presents Charles Tansley's point of view at times, Tansley is clearly a minor character. Even the modernist narratives most celebrated for their experimentation tend to maintain a recognizable hierarchy among characters. In James Joyce's *Ulysses,* Leopold Bloom and Stephen Dedalus are major, with Molly Bloom emerging suddenly from a minor into a major role in the concluding chapter, but Buck Mulligan, Mr. Deasy, Gerty MacDowell, Mrs. Purefoy, and Simon Dedalus are recognizably minor.

The equal status of six major figures is a generally unregarded way that *The Waves* unsettles familiar habits of reading. The most obvious difficulty the novel presents, however, is its structure. This structure is markedly different from that of virtually any other piece of prose fiction, long or short. It is not difficult to comprehend, but so unfamiliar that it presents readers with immediate problems of discerning tone: of how to evaluate, identify, find meanings and emphases, and feel. Indeed, when Woolf wrote about her conception of *The Waves,* she often rejected the word *novel,* casting about for a more accurate genre description. In a famous diary entry, she proposed that her work in progress was "an abstract mystical eyeless book: a playpoem" (November 7, 1928, *Diary* 3: 203). "Playpoem" expands the categories, adding drama and poetry to the third major genre, fiction, and suggesting that the innovations of *The Waves* require

us to read it keeping in mind the conventions of all three major
Western literary forms.

The Shape of *The Waves*

"ABSTRACT, MYSTICAL, EYELESS"—what kind of book is that?
Woolf's own description of *The Waves* suggests some of its difference from most novels, which almost by definition are concrete, empirical, and full of precise social observation. A reader
of a novel generally can answer the question "What is it about?"
But a reader of *The Waves* flounders: "Well, it's about these six
people, and the sun rises and goes up and then goes down until
it sets at the end of their lives."

Hardly a compelling plot, but plot is not the source of fascination in *The Waves,* any more than plot is what one looks for
in a lyric poem. Woolf had for a long time chafed at the restrictions imposed by common understandings of plot in novels. As
early as her 1919 essay "Modern Novels," she protested, "If one
were free and could set down what one chose, there would be
no plot"—and she went on to suggest that under such ideal
conditions the writer would need to provide "little probability"
and could be allowed "a vague general confusion in which the
clear-cut features of the tragic, the comic, the passionate, and
the lyrical were dissolved beyond the possibility of separate recognition" (*Essays* 3: 33). These pleas for liberation from genre conventions look forward to her achievement in *Jacob's Room, Mrs.
Dalloway, To the Lighthouse,* and *Orlando,* but have particular ap-
plication to *The Waves.* In 1930 she wrote to the composer Ethel
Smyth that in working on this most experimental of her novels
she was "writing to a rhythm and not to a plot," although the
process was "completely opposed to the tradition of fiction and
I am casting about all the time for some rope to throw the

reader" (August 28, 1930, *Letters* 4: 204). That "rope" for a reader who might otherwise drown in *The Waves* was a structure that emerged only in the third draft, a pattern of two alternating narrative strategies.

The first of these strategies was external description by an impersonal third-person narrator, a method she had used in parts of the 1919 short story "Kew Gardens" and in the "Time Passes" section of *To the Lighthouse*. *The Waves* opens, "*The sun had not yet risen. The sea was indistinguishable from the sky . . .*" This scene of what Woolf provisionally termed "insensitive nature" (January 26, 1930, *Diary* 3: 285) extends in this first italicized passage to include a seaside house and garden, constituting a background for everything else in the novel. *Background*, however, is a visual term, and for Woolf, metaphors from music are even more important structural principles of this novel written "to a rhythm." The *sound* of waves permeates this descriptive passage, to which Woolf gave the theatrical and musical name of interlude: "*The wave paused, and then drew out again, sighing like a sleeper whose breath comes and goes unconsciously*" (3). In ensuing interludes the waves "*fell with muffled thuds, like logs falling, on the shore,*" "*drummed on the shore,*" "*fell again, like the thud of a great beast stamping,*" "*rolled back sighing over the shingle,*" and finally "*broke on the shore*" (19, 53, 108, 174, 220). The sound of the waves is like a continuous bass line underlying a piece of music: fundamental, repetitive, and suggesting eternity.

Struggling with the structure of her novel in the middle of 1929, Woolf asked herself, "Could one not get the waves to be heard all through?" (June 23, 1929, *Diary* 3: 236). But only when she arrived at the way she would present the human part of the novel—the actions, thoughts, and feelings of six friends through the course of their lives—did she resolve the problem of how to suggest the waves' continuous presence. Her drafts show her initially working with a vaguely embodied narrator, a "she" who announces near the beginning of the project, "I am telling my-self the story of the world from the beginning; . . . I am not con-cerned with the single life" (*Two Holograph Drafts* 6). In the first draft, this "story of the world" mixes descriptions of sea and landscape with remarks about a number of children, some of them prototypes of the "speaking" characters in the final ver-sion, and the one important silent character, the charismatic Percival. Only much later did Woolf decide to separate the "in-sensitive nature" descriptions from the characters. On August 20, 1930, she wrote in her diary, "The Waves is I think resolv-ing itself . . . into a series of dramatic soliloquies. The thing is to keep them running homogeneously in & out, in the rhythm of the waves" (*Diary* 3: 312).

The second narrative strategy of *The Waves* is thus dramatic soliloquy: nine sections of first-person self-narration, typo-graphically signaled by being in regular rather than italic type-face. The passages of self-narration consist of "speeches" by individual characters, presented within quotation marks and identified by narrative tags using the verb "said": "'I see a ring,' said Bernard"; "'Now the wind lifts the blind,' said Susan" (4, 69). As the examples show, the soliloquies are mainly in the present tense, but not the progressive present of most spoken English (in which Susan would say, "Now the wind is lifting the blind"). As Dorrit Cohn observes, the characteristic tense of the soliloquies in *The Waves* is the simple present, "the tense re-served for English poetry," for which Cohn uses the name "lyric present" (Cohn 264). Like the speakers of many lyric poems, particularly poems of Percy Bysshe Shelley, the most quoted writer in *The Waves*, the self-narrating characters present their immediate impressions and thoughts—and also their immedi-ate actions—in a grammar that is simple but not colloquial, heightened but not ornamented, direct but not artless. "I fall upon the thorns of life! I bleed!" cries the speaker in Shelley's great "Ode to the West Wind." In *The Waves,* Rhoda exclaims, "Oh, this is pain, this is anguish! I faint, I fail" (see the note to page 40). Both speakers "speak" only metaphorically, in that their utterances are not dialogue addressed to other characters, nor are they precisely internal monologue or the kind of soliloquy addressed to an audience in a dramatic performance. The exclamations are rhetorically stylized and, most important, not individualized or "characteristic." Both Shelley's speaker and Rhoda narrate an immediate but abstract experience: not a literal fall, faint, or (physical) failure but a psychological and metaphysical event that readers are implicitly invited to universalize as well as sympathize with. Like Shelley's speaker, Rhoda is hurt by "life," not simply by individual mishaps.

In final form, *The Waves* consists of nine one- to two-page interludes set in italic type, each introducing a longer section of soliloquies set in regular type. The first interlude shows the sun rising; the second shows the sun higher in the sky; and so on to noon in the fifth interlude; and then the slow decline to sunset, with darkness covering the landscape of sea and shore at the beginning of the ninth interlude. The scope of the scene described becomes radically larger in the fifth interlude, where the point of view seems to move back to encompass a large section of the globe. This description notes the sun's effect on *"desolate cairns," "dark-green jungle-trees," "smooth gilt mosque[s],"* and *"long-breasted, white-haired women who knelt in the river bed beating wrinkled cloths upon stones,"* before moving *"further north"* to *"cloudier and rainier countries"* (107). The abrupt expansion of focus to reveal a vista of southern European, Middle Eastern, or Far Eastern scenes occurs in other of Woolf's novels, notably *Jacob's Room* (44). Here, it is part of a web of references within the text to Britain's colonies and former colonies and to the rise of Western fascism—themes charged with political and social implications within a novel that in general avoids reference to historical and

social markers. These themes have attracted considerable critical attention during the past twenty years (McIntire, Berman,
McGee, Marcus 1992; see also "The Silence of Percival," beginning on page lv).

The nine interludes thus present stages of a single day, from
sunrise to sunset and full darkness. They frame the soliloquy sections with a distanced, disinterested account of one day, a strategy linking *The Waves* with two other classic modernist novels
that present the course of a single day, James Joyce's *Ulysses*
(1922) and Woolf's own *Mrs. Dalloway* (1925). In the soliloquies
that follow each interlude, the periods in the lives of the characters are presented sequentially and coincide metaphorically with
times of day described. The sun's rising introduces them as small
children at school; the early morning finds them going off to
board at secondary schools; and so on. In the first eight sections,
most of the characters speak at least once: Only Rhoda and
Bernard are absent from the sixth section. In the ninth section, a
single character, Bernard, tries to "sum up" all their lives from the
vantage of late middle age (176). A human life parallels a single
day, with all the connotations of transience, insignificance, repetition, and universality that this ancient metaphor carries with it.

How can a novel with such a general, not to say collective,
focus sustain interest? The answer will lie with individual readers' preferences and tolerances, but it might also be noted that
one of the modernist works lying closest in its aims and concerns to *The Waves* is not only widely read but loved as well as
admired. The long poem *The Waste Land,* written by Leonard
and Virginia Woolf's close friend T. S. Eliot and published in
1923 by the Woolfs' Hogarth Press, contains a number of narratives held together by an abstract frame, and a number of
characters who voice concerns of apocalyptic, universal, but
also poignantly personal and social importance. In "Letter to a
Young Poet," an essay that Virginia Woolf wrote right after

finishing *The Waves,* she counseled the aspiring poet of 1931 to return to the example of Shakespeare and "to embark upon a long poem in which people as unlike yourself as possible talk at the tops of their voices" (224). The prescription sounds remarkably like Eliot's practice in *The Waste Land* as well as her own practice in her "playpoem," with the qualification in both cases that the fictional people are in certain respects very like their creators, while in many other respects, of course, "as unlike [them] as possible." Her concern in this essay, as in so many of her important modernist manifestos, was finding an adequate literary form for an experience that paradoxically was at once definitively modern and eternal. In *The Waves,* she did not try to create suspense, excitement, and, as she wrote in "Modern Novels," "an air of probability so impeccable that if all [her] figures were to come to life they would find themselves dressed down to the last button in the fashion of the hour" (*Essays* 3: 33). Rather, we can gather that her hybrid, alternative fictional form was the product of what she called in "Character in Fiction" "the appalling effort of saying what I meant" (*Essays* 3: 432).

Voicing the Characters: Motifs and Allusions

ARE THERE characters in *The Waves?* After reading a laudatory review of the novel in the London *Times Literary Supplement,* Woolf noted, "Odd, that they . . . shd. praise my characters when I meant to have none" (October 8, 1931, *Diary* 4: 47). The comment is often quoted to suggest that Rhoda, Susan, Neville, Louis, Jinny, and Bernard are somehow not "real" within the fictional universe, or that they mask some underlying reality, other than the obvious reality that Virginia Woolf created and gave voice to them all. These six "speakers" do violate a number of common conventions for writing and understanding characters.

But it would be difficult to regard them as evidence that characters do not exist in *The Waves,* or—despite Bernard's evocation of "the body of the complete human being whom we have failed to be, but at the same time, cannot forget" (205)—that they can be regarded merely as symbols or parts of a whole. A modernist innovator who had proclaimed character the most important part of the novel, Woolf wrote in her 1924 manifesto "Character in Fiction," "I believe that all novels . . . deal with character, and that it is to express character—not to preach doctrines, sing songs, or celebrate the glories of the British Empire, that the form of the novel, so clumsy, verbose, and undramatic, so rich, elastic, and alive, has been evolved" (*Essays* 3: 425). It makes sense, then, to ask in what *way* Woolf meant to have no characters in *The Waves,* or in what respects these are not usual characters.

The major problem with thinking of the six "speaking" friends as characters is not only that their soliloquies are in rhetorically heightened language that no one would (or could) ever use in life, but also that there are no significant idiomatic differences *among* the various characters' utterances. Social, sexual Jinny at her first grown-up party observes with fine poetic accuracy, "Wine has a drastic, an astringent taste. I cannot help wincing as I drink. Scent and flowers, radiance and heat, are distilled here to a fiery, to a yellow liquid" (74). Scholarly, precise Neville enunciates a brilliant critical precept (perhaps useful to readers of this novel) using a brilliant extended simile: "To read this poem one must have myriad eyes, like one of those lamps that turn on slabs of racing water at midnight in the Atlantic, when perhaps only a spray of seaweed pricks the surface, or suddenly the waves gape and up shoulders a monster. One must put aside antipathies and jealousies and not interrupt" (145). In the story told by the soliloquies, Neville is understandably reading a poem—he is a scholar and eventually an Oxbridge don, who reads extensively and secretly wants to be a poet; whereas Jinny, who plays excellent tennis and otherwise pirouettes through school, apparently reads little other than magazines. Yet Jinny here "speaks" as vividly and exactly as Neville and with at least as much meticulous regard for parallelism, cadences, and meaningful distortions of syntax: "a drastic, an astringent taste"; "a fiery . . . a yellow liquid." If the usual conventions of characterization applied, we would have either to hypothesize that Jinny had a secret life with many volumes of poetry and a thesaurus, or to conclude that her diction and phrasing fail to fit her character. The latter is closer to the case, of course, but given this definition of "fit" it is also the case that Neville's diction and phrasing are inappropriate for *his* character . . . but only if to be a character, one must display "characteristic," individuated speech mannerisms.

Yet while Rhoda, Louis, Jinny, Bernard, Neville, and Susan all speak in the same idiom throughout *The Waves*—an adult, educated, literary, elevated discourse in the "lyric present" tense—they are individuated by other means. Indeed, individuation is a crucial part of their stories and occupies the first several sections of the novel. Woolf's technique of presentation carefully distinguishes them by associating each with a group of identifying phrases, which are developed and elaborated as the speakers grow older and are sometimes woven with other identifying phrases or passed to another speaker. Susan's "I love, I hate"— from Catullus's "Odi et amo" (9, see note), Louis's "ring of beaten steel" signifying his apprehension of the civilization and poetic tradition undergirding the everyday, Neville's vision of death as the "apple trees . . . which we cannot pass," Bernard's "linked phrases in which I run together whatever happens" (34), and Rhoda's cry, "—Oh! to whom?"—from Shelley's "The Question"—both describe and delimit character. These phrases function like leitmotivs in the operas of Richard Wagner, some of which Woolf reviewed for the London *Times* (see the note to page 24). In Wagner's *musik-drama,* characters and major feelings or ideas are signaled by musical passages that recur in different keys and modes and can be interwoven with other leitmotivs. In *The Waves,* similar verbal motifs introduce a character and bring certain of her or his concerns to the fore in various contexts. They also signal the importance of childhood in the formation of subjectivity, as all are carried forward from very early in life—that is, from the first two sections. The characters grow and develop through repeated returns to childhood incidents or impressions. Many of these incidents and impressions are by social standards unimportant: not the stuff of events in the narratives of daily life, not even elements of plot according to the conventions of realist fiction. They are important to the speakers and central to their identities, however, another indication that *The Waves,* like the other novels of Woolf's great middle period, is motivated by the lure of character.

One effect this mode of presentation enables is a high degree of self-consciousness among the speakers, along with an ability to articulate this self-consciousness powerfully. Characters communicate feelings and thoughts, sometimes along with the information that they are *incapable* of such communication. This particular quality of Woolf's technique is perhaps clearest when Susan "*says,*" "The only sayings I understand are cries of love, hate, rage and pain" (95), or Jinny "*says,*" "[M]y imagination is the bodies [*sic*]. I can imagine nothing beyond the circle cast by my body" (93).

Similarly, even when very young, the characters allude to works of Greek, Latin, and British literature. Not only does Susan's "I love, I hate" come from Catullus but Rhoda's apparently involuntary cry as she jerks suddenly awake, "Oh, but I sink, I fall!" refers to Shelley's 1821 poem *Epipsychidion* and is part of a skein of references to poetry by Shelley and, to a lesser extent, Byron that, as Gillian Beer notes, forms an elegiac substratum both for Rhoda's character and for the novel as a whole (18, see note; Beer, "Life of Anybody" 85). These references help construct Rhoda as a poetic and prophetic figure, giving her a range of articulation only ostensibly at odds with her vulnerable, outcast status. The implication is that precisely because she is always uneasy with ordinary social life, she is in a position to see what others cannot. Her great modernist dirge for Percival at the center of the book shows that at crucial moments she can penetrate appearances to "the thing that lies beneath the semblance of the thing" (118, see note). The other character who feels himself an outsider, Louis, also uses a great deal of allusive language—in his case referring to the poems and criticism of T. S. Eliot, the friend on whom he was to some extent modeled. Julia Briggs suggests many respects in which Louis is built out of references to Eliot's poems, especially *The Waste Land,* and how thoroughly *The Waves* is saturated by his influence (Briggs 250–52). The notes to this edition suggest in addition how references to nursery rhymes, Shakespeare's plays and sonnets, hymns, religious meditations, and poetry from classical Greek and Latin sources to the present day enrich and complicate the "speech" and personalities of the six characters.

Sources of the Characters

SHORTLY AFTER the publication of *Mrs. Dalloway,* Woolf wrote a diary entry reporting the judgment of her close friend Lytton Strachey on the character of Clarissa: "I alternately laugh at her, & cover her, very remarkably, with myself" (June 18, 1925, *Diary* 3: 32). In many respects, Woolf did similar things with the six "speaking" characters of *The Waves.* She distanced herself from them, both conceiving them as types and modeling some of them on friends and relatives. But she also covered them with herself, not just in the obvious sense that as a writer she imaginatively inhabited them, but also in the more intimate sense of giving some of them her own formative experiences.

For instance, an important observation from her diary of 1926 introduces the image of a few words spoken into a lengthy silence, words "mystical" in their inexplicable silence: "One sees a fin passing far out" (September 30, 1926, *Diary* 3: 113). In *The Waves*, Bernard refers to silence broken by a few words, "as if a fin rose in the wastes of silence; then the fin, the thought, sinks back into the depths spreading round it a little ripple of satisfaction, content" (202). He comes up with this image in a moment of "escape," and promptly records it in his notebook of "useful" phrases (25): "I see far out a waste of water. A fin turns. This bare visual impression is unattached to any line of reason, it springs up as one might see the fin of a porpoise on the horizon. Visual impressions often communicate thus briefly statements that we shall in time to come uncover and coax into words. I note under F., therefore, 'Fin in a waste of waters'" (137–38).

Woolf used Bernard's recurrent phrase to describe the project of *The Waves* as a whole, writing about her completion of the manuscript, "I have netted that fin in the waste of water which appeared to me over the marshes out of my window at Rodmell" (February 7, 1931, *Diary* 4: 10). And she also gave to Bernard her own writerly predilection for turning events into phrases. "I say to myself instinctively 'What's the phrase for that?'" she reported after describing a flight of birds in a diary entry (August 12, 1928, *Diary* 3: 191). But Bernard is very unlike her in other ways. His own gift for phrasemaking is social. He observes, "[I]f I find myself in company with other people, words at once make smoke rings—see how phrases at once begin to wreathe off my lips" (47–48). His forte is conversation, not literature, and although he aspires to write a truly comprehensive novel—"My book will certainly run to many volumes embracing every known

variety of man and woman" (48)—he admits, "When I cannot
see words curling like rings of smoke round me I am in darkness—I am nothing. When I am alone I fall into lethargy...I
only come into existence when the plumber, or the horse-
dealers, or whoever it may be, says something which sets me
alight. Then how lovely the smoke of my phrase is, rising and
falling, flaunting and falling..." (96).

In all these respects, Bernard resembles a close friend of the
Woolfs, the critic and editor Desmond MacCarthy, who was always about to write a novel, and whom Virginia described as
someone "the younger generation" would say "was the most
gifted of us all. But why did he never do anything? they will
ask" (February 18, 1919, *Diary* 1: 241–42). As MacCarthy and his
friends grew older, it became clearer and clearer that although he
talked enthrallingly and wrote intelligent reviews, he never would
"do anything" in the field of fiction writing. At one point in 1919,
members of the Bloomsbury Group hired a stenographer to sit
with them and transcribe his conversation in shorthand, with the
idea that if MacCarthy produced nothing else, a literary work
might be made out of his talk. But Virginia wrote to Vanessa that
the stenographer reported, "It is the dullest thing you can imagine to read," and the project was abandoned (May 22, 1921, *Letters* 2: 471). An irritable comment in a 1925 diary suggests how
his character may have provided Woolf with some of the impe-
tus to write *The Waves*. She wrote of Desmond, who had left her
with "intense depression," "I have just made this beautiful
image—how he is like a wave that never breaks, but lollops one
this way & that way & the sail hangs on ones mast & the sun
beats down" (June 5, 1925, *Diary* 3: 27).

Bernard is a useful sort of writer to contrast with her own
aims and practices. In her memoir "A Sketch of the Past," she
makes clear that her own proclivity for "putting it into words" is
an unveiling that reveals a "token of some real thing behind ap-

pearances," which the words "make ... real" (*Moments of Being*
72). Bernard's fertility as raconteur, on the contrary, often leads
him to overlay experience with entertaining stories, veiling rather
than unveiling reality: "My mind hums hither and thither with its
veil of words for everything" (85). His question in the seventh
section, "Are there stories?" (136) is the great experimental
writer's fundamental query—which is to say it is Woolf's own.
In context, however, Bernard's question is (also) self-critical, and
directs us to attend to the mode in which the first eight sections
of *The Waves* present the lives of the friends, in comparison with
Bernard's single-voiced summing-up, which begins in the mode
of one of the oldest stories, "In the beginning, there was the
nursery" (177, see note).

Woolf gave her own formative experiences to more characters than Bernard. Neville, who embodies the precision, physical
fragility, homosexuality, and caustic wit of the biographer Lytton
Strachey, has her childhood memory of hearing about an unexpected, violent death and associating it with an unpassable apple
tree, which becomes a symbol for mortality: "[W]e are doomed,
all of us by the apple trees, by the immitigable tree which we
cannot pass" (16, see note for page 15; see also "Sketch" 71).
And the shy, visionary Rhoda is given Woolf's early, portentous
recognition of "reality" when faced by a puddle, although
Rhoda's version is more ominous. Woolf's account of her own
experience with the puddle occurs in the same diary entry where
she first described the "fin passing far out." This memory is
similarly "mystical," undecipherable, and momentous: "The in-
teresting thing is that in all my feeling and thinking I have never
come up against this before. Life is, soberly & accurately, the
oddest affair; has in it the essence of reality. I used to feel this
as a child—couldn't step across a puddle once, I remember, for
thinking how strange—what am I? etc." (September 30, 1926,
Diary 3: 113; see also "Sketch" 78). More bleakly, Rhoda recalls

of the puddle, "I could not cross it. Identity failed me. We are nothing, I said, and fell" (45, see note).

Rhoda also seems to embody Woolf's bisexuality, as an adolescent cherishing an unarticulated crush on the headmistress of her school (31) and searching in vain for the object of her desire. Her reiterated cry, "Oh! to whom?" expresses a longing that not only dare not speak its name, but is culturally unintelligible in the fictional universe she inhabits. As a consequence she has "no end in view," living in a world of discrete, apocalyptic moments (Hite). Unlike Woolf, she does not create in words or any other medium, although in the drafts Woolf played with the possibility of developing her as a fiction writer, who escaped from the uncertainties of the world by starting in an exercise book "a story" in which "the world was different," and who after "the puddle experience" tries to treat it as a moment of being, "when the pulse in her head seemed to beat a million to a minute & her brain to expand so that she was able to understand everything" (*Two Holograph Drafts* 33, 142). She remains a character who both fears and resists the everyday: the predictable, reassuring routine in which, as Bernard says, "Tuesday follows Monday" (190) and, as Woolf writes in "A Sketch of the Past," time passes embedded in "a kind of nondescript cotton wool" (70).

Of all the characters in *The Waves*, Louis is recognizable to the most readers as based on a real-life person, the great poet T. S. Eliot. The Australian whose father is "a banker in Brisbane" (12) translates easily into the American who hailed from Saint Louis and who, like his fictional counterpart, went "vaguely, to make money vaguely," and found himself a Keatsian businessman "half in love with the typewriter and the telephone" (121, see note). Eliot worked with conspicuous success at Lloyds Bank and later at Faber and Faber publishers, although his friends, among them the Woolfs, tried to rescue him with a regular stipend that would allow him to write poetry and criticism full-time. Like the author of "Tradition and the Individual Talent," Louis regards his own efforts as intertwined with a literary history that reshapes itself with every enduring new poem: "My destiny has been that I remember and must weave together, must plait into one cable the many threads, the thin, the thick, the broken, the enduring of our long history, of our tumultuous and varied day" (148). And like the author of "Rhapsody on a Windy Night," "Preludes," "Sweeney Among the Nightingales," "Morning at the Window," and *The Waste Land*— all poems published by Leonard and Virginia Woolf's Hogarth Press—he prefers the modern, urban "view over chimney-pots; cats scraping their mangy sides upon blistered chimney-stacks; broken windows; and the hoarse clangour of bells from the steeple of some brick chapel" (161). Bernard offers a sketch of him as "[p]rim, suspicious, lifting his feet like a crane" (180), a representation that anticipates the even less flattering description that Eliot wrote of himself in 1933:

How unpleasant to meet Mr. Eliot!
With his features of clerical cut,
And his brow so grim
And his mouth so prim
And his conversation, so nicely
Restricted to What Precisely
And If and Perhaps and But. ("Five-Finger Exercises" 135)

Yet Louis is a sympathetic character, deeply informed by the "positively familiar & jocular & friendly" "Tom," whom Virginia Woolf grew to know beneath the stiff exterior of Mr. Eliot (March 12, 1922, *Diary* 2: 170).

Woolf seems to have developed her first ideas about *The Waves* from a letter she received from her sister, Vanessa Bell, who was then living in Cassis, in the south of France. Vanessa described the intrusion of "a huge moth—half a foot, literally, across," which she finally killed to provide the children with a specimen. She then found that another moth had followed, "a better specimen," and worried that if one female were inside the room, all the males in the area would follow—perhaps a portent of Jinny's strangely potent powers, as Woolf depicts them in *The Waves*. Vanessa then added, through a largely associative connection, "I wish you would write a book about the maternal instinct. In all my wide reading I haven't yet found it properly explored. . . . Of course it is one of the worst of the passions, animal and remorseless" (*Selected Letters of Vanessa Bell*, May 3, 1927: 314–15). Vanessa's mixture of moths and mothers prompted Woolf to begin her novel, which for several years was titled "The Moths." Although early drafts sketched a kind of evolutionary seascape in which generations of mothers gave birth, "groan[ing] & fall[ing] ~~back~~ . . . Like one wave, ~~& then~~ succeeding another . . . endlessly sinking & falling as far as the eye can stretch" (*Two Holograph Drafts* 7), the final version says little of maternity, replacing the hierarchies and exclusiveness of blood relations with the horizontal bonds of friendship. The one character who does display the "animal and remorseless" nature of the maternal instinct is Susan, who resembles Vanessa herself in her physical features and love of country life. Susan does not, however, have Vanessa's talent for or interest in the visual arts, and she is fundamentally possessive rather than trying, like Bell, to accommodate a range of sexual and familial relationships. Susan forecasts a maternal role for herself that threatens the connection among the friends: "I shall be debased and hidebound by the bestial and beautiful passion of maternity. I shall push the fortunes of my children unscrupulously. I shall hate those who see their faults. I shall lie basely to help them. I shall let them wall me away from you, from you and from you" (95). But although Susan is the character who shares fewest of the

Bloomsbury values of tolerance and generosity, she does draw on her author's own experiences. Virginia Woolf loved both city and country, and if Jinny is the city denizen, Susan is the rural walker, who in a moment of early morning happiness can say, "I think I am the field, I am the barn, I am the trees; mine are the flocks of birds, and this young hare who leaps, at the last moment when I step almost on him" (70).

Jinny bears Woolf's childhood nickname but also resembles the younger partners of older friends: Clive Bell's lover Mary Hutchinson (Hussey, *A to Z* 131) and John Maynard Keynes's wife, Lydia Lopokova. Her pleasure in the details of modern city life and her bravery in the face of aging and mortality are qualities Woolf admired and shared (140–41). In general, however, this intensely unintellectual, heterosexual, sensual, and social character may seem at the furthest remove from popular images of the restrained, somewhat dowdy genius of Bloomsbury. But Virginia Woolf took great pleasure in flirting with certain men, an activity she described memorably in "Old Bloomsbury" as "showing off, which is not copulating, necessarily, nor altogether being in love" (194). The magical raising of the arm and the unvoiced "Come!" with which Jinny, like a female moth or nightingale, summons young men is something she represents fully with a bare minimum of description. And there are few passages in literature that describe the pleasure and confidence of awakening female sexuality as surely as Jinny's moment in the train leaving school: "My body instantly of its own accord puts forth a frill under his gaze" (44).

The Silence of Percival

WOOLF'S INNOVATIVE mode of presenting the six "speaking" characters makes it impossible for any one of them to be mysterious. Because the soliloquies directly present attitudes, motivations, and desires that may be conscious, unconscious, or somewhere on the spectrum in between, readers know how a speaker feels, what a speaker intends, and often how a speaker will act, even when that speaker is somewhat successful in deluding himself or herself. "Yes, all is propitious. I am now in the mood. I can write the letter straight off which I have begun ever so many times," Bernard announces: a bit of self-narration intended to be a self-fulfilling prophecy. He is the character most given to such optimistic pronouncements about his own behavior and abilities, inclined to take the word for the deed. "I am writing the first thing that comes into my head without troubling to put the paper straight. It is going to be a brilliant sketch"—but of course the letter never materializes, despite "a sip of Byron" for mood (55–56). Armed with a collection of phrases that seem to include some thundering clichés, and with a penchant for self-recounting that leads him at times to imagine a future biographer who will represent him in the most conventionally flattering terms, Bernard can assure himself that, for instance, he possesses the best parts of both gender stereotypes: "'joined to the sensibility of a woman' (I am here quoting my own biographer) 'Bernard possessed the logical sobriety of a man'" (54). His bravado, compounded of sociability, self-absorption, and what Neville describes as "the story which he never stops telling himself" (49), is guileless and wholly available to readers, who witness his oscillations between mild self-deception and mild self-criticism until, in the closing section, he discovers his mortality in a moment of eclipse when he loses the object of biographical narration and becomes "[a] man without a self" (211). All the characters are similarly exposed in their most apparently private motives, illusions, and fears. Even Louis and Rhoda, who are anxious about revealing their differences from what they see as the human norm and who both claim to be "the weakest, the youngest of them all" (69, 76), are open to the reader's full inspection, even as they try to disguise their unease from the others. Indeed, they must narrate both their unease and their attempts to disguise it: "I pull on my stockings as I see them pull on theirs. I wait for you to speak and then speak like you"; "I prop my book against a bottle of Worcester sauce and try to look like the rest" (94, 66).

One character in *The Waves,* however, is mysterious precisely because he does not "speak" at all. The resonantly named Percival appears for the first time in the school chapel as the object of Neville's sidelong gaze, flicking his hand to the back of his neck and having this gesture imitated by others (24). At college with Bernard and Neville, he inspires intense adoration, devotion, desire, emulation, and jealousy. As their adult lives begin, the six "speakers" celebrate him at a farewell dinner before he goes to India. By the beginning of the central fifth section— noon of the day described by the interludes—he is dead, victim of a meaningless accident. He is never forgotten. At the close of the novel, when Bernard resolves to fight his last enemy, Death, he likens himself to Percival, riding against death "with my spear couched and my hair flying back like a young man's, like Percival's, when he galloped in India" (220, see note).

Like Jacob in *Jacob's Room,* Percival is modeled to a degree on Virginia Woolf's older brother, Thoby Stephen, who died of typhoid fever after a visit to Greece in 1906 (see the preface, page xii). Of the many family deaths she suffered while young, Thoby's was in many respects the most significant because it led her to formulate her stance of resistance and her view of reality as a particular kind of experience or force. When at work on *The Waves,* she wrote in a diary entry of "walking up this street, engaged with my anguish, as I was after Thoby died—alone; fighting something alone." This mode of fighting, her response to this bereavement, became a recipe for living: "If I never felt these extraordinarily pervasive strains—of unrest or rest or happiness or discomfort—I should float down into acquiescence. Here is something to fight: & when I wake early I say to myself Fight, fight" (October 11, 1929, *Diary* 3: 260). Woolf made the connection between Percival and Thoby clear at the conclusion of *The Waves,* not only because Bernard expresses her attitude of "Fight, fight" but because she contemplated writing "Julian Thoby Stephen 1881–1906 on the first page" (220, see note; February 7, 1931, *Diary* 4: 10). Like *Jacob's Room,* then, *The Waves* was in part a requiem for her brother.

But like Jacob in the earlier novel—and like Thoby Stephen, whom Woolf pictured later as an "inheritor" of literary, academic, and professional tradition ("Sketch" 139)—Percival is explicitly privileged, a member of the ruling class who, unlike women of any class, is educated to rule. Like Jacob again, he is strangely unknowable, as much an absence defined by the yearning figures who surround him as a present character. Apparently large, beautiful, athletic, charismatic, unintellectual, unreflective, conventional, and a natural leader, he inspires obedience, respect, adoration, and, according to Louis, poetry (27). With no represented interiority, he seems almost to have no interior. Neville describes him in a boat, "lounging on the cushions, monolithic, in giant repose," and observes, "[H]e is always the first to detect insincerity; and is brutal in the extreme" (58, 26). Louis adores "his magnificence" and decries his "slovenly accents" (25). Bernard hypothesizes long after his death that Percival might have emerged in his colonial administrative post as a rebel: "He would have done justice. He would have protected. About the age of forty he would have shocked the authorities" (180). The peroration anticipates some of Woolf's comments on Thoby in "A Sketch of the Past": In college he was "already, in anticipation, a law maker" ("Sketch" 139).

And in a very odd moment during the farewell dinner,

Bernard describes Percival as "a God" (98). The epithet fits some of the imagery associated with this silent monolith, whose name (Percival, Parzifal, or Parsifal, depending on the language) harks back to Arthurian tradition, where it is associated with purity, innocence, bravery, quest, the Holy Grail—an ultimate object of desire in Christian folklore—and a kind of idiocy: Percival is known in the Grail legend as the Fool (see the note to page 24). The Arthurian Percival lurks in the background of *The Waste Land* as the knight whose question, had he asked it, could have cured the Fisher King. Further, according to Julia Briggs, in *The Waves* Percival occupies the place of the sun hero, or year hero in primitive religions: the god-man who is destroyed and falls back to earth when the sun is at its zenith (Briggs 254). Yet although the way Percival is presented keeps him radically separate rather than enmeshed in the fine web of relationships and ideas that we see among the others, he is not, within the value system of the novel, clearly godlike. His conventionality, leadership, charisma, and especially his choice of career in colonial administration may inspire unease in readers, especially those familiar with Virginia Woolf's own positions, expressed both in private writings like diaries and letters and in published writings like the long essays *A Room of One's Own* and *Three Guineas,* on imperialism and on masculine privilege and dominance.

The speech in which Bernard terms Percival "a God" occurs during the farewell dinner and, like the story of Elvedon that Bernard told Susan when both were children (10), constructs a fantasy of an alternative place. "I see India," Bernard begins, and goes on to describe a landscape of "ramshackle pagodas," "bullocks who drag a low cart," natives "chattering excitedly" over an accident, and an "old man in a ditch" who "continues to chew betel and to contemplate his navel." Into this hackneyed setting, presumably familiar to the listeners from colonial adventure stories, comes Percival, a shabby hero in the

tradition of the two wanderers in Rudyard Kipling's "The Man
Who Would Be King" or the more ethical and ironic Marlow in
Joseph Conrad's *Heart of Darkness,* riding "a flea-bitten mare"
and dealing with the upset oxcart by "applying the standards of
the West, by using the violent language that is natural to him."
Bernard's conclusion is grandiose and memorable: "The Oriental problem is solved" (98).

The phrase "the Oriental problem" historically described
various troubled European relations with Middle Eastern, South
Asian, and East Asian colonies, with the word *Oriental* homogenizing all such countries into one problematic other. The details
of Bernard's fantasy are also homogenizing and stereotypical,
built on romantic clichés of Empire thoroughly debunked by the
people in the Woolfs' circle, including Leonard Woolf, who had
been a colonial administrator in Ceylon and decided there that
imperialism was a mistake (see the note to page 98; L. Woolf,
Growing). It seems likely, then, that the passage is satiric. But who
does the satirizing, and at whose expense? Is Bernard a critic of
empire here? His story is exaggerated and affably funny, of
course, but he says nothing, here or later, to suggest that he believes Percival should not have a career adventuring in the
colonies and setting natives right. Immediately after he finishes,
Rhoda treats his story as a reverent encomium and echoes its
sentiments (99). Does the satire occur, then, at the expense of all
the characters, and is Woolf presenting all the speakers, as well
as Percival, as collusive in a racist fantasy? If so, what are readers
supposed to think and feel about them, at this moment and else-
where? Or should we conclude that the passage is not, in fact,
satiric, and that Woolf herself simply endorses here what the editor of the holograph *Waves* manuscripts, J. W. Graham, calls "the
irrational adherence to traditional values so apparent in the conventional Percival, the strong, silent youth who goes to a far
country in the service of Empire, as one of its culture heroes"

(Graham, "Heroic Theme" 313)? Part of the design of *The Waves* is that such questions can, indeed must, be asked—and cannot be easily answered.

The Absence of Tonal Cues in *The Waves*

THE PROBLEM with all such attempts to interpret this particular moment is that there are no clear signals within the text to show readers where values should be assigned. For example, Woolf could have used a more extended third-person narrator to go beyond the words "said Bernard," adding reliable information about Bernard's intentions in telling the story. The decision to structure the novel from soliloquies "running homogeneously in & out, in the rhythm of the waves" ruled out such uses of the narrator. The decision to give the characters a functional equality, at least until the closing section, in which Bernard alone "speaks," makes it difficult to privilege one or two of the characters over the others as having authorial sanction: as voicing views and values that express attitudes held by Woolf herself. Furthermore, the rhetorically heightened "speeches" contain the characters in the lyric present, representing them at some points as communicating (e.g., 59–64 and 166, see note) but keeping their utterances more solitary than social.

The episode of "the Oriental problem" is thus important because it is a particularly pressing example of an effect that Woolf put a great deal of effort into achieving throughout *The Waves*. It is simplest to describe this effect negatively: as an *absence* of those tonal cues that in most fiction are crucial to locating the author's values and thus help readers discover what they are supposed to think and feel about the events and characters in a story. But in the long process of writing *The Waves*, Virginia Woolf came to regard effacing or minimizing such cues as part of the positive task faced by the modern experimental writer.

In a diary entry as she was beginning to conceptualize *The Waves*, she wrote of the need to "eliminate all waste, deadness, superfluity: to give the moment whole; whatever it includes." Her notion of "the moment" was that it was "saturated"—it must "include nonsense, fact, sordidity: but made transparent" (November 28, 1928, *Diary* 3: 209–10). What might transparency entail? In an essay written the year before, she had in effect called for a novel like *The Waves*, which like poetry would "say the simple things which are so tremendous" but would also "take the mould of that queer conglomeration of incongruous things—the modern mind" that is "full of monstrous, hybrid, unmanageable emotions" ("Narrow Bridge" 20, 19–20, 12). Such a novel would be revolutionary in its concern for "the relation of the mind to general ideas and its soliloquy in solitude," and in its *lack* of concern for "the incessant, the remorseless analysis" of interpersonal relations, especially romantic relations (19). In the process of formulating her most experimental novel, she seems also to have erased much of the "remorseless analysis" of motives and values that has so much to do with long-standing traditions of prose fiction. Motives and values are in play in *The Waves*, but they are not specified or settled. They are raised as part of a very different project, which stands "further back from life," expressing "the feeling and ideas of the characters closely and vividly, but from a different angle" ("Narrow Bridge" 18).

Readers plunged into the saturated lyric present of *The Waves* are not thereby removed from questions of ethics or politics, but they do view those questions from a different angle. Not only the problems of empire and the future of Western Europe, but, more obviously, questions about gender and class intrude without a clear indication of what one is supposed to believe or how one is supposed to feel about them. Virginia

Woolf's most influential political positions were feminist, and she was most interested in women as writers (*A Room of One's Own,* "Women and Fiction") and as people deserving to be educated and to enter the professions (*Three Guineas,* "Professions for Women"). How should we regard the gender distinctions in this novel, where the privileges of education and writing (and all the discussions of writing) go entirely to the men? Another question: How should we read Louis's colonial status and his banker father's failure, details that suggest wide differences in class as well as national identity? Earlier drafts of *The Waves* began with children of many classes, some destined to become servants while others were educated to rule (*Two Holograph Drafts* 108). How does class figure in *The Waves,* then, and what attitudes are readers supposed to take to it? Still another question: How should readers take Bernard's claim to "sum up" in the last section? What authority does his single-voiced narration give him? Does his version supplant the earlier versions, augment them, correct them (there is some conflict), and to what end? Finally, how should one read the ending?

This introduction does not aim somehow to answer these questions, nor does it embrace the alternative position of dismissing them as irrelevant to Woolf's project. By downplaying or omitting the most generally expected tonal cues, Virginia Woolf gave readers tremendous latitude to make choices about how to read *The Waves.* One way to make such choices obviously could be to select elements of the novel that support a preferred thesis. Certain characters and attitudes could be declared right and admirable, others untrustworthy or ridiculous. But the extreme density of the descriptions, the intensity of the passions, and the play of humor, resentment, abjection, care, infatuation, interest, vivacity, depression, and courage within phrases, sentences, and soliloquies, as well as among the speakers, suggest that rather than rushing to decide where to assign value, we might try instead to absorb all the disparate elements of the saturated moment. In an essay called "How Should One Read a Book?" Woolf recognized the necessity for readers to "pass judgment upon these multitudinous impressions" gained from reading: "we must make of these fleeting shapes one that is hard and lasting." But for her this step is the last in the reading process, to be delayed until the experience of reading permeates all levels of consciousness and unconsciousness. She counseled, "Wait for the dust of reading to settle; for the conflict and the questioning to die down. . . . Then suddenly without our willing it . . . the book will return, but differently" ("How Should One Read" 266–67). The way to begin the process that ends with a grasp of "the book as a whole" involves a kind of cooperative effort in which the reader draws as close as possible to the writer in order to apprehend the words on the page exactly: "Do not dictate to your author; try to become him. Be his fellow-worker and accomplice . . . if you open your mind as widely as possible, then signs and hints of almost imperceptible fineness, from the twist and turn of the first sentences, will bring you into the presence of a human being unlike any other" ("How Should One Read" 259).

In Virginia Woolf's fiction, and especially in *The Waves,* sentences do "twist and turn," constantly changing direction, intensity, implication, and emotional effect. Attentiveness to phrases and sentences, to ways in which narrative strategies move us into intimate contact with characters or suddenly remove us to an ironic distance, and to the patterns created by repetition and allusion enable the novel's effects: the ways it feels, means, and creates its values. As numerous critics and common readers have testified, the experience can be rich and moving, and may even shift customary attitudes and angles of perception. Neville's observations on reading may be helpful to the reader of the book in which he appears. "One must be sceptical, but throw caution to the winds," he advises, perhaps paradoxically, "and when the door opens accept absolutely." The aim, he tells us, is to "let down one's net deeper and deeper and gently draw in and bring to the surface what he said and she said and make poetry" (145).

I want especially to thank Debra Fried, Mark Hussey, and Brian Kang for their help.

WORKS CITED

Beer, Gillian. "*The Waves*: 'The Life of Anybody.'" In *Virginia Woolf: The Common Ground,* 74–91. Ann Arbor: University of Michigan Press, 1996.

Bell, Vanessa. *Selected Letters of Vanessa Bell.* Edited by Regina Marler. New York: Pantheon, 1993.

Berman, Jessica. "Of Oceans and Opposition: *The Waves,* Oswald Mosley, and the New Party." In *Virginia Woolf and Fascism: Resisting the Dictators' Seduction.* Edited by Merry M. Pawlowski, 105–21. Basingstoke, England: Palgrave, 2002.

Briggs, Julia. *Virginia Woolf: An Inner Life.* Orlando: Harcourt, 2005.

Caughie, Pamela L. *Virginia Woolf and Postmodernism: Literature in Quest and Question of Itself.* Urbana and Chicago: University of Illinois Press, 1991.

Cohn, Dorrit. *Transparent Minds: Narrative Modes for Presenting Consciousness in Fiction.* Princeton and New York: Princeton University Press, 1978.

Conrad, Joseph. *Heart of Darkness.* Edited by Robert Hampson. London and New York: Penguin, 1997.

Cuddy-Keane, Melba. *Virginia Woolf, the Intellectual, and the Public Sphere.* Cambridge: Cambridge University Press, 2003.

DuPlessis, Rachel Blau. "Woolfenstein." In *Breaking the Sequence: Women's Experimental Fiction.* Edited by Ellen G. Friedman and Miriam Fuchs, 99–114. Princeton, NJ: Princeton University Press, 1989.

———. *Writing Beyond the Ending: Narrative Strategies of Twentieth-Century Women Writers.* Bloomington: Indiana University Press, 1985.

Eliot, T. S. "Five-Finger Exercises." In *Collected Poems, 1909–1962,* 135. New York: Harcourt, Brace and World, 1970.

———. "Tradition and the Individual Talent." In *Selected Essays, 1917–1932,* 3–11. New York: Harcourt Brace, 1932.

Forster, E. M. *Virginia Woolf.* New York: Harcourt, Brace and Company, 1942.

Graham, J. W. "Manuscript Revision and the Heroic Theme of *The Waves.*" *Twentieth Century Literature* 29.3 (Fall 1983): 312–32.

Hite, Molly. "Virginia Woolf's Two Bodies." *Genders* 31 (2000). www .genders.org/g31/g31_hite.html.

Hussey, Mark. *The Singing of the Real World: The Philosophy of Virginia Woolf's Fiction.* Columbus: Ohio State University Press, 1986.

———. *Virginia Woolf A to Z: A Comprehensive Reference for Students, Teachers, and Common Readers to Her Life, Works, and Critical Reception.* New York: Facts on File, 1995.

Kipling, Rudyard. "The Man Who Would Be King." In *The Man Who Would Be King, and Other Stories,* 244–79. Oxford: Oxford University Press, 1987.

Laurence, Patricia Ondek. *The Reading of Silence: Virginia Woolf in the English Tradition.* Stanford, CA: Stanford University Press, 1991.

Marcus, Jane. "Britannia Rules *The Waves.*" In *Decolonizing Tradition: New Views of Twentieth-Century "British" Literary Canons.* Edited by Karen R. Lawrence, 136–62. Urbana: University of Illinois Press, 1992.

———. *Virginia Woolf and the Languages of Patriarchy.* Bloomington: Indiana University Press, 1987.

McGee, Patrick. "The Politics of Modernist Form: Or, Who Rules *The Waves?*" *Modern Fiction Studies* 38.3 (Autumn 1992): 631–50.

McIntire, Gabrielle. "Heteroglossia, Monologism, and Fascism: Bernard Reads *The Waves.*" *Narrative* 13.1 (January 2005): 29–45.

Minow-Pinkney, Makiko. "*The Waves.*" In *Virginia Woolf and the Problem of the Subject: Feminine Writing in the Major Novels,* 152–86. New Brunswick, NJ: Rutgers University Press, 1987.

Woolf, Leonard. *Growing: An Autobiography of the Years 1904 to 1911.* New York: Harcourt, Brace & World, 1962.

Woolf, Virginia. "Character in Fiction." In *The Essays of Virginia Woolf.* Vol. 3. Edited by Andrew McNeillie, 420–38. San Diego: Harcourt Brace Jovanovich, 1988.

———. "How Should One Read a Book?" In *The Second Common Reader.* Edited and introduced by Andrew McNeillie, 258–70. San Diego: Harcourt, 1986.

———. *Jacob's Room.* New York: Harvest/Harcourt, 1990.

———. "Letter to a Young Poet." In *The Death of the Moth and Other Essays,* 208–26. New York: Harcourt Brace & Co., 1970.

———. "Modern Novels." In *The Essays of Virginia Woolf.* Vol. 3. Edited by Andrew McNeillie, 30–37. San Diego: Harcourt Brace Jovanovich, 1988.

————. *Mrs. Dalloway.* Annotated and with an introduction by Bonnie Kime Scott. Orlando: Harcourt, 2005.

————. "The Narrow Bridge of Art." In *Granite and Rainbow,* 11–23. New York: Harcourt Brace Jovanovich, 1958.

————. "Old Bloomsbury." In *Moments of Being.* Edited by Jeanne Schulkind, 181–201. San Diego: Harcourt Brace Jovanovich, 1985.

————. "Professions for Women." In *The Death of the Moth and Other Essays,* 235–42. New York: Harcourt Brace Jovanovich, 1972.

————. *A Room of One's Own.* Annotated and with an introduction by Susan Gubar. Orlando: Harcourt, 2005.

————. "A Sketch of the Past." In *Moments of Being.* Edited by Jeanne Schulkind, 64–159. San Diego: Harcourt Brace Jovanovich, 1985.

————. *Three Guineas.* Annotated and with an introduction by Jane Marcus. Orlando: Harcourt, 2006.

————. *To the Lighthouse.* Annotated and with an introduction by Mark Hussey. Orlando: Harcourt, 2005.

————. *The Waves: The Two Holograph Drafts.* Transcribed and edited by J. W. Graham. Toronto: University of Toronto Press, 1976.

————. "Women and Fiction." In *Granite and Rainbow,* 76–84. New York: Harcourt Brace Jovanovich, 1975. Originally published in 1958.

The Waves

*T*HE SUN *had not yet risen. The sea was indistinguishable from the sky, except that the sea was slightly creased as if a cloth had wrinkles in it. Gradually as the sky whitened a dark line lay on the horizon dividing the sea from the sky and the grey cloth became barred with thick strokes moving, one after another, beneath the surface, following each other, pursuing each other, perpetually.*

As they neared the shore each bar rose, heaped itself, broke and swept a thin veil of white water across the sand. The wave paused, and then drew out again, sighing like a sleeper whose breath comes and goes unconsciously. Gradually the dark bar on the horizon became clear as if the sediment in an old wine-bottle had sunk and left the glass green. Behind it, too, the sky cleared as if the white sediment there had sunk, or as if the arm of a woman couched beneath the horizon had raised a lamp and flat bars of white, green and yellow, spread across the sky like the blades of a fan. Then she raised her lamp higher and the air seemed to become fibrous and to tear away from the green surface flickering and flaming in red and yellow fibres like the smoky fire that roars from a bonfire. Gradually the fibres of the burning bonfire were fused into one haze, one incandescence which lifted the weight of the woollen grey sky on top of it and turned it to a million atoms of soft blue. The surface of the sea slowly became transparent and lay rippling and sparkling until the dark stripes were almost rubbed out. Slowly the arm that held the lamp raised it higher and then higher until a broad flame became visible; an arc of fire burnt on the rim of the horizon, and all round it the sea blazed gold.

sunrise

The light struck upon the trees in the garden, making one leaf transparent and then another. One bird chirped high up; there was a pause; another chirped lower down. The sun sharpened the walls of the house, and rested like the tip of a fan upon a white blind and made a blue fingerprint of shadow under the leaf by the bedroom window. The blind stirred slightly, but all within was dim and unsubstantial. The birds sang their blank melody outside.

"I SEE a ring," said Bernard, "hanging above me. It quivers and hangs in a loop of light."

"I see a slab of pale yellow," said Susan, "spreading away until it meets a purple stripe."

"I hear a sound," said Rhoda, "cheep, chirp; cheep, chirp; going up and down."

"I see a globe," said Neville, "hanging down in a drop against the enormous flanks of some hill."

"I see a crimson tassel," said Jinny, "twisted with gold threads."

"I hear something stamping," said Louis. "A great beast's foot is chained. It stamps, and stamps, and stamps."

"Look at the spider's web on the corner of the balcony," said Bernard. "It has beads of water on it, drops of white light."

"The leaves are gathered round the window like pointed ears," said Susan.

"A shadow falls on the path," said Louis, "like an elbow bent."

"Islands of light are swimming on the grass," said Rhoda. "They have fallen through the trees."

"The birds' eyes are bright in the tunnels between the leaves," said Neville.

"The stalks are covered with harsh, short hairs," said Jinny, "and drops of water have stuck to them."

"A caterpillar is curled in a green ring," said Susan, "notched with blunt feet."

"The grey-shelled snail draws across the path and flattens the blades behind him," said Rhoda.

"And burning lights from the window-panes flash in and out on the grasses," said Louis.

"Stones are cold to my feet," said Neville. "I feel each one, round or pointed, separately."

"The back of my hand burns," said Jinny, "but the palm is clammy and damp with dew."

"Now the cock crows like a spurt of hard, red water in the white tide," said Bernard.

"Birds are singing up and down and in and out all round us," said Susan.

"The beast stamps; the elephant with its foot chained; the great brute on the beach stamps," said Louis.

"Look at the house," said Jinny, "with all its windows white with blinds."

"Cold water begins to run from the scullery tap," said Rhoda, "over the mackerel in the bowl."

"The walls are cracked with gold cracks," said Bernard, "and there are blue, finger-shaped shadows of leaves beneath the windows."

"Now Mrs. Constable pulls up her thick, black stockings," said Susan.

"When the smoke rises, sleep curls off the roof like a mist," said Louis.

"The birds sang in chorus first," said Rhoda. "Now the scullery door is unbarred. Off they fly. Off they fly like a fling of seed. But one sings by the bedroom window alone."

"Bubbles form on the floor of the saucepan," said Jinny. "Then they rise, quicker and quicker in a silver chain to the top."

"Now Biddy scrapes the fish-scales with a jagged knife on to a wooden board," said Neville.

"The dining-room window is dark blue now," said Bernard, "and the air ripples above the chimneys."

"A swallow is perched on the lightning-conductor," said Susan. "And Biddy has smacked down the bucket on the kitchen flags."

"That is the first stroke of the church bell," said Louis. "Then the others follow; one, two; one, two; one, two."

"Look at the table-cloth, flying white along the table," said

Rhoda. "Now there are rounds of white china, and silver streaks beside each plate."

"Suddenly a bee booms in my ear," said Neville. "It is here; it is past."

"I burn, I shiver," said Jinny, "out of this sun, into this shadow."

"Now they have all gone," said Louis. "I am alone. They have gone into the house for breakfast, and I am left standing by the wall among the flowers. It is very early, before lessons. Flower after flower is specked on the depths of green. The petals are harlequins. Stalks rise from the black hollows beneath. The flowers swim like fish made of light upon the dark, green waters. I hold a stalk in my hand. I am the stalk. My roots go down to the depths of the world, through earth dry with brick, and damp earth, through veins of lead and silver. I am all fibre. All tremors shake me, and the weight of the earth is pressed to my ribs. Up here my eyes are green leaves, unseeing. I am a boy in grey flannels with a belt fastened by a brass snake up here. Down there my eyes are the lidless eyes of a stone figure in a desert by the Nile. I see women passing with red pitchers to the river; I see camels swaying and men in turbans. I hear tramplings, tremblings, stirrings round me.

"Up here Bernard, Neville, Jinny and Susan (but not Rhoda) skim the flower-beds with their nets. They skim the butterflies from the nodding tops of the flowers. They brush the surface of the world. Their nets are full of fluttering wings. 'Louis! Louis! Louis!' they shout. But they cannot see me. I am on the other side of the hedge. There are only little eyeholes among the leaves. Oh, Lord, let them pass. Lord, let them lay their butterflies on a pocket-handkerchief on the gravel. Let them count out their tortoise-shells, their red admirals and cabbage whites. But let me be unseen. I am green as a yew tree in the shade of the hedge. My hair is made of leaves. I am rooted to the middle of the earth.

masturbation

My body is a stalk. I press the stalk. A drop oozes from the hole at the mouth and slowly, thickly, grows larger and larger. Now something pink passes the eyehole. Now an eyebeam is slid through the chink. Its beam strikes me. I am a boy in a grey flannel suit. She has found me. I am struck on the nape of the neck. She has kissed me. All is shattered."

"I was running," said Jinny, "after breakfast. I saw leaves moving in a hole in the hedge. I thought, 'That is a bird on its nest.' I parted them and looked; but there was no bird on a nest. The leaves went on moving. I was frightened. I ran past Susan, past Rhoda, and Neville and Bernard in the tool-house talking. I cried as I ran, faster and faster. What moved the leaves? What moves my heart, my legs? And I dashed in here, seeing you green as a bush, like a branch, very still, Louis, with your eyes fixed. 'Is he dead?' I thought, and kissed you, with my heart jumping under my pink frock like the leaves, which go on moving, though there is nothing to move them. Now I smell geraniums; I smell earth mould. I dance. I ripple. I am thrown over you like a net of light. I lie quivering flung over you."

"Through the chink in the hedge," said Susan, "I saw her kiss him. I raised my head from my flower-pot and looked through a chink in the hedge. I saw her kiss him. I saw them, Jinny and Louis, kissing. Now I will wrap my agony inside my pocket-handkerchief. It shall be screwed tight into a ball. I will go to the beech wood alone, before lessons. I will not sit at a table, doing sums. I will not sit next Jinny and next Louis. I will take my anguish and lay it upon the roots under the beech trees. I will examine it and take it between my fingers. They will not find me. I shall eat nuts and peer for eggs through the brambles and my hair will be matted and I shall sleep under hedges and drink water from ditches and die there."

"Susan has passed us," said Bernard. "She has passed the tool-house door with her handkerchief screwed into a ball. She

Jinny kisses Louis

Susan saw kiss (anguish/agony)

was not crying, but her eyes, which are so beautiful, were narrow as cats' eyes before they spring. I shall follow her, Neville. I shall go gently behind her, to be at hand, with my curiosity, to comfort her when she bursts out in a rage and thinks, 'I am alone.'

"Now she walks across the field with a swing, nonchalantly, to deceive us. Then she comes to the dip; she thinks she is unseen; she begins to run with her fists clenched in front of her. Her nails meet in the ball of her pocket-handkerchief. She is making for the beech woods out of the light. She spreads her arms as she comes to them and takes to the shade like a swimmer. But she is blind after the light and trips and flings herself down on the roots under the trees, where the light seems to pant in and out, in and out. The branches heave up and down. There is agitation and trouble here. There is gloom. The light is fitful. There is anguish here. The roots make a skeleton on the ground, with dead leaves heaped in the angles. Susan has spread her anguish out. Her pocket-handkerchief is laid on the roots of the beech trees and she sobs, sitting crumpled where she has fallen."

"I saw her kiss him," said Susan. "I looked between the leaves and saw her. She danced in flecked with diamonds light as dust. And I am squat, Bernard, I am short. I have eyes that look close to the ground and see insects in the grass. The yellow warmth in my side turned to stone when I saw Jinny kiss Louis. I shall eat grass and die in a ditch in the brown water where dead leaves have rotted."

"I saw you go," said Bernard. "As you passed the door of the tool-house I heard you cry, 'I am unhappy.' I put down my knife. I was making boats out of firewood with Neville. And my hair is untidy, because when Mrs. Constable told me to brush it there was a fly in a web, and I asked, 'Shall I free the fly? Shall I let the fly be eaten?' So I am late always. My hair is unbrushed and these chips of wood stick in it. When I heard you cry I followed you, and saw you put down your handkerchief, screwed up, with its rage, with its hate, knotted in it. But soon that will cease. Our bodies are close now. You hear me breathe. You see the beetle too carrying off a leaf on its back. It runs this way, then that way, so that even your desire while you watch the beetle, to possess one single thing (it is Louis now) must waver, like the light in and out of the beech leaves; and then words, moving darkly, in the depths of your mind will break up this knot of hardness, screwed in your pocket-handkerchief."

from a poem

"I love," said Susan, "and I hate. I desire one thing only. My eyes are hard. Jinny's eyes break into a thousand lights. Rhoda's are like those pale flowers to which moths come in the evening. Yours grow full and brim and never break. But I am already set on my pursuit. I see insects in the grass. Though my mother still knits white socks for me and hems pinafores and I am a child, I love and I hate."

"The Moths" = orig. title

"But when we sit together, close," said Bernard, "we melt into each other with phrases. We are edged with mist. We make an unsubstantial territory."

"I see the beetle," said Susan. "It is black, I see; it is green, I see; I am tied down with single words. But you wander off; you slip away; you rise up higher, with words and words in phrases."

"Now," said Bernard, "let us explore. There is the white house lying among the trees. It lies down there ever so far beneath us. We shall sink like swimmers just touching the ground with the tips of their toes. We shall sink through the green air of the leaves, Susan. We sink as we run. The waves close over us, the beech leaves meet above our heads. There is the stable clock with its gilt hands shining. Those are the flats and heights of the roofs of the great house. There is the stable-boy clattering in the yard in rubber-boots. That is Elvedon.

Elv.= Brit. Imperialism

"Now we have fallen through the tree-tops to the earth. The air no longer rolls its long, unhappy, purple waves over us. We touch earth; we tread ground. That is the close-clipped hedge of the ladies' garden. There they walk at noon, with scissors, clipping roses. Now we are in the ringed wood with the wall round it. This is Elvedon. I have seen signposts at the cross-roads with one arm pointing 'To Elvedon.' No one has been there. The ferns smell very strong, and there are red funguses growing beneath them. Now we wake the sleeping daws who have never seen a human form; now we tread on rotten oak apples, red with age and slippery. There is a ring of wall round this wood; nobody comes here. Listen! That is the flop of a giant toad in the undergrowth; that is the patter of some primeval fir-cone falling to rot among the ferns.

"Put your foot on this brick. Look over the wall. That is Elvedon. The lady sits between the two long windows, writing. The gardeners sweep the lawn with giant brooms. We are the first to come here. We are the discoverers of an unknown land. Do not stir; if the gardeners saw us they would shoot us. We should be nailed like stoats to the stable door. Look! Do not move. Grasp the ferns tight on the top of the wall."

woman: novelist

"I see the lady writing. I see the gardeners sweeping," said Susan. "If we died here, nobody would bury us."

"Run!" said Bernard. "Run! The gardener with the black beard has seen us! We shall be shot! We shall be shot like jays and pinned to the wall! We are in a hostile country. We must escape to the beech wood. We must hide under the trees. I turned a twig as we came. There is a secret path. Bend as low as you can. Follow without looking back. They will think we are foxes. Run!

"Now we are safe. Now we can stand upright again. Now we can stretch our arms in this high canopy, in this vast wood. I hear nothing. That is only the murmur of the waves in the air.

That is a wood-pigeon breaking cover in the tops of the beech trees. The pigeon beats the air; the pigeon beats the air with wooden wings."

"Now you trail away," said Susan, "making phrases. Now you mount like an air-ball's string, higher and higher through the layers of the leaves, out of reach. Now you lag. Now you tug at my skirts, looking back, making phrases. You have escaped me. Here is the garden. Here is the hedge. Here is Rhoda on the path rocking petals to and fro in her brown basin."

"All my ships are white," said Rhoda. "I do not want red petals of hollyhocks or geranium. I want white petals that float when I tip the basin up. I have a fleet now swimming from shore to shore. I will drop a twig in as a raft for a drowning sailor. I will drop a stone in and see bubbles rise from the depths of the sea. Neville has gone and Susan has gone; Jinny is in the kitchen garden picking currants with Louis perhaps. I have a short time alone, while Miss Hudson spreads our copy-books on the school-room table. I have a short space of freedom. I have picked all the fallen petals and made them swim. I have put raindrops in some. I will plant a lighthouse here, a head of Sweet Alice. And I will now rock the brown basin from side to side so that my ships may ride the waves. Some will founder. Some will dash themselves against the cliffs. One sails alone. That is my ship. It sails into icy caverns where the sea-bear barks and stalac- tites swing green chains. The waves rise; their crests curl; look at the lights on the mastheads. They have scattered, they have foundered, all except my ship which mounts the wave and sweeps before the gale and reaches the islands where the par- rots chatter and the creepers . . ."

"Where is Bernard?" said Neville. "He has my knife. We were in the tool-shed making boats, and Susan came past the door. And Bernard dropped his boat and went after her taking my knife, the sharp one that cuts the keel. He is like a dangling

wire, a broken bell-pull, always twangling. He is like the seaweed
hung outside the window, damp now, now dry. He leaves me in
the lurch; he follows Susan; and if Susan cries he will take my
knife and tell her stories. The big blade is an emperor; the broken blade a Negro. I hate dangling things; I hate dampish things.
I hate wandering and mixing things together. Now the bell rings
and we shall be late. Now we must drop our toys. Now we must
go in together. The copy-books are laid out side by side on the
green baize table."

"I will not conjugate the verb," said Louis, "until Bernard
has said it. My father is a banker in Brisbane and I speak with
an Australian accent. I will wait and copy Bernard. He is English. They are all English. Susan's father is a clergyman. Rhoda
has no father. Bernard and Neville are the sons of gentlemen.
Jinny lives with her grandmother in London. Now they suck
their pens. Now they twist their copy-books, and, looking sideways at Miss Hudson, count the purple buttons on her bodice.
Bernard has a chip in his hair. Susan has a red look in her eyes.
Both are flushed. But I am pale; I am neat, and my knickerbock-
ers are drawn together by a belt with a brass snake. I know the
lesson by heart. I know more than they will ever know. I know
my cases and my genders; I could know everything in the world
if I wished. But I do not wish to come to the top and say my
lesson. My roots are threaded, like fibres in a flower-pot, round
and round about the world. I do not wish to come to the top and
live in the light of this great clock, yellow-faced, which ticks and
ticks. Jinny and Susan, Bernard and Neville bind themselves
into a thong with which to lash me. They laugh at my neatness,
at my Australian accent. I will now try to imitate Bernard softly
lisping Latin."

"Those are white words," said Susan, "like stones one picks
up by the seashore."

[handwritten marginalia: "Neville jealous?", "Louis is Aussie. Worried abt diff.", "Wm TS — Eliot", "latin dec:", "(class)", "Not a gentleman"]

"They flick their tails right and left as I speak them," said Bernard. "They wag their tails; they flick their tails; they move through the air in flocks, now this way, now that way, moving all together, now dividing, now coming together."

"Those are yellow words, those are fiery words," said Jinny. "I should like a fiery dress, a yellow dress, a fulvous dress to wear in the evening." *Tawny*

"Each tense," said Neville, "means differently. There is an order in this world; there are distinctions, there are differences in this world, upon whose verge I step. For this is only a beginning."

"Now Miss Hudson," said Rhoda, "has shut the book. Now the terror is beginning. Now taking her lump of chalk she draws figures, six, seven, eight, and then a cross and then a line on the blackboard. What is the answer? The others look; they look with understanding. Louis writes; Susan writes; Neville writes; Jinny writes; even Bernard has now begun to write. But I cannot write. I see only figures. The others are handing in their answers, one by one. Now it is my turn. But I have no answer. The others are allowed to go. They slam the door. Miss Hudson goes. I am left alone to find an answer. The figures mean nothing now. Meaning has gone. The clock ticks. The two hands are convoys marching through a desert. The black bars on the clock face are green oases. The long hand has marched ahead to find water. The other painfully stumbles among hot stones in the desert. It will die in the desert. The kitchen door slams. Wild dogs bark far away. Look, the loop of the figure is beginning to fill with time; it holds the world in it. I begin to draw a figure and the world is looped in it, and I myself am outside the loop; which I now join—so—and seal up, and make entire. The world is entire, and I am outside of it, crying, 'Oh, save me, from being blown for ever outside the loop of time!'"

*solitude is prison & refuge
wants to be left alone and saved.*

No one notices her.
Rhoda is "unseen", but
seen. ↓

14   *The Waves*

"There Rhoda sits staring at the blackboard," said Louis, "in the schoolroom, while we ramble off, picking here a bit of thyme, pinching here a leaf of southernwood while Bernard tells a story. Her shoulder-blades meet across her back like the wings of a small butterfly. And as she stares at the chalk figures, her mind lodges in those white circles; it steps through those white loops into emptiness, alone. They have no meaning for her. She has no answer for them. She has no body as the others have. And I, who speak with an Australian accent, whose father is a banker in Brisbane, do not fear her as I fear the others."

"Let us now crawl," said Bernard, "under the canopy of the currant leaves, and tell stories. Let us inhabit the underworld. Let us take possession of our secret territory, which is lit by pendant currants like candelabra, shining red on one side, black on the other. Here, Jinny, if we curl up close, we can sit under the canopy of the currant leaves and watch the censers swing. This is our universe. The others pass down the carriage-drive. The skirts of Miss Hudson and Miss Curry sweep by like candle extinguishers. Those are Susan's white socks. Those are Louis' neat sand-shoes firmly printing the gravel. Here come warm gusts of decomposing leaves, of rotting vegetation. We are in a swamp now; in a malarial jungle. There is an elephant white with maggots, killed by an arrow shot dead in its eye. The bright eyes of hopping-birds—eagles, vultures—are apparent. They take us for fallen trees. They pick at a worm—that is a hooded cobra—and leave it with a festering brown scar to be mauled by lions. This is our world, lit with crescents and stars of light; and great petals half transparent block the openings like purple windows. Everything is strange. Things are huge and very small. The stalks of flowers are thick as oak trees. Leaves are high as the domes of vast cathedrals. We are giants, lying here, who can make forests quiver."

"This is here," said Jinny, "this is now. But soon we shall go. Soon Miss Curry will blow her whistle. We shall walk. We shall part. You will go to school. You will have masters wearing crosses with white ties. I shall have a mistress in a school on the East Coast who sits under a portrait of Queen Alexandra. That is where I am going, and Susan and Rhoda. This is only here; this is only now. Now we lie under the currant bushes and every time the breeze stirs we are mottled all over. My hand is like a snake's skin. My knees are pink floating islands. Your face is like an apple tree netted under."

"The heat is going," said Bernard, "from the Jungle. The leaves flap black wings over us. Miss Curry has blown her whistle on the terrace. We must creep out from the awning of the currant leaves and stand upright. There are twigs in your hair, Jinny. There is a green caterpillar on your neck. We must form, two by two. Miss Curry is taking us for a brisk walk, while Miss Hudson sits at her desk settling her accounts."

"It is dull," said Jinny, "walking along the high road with no windows to look at, with no bleared eyes of blue glass let into the pavement."

"We must form into pairs," said Susan, "and walk in order, not shuffling our feet, not lagging, with Louis going first to lead us, because Louis is alert and not a wool-gatherer."

"Since I am supposed," said Neville, "to be too delicate to go with them, since I get so easily tired and then am sick, I will use this hour of solitude, this reprieve from conversation, to coast round the purlieus of the house and recover, if I can, by standing on the same stair half-way up the landing, what I felt when I heard about the dead man through the swing-door last night when cook was shoving in and out the dampers. He was found with his throat cut. The apple-tree leaves became fixed in the sky; the moon glared; I was unable to lift my foot up the stair. He was found in the gutter. His blood gurgled down the gutter. His jowl was white as a dead codfish. I shall call this stricture, this rigidity, 'death among the apple trees' for ever. There

semi-autobio VW

were the floating, pale-grey clouds; and the immitigable tree; the implacable tree with its greaved silver bark. The ripple of my life was unavailing. I was unable to pass by. There was an obstacle. 'I cannot surmount this unintelligible obstacle,' I said. And the others passed on. But we are doomed, all of us by the apple trees, by the immitigable tree which we cannot pass.

"Now the stricture and rigidity are over; and I will continue to make my survey of the purlieus of the house in the late afternoon, in the sunset, when the sun makes oleaginous spots on the linoleum, and a crack of light kneels on the wall, making the chair legs look broken."

"I saw Florrie in the kitchen garden," said Susan, "as we came back from our walk, with the washing blown out round her, the pyjamas, the drawers, the night-gowns blown tight. And Ernest kissed her. He was in his green baize apron, cleaning silver; and his mouth was sucked like a purse in wrinkles and he seized her with the pyjamas blown out hard between them. He was blind as a bull, and she swooned in anguish, only little veins streaking her white cheeks red. Now though they pass plates of bread and butter and cups of milk at tea-time I see a crack in the earth and hot steam hisses up; and the urn roars as Ernest roared, and I am blown out hard like the pyjamas, even while my teeth meet in the soft bread and butter, and I lap the sweet milk. I am not afraid of heat, nor of the frozen winter. Rhoda dreams, sucking a crust soaked in milk; Louis regards the wall opposite with snail-green eyes; Bernard moulds his bread into pellets and calls them 'people.' Neville with his clean and decisive ways has finished. He has rolled his napkin and slipped it through the silver ring. Jinny spins her fingers on the table-cloth, as if they were dancing in the sunshine, pirouetting. But I am not afraid of the heat or of the frozen winter."

"Now," said Louis, "we all rise; we all stand up. Miss Curry spreads wide the black book on the harmonium. It is difficult not to weep as we sing, as we pray that God may keep us safe while we sleep, calling ourselves little children. When we are sad and trembling with apprehension it is sweet to sing together, leaning slightly, I towards Susan, Susan towards Bernard, clasping hands, afraid of much, I of my accent, Rhoda of figures; yet resolute to conquer."

"We troop upstairs like ponies," said Bernard, "stamping, clattering one behind another to take our turns in the bathroom. We buffet, we tussle, we spring up and down on the hard, white beds. My turn has come. I come now.

"Mrs. Constable, girt in a bath-towel, takes her lemon-coloured sponge and soaks it in water; it turns chocolate-brown; it drips; and, holding it high above me, shivering beneath her, she squeezes it. Water pours down the runnel of my spine. Bright arrows of sensation shoot on either side. I am covered with warm flesh. My dry crannies are wetted; my cold body is warmed; it is sluiced and gleaming. Water descends and sheets me like an eel. Now hot towels envelop me, and their roughness, as I rub my back, makes my blood purr. Rich and heavy sensations form on the roof of my mind; down showers the day—the woods; and Elvedon; Susan and the pigeon. Pouring down the walls of my mind, running together, the day falls copious, resplendent. Now I tie my pyjamas loosely round me, and lie under this thin sheet afloat in the shallow light which is like a film of water drawn over my eyes by a wave. I hear through it far off, far away, faint and far, the chorus beginning; wheels; dogs; men shouting; church bells; the chorus beginning."

"As I fold up my frock and my chemise," said Rhoda, "so I put off my hopeless desire to be Susan, to be Jinny. But I will stretch my toes so that they touch the rail at the end of the bed; I will assure myself, touching the rail, of something hard. Now I cannot sink; cannot altogether fall through the thin sheet now. Now I spread my body on this frail mattress and hang suspended.

I am above the earth now. I am no longer upright, to be knocked against and damaged. All is soft, and bending. Walls and cupboards whiten and bend their yellow squares on top of which a pale glass gleams. Out of me now my mind can pour. I can think of my Armadas sailing on the high waves. I am relieved of hard contacts and collisions. I sail on alone under the white cliffs. Oh, but I sink, I fall! That is the corner of the cupboard; that is the nursery looking-glass. But they stretch, they elongate. I sink down on the black plumes of sleep; its thick wings are pressed to my eyes. Travelling through darkness I see the stretched flower-beds, and Mrs. Constable runs from behind the corner of the pampas-grass to say my aunt has come to fetch me in a carriage. I mount; I escape; I rise on spring-heeled boots over the tree-tops. But I am now fallen into the carriage at the hall door, where she sits nodding yellow plumes with eyes hard like glazed marbles. Oh, to awake from dreaming! Look, there is the chest of drawers. Let me pull myself out of these waters. But they heap themselves on me; they sweep me between their great shoulders; I am turned; I am tumbled; I am stretched, among these long lights, these long waves, these endless paths, with people pursuing, pursuing."

midday or early a.m.

*T*HE SUN rose higher. Blue waves, green waves swept a quick fan over the beach, circling the spike of sea-holly and leaving shallow pools of light here and there on the sand. A faint black rim was left behind them. The rocks which had been misty and soft hardened and were marked with red clefts.

Sharp stripes of shadow lay on the grass, and the dew dancing on the tips of the flowers and leaves made the garden like a mosaic of single sparks not yet formed into one whole. The birds, whose breasts were specked canary and rose, now sang a strain or two together, wildly, like skaters rollicking arm-in-arm, and were suddenly silent, breaking asunder.

The sun laid broader blades upon the house. The light touched something green in the window corner and made it a lump of emerald, a cave of pure green like stoneless fruit. It sharpened the edges of chairs and tables and stitched white table-cloths with fine gold wires. As the light increased a bud here and there split asunder and shook out flowers, green veined and quivering, as if the effort of opening had set them rocking, and pealing a faint carillon as they beat their frail clappers against their white walls. Everything became softly amorphous, as if the china of the plate flowed and the steel of the knife were liquid. Meanwhile the concussion of the waves breaking fell with muffled thuds, like logs falling, on the shore.

"Now," said Bernard, "the time has come. The day has come. The cab is at the door. My huge box bends George's bandy-legs even wider. The horrible ceremony is over, the tips, and the good-byes in the hall. Now there is this gulping ceremony with my mother, this hand-shaking ceremony with my father; now I must go on waving, I must go on waving, till we turn the corner. Now that ceremony is over. Heaven be praised, all ceremonies are over. I am alone; I am going to school for the first time.

"Everybody seems to be doing things for this moment only; and never again. Never again. The urgency of it all is fearful. Everybody knows I am going to school, going to school for the first time. 'That boy is going to school for the first time,' says the housemaid, cleaning the steps. I must not cry. I must behold them indifferently. Now the awful portals of the station gape; 'the moon-faced clock regards me.' I must make phrases and phrases and so interpose something hard between myself and the stare of housemaids, the stare of clocks, staring faces, indifferent faces, or I shall cry. There is Louis, there is Neville in long coats, carrying handbags, by the booking-office. They are composed. But they look different."

"Here is Bernard," said Louis. "He is composed; he is easy. He swings his bag as he walks. I will follow Bernard, because he is not afraid. We are drawn through the booking-office on to the platform as a stream draws twigs and straws round the piers of a bridge. There is the very powerful, bottle-green engine without a neck, all back and thighs, breathing steam. The guard blows his whistle; the flag is dipped; without an effort, of its own momentum, like an avalanche started by a gentle push, we start forward. Bernard spreads a rug and plays knucklebones. Neville reads. London crumbles. London heaves and surges. There is a bristling of chimneys and towers. There a white church; there a mast among the spires. There a canal. Now there are open spaces with asphalt paths upon which it is strange that people should now be walking. There is a hill striped with red houses. A man crosses a bridge with a dog at his heels. Now the red boy begins firing at a pheasant. The blue boy shoves him aside. 'My uncle is the best shot in England. My cousin is Master of Foxhounds.' Boasting begins. And I cannot boast, for my father is a banker in Brisbane, and I speak with an Australian accent."

"After all this hubbub," said Neville, "all this scuffling and hubbub, we have arrived. This is indeed a moment—this is indeed a solemn moment. I come, like a lord to his halls appointed. That is our founder; our illustrious founder, standing in the courtyard with one foot raised. I salute our founder. A noble Roman air hangs over these austere quadrangles. Already the lights are lit in the form rooms. Those are laboratories perhaps; and that a library, where I shall explore the exactitude of the Latin language, and step firmly upon the well-laid sentences, and pronounce the explicit, the sonorous hexameters of Virgil; of Lucretius; and chant with a passion that is never obscure or formless the loves of Catullus, reading from a big book, a quarto with margins. I shall lie, too, in the fields among the tickling grasses. I shall lie with my friends under the towering elm trees.

"Behold, the Headmaster. Alas, that he should excite my ridicule. He is too sleek, he is altogether too shiny and black, like some statue in a public garden. And on the left side of his waistcoat, his taut, his drum-like waistcoat, hangs a crucifix."

"Old Crane," said Bernard, "now rises to address us. Old Crane, the Headmaster, has a nose like a mountain at sunset, and a blue cleft in his chin, like a wooded ravine, which some tripper has fired; like a wooded ravine seen from the train window. He sways slightly, mouthing out his tremendous and sonorous words. I love tremendous and sonorous words. But his words are too hearty to be true. Yet he is by this time convinced of their truth. And when he leaves the room, lurching rather heavily

from side to side, and hurls his way through the swing-doors, all
the masters, lurching rather heavily from side to side, hurl themselves also through the swing-doors. This is our first night at
school, apart from our sisters."

"THIS IS MY first night at school," said Susan, "away from my
father, away from my home. My eyes swell; my eyes prick with
tears. I hate the smell of pine and linoleum. I hate the wind-
bitten shrubs and the sanitary tiles. I hate the cheerful jokes and
the glazed look of every one. I left my squirrel and my doves for
the boy to look after. The kitchen door slams, and shot patters
among the leaves when Percy fires at the rocks. All here is false;
all is meretricious. Rhoda and Jinny sit far off in brown serge,
and look at Miss Lambert who sits under a picture of Queen
Alexandra reading from a book before her. There is also a blue
scroll of needlework embroidered by some old girl. If I do not
purse my lips, if I do not screw my handkerchief, I shall cry."

    "The purple light," said Rhoda, "in Miss Lambert's ring
passes to and fro across the black stain on the white page of the
Prayer Book. It is a vinous, it is an amorous light. Now that our
boxes are unpacked in the dormitories, we sit herded together
under maps of the entire world. There are desks with wells for
the ink. We shall write our exercises in ink here. But here I am
nobody. I have no face. This great company, all dressed in
brown serge, has robbed me of my identity. We are all callous,
unfriended. I will seek out a face, a composed, a monumental
face, and will endow it with omniscience, and wear it under my
dress like a talisman and then (I promise this) I will find some
dingle in a wood where I can display my assortment of curious
treasures. I promise myself this. So I will not cry."

    "That dark woman," said Jinny, "with high cheek-bones, has
a shiny dress, like a shell, veined, for wearing in the evening. That
is nice for summer, but for winter I should like a thin dress shot

with red threads that would gleam in the firelight. Then when the lamps were lit, I should put on my red dress and it would be thin as a veil, and would wind about my body, and billow out as I came into the room, pirouetting. It would make a flower shape as I sank down, in the middle of the room, on a gilt chair. But Miss Lambert wears an opaque dress, that falls in a cascade from her snow-white ruffle as she sits under a picture of Queen Alexandra pressing one white finger firmly on the page. And we pray."

"NOW WE MARCH, two by two," said Louis, "orderly, processional, into chapel. I like the dimness that falls as we enter the sacred building. I like the orderly progress. We file in; we seat ourselves. We put off our distinctions as we enter. I like it now, when, lurching slightly, but only from his momentum, Dr. Crane mounts the pulpit and reads the lesson from a Bible spread on the back of the brass eagle. I rejoice; my heart expands in his bulk, in his authority. He lays the whirling dust clouds in my tremulous, my ignominiously agitated mind—how we danced round the Christmas tree and handing parcels they forgot me, and the fat woman said, 'This little boy has no present,' and gave me a shiny Union Jack from the top of the tree, and I cried with fury—to be remembered with pity. Now all is laid by his authority, his crucifix, and I feel come over me the sense of the earth under me, and my roots going down and down till they wrap themselves round some hardness at the centre. I recover my continuity, as he reads. I become a figure in the procession, a spoke in the huge wheel that turning, at last erects me, here and now. I have been in the dark; I have been hidden; but when the wheel turns (as he reads) I rise into this dim light where I just perceive, but scarcely, kneeling boys, pillars and memorial brasses. There is no crudity here, no sudden kisses."

"The brute menaces my liberty," said Neville, "when he prays. Unwarmed by imagination, his words fall cold on my head like paving-stones, while the gilt cross heaves on his waist-coat. The words of authority are corrupted by those who speak them. I gibe and mock at this sad religion, at these tremulous, grief-stricken figures advancing, cadaverous and wounded, down a white road shadowed by fig trees where boys sprawl in the dust—naked boys; and goat-skins distended with wine hang at the tavern door. I was in Rome travelling with my father at Easter; and the trembling figure of Christ's mother was borne niddle-noddling along the streets; there went by also the stricken figure of Christ in a glass case.

"Now I will lean sideways as if to scratch my thigh. So I shall see Percival. There he sits, upright among the smaller fry. He breathes through his straight nose rather heavily. His blue, and oddly inexpressive eyes, are fixed with pagan indifference upon the pillar opposite. He would make an admirable churchwarden. He should have a birch and beat little boys for misdemeanours. He is allied with the Latin phrases on the memorial brasses. He sees nothing; he hears nothing. He is remote from us all in a pagan universe. But look—he flicks his hand to the back of his neck. For such gestures one falls hopelessly in love for a lifetime. Dalton, Jones, Edgar and Bateman flick their hands to the backs of their necks likewise. But they do not succeed."

"At last," said Bernard, "the growl ceases. The sermon ends. He has minced the dance of the white butterflies at the door to powder. His rough and hairy voice is like an unshaven chin. Now he lurches back to his seat like a drunken sailor. It is an action that all the other masters will try to imitate; but, being flimsy, being floppy, wearing grey trousers, they will only succeed in making themselves ridiculous. I do not despise them. Their antics seem pitiable in my eyes. I note the fact for future reference with many others in my notebook. When I am grown up I shall carry a notebook—a fat book with many pages, methodically lettered. I shall enter my phrases. Under B shall come

'Butterfly powder.' If, in my novel, I describe the sun on the window-sill, I shall look under B and find butterfly powder. That will be useful. The tree 'shades the window with green fingers.' That will be useful. But alas! I am so soon distracted—by a hair like twisted candy, by Celia's Prayer Book, ivory covered. Louis can contemplate nature, unwinking, by the hour. Soon I fail, unless talked to. 'The lake of my mind, unbroken by oars, heaves placidly and soon sinks into an oily somnolence.' That will be useful."

"Now we move out of this cool temple, into the yellow playing-fields," said Louis. "And, as it is a half-holiday (the Duke's birthday) we will settle among the long grasses, while they play cricket. Could I be 'they' I would choose it; I would buckle on my pads and stride across the playing-field at the head of the batsmen. Look now, how everybody follows Percival. He is heavy. He walks clumsily down the field, through the long grass, to where the great elm trees stand. His magnificence is that of some mediaeval commander. A wake of light seems to lie on the grass behind him. Look at us trooping after him, his faithful servants, to be shot like sheep, for he will certainly attempt some forlorn enterprise and die in battle. My heart turns rough; it abrades my side like a file with two edges; one, that I adore his magnificence; the other I despise his slovenly accents—I who am so much his superior—and am jealous."

"And now," said Neville, "let Bernard begin. Let him burble on, telling us stories, while we lie recumbent. Let him describe what we have all seen so that it becomes a sequence. Bernard says there is always a story. I am a story. Louis is a story. There is the story of the boot-boy, the story of the man with one eye, the story of the woman who sells winkles. Let him burble on with his story while I lie back and regard the stiff-legged figures of the padded batsmen through the trembling grasses. It seems as if the whole world were flowing and curving—on the earth the trees, in the sky the clouds. I look up, through the trees, into the sky. The match seems to be played up there. Faintly among the soft, white clouds I hear the cry 'Run,' I hear the cry 'How's that?' The clouds lose tufts of whiteness as the breeze dishevels them. If that blue could stay for ever; if that hole could remain for ever; if this moment could stay for ever—

"But Bernard goes on talking. Up they bubble—images. 'Like a camel,' . . . 'a vulture.' The camel is a vulture; the vulture a camel; for Bernard is a dangling wire, loose, but seductive. Yes, for when he talks, when he makes his foolish comparisons, a lightness comes over one. One floats, too, as if one were that bubble; one is freed; I have escaped, one feels. Even the chubby little boys (Dalton, Larpent and Baker) feel the same abandonment. They like this better than the cricket. They catch the phrases as they bubble. They let the feathery grasses tickle their noses. And then we all feel Percival lying heavy among us. His curious guffaw seems to sanction our laughter. But now he has rolled himself over in the long grass. He is, I think, chewing a stalk between his teeth. He feels bored; I too feel bored. Bernard at once perceives that we are bored. I detect a certain effort, an extravagance in his phrase, as if he said 'Look!' but Percival says 'No.' For he is always the first to detect insincerity; and is brutal in the extreme. The sentence tails off feebly. Yes, the appalling moment has come when Bernard's power fails him and there is no longer any sequence and he sags and twiddles a bit of string and falls silent, gaping as if about to burst into tears. Among the tortures and devastations of life is this then—our friends are not able to finish their stories."

"Now let me try," said Louis, "before we rise, before we go to tea, to fix the moment in one effort of supreme endeavour. This shall endure. We are parting; some to tea; some to the nets; I to show my essay to Mr. Barker. This will endure. From discord, from hatred (I despise dabblers in imagery—I resent the

power of Percival intensely) my shattered mind is pieced together by some sudden perception. I take the trees, the clouds,
to be witnesses of my complete integration. I, Louis, I, who
shall walk the earth these seventy years, am born entire, out of
hatred, out of discord. Here on this ring of grass we have sat
together, bound by the tremendous power of some inner compulsion. The trees wave, the clouds pass. The time approaches
when these soliloquies shall be shared. We shall not always give
out a sound like a beaten gong as one sensation strikes and then
another. Children, our lives have been gongs striking; clamour
and boasting; cries of despair; blows on the nape of the neck in
gardens.

"Now grass and trees, the travelling air blowing empty
spaces in the blue which they then recover, shaking the leaves
which then replace themselves, and our ring here, sitting, with
our arms binding our knees, hint at some other order, and better, which makes a reason everlastingly. This I see for a second,
and shall try tonight to fix in words, to forge in a ring of steel,
though Percival destroys it, as he blunders off, crushing the
grasses, with the small fry trotting subservient after him. Yet it
is Percival I need; for it is Percival who inspires poetry."

"FOR HOW many months," said Susan, "for how many years,
have I run up these stairs, in the dismal days of winter, in the
chilly days of spring? Now it is midsummer. We go upstairs to
change into white frocks to play tennis—Jinny and I with
Rhoda following after. I count each step as I mount, counting
each step something done with. So each night I tear off the old
day from the calendar, and screw it tight into a ball. I do this
vindictively, while Betty and Clara are on their knees. I do not
pray. I revenge myself upon the day. I wreak my spite upon its
image. You are dead now, I say, school day, hated day. They have
made all the days of June—this is the twenty-fifth—shiny and

orderly, with gongs, with lessons, with orders to wash, to change, to work, to eat. We listen to missionaries from China. We drive off in brakes along the asphalt pavement, to attend concerts in halls. We are shown galleries and pictures.

"At home the hay waves over the meadows. My father leans upon the stile, smoking. In the house one door bangs and then another, as the summer air puffs along the empty passages. Some old picture perhaps swings on the wall. A petal drops from the rose in the jar. The farm wagons strew the hedges with tufts of hay. All this I see, I always see, as I pass the looking-glass on the landing, with Jinny in front and Rhoda lagging behind. Jinny dances. Jinny always dances in the hall on the ugly, the encaustic tiles; she turns cartwheels in the playground; she picks some flower forbiddenly, and sticks it behind her ear so that Miss Perry's dark eyes smoulder with admiration, for Jinny, not me. Miss Perry loves Jinny; and I could have loved her, but now love no one, except my father, my doves and the squirrel whom I left in the cage at home for the boy to look after."

"I hate the small looking-glass on the stairs," said Jinny. "It shows our heads only; it cuts off our heads. And my lips are too wide, and my eyes are too close together; I show my gums too much when I laugh. Susan's head, with its fell look, with its grass-green eyes which poets will love, Bernard said, because they fall upon close white stitching, put mine out; even Rhoda's face mooning, vacant, is completed, like those white petals she used to swim in her bowl. So I skip up the stairs past them, to the next landing, where the long glass hangs, and I see myself entire. I see my body and head in one now; for even in this serge frock they are one, my body and my head. Look, when I move my head I ripple all down my narrow body; even my thin legs ripple like a stalk in the wind. I flicker between the set face of Susan and Rhoda's vagueness; I leap like one of those flames that run between the cracks of the earth; I move, I dance; I never cease to move and to dance. I move like the leaf that moved in the hedge as a child and frightened me. I dance over these streaked, these impersonal, distempered walls with their yellow skirting as firelight dances over teapots. I catch fire even from women's cold eyes. When I read, a purple rim runs round the black edge of the textbook. Yet I cannot follow any word through its changes. I cannot follow any thought from present to past. I do not stand lost, like Susan, with tears in my eyes remembering home; or lie, like Rhoda, crumpled among the ferns, staining my pink cotton green, while I dream of plants that flower under the sea, and rocks through which the fish swim slowly. I do not dream.

"Now let us be quick. Now let me be the first to pull off these coarse clothes. Here are my clean white stockings. Here are my new shoes. I bind my hair with a white ribbon, so that when I leap across the court the ribbon will stream out in a flash, yet curl round my neck, perfectly in its place. Not a hair shall be untidy."

"That is my face," said Rhoda, "in the looking-glass behind Susan's shoulder—that face is my face. But I will duck behind her to hide it, for I am not here. I have no face. Other people have faces; Susan and Jinny have faces; they are here. Their world is the real world. The things they lift are heavy. They say Yes, they say No; whereas I shift and change and am seen through in a second. If they meet a housemaid she looks at them without laughing. But she laughs at me. They know what to say if spoken to. They laugh really; they get angry really; while I have to look first and do what other people do when they have done it.

"See now with what extraordinary certainty Jinny pulls on her stockings, simply to play tennis. That I admire. But I like Susan's way better, for she is more resolute, and less ambitious of distinction than Jinny. Both despise me for copying what they do; but Susan sometimes teaches me, for instance, how to tie a bow, while Jinny has her own knowledge but keeps it to herself. They have friends to sit by. They have things to say privately in corners. But I attach myself only to names and faces; and hoard them like amulets against disaster. I choose out across the hall some unknown face and can hardly drink my tea when she whose name I do not know sits opposite. I choke. I am rocked from side to side by the violence of my emotion. I imagine these nameless, these immaculate people, watching me from behind bushes. I leap high to excite their admiration. At night, in bed, I excite their complete wonder. I often die pierced with arrows to win their tears. If they should say, or I should see from a label on their boxes that they were in Scarborough last holidays, the whole town runs gold, the whole pavement is illuminated. Therefore I hate looking-glasses which show me my real face. Alone, I often fall down into nothingness. I must push my foot stealthily lest I should fall off the edge of the world into nothingness. I have to bang my hand against some hard door to call myself back to the body."

"We are late," said Susan. "We must wait our turn to play. We will pitch here in the long grass and pretend to watch Jinny and Clara, Betty and Mavis. But we will not watch them. I hate watching other people play games. I will make images of all the things I hate most and bury them in the ground. This shiny pebble is Madame Carlo, and I will bury her deep because of her fawning and ingratiating manners, because of the sixpence she gave me for keeping my knuckles flat when I played my scales. I buried her sixpence. I would bury the whole school; the gymnasium; the classroom; the dining-room that always smells of meat, and the chapel. I would bury the red-brown tiles and the oily portraits of old men—benefactors, founders of schools. There are some trees I like; the cherry tree with lumps of clear gum on the bark; and one view from the attic towards some far hills. Save for these, I would bury it all as I bury these ugly stones that are always scattered about this briny coast, with its piers and its trippers. At home, the waves are mile long. On winter nights we hear them booming. Last Christmas a man was drowned sitting alone in his cart."

"When Miss Lambert passes," said Rhoda, "talking to the clergyman, the others laugh and imitate her hunch behind her back; yet everything changes and becomes luminous. Jinny leaps higher too when Miss Lambert passes. Suppose she saw that daisy, it would change. Wherever she goes, things are changed under her eyes; and yet when she has passed is not the thing the same again? Miss Lambert is taking the clergyman through the wicket-gate to her private garden; and when she comes to the pond, she sees a frog on a leaf, and that will change. All is solemn, all is pale where she stands, like a statue in a grove. She lets her tasselled silken cloak slip down, and only her purple ring still glows, her vinous, her amethystine ring. There is this mystery about people when they leave us. When they leave us I can companion them to the pond and make them stately. When Miss Lambert passes, she makes the daisy change; and everything runs like streaks of fire when she carves the beef. Month by month things are losing their hardness; even my body now lets the light through; my spine is soft like wax near the flame of the candle. I dream; I dream."

"I have won the game," said Jinny. "Now it is your turn. I must throw myself on the ground and pant. I am out of breath with running, with triumph. Everything in my body seems thinned out with running and triumph. My blood must be bright red, whipped up, slapping against my ribs. My soles tingle, as if wire rings opened and shut in my feet. I see every blade of grass very clear. But the pulse drums so in my forehead, behind my eyes, that everything dances—the net, the grass; your faces leap like butterflies; the trees seem to jump up and down. There is nothing staid, nothing settled in this universe. All is rippling, all is dancing; all is quickness and triumph. Only, when I have lain alone on the hard ground, watching you play your game, I begin to feel the wish to be singled out; to be summoned, to be called away by one person who comes to find me, who is attracted towards me, who cannot keep himself from me, but comes to where I sit on my gilt chair, with my frock billowing round me like a flower. And withdrawing into an alcove, sitting alone on a balcony we talk together.

"Now the tide sinks. Now the trees come to earth; the brisk waves that slap my ribs rock more gently, and my heart rides at anchor, like a sailing-boat whose sails slide slowly down on to the white deck. The game is over. We must go to tea now."

"THE BOASTING boys," said Louis, "have gone now in a vast team to play cricket. They have driven off in their great brake, singing in chorus. All their heads turn simultaneously at the corner by the laurel bushes. Now they are boasting. Larpent's brother played football for Oxford; Smith's father made a century at Lords. Archie and Hugh; Parker and Dalton; Larpent and Smith; then again Archie and Hugh; Parker and Dalton; Larpent and Smith—the names repeat themselves; the names are the same always. They are the volunteers; they are the cricketers; they are the officers of the Natural History Society. They are always forming into fours and marching in troops with badges on their caps; they salute simultaneously passing the figure of their general. How majestic is their order, how beautiful is their obedience! If I could follow, if I could be with them I would sacrifice all I know. But they also leave butterflies trembling with their wings pinched off; they throw dirty pocket-handkerchiefs clotted with blood screwed up into corners. They make little boys sob in dark passages. They have big red ears that stand out under their caps. Yet that is what we wish to be, Neville and I. I watch them go with envy. Peeping from behind a curtain, I note the simultaneity of their movements with delight. If my legs were reinforced by theirs, how they would run! If I had been with them and won matches and rowed in great races, and galloped all day, how I should thunder out songs at midnight! In what a torrent the words would rush from my throat!"

"Percival has gone now," said Neville. "He is thinking of nothing but the match. He never waved his hand as the brake turned the corner by the laurel bush. He despises me for being too weak to play (yet he is always kind to my weakness). He despises me for not caring if they win or lose except that he cares. He takes my devotion; he accepts my tremulous, no doubt abject offering, mixed with contempt as it is for his mind. For he cannot read. Yet when I read Shakespeare or Catullus, lying in the long grass, he understands more than Louis. Not the words—but what are words? Do I not know already how to rhyme, how to imitate Pope, Dryden, even Shakespeare? But I cannot stand all day in the sun with my eyes on the ball; I cannot feel the flight of the ball through my body and think only of the ball. I shall be a clinger to the outsides of words all my life. Yet I could not live with him and suffer his stupidity. He will coarsen and snore. He will marry and there will be scenes of tenderness at breakfast. But now he is young. Not a thread, not a sheet of paper lies between him and the sun, between him and the rain, between him and the moon as he lies naked, tumbled, hot, on his bed. Now as they drive along the high road in their brake his face is mottled red and yellow. He will throw off his coat and stand with his legs apart, with his hands ready, watching the wicket. And he will pray, 'Lord, let us win'; he will think of one thing only, that they should win.

"How could I go with them in a brake to play cricket? Only Bernard could go with them, but Bernard is too late to go with them. He is always too late. He is prevented by his incorrigible moodiness from going with them. He stops, when he washes his hands, to say, 'There is a fly in that web. Shall I rescue that fly; shall I let the spider eat it?' He is shaded with innumerable perplexities, or he would go with them to play cricket, and would lie in the grass, watching the sky, and would start when the ball was hit. But they would forgive him; for he would tell them a story."

"They have bowled off," said Bernard, "and I am too late to go with them. The horrid little boys, who are also so beautiful, whom you and Louis, Neville, envy so deeply, have bowled off with their heads all turned the same way. But I am unaware of these profound distinctions. My fingers slip over the keyboard without knowing which is black and which white. Archie makes easily a hundred; I by a fluke make sometimes fifteen. But what is the difference between us? Wait though, Neville; let me talk. The bubbles are rising like the silver bubbles from the floor of a saucepan; image on top of image. I cannot sit down to my book, like Louis, with ferocious tenacity. I must open the little trap-door and let out these linked phrases in which I run together whatever happens so that instead of incoherence there is perceived a wandering thread, lightly joining one thing to another. I will tell you the story of the doctor.

"When Dr. Crane lurches through the swing-doors after prayers he is convinced, it seems, of his immense superiority; and indeed, Neville, we cannot deny that his departure leaves us not only with a sense of relief, but also with a sense of something removed, like a tooth. Now let us follow him as he heaves through the swing-door to his own apartments. Let us imagine him in his private room over the stables undressing. He unfastens his sock suspenders (let us be trivial, let us be intimate). Then with a characteristic gesture (it is difficult to avoid these ready-made phrases, and they are, in his case, somehow appropriate) he takes the silver, he takes the coppers from his trouser pockets and places them there, and there, on his dressing-table. With both arms stretched on the arms of his chair he reflects (this is his private moment; it is here we must try to catch him) shall he cross the pink bridge into his bedroom or shall he not cross it? The two rooms are united by a bridge of rosy light from the lamp at the bedside where Mrs. Crane lies with her hair on the pillow reading a French memoir. As she reads, she sweeps her hand with an abandoned and despairing gesture over her forehead, and sighs, 'Is this all?' comparing herself with some French duchess. Now, says the doctor, in two years I shall retire. I shall clip yew hedges in a west country garden. An admiral I might have been; or a judge; not a schoolmaster. What forces, he asks, staring at the gas-fire with his shoulders hunched up more hugely than we know them (he is in his shirt-sleeves remember) have brought me to this? What vast forces? he thinks, getting into the stride of his majestic phrases as he looks over his shoulder at the window. It is a stormy night; the branches of the chestnut trees are ploughing up and down. Stars flash between them. What vast forces of good and evil have brought me here? he asks, and sees with sorrow that his chair has worn a little hole in the pile of the purple carpet. So there he sits, swinging his braces. But stories that follow people into their private rooms are difficult. I cannot go on with this story. I twiddle a piece of string; I turn over four or five coins in my trouser pocket."

"Bernard's stories amuse me," said Neville, "at the start. But when they tail off absurdly and he gapes, twiddling a bit of string, I feel my own solitude. He sees every one with blurred edges. Hence I cannot talk to him of Percival. I cannot expose my absurd and violent passion to his sympathetic understanding. It, too, would make a 'story.' I need some one whose mind falls like a chopper on a block; to whom the pitch of absurdity is sublime; and a shoe-string adorable. To whom can I expose the urgency of my own passion? Louis is too cold, too universal. There is nobody—here among these grey arches, and moaning pigeons, and cheerful games and tradition and emulation, all so skilfully organised to prevent feeling alone. Yet I am struck still as I walk by sudden premonitions of what is to come. Yesterday, passing the open door leading into the private garden, I saw Fenwick with his mallet raised. The steam from the tea-urn rose in the middle of the lawn. There were banks of blue flowers. Then suddenly descended upon me the obscure, the mystic sense of adoration, of completeness that triumphed over chaos. Nobody saw my poised and intent figure as I stood at the open door. Nobody guessed the need I had to offer my being to one god; and perish, and disappear. His mallet descended; the vision broke.

"Should I seek out some tree? Should I desert these form rooms and libraries, and the broad yellow page in which I read Catullus, for woods and fields? Should I walk under beech trees, or saunter along the river bank, where the trees meet united like lovers in the water? But nature is too vegetable, too vapid. She has only sublimities and vastitudes and water and leaves. I begin to wish for firelight, privacy, and the limbs of one person."

"I begin to wish," said Louis, "for night to come. As I stand here with my hand on the grained oak panel of Mr. Wickham's door I think myself the friend of Richelieu, or the Duke of St. Simon holding out a snuff-box to the King himself. It is my privilege. My witticisms 'run like wildfire through the court.' Duchesses tear emeralds from their ear-rings out of admiration—but these rockets rise best in darkness, in my cubicle at night. I am now a boy only with a colonial accent holding my knuckles against Mr. Wickham's grained oak door. The day has been full of ignominies and triumphs concealed from fear of laughter. I am the best scholar in the school. But when darkness comes I put off this unenviable body—my large nose, my thin lips, my colonial accent—and inhabit space. I am then Virgil's companion, and Plato's. I am then the last scion of one of the great houses of France. But I am also one who will force himself to desert these windy and moonlit territories, these midnight wanderings, and confront grained oak doors. I will achieve in my life—Heaven grant that it be not long—some gigantic amalgamation between the two discrepancies so hideously apparent to me. Out of my suffering I will do it. I will knock. I will enter."

"I HAVE TORN off the whole of May and June," said Susan, "and twenty days of July. I have torn them off and screwed them up so that they no longer exist, save as a weight in my side. They have been crippled days, like moths with shrivelled wings unable to fly. There are only eight days left. In eight days' time I shall get out of the train and stand on the platform at six-twenty-five. Then my freedom will unfurl, and all these restrictions that wrinkle and shrivel—hours and order and discipline, and being here and there exactly at the right moment—will crack asunder. Out the day will spring, as I open the carriage-door and see my father in his old hat and gaiters. I shall tremble. I shall burst into tears. Then next morning I shall get up at dawn. I shall let myself out by the kitchen door. I shall walk on the moor. The great horses of the phantom riders will thunder behind me and stop suddenly. I shall see the swallow skim the grass. I shall throw myself on a bank by the river and watch the fish slip in and out among the reeds. The palms of my hands will be printed with pine-needles. I shall there unfold and take out whatever it is I have made here; something hard. For something has grown in me here, through the winters and summers, on staircases, in bedrooms. I do not want, as Jinny wants, to be admired. I do not want people, when I come in, to look up with admiration. I want to give, to be given, and solitude in which to unfold my possessions.

"Then I shall come back through the trembling lanes under the arches of the nut leaves. I shall pass an old woman wheeling a perambulator full of sticks; and the shepherd. But we shall not speak. I shall come back through the kitchen garden, and see the curved leaves of the cabbages pebbled with dew, and the house in the garden, blind with curtained windows. I shall go upstairs to my room, and turn over my own things, locked carefully in the wardrobe; my shells; my eggs; my curious grasses. I shall feed my doves and my squirrel. I shall go to the kennel and comb my spaniel. So gradually I shall turn over the hard thing that has grown here in my side. But here bells ring; feet shuffle perpetually."

"I hate darkness and sleep and night," said Jinny, "and lie longing for the day to come. I long that the week should be all one day without divisions. When I wake early—and the birds wake me—I lie and watch the brass handles on the cupboard grow clear; then the basin; then the towel-horse. As each thing in the bedroom grows clear, my heart beats quicker. I feel my body harden, and become pink, yellow, brown. My hands pass over my legs and body. I feel its slopes, its thinness. I love to hear the gong roar through the house and the stir begin—here a thud, there a patter. Doors slam; water rushes. Here is another day, here is another day, I cry, as my feet touch the floor. It may be a bruised day, an imperfect day. I am often scolded. I am often in disgrace for idleness, for laughing; but even as Miss Matthews grumbles at my feather-headed carelessness, I catch sight of something moving—a speck of sun perhaps on a picture, or the donkey drawing the mowing-machine across the lawn; or a sail that passes between the laurel leaves, so that I am never cast down. I cannot be prevented from pirouetting behind Miss Matthews into prayers.

"Now, too, the time is coming when we shall leave school and wear long skirts. I shall wear necklaces and a white dress without sleeves at night. There will be parties in brilliant rooms; and one man will single me out and will tell me what he has told no other person. He will like me better than Susan or Rhoda. He will find in me some quality, some peculiar thing. But I shall not let myself be attached to one person only. I do not want to be fixed, to be pinioned. I tremble, I quiver, like the leaf in the hedge, as I sit dangling my feet, on the edge of the bed, with a new day to break open. I have fifty years, I have sixty years to spend. I have not yet broken into my hoard. This is the beginning."

"There are hours and hours," said Rhoda, "before I can put out the light and lie suspended on my bed above the world, before I can let the day drop down, before I can let my tree grow, quivering in green pavilions above my head. Here I cannot let it grow. Somebody knocks through it. They ask questions, they interrupt, they throw it down.

"Now I will go to the bathroom and take off my shoes and wash; but as I wash, as I bend my head down over the basin, I will let the Russian Empress's veil flow about my shoulders. The diamonds of the Imperial crown blaze on my forehead. I hear the roar of the hostile mob as I step out on to the balcony. Now I dry my hands, vigorously, so that Miss, whose name I forget, cannot suspect that I am waving my fist at an infuriated mob. 'I am your Empress, people.' My attitude is one of defiance. I am fearless. I conquer.

"But this is a thin dream. This is a papery tree. Miss Lambert blows it down. Even the sight of her vanishing down the corridor blows it to atoms. It is not solid; it gives me no satisfaction—this Empress dream. It leaves me, now that it has fallen, here in the passage rather shivering. Things seem paler. I will go now into the library and take out some book, and read and look; and read again and look. Here is a poem about a hedge. I will wander down it and pick flowers, green cowbind and the moonlight coloured may, wild roses and ivy serpentine. I will clasp them in my hands and lay them on the desk's shiny surface. I will sit by the river's trembling edge and look at the water-lilies, broad and bright, which lit the oak that overhung the hedge with moonlight beams of their own watery light. I will pick flowers; I will bind flowers in one garland and clasp them and present them—Oh! to whom? There is some check in the flow of my being; a deep stream presses on some obstacle; it jerks; it tugs; some knot in the centre resists. Oh, this is pain, this is anguish! I faint, I fail. Now my body thaws; I am un-sealed, I am incandescent. Now the stream pours in a deep tide fertilising, opening the shut, forcing the tight-folded, flooding free. To whom shall I give all that now flows through me, from my warm, my porous body? I will gather my flowers and present them—Oh! to whom?

"Sailors loiter on the parade, and amorous couples; the om-nibuses rattle along the sea front to the town. I will give; I will enrich; I will return to the world this beauty. I will bind my flow-ers in one garland and advancing with my hand outstretched will present them—Oh! to whom?"

"NOW WE have received," said Louis, "for this is the last day of the last term—Neville's and Bernard's and my last day—what-ever our masters have had to give us. The introduction has been made; the world presented. They stay, we depart. The great Doctor, whom of all men I most revere, swaying a little from side to side among the tables, the bound volumes, has dealt out Horace, Tennyson, the complete works of Keats and Matthew Arnold suitably inscribed. I respect the hand which gave them. He speaks with complete conviction. To him his words are true, though not to us. Speaking in the gruff voice of deep emotion, fiercely, tenderly, he has told us that we are about to go. He has bid us 'quit ourselves like men.' (On his lips quotations from the

Bible, from the *Times,* seem equally magnificent.) Some will do
this; others that. Some will not meet again. Neville, Bernard and
I shall not meet here again. Life will divide us. But we have
formed certain ties. Our boyish, our irresponsible years are over.
But we have forged certain links. Above all, we have inherited
traditions. These stone flags have been worn for six hundred
years. On these walls are inscribed the names of men of war, of
statesmen, of some unhappy poets (mine shall be among them).
Blessings be on all traditions, on all safeguards and circumscrip-
tions! I am most grateful to you men in black gowns, and you,
dead, for your leading, for your guardianship; yet after all, the
problem remains. The differences are not yet solved. Flowers
toss their heads outside the window. I see wild birds, and im-
pulses wilder than the wildest birds strike from my wild heart.
My eyes are wild; my lips tight pressed. The bird flies; the flower
dances; but I hear always the sullen thud of the waves; and the
chained beast stamps on the beach. It stamps and stamps."

"This is the final ceremony," said Bernard. "This is the last
of all our ceremonies. We are overcome by strange feelings. The
guard holding his flag is about to blow his whistle; the train
breathing steam in another moment is about to start. One wants
to say something, to feel something, absolutely appropriate to
the occasion. One's mind is primed; one's lips are pursed. And
then a bee drifts in and hums round the flowers in the bouquet
which Lady Hampton, the wife of the General, keeps smelling
to show her appreciation of the compliment. If the bee were to
sting her nose? We are all deeply moved; yet irreverent; yet pen-
itent; yet anxious to get it over; yet reluctant to part. The bee
distracts us; its casual flight seems to deride our intensity. Humming vaguely, skimming widely, it is settled now on the carnation. Many of us will not meet again. We shall not enjoy certain
pleasures again, when we are free to go to bed, or to sit up, when
I need no longer smuggle in bits of candle ends and immoral

literature. The bee now hums round the head of the great Doctor. Larpent, John, Archie, Percival, Baker and Smith—I have liked them enormously. I have known one mad boy only. I have hated one mean boy only. I enjoy in retrospect my terribly awkward breakfasts at the Headmaster's table with toast and marmalade. He alone does not notice the bee. If it were to settle on his nose he would flick it off with one magnificent gesture. Now he has made his joke; now his voice has almost broken but not quite. Now we are dismissed—Louis, Neville and I for ever. We take our highly-polished books scholastically inscribed in a little crabbed hand. We rise, we disperse; the pressure is removed. The bee has become an insignificant, a disregarded insect, flown through the open window into obscurity. Tomorrow we go."

"We are about to part," said Neville. "Here are the boxes; here are the cabs. There is Percival in his billycock hat. He will forget me. He will leave my letters lying about among guns and dogs unanswered. I shall send him poems and he will perhaps reply with a picture post card. But it is for that that I love him. I shall propose meeting—under a clock, by some Cross; and shall wait, and he will not come. It is for that that I love him. Oblivious, almost entirely ignorant, he will pass from my life. And I shall pass, incredible as it seems, into other lives; this is only an escapade perhaps, a prelude only. I feel already, though I cannot endure the Doctor's pompous mummery, and faked emotions, that things we have only dimly perceived draw near. I shall be free to enter the garden where Fenwick raises his mallet. Those who have despised me shall acknowledge my sovereignty. But by some inscrutable law of my being sovereignty and the possession of power will not be enough; I shall always push through curtains to privacy, and want some whispered words alone. Therefore I go, dubious, but elate; apprehensive of intolerable pain; yet I think bound in my adventuring to conquer after huge suffering, bound, surely, to discover my desire in the

end. There, for the last time, I see the statue of our pious
founder with the doves about his head. They will wheel for ever
about his head, whitening it, while the organ moans in the
chapel. So I take my seat; and, when I have found my place in
the corner of our reserved compartment, I will shade my eyes
with a book to hide one tear; I will shade my eyes to observe;
to peep at one face. It is the first day of the summer holidays."

"IT IS THE first day of the summer holidays," said Susan. "But
the day is still rolled up. I will not examine it until I step out on
to the platform in the evening. I will not let myself even smell
it until I smell the cold green air off the fields. But already these
are not school fields; these are not school hedges; the men in
these fields are doing real things; they fill carts with real hay; and
those are real cows, not school cows. But the carbolic smell of
corridors and the chalky smell of schoolrooms is still in my nostrils. The glazed, shiny look of matchboard is still in my eyes. I
must wait for fields and hedges, and woods and fields, and steep
railway cuttings, sprinkled with gorse bushes, and trucks in sid-
ings, and tunnels and suburban gardens with women hanging
out washing, and then fields again and children swinging on
gates to cover it over, to bury it deep, this school that I have
hated.

"I will not send my children to school nor spend a night all
my life in London. Here in this vast station everything echoes
and booms hollowly. The light is like the yellow light under an
awning. Jinny lives here. Jinny takes her dog for walks on these
pavements. People here shoot through the streets silently. They
look at nothing but shop-windows. Their heads bob up and
down all at about the same height. The streets are laced together
with telegraph wires. The houses are all glass, all festoons and
glitter; now all front doors and lace curtains, all pillars and white
steps. But now I pass on, out of London again; the fields begin

again; and the houses, and women hanging washing, and trees and fields. London is now veiled, now vanished, now crumbled, now fallen. The carbolic and the pitch-pine begin to lose their savour. I smell corn and turnips. I undo a paper packet tied with a piece of white cotton. The egg shells slide in to the cleft between my knees. Now we stop at station after station, rolling out milk cans. Now women kiss each other and help with baskets. Now I will let myself lean out of the window. The air rushes down my nose and throat—the cold air, the salt air with the smell of turnip fields in it. And there is my father, with his back turned, talking to a farmer. I tremble. I cry. There is my father in gaiters. There is my father."

"I sit snug in my own corner going North," said Jinny, "in this roaring express which is yet so smooth that it flattens hedges, lengthens hills. We flash past signal-boxes; we make the earth rock slightly from side to side. The distance closes for ever in a point; and we for ever open the distance wide again. The telegraph poles bob up incessantly; one is felled, another rises. Now we roar and swing into a tunnel. The gentleman pulls up the window. I see reflections on the shining glass which lines the tunnel. I see him lower his paper. He smiles at my reflection in the tunnel. My body instantly of its own accord puts forth a frill under his gaze. My body lives a life of its own. Now the black window glass is green again. We are out of the tunnel. He reads his paper. But we have exchanged the approval of our bodies. There is then a great society of bodies, and mine is introduced; mine has come into the room where the gilt chairs are. Look— all the windows of the villas and their white-tented curtains dance; and the men sitting in the hedges in the cornfields with knotted blue handkerchiefs are aware too, as I am aware, of heat and rapture. One waves as we pass him. There are bowers and arbours in these villa gardens and young men in shirt-sleeves on ladders trimming roses. A man on a horse canters over the field.

His horse plunges as we pass. And the rider turns to look at us. We roar again through blackness. And I lie back; I give myself up to rapture; I think that at the end of the tunnel I enter a lamp-lit room with chairs into one of which I sink, much admired, my dress billowing round me. But behold, looking up, I meet the eyes of a sour woman, who suspects me of rapture. My body shuts in her face, impertinently, like a parasol. I open my body, I shut my body at my will. Life is beginning. I now break into my hoard of life."

"It is the first day of the summer holidays," said Rhoda. "And now, as the train passes by these red rocks, by this blue sea, the term, done with, forms itself into one shape behind me. I see its colour. June was white. I see the fields white with daisies, and white with dresses; and tennis courts marked with white. Then there was wind and violent thunder. There was a star riding through clouds one night, and I said to the star, 'Consume me.' That was at midsummer, after the garden party, and my humiliation at the garden party. Wind and storm coloured July. Also, in the middle, cadaverous, awful, lay the grey puddle in the courtyard, when, holding an envelope in my hand, I carried a message. I came to the puddle. I could not cross it. Identity failed me. We are nothing, I said, and fell. I was blown like a feather. I was wafted down tunnels. Then very gingerly, I pushed my foot across. I laid my hand against a brick wall. I returned very painfully, drawing myself back into my body over the grey, cadaverous space of the puddle. This is life then to which I am committed.

"So I detach the summer term. With intermittent shocks, sudden as the springs of a tiger, life emerges heaving its dark crest from the sea. It is to this we are attached; it is to this we are bound, as bodies to wild horses. And yet we have invented devices for filling up the crevices and disguising these fissures. Here is the ticket collector. Here are two men; three women;

there is a cat in a basket; myself with my elbow on the window-sill—this is here and now. We draw on, we make off, through whispering fields of golden corn. Women in the fields are surprised to be left behind there, hoeing. The train now stamps heavily, breathes stertorously, as it climbs up and up. At last we are on the top of the moor. Only a few wild sheep live here; a few shaggy ponies; yet we are provided with every comfort; with tables to hold our newspapers, with rings to hold our tumblers. We come carrying these appliances with us over the top of the moor. Now we are on the summit. Silence will close behind us. If I look back over that bald head, I can see silence already closing and the shadows of clouds chasing each other over the empty moor; silence closes over our transient passage. This I say is the present moment; this is the first day of the summer holidays. This is part of the emerging monster to whom we are attached."

"NOW WE are off," said Louis. "Now I hang suspended without attachments. We are nowhere. We are passing through England in a train. England slips by the window, always changing from hill to wood, from rivers and willows to towns again. And I have no firm ground to which I go. Bernard and Neville, Percival, Archie, Larpent and Baker go to Oxford or Cambridge, to Edinburgh, Rome, Paris, Berlin, or to some American University. I go vaguely, to make money vaguely. Therefore a poignant shadow, a keen accent, falls on these golden bristles, on these poppy-red fields, this flowing corn that never overflows its boundaries; but runs rippling to the edge. This is the first day of a new life, another spoke of the rising wheel. But my body passes vagrant as a bird's shadow. I should be transient as the shadow on the meadow, soon fading, soon darkening and dying there where it meets the wood, were it not that I coerce my brain to form in my forehead; I force myself to state, if only in one line of unwritten poetry, this moment; to mark this inch in the long, long history that began in Egypt, in the time of the Pharaohs, when women carried red pitchers to the Nile. I seem already to have lived many thousand years. But if I now shut my eyes, if I fail to realise the meeting-place of past and present, that I sit in a third-class railway carriage full of boys going home for the holidays, human history is defrauded of a moment's vision. Its eye, that would see through me, shuts—if I sleep now, through slovenliness, or cowardice, burying myself in the past, in the dark; or acquiesce, as Bernard acquiesces, telling stories; or boast, as Percival, Archie, John, Walter, Lathom, Larpent, Roper, Smith boast—the names are the same always, the names of the boasting boys. They are all boasting, all talking, except Neville, who slips a look occasionally over the edge of a French novel, and so will always slip into cushioned firelit rooms, with many books and one friend, while I tilt on an office chair behind a counter. Then I shall grow bitter and mock at them. I shall envy them their continuance down the safe traditional ways under the shade of old yew trees while I consort with cockneys and clerks, and tap the pavements of the city.

"But now disembodied, passing over fields without lodgment—(there is a river; a man fishes; there is a spire, there is the village street with its bow-windowed inn)—all is dreamlike and dim to me. These hard thoughts, this envy, this bitterness, make no lodgment in me. I am the ghost of Louis, an ephemeral passer-by, in whose mind dreams have power, and garden sounds when in the early morning petals float on fathomless depths, and the birds sing. I dash and sprinkle myself with the bright waters of childhood. Its thin veil quivers. But the chained beast stamps and stamps on the shore."

"Louis and Neville," said Bernard, "both sit silent. Both are absorbed. Both feel the presence of other people as a separating wall. But if I find myself in company with other people, words at once make smoke rings—see how phrases at once begin to wreathe off my lips. It seems that a match is set to a fire; something burns. An elderly and apparently prosperous man, a traveller, now gets in. And I at once wish to approach him; I instinctively dislike the sense of his presence, cold, unassimilated, among us. I do not believe in separation. We are not single. Also I wish to add to my collection of valuable observations upon the true nature of human life. My book will certainly run to many volumes embracing every known variety of man and woman. I fill my mind with whatever happens to be the contents of a room or a railway carriage as one fills a fountain-pen in an inkpot. I have a steady unquenchable thirst. Now I feel by imperceptible signs, which I cannot yet interpret but will later, that his defiance is about to thaw. His solitude shows signs of cracking. He has passed a remark about a country house. A smoke ring issues from my lips (about crops) and circles him, bringing him into contact. The human voice has a disarming quality—(we are not single, we are one). As we exchange these few but amiable remarks, about country houses, I furbish him up and make him concrete. He is indulgent as a husband but not faithful; a small builder who employs a few men. In local society he is important; is already a councillor, and perhaps in time will be mayor. He wears a large ornament, like a double tooth torn up by the roots, made of coral, hanging at his watch-chain. Walter J. Trumble is the sort of name that would fit him. He has been in America, on a business trip with his wife, and a double room in a smallish hotel cost him a whole month's wages. His front tooth is stopped with gold.

"The fact is that I have little aptitude for reflection. I require the concrete in everything. It is so only that I lay hands upon the world. A good phrase, however, seems to me to have an independent existence. Yet I think it is likely that the best are made in solitude. They require some final refrigeration which I cannot give them dabbling always in warm soluble words. My method, nevertheless, has certain advantages over theirs. Neville is repelled by the grossness of Trumble. Louis, glancing, tripping with the high step of a disdainful crane, picks up words as if in sugar-tongs. It is true that his eyes—wild, laughing, yet desperate—express something that we have not gauged. There is about both Neville and Louis a precision, an exactitude that I admire and shall never possess. Now I begin to be aware that action is demanded. We approach a junction; at a junction I have to change. I have to board a train for Edinburgh. I cannot precisely lay fingers on this fact—it lodges loosely among my thoughts like a button, like a small coin. Here is the jolly old boy who collects tickets. I had one—I had one certainly. But it does not matter. Either I shall find it, or I shall not find it. I examine my note-case. I look in all my pockets. These are the things that for ever interrupt the process upon which I am eternally engaged of finding some perfect phrase that fits this very moment exactly."

"Bernard has gone," said Neville, "without a ticket. He has escaped us, making a phrase, waving his hand. He talked as easily to the horse-breeder or to the plumber as to us. The plumber accepted him with devotion. 'If he had a son like that,' he was thinking, 'he would manage to send him to Oxford.' But what did Bernard feel for the plumber? Did he not only wish to continue the sequence of the story which he never stops telling himself? He began it when he rolled his bread into pellets as a child. One pellet was a man, one was a woman. We are all pellets. We are all phrases in Bernard's story, things he writes down in his notebook under A or under B. He tells our story with extraordinary understanding, except of what we most feel. For he does not need us. He is never at our mercy. There he is, waving his arms on the platform. The train has gone without him. He has missed his connection. He has lost his ticket. But that does not matter. He will talk to the barmaid about the nature of human destiny. We are off; he has forgotten us already; we pass out of his view; we go on, filled with lingering sensations, half bitter, half sweet, for he is somehow to be pitied breasting the world with half-finished phrases, having lost his ticket; he is also to be loved.

"Now I pretend again to read. I raise my book, till it almost covers my eyes. But I cannot read in the presence of horse-dealers and plumbers. I have no power of ingratiating myself. I do not admire that man; he does not admire me. Let me at least be honest. Let me denounce this piffling, trifling, self-satisfied world; these horse-hair seats; these coloured photographs of piers and parades. I could shriek aloud at the smug self-satisfaction, at the mediocrity of this world, which breeds horse-dealers with coral ornaments hanging from their watch-chains. There is that in me which will consume them entirely. My laughter shall make them twist in their seats; shall drive them howling before me. No; they are immortal. They triumph. They will make it impossible for me always to read Catullus in a third-class railway carriage. They will drive me in October to take refuge in one of the universities, where I shall become a don; and go with schoolmasters to Greece; and lecture on the ruins of the Parthenon. It would be better to breed horses and live in one of those red villas than to run in and out of the skulls of Sophocles and Euripides like a maggot, with a high-minded wife, one of those University women. That, however, will be my fate. I shall suffer. I am already at eighteen capable of such contempt that horse-breeders hate me. That is my triumph; I do not compromise. I am not timid; I have no accent. I do not finick about fearing what people think of 'my father a banker at Brisbane' like Louis.

"Now we draw near the centre of the civilised world. There are the familiar gasometers. There are the public gardens intersected by asphalt paths. There are the lovers lying shamelessly mouth to mouth on the burnt grass. Percival is now almost in Scotland; his train draws through the red moors; he sees the long line of the border hills and the Roman wall. He reads a detective novel, yet understands everything.

"The train slows and lengthens, as we approach London, the centre, and my heart draws out too, in fear, in exultation. I am about to meet—what? What extraordinary adventure waits me, among these mail vans, these porters, these swarms of people calling taxis? I feel insignificant, lost, but exultant. With a soft shock we stop. I will let the others get out before me. I will sit still one moment before I emerge into that chaos, that tumult. I will not anticipate what is to come. The huge uproar is in my ears. It sounds and resounds under this glass roof like the surge of a sea. We are cast down on the platform with our handbags. We are whirled asunder. My sense of self almost perishes; my contempt. I become drawn in, tossed down, thrown sky-high. I step out on to the platform, grasping tightly all that I possess—one bag."

*T*HE SUN rose. Bars of yellow and green fell on the shore gilding the ribs of the eaten-out boat and making the sea-holly and its mailed leaves gleam blue as steel. Light almost pierced the thin swift waves as they raced fan-shaped over the beach. The girl who had shaken her head and made all the jewels, the topaz, the aquamarine, the water-coloured jewels with sparks of fire in them dance, now bared her brows and with wide-opened eyes drove a straight pathway over the waves. Their quivering mackerel sparkling was darkened; they massed themselves; their green hollows deepened and darkened and might be traversed by shoals of wandering fish. As they splashed and drew back they left a black rim of twigs and cork on the shore and straws and sticks of wood as if some light shallop had foundered and burst its sides and the sailor had swum to land and bounded up the cliff and left his frail cargo to be washed ashore.

In the garden the birds that had sung erratically and spasmodically in the dawn on that tree, on that bush, now sang together in chorus, shrill and sharp; now together, as if conscious of companionship, now alone as if to the pale blue sky. They swerved, all in one flight, when the black cat moved among the bushes, when the cook threw cinders on the ash heap and startled them. Fear was in their song, and apprehension of pain, and joy to be snatched quickly now at this instant. Also they sang emulously in the clear morning air, swerving high over the elm tree, singing together as they chased each other, escaping, pursuing, pecking each other as they turned high in the air. And then tiring of pursuit and flight, lovelily they came descending, delicately declining, dropped down and sat silent on the tree, on the wall, with their bright eyes glancing, and their heads turned this way, that way; aware, awake; intensely conscious of one thing, one object in particular.

Perhaps it was a snail shell, rising in the grass like a grey cathedral, a swelling building burnt with dark rings and shadowed green by the grass. Or perhaps they saw the splendour of the flowers making a light of flowing purple over the beds, through which dark tunnels of purple shade were driven between the stalks. Or they fixed their gaze on the small bright apple leaves, dancing yet withheld, stiffly sparkling among the pink-tipped *blossoms. Or they saw the rain drop on the hedge, pendent but not falling, with a whole house bent in it, and towering elms; or, gazing straight at the sun, their eyes became gold beads.*

Now glancing this side, that side, they looked deeper, beneath the flowers, down the dark avenues into the unlit world where the leaf rots and the flower has fallen. Then one of them, beautifully darting, accurately alighting, spiked the soft, monstrous body of the defenceless worm, pecked again and yet again, and left it to fester. Down there among the roots where the flowers decayed, gusts of dead smells were wafted; drops formed on the bloated sides of swollen things. The skin of rotten fruit broke, and matter oozed too thick to run. Yellow excretions were exuded by slugs and now and again an amorphous body with a head at either end swayed slowly from side to side. The gold-eyed birds darting in between the leaves observed that purulence, that wetness, quizzically. Now and then they plunged the tips of their beaks savagely into the sticky mixture.

Now, too, the rising sun came in at the window, touching the red-edged curtain and began to bring out circles and lines. Now in the growing light its whiteness settled in the plate; the blade condensed its gleam. Chairs and cupboards loomed behind so that though each was separate they seemed inextricably involved. The looking-glass whitened its pool upon the wall. The real flower on the window-sill was attended by a phantom flower. Yet the phantom was part of the flower for when a bud broke free, the paler flower in the glass opened a bud too.

The wind rose. The waves drummed on the shore, like turbaned warriors, like turbaned men with poisoned assegais who, whirling their arms on high, advance upon the feeding flocks, the white sheep.

'THE COMPLEXITY of things becomes more close," said Bernard, "here at college, where the stir and pressure of life are so extreme, where the excitement of mere living becomes daily more urgent. Every hour something new is unburied in the great bran pie. What am I? I ask. This? No, I am that. Especially now, when I have left a room, and people talking, and the stone flags ring out with my solitary footsteps, and I behold the moon rising, sublimely, indifferently, over the ancient chapel—then it becomes clear that I am not one and simple, but complex and many. Bernard in public, bubbles; in private, is secretive. That is what they do not understand, for they are now undoubtedly discussing me, saying I escape them, am evasive. They do not understand that I have to effect different transitions; have to cover the entrances and exits of several different men who alternately act their parts as Bernard. I am abnormally aware of circumstances. I can never read a book in a railway carriage without asking, Is he a builder? Is she unhappy? I was aware today acutely that poor Simes, with his pimple was feeling, how bitterly, that his chance of making a good impression upon Billy Jackson was remote. Feeling this painfully I invited him to dinner with ardour. This he will attribute to an admiration which is not mine. That is true. But 'joined to the sensibility of a woman' (I am here quoting my own biographer) 'Bernard possessed the logical sobriety of a man.' Now people who make a single impression, and that, in the main, a good one (for there seems to be a virtue in simplicity) are those who keep their equilibrium in mid-stream. (I instantly see fish with their noses one way, the stream rushing past another.) Canon, Lycett, Peters, Hawkins, Larpent, Neville—all fish in mid-stream. But you understand, you, my self, who always comes at a call (that would be a harrowing experience to call and for no one to come; that would make the midnight hollow, and explains the expression of old men in clubs—they have given up calling for a self who does not come) you understand that I am only superficially represented by what I was saying tonight. Underneath, and, at the moment when I am most disparate, I am also integrated. I sympathise effusively; I also sit like a toad in a hole, receiving with perfect coldness whatever comes. Very few of you who are now discussing me have the double capacity to feel, to reason. Lycett, you see, believes in running after hares; Hawkins has spent a most industrious afternoon in the library. Peters has his young lady at the circulating library. You are all engaged, involved, drawn in, and absolutely energised to the top of your bent—all save Neville, whose mind is far too complex to be roused by any single activity. I also am too complex. In my case something remains floating, unattached.

"Now, as a proof of my susceptibility to atmosphere, here, as I come into my room, and turn on the light, and see the sheet of paper, the table, my gown lying negligently over the back of the chair, I feel that I am that dashing yet reflective man, that bold and deleterious figure, who, lightly throwing off his cloak, seizes his pen and at once flings off the following letter to the girl with whom he is passionately in love.

"Yes, all is propitious. I am now in the mood. I can write the letter straight off which I have begun ever so many times. I have just come in; I have flung down my hat and my stick; I am writing the first thing that comes into my head without troubling to put the paper straight. It is going to be a brilliant sketch which, she must think, was written without a pause, without an erasure. Look how unformed the letters are—there is a careless blot. All must be sacrificed to speed and carelessness. I will write a quick, running, small hand, exaggerating the down stroke of the 'y' and crossing the 't' thus — with a dash. The date shall be only Tuesday, the 17th, and then a question mark. But also I must give her the impression that though he—for this is not myself—is writing in such an off-hand, such a slap-dash

way, there is some subtle suggestion of intimacy and respect. I
must allude to talks we have had together—bring back some remembered scene. But I must seem to her (this is very important) to be passing from thing to thing with the greatest ease in
the world. I shall pass from the service for the man who was
drowned (I have a phrase for that) to Mrs. Moffat and her sayings (I have a note of them) and so to some reflections apparently casual but full of profundity (profound criticism is often
written casually) about some book I have been reading, some
out-of-the-way book. I want her to say as she brushes her hair
or puts out the candle, 'Where did I read that? Oh, in Bernard's
letter.' It is the speed, the hot, molten effect, the lava flow of
sentence into sentence that I need. Who am I thinking of?
Byron of course. I am, in some ways, like Byron. Perhaps a sip
of Byron will help to put me in the vein. Let me read a page.
No; this is dull; this is scrappy. This is rather too formal. Now
I am getting the hang of it. Now I am getting his beat into my
brain (the rhythm is the main thing in writing). Now, without
pausing I will begin, on the very lilt of the stroke—

"Yet it falls flat. It peters out. I cannot get up steam enough
to carry me over the transition. My true self breaks off from my
assumed. And if I begin to re-write it, she will feel, 'Bernard is
posing as a literary man; Bernard is thinking of his biographer'
(which is true). No, I will write the letter tomorrow directly after
breakfast.

"Now let me fill my mind with imaginary pictures. Let me
suppose that I am asked to stay at Restover, King's Laughton,
Station Langley three miles. I arrive in the dusk. In the courtyard of this shabby but distinguished house there are two or
three dogs, slinking, long legged. There are faded rugs in the
hall; a military gentleman smokes a pipe as he paces the terrace.
The note is of distinguished poverty and military connections.
A hunter's hoof on the writing-table—a favourite horse. 'Do

you ride?' 'Yes, sir, I love riding.' 'My daughter expects us in the drawing-room.' My heart pounds against my ribs. She is standing at a low table; she has been hunting; she munches sandwiches like a tomboy. I make a fairly good impression on the Colonel. I am not too clever, he thinks; I am not too raw. Also I play billiards. Then the nice maid who has been with the family thirty years comes in. The pattern on the plates is of Oriental long-tailed birds. Her mother's portrait in muslin hangs over the fireplace. I can sketch the surroundings up to a point with extraordinary ease. But can I make it work? Can I hear her voice—the precise tone with which, when we are alone, she says 'Bernard'? And then what next?

"The truth is that I need the stimulus of other people. Alone, over my dead fire, I tend to see the thin places in my own stories. The real novelist, the perfectly simple human being, could go on, indefinitely, imagining. He would not integrate, as I do. He would not have this devastating sense of grey ashes in a burnt-out grate. Some blind flaps in my eyes. Everything becomes impervious. I cease to invent.

"Let me recollect. It has been on the whole a good day. The drop that forms on the roof of the soul in the evening is round, many-coloured. There was the morning, fine; there was the afternoon, walking. I like views of spires across grey fields. I like glimpses between people's shoulders. Things kept popping into my head. I was imaginative, subtle. After dinner, I was dramatic. I put into concrete form many things that we had dimly observed about our common friends. I made my transitions easily. But now let me ask myself the final question, as I sit over this grey fire, with its naked promontories of black coal, which of these people am I? It depends so much upon the room. When I say to myself, 'Bernard,' who comes? A faithful, sardonic man, disillusioned, but not embittered. A man of no particular age or calling. Myself, merely. It is he who now takes the poker and rattles the cinders so that they fall in showers through the grate. 'Lord,' he says to himself, watching them fall, 'what a pother!' and then he adds, lugubriously, but with some sense of consolation, 'Mrs. Moffat will come and sweep it all up —' I fancy I shall often repeat to myself that phrase, as I rattle and bang through life, hitting first this side of the carriage then the other, 'Oh, yes, Mrs. Moffat will come and sweep it all up.' And so to bed."

"In a world which contains the present moment," said Neville, "why discriminate? Nothing should be named lest by so doing we change it. Let it exist, this bank, this beauty, and I, for one instant, steeped in pleasure. The sun is hot. I see the river. I see trees specked and burnt in the autumn sunlight. Boats float past, through the red, through the green. Far away a bell tolls, but not for death. There are bells that ring for life. A leaf falls, from joy. Oh, I am in love with life! Look how the willow shoots its fine sprays into the air! Look how through them a boat passes, filled with indolent, with unconscious, with powerful young men. They are listening to the gramophone; they are eating fruit out of paper bags. They are tossing the skins of bananas, which then sink eel-like, into the river. All they do is beautiful. There are cruets behind them and ornaments; their rooms are full of oars and oleographs but they have turned all to beauty. That boat passes under the bridge. Another comes. Then another. That is Percival, lounging on the cushions, monolithic, in giant repose. No, it is only one of his satellites, imitating his monolithic, his giant repose. He alone is unconscious of their tricks, and when he catches them at it he buffets them good-humouredly with a blow of his paw. They, too, have passed under the bridge through 'the fountains of the pendent trees,' through its fine strokes of yellow and plum colour. The breeze stirs; the curtain quivers; I see behind the leaves the grave, yet eternally joyous buildings, which seem porous, not gravid; light, though set so immemorially in the ancient turf.

Now begins to rise in me the familiar rhythm; words that have lain dormant now lift, now toss their crests, and fall and rise, and fall and rise again. I am a poet, yes. Surely I am a great poet. Boats and youth passing and distant trees, 'the falling fountains of the pendent trees.' I see it all. I feel it all. I am inspired. My eyes fill with tears. Yet even as I feel this, I lash my frenzy higher and higher. It foams. It becomes artificial, insincere. Words and words and words, how they gallop—how they lash their long manes and tails, but for some fault in me I cannot give myself to their backs; I cannot fly with them, scattering women and string bags. There is some flaw in me—some fatal hesitancy, which, if I pass it over, turns to foam and falsity. Yet it is incredible that I should not be a great poet. What did I write last night if it was not poetry? Am I too fast, too facile? I do not know. I do not know myself sometimes, or how to measure and name and count out the grains that make me what I am.

"Something now leaves me; something goes from me to meet that figure who is coming, and assures me that I know him before I see who it is. How curiously one is changed by the addition, even at a distance, of a friend. How useful an office one's friends perform when they recall us. Yet how painful to be recalled, to be mitigated, to have one's self adulterated, mixed up, become part of another. As he approaches I become not myself but Neville mixed with somebody—with whom?— with Bernard? Yes, it is Bernard, and it is to Bernard that I shall put the question, Who am I?"

"How strange," said Bernard, "the willow looks seen together. I was Byron, and the tree was Byron's tree, lachrymose, down-showering, lamenting. Now that we look at the tree together, it has a combed look, each branch distinct, and I will tell you what I feel, under the compulsion of your clarity.

"I feel your disapproval, I feel your force. I become, with you, an untidy, an impulsive human being whose bandanna handkerchief is for ever stained with the grease of crumpets. Yes, I hold Gray's *Elegy* in one hand; with the other I scoop out the bottom crumpet, that has absorbed all the butter and sticks to the bottom of the plate. This offends you; I feel your distress acutely. Inspired by it and anxious to regain your good opinion, I proceed to tell you how I have just pulled Percival out of bed; I describe his slippers, his table, his guttered candle; his surly and complaining accents as I pull the blanket off his feet; he burrowing, like some vast cocoon meanwhile. I describe all this in such a way that, centred as you are upon some private sorrow (for a hooded shape presides over our encounter) you give way, you laugh and delight in me. My charm and flow of language, unexpected and spontaneous as it is delights me too. I am astonished, as I draw the veil off things with words, how much, how infinitely more than I can say I have observed. More and more bubbles into my mind as I talk, images and images. This, I say to myself, is what I need; why, I ask, can I not finish the letter that I am writing? For my room is always scattered with unfinished letters. I begin to suspect, when I am with you, that I am among the most gifted of men. I am filled with the delight of youth, with potency, with the sense of what is to come. Blundering, but fervid, I see myself buzzing round flowers, humming down scarlet cups, making blue funnels resound with my prodigious booming. How richly I shall enjoy my youth (you make me feel). And London. And freedom. But stop. You are not listening. You are making some protest, as you slide with an inexpressibly familiar gesture, your hand along your knee. By such signs we diagnose our friends' diseases. 'Do not, in your affluence and plenty,' you seem to say, 'pass me by.' 'Stop,' you say. 'Ask me what I suffer.'

"Let me then create you. (You have done as much for me.) You lie on this hot bank, in this lovely, this fading, this still bright October day, watching boat after boat float through the combed-out twigs of the willow tree. And you wish to be a poet; and you wish to be a lover. But the splendid clarity of your intelligence, and the remorseless honesty of your intellect (these Latin words I owe you; these qualities of yours make me shift a little uneasily and see the faded patches, the thin strands in my own equipment) bring you to a halt. You indulge in no mystifications. You do not fog yourself with rosy clouds, or yellow.

"Am I right? Have I read the little gesture of your left hand correctly? If so, give me your poems; hand over the sheets you wrote last night in such a fervour of inspiration that you now feel a little sheepish. For you distrust inspiration, yours or mine. Let us go back together, over the bridge, under the elm trees, to my room, where, with walls round us and red serge curtains drawn, we can shut out these distracting voices, scents and savours of lime trees, and other lives; these pert shop-girls, disdainfully tripping, these shuffling, heavy-laden old women; these furtive glimpses of some vague and vanishing figure — it might be Jinny, it might be Susan, or was that Rhoda disappearing down the avenue? Again, from some slight twitch I guess your feeling; I have escaped you; I have gone buzzing like a swarm of bees, endlessly vagrant, with none of your power of fixing remorselessly upon a single object. But I will return."

"When there are buildings like these," said Neville, "I cannot endure that there should be shop-girls. Their titter, their gossip, offends me; breaks into my stillness, and nudges me, in moments of purest exultation, to remember our degradation.

"But now we have regained our territory after that brief brush with the bicycles and the lime scent and the vanishing figures in the distracted street. Here we are masters of tranquillity and order; inheritors of proud tradition. The lights are beginning to make yellow slits across the square. Mists from the river are filling these ancient spaces. They cling, gently, to the hoary stone. The leaves now are thick in country lanes, sheep cough

in the damp fields; but here in your room we are dry. We talk
privately. The fire leaps and sinks, making some knob bright.

"You have been reading Byron. You have been marking the
passages that seem to approve of your own character. I find
marks against all those sentences which seem to express a sardonic yet passionate nature; a moth-like impetuosity dashing itself against hard glass. You thought, as you drew your pencil
there, 'I too throw off my cloak like that. I too snap my fingers
in the face of destiny.' Yet Byron never made tea as you do, who
fill the pot so that when you put the lid on the tea spills over.
There is a brown pool on the table—it is running among your
books and papers. Now you mop it up, clumsily, with your
pocket-handkerchief. You then stuff your handkerchief back
into your pocket—that is not Byron; that is you; that is so es-
sentially you that if I think of you in twenty years' time, when
we are both famous, gouty and intolerable, it will be by that
scene: and if you are dead, I shall weep. Once you were Tolstoi's young man; now you are Byron's young man; perhaps you
will be Meredith's young man; then you will visit Paris in the
Easter vacation and come back wearing a black tie, some detestable Frenchman whom nobody has ever heard of. Then I
shall drop you.

"I am one person—myself. I do not impersonate Catullus,
whom I adore. I am the most slavish of students, with here a
dictionary; there a notebook in which I enter curious uses of the
past participle. But one cannot go on for ever cutting these ancient inscriptions clearer with a knife. Shall I always draw the red
serge curtain close and see my book, laid like a block of marble,
pale under the lamp? That would be a glorious life, to addict
oneself to perfection; to follow the curve of the sentence wherever it might lead, into deserts, under drifts of sand, regardless
of lures, of seductions; to be poor always and unkempt; to be
ridiculous in Piccadilly.

"But I am too nervous to end my sentence properly. I speak quickly, as I pace up and down, to conceal my agitation. I hate your greasy handkerchiefs—you will stain your copy of *Don Juan*. You are not listening to me. You are making phrases about Byron. And while you gesticulate, with your cloak, your cane, I am trying to expose a secret told to nobody yet; I am asking you (as I stand with my back to you) to take my life in your hands and tell me whether I am doomed always to cause repulsion in those I love?

"I stand with my back to you fidgeting. No, my hands are now perfectly still. Precisely, opening a space in the bookcase, I insert *Don Juan;* there. I would rather be loved, I would rather be famous than follow perfection through the sand. But am I doomed to cause disgust? Am I a poet? Take it. The desire which is loaded behind my lips, cold as lead, fell as a bullet, the thing I aim at shop-girls, women, the pretence, the vulgarity of life (because I love it) shoots at you as I throw—catch it—my poem."

"He has shot like an arrow from the room," said Bernard. "He has left me his poem. O friendship, I too will press flowers between the pages of Shakespeare's sonnets! O friendship, how piercing are your darts—there, there, again there. He looked at me, turning to face me; he gave me his poem. All mists curl off the roof of my being. That confidence I shall keep to my dying day. Like a long wave, like a roll of heavy waters, he went over me, his devastating presence—dragging me open, laying bare the pebbles on the shore of my soul. It was humiliating; I was turned to small stones. All semblances were rolled up. 'You are not Byron; you are your self.' To be contracted by another person into a single being—how strange.

"How strange to feel the line that is spun from us lengthening its fine filament across the misty spaces of the intervening world. He is gone; I stand here, holding his poem. Between us is this line. But now, how comfortable, how reassuring to feel

that alien presence removed, that scrutiny darkened and hooded
over! How grateful to draw the blinds, and admit no other presence; to feel returning from the dark corners in which they took
refuge, those shabby inmates, those familiars, whom, with his
superior force, he drove into hiding. The mocking, the observant spirits who, even in the crisis and stab of the moment
watched on my behalf, now come flocking home again. With
their addition, I am Bernard; I am Byron; I am this, that and the
other. They darken the air and enrich me, as of old with their
antics, their comments, and cloud the fine simplicity of my moment of emotion. For I am more selves than Neville thinks. We
are not simple as our friends would have us to meet their needs.
Yet love is simple.

"Now they have returned, my inmates, my familiars. Now
the stab, the rent in my defences that Neville made with his astonishing fine rapier is repaired. I am almost whole now; and see
how jubilant I am, bringing into play all that Neville ignores in
me. I feel, as I look from the window, parting the curtains, 'That
would give him no pleasure; but it rejoices me.' (We use our
friends to measure our own stature.) My scope embraces what
Neville never reaches. They are shouting hunting-songs over
the way. They are celebrating some run with the beagles. The
little boys in caps who always turned at the same moment when
the brake went round the corner are clapping each other on the
shoulder and boasting. But Neville, delicately avoiding interference, stealthily, like a conspirator, hastens back to his room. I
see him sunk in his low chair gazing at the fire which has assumed for the moment an architectural solidity. If life, he thinks,
could wear that permanence, if life could have that order—for
above all he desires order, and detests my Byronic untidiness;
and so draws his curtain; and bolts his door. His eyes (for he is
in love; the sinister figure of love presided at our encounter) fill
with longing; fill with tears. He snatches the poker and with one

blow destroys that momentary appearance of solidity in the burning coals. All changes. And youth and love. The boat has floated through the arch of the willows and is now under the bridge. Percival, Tony, Archie, or another, will go to India. We shall not meet again. Then he stretches his hand for his copy-book—a neat volume bound in mottled paper—and writes feverishly long lines of poetry, in the manner of whomever he admires most at the moment.

"But I want to linger; to lean from the window; to listen. There again comes that rollicking chorus. They are now smashing china—that also is the convention. The chorus, like a torrent jumping rocks, brutally assaulting old trees, pours with splendid abandonment headlong over precipices. On they roll; on they gallop; after hounds, after footballs; they pump up and down attached to oars like sacks of flour. All divisions are merged—they act like one man. The gusty October wind blows the uproar in bursts of sound and silence across the court. Now again they are smashing the china—that is the convention. An old, unsteady woman carrying a bag trots home under the fire-red windows. She is half afraid that they will fall on her and tumble her into the gutter. Yet she pauses as if to warm her knobbed, her rheumaticky hands at the bonfire which flares away with streams of sparks and bits of blown paper. The old woman pauses against the lit window. A contrast. That I see and Neville does not see; that I feel and Neville does not feel. Hence he will reach perfection, and I shall fail and shall leave nothing behind me but imperfect phrases littered with sand.

"I think of Louis now. What malevolent yet searching light would Louis throw upon this dwindling autumn evening, upon this china smashing and trolling of hunting-songs, upon Neville, Byron and our life here? His thin lips are somewhat pursed; his cheeks are pale; he pores in an office over some obscure commercial document. 'My father, a banker at Brisbane'—being ashamed of him he always talks of him—failed. So he sits in an office, Louis the best scholar in the school. But I seeking contrasts often feel his eye on us, his laughing eye, his wild eye, adding us up like insignificant items in some grand total which he is for ever pursuing, in his office. And one day taking a fine pen and dipping it in red ink, the addition will be complete; our total will be known; but it will not be enough.

"Bang! They have thrown a chair now against the wall. We are damned then. My case is dubious too. Am I not indulging in unwarranted emotions? Yes, as I lean out of the window and drop my cigarette so that it twirls lightly to the ground I feel Louis watching even my cigarette. And Louis says, 'That means something. But what?'"

"People go on passing," said Louis. "They pass the window of this eating-shop incessantly. Motor-cars, vans, motor-omnibuses; and again motor-omnibuses, vans, motor-cars—they pass the window. In the background I perceive shops and houses; also the grey spires of a city church. In the foreground are glass shelves set with plates of buns and ham sandwiches. All is somewhat obscured by steam from a tea-urn. A meaty, vapourish smell of beef and mutton, sausages and mash, hangs down like a damp net in the middle of the eating-house. I prop my book against a bottle of Worcester sauce and try to look like the rest.

"Yet I cannot. (They go on passing, they go on passing in disorderly procession.) I cannot read my book, or order my beef, with conviction. I repeat, 'I am an average Englishman; I am an average clerk,' yet I look at the little men at the next table to be sure that I do what they do. Supple-faced, with rippling skins, that are always twitching with the multiplicity of their sensations, prehensile like monkeys, greased to this particular moment, they are discussing with all the right gestures the sale of a piano. It blocks up the hall; so he would take a tenner. People go on passing; they go on passing against the spires of the church and the plates of ham sandwiches. The streamers of my consciousness waver out and are perpetually torn and distressed by their disorder. I cannot therefore concentrate on my dinner. 'I would take a tenner. The case is handsome; but it blocks up the hall.' They dive and plunge like guillemots whose feathers are slippery with oil. All excesses beyond that norm are vanity. That is the mean; that is the average. Meanwhile the hats bob up and down; the door perpetually shuts and opens. I am conscious of flux, of disorder; of annihilation and despair. If this is all, this is worthless. Yet I feel, too, the rhythm of the eating-house. It is like a waltz tune, eddying in and out, round and round. The waitresses, balancing trays, swing in and out, round and round, dealing plates of greens, of apricot and custard, dealing them at the right time, to the right customers. The average men, including her rhythm in their rhythm ('I would take a tenner; for it blocks up the hall') take their greens, take their apricots and custard. Where then is the break in this continuity? What the fissure through which one sees disaster? The circle is unbroken; the harmony complete. Here is the central rhythm; here the common mainspring. I watch it expand, contract; and then expand again. Yet I am not included. If I speak, imitating their accent, they prick their ears, waiting for me to speak again, in order that they may place me— if I come from Canada or Australia, I, who desire above all things to be taken to the arms with love, an alien, external. I, who would wish to feel close over me the protective waves of the ordinary, catch with the tail of my eye some far horizon; am aware of hats bobbing up and down in perpetual disorder. To me is addressed the plaint of the wandering and distracted spirit—(a woman with bad teeth falters at the counter). Bring us back to the fold, we who pass so disjectedly, bobbing up and down, past windows with plates of ham sandwiches in the foreground. Yes; I will reduce you to order.

"I will read in the book that is propped against the bottle of Worcester sauce. It contains some forged rings, some perfect statements, a few words, but poetry. You, all of you, ignore it. What the dead poet said, you have forgotten. And I cannot translate it to you so that its binding power ropes you in, and makes it clear to you that you are aimless; and the rhythm is cheap and worthless; and so remove that degradation which, if you are unaware of your aimlessness, pervades you, making you senile, even while you are young. To translate that poem so that it is easily read is to be my endeavour. I, the companion of Plato, of Virgil, will knock at the grained oak door. I oppose to what is passing this ramrod of beaten steel. I will not submit to this aimless passing of billycock hats and Homburg hats and all the plumed and variegated head-dresses of women. (Susan, whom I respect, would wear a plain straw hat on a summer's day.) And the grinding and the steam that runs in unequal drops down the window pane; and the stopping and the starting with a jerk of motor-omnibuses; and the hesitations at counters; and the words that trail drearily without human meaning; I will reduce you to order.

"My roots go down through veins of lead and silver, through damp, marshy places that exhale odours to a knot made of oak roots bound together in the centre. Sealed and blind, with each stopping my ears, I have yet heard rumours of wars; and the nightingale; have felt the hurrying of many troops of men flocking hither and thither in quest of civilisation like flocks of birds migrating seeking the summer; I have seen women carrying red pitchers to the banks of the Nile. I woke in a garden, with a blow on the nape of my neck, a hot kiss, Jinny's; remembering all this as one remembers confused cries and toppling pillars and shafts of red and black in some nocturnal conflagration. I am for ever sleeping and waking. Now I sleep; now I wake. I see the gleaming tea-urn; the glass cases full of pale-yellow sandwiches; the

men in round coats perched on stools at the counter; and also
behind them, eternity. It is a stigma burnt on my quivering flesh
by a cowled man with a red-hot iron. I see this eating-shop
against the packed and fluttering birds' wings, many feathered,
folded, of the past. Hence my pursed lips, my sickly pallor; my
distasteful and uninviting aspect as I turn my face with hatred
and bitterness upon Bernard and Neville, who saunter under
yew trees; who inherit arm-chairs; and draw their curtains close,
so that lamplight falls on their books.

"Susan, I respect; because she sits stitching. She sews under
a quiet lamp in a house where the corn sighs close to the window and gives me safety. For I am the weakest, the youngest of
them all. I am a child looking at his feet and the little runnels
that the stream has made in the gravel. That is a snail, I say, that
is a leaf. I delight in the snails; I delight in the leaf. I am always
the youngest, the most innocent, the most trustful. You are
all protected. I am naked. When the waitress with the plaited
wreaths of hair swings past, she deals you your apricots and custard unhesitatingly, like a sister. You are her brothers. But when
I get up, brushing the crumbs from my waistcoat, I slip too large
a tip, a shilling, under the edge of my plate, so that she may not
find it till I am gone, and her scorn, as she picks it up with
laughter, may not strike on me till I am past the swing-doors."

"NOW THE wind lifts the blind," said Susan. "Jars, bowls, matting and the shabby arm-chair with the hole in it are now become distinct. The usual faded ribbons sprinkle the wall-paper.
The bird chorus is over, only one bird now sings close to the
bedroom window. I will pull on my stockings and go quietly
past the bedroom doors, and down through the kitchen, out
through the garden past the greenhouse into the field. It is still
early morning. The mist is on the marshes. The day is stark and
stiff as a linen shroud. But it will soften; it will warm. At this

hour, this still early hour, I think I am the field, I am the barn, I am the trees; mine are the flocks of birds, and this young hare who leaps, at the last moment when I step almost on him. Mine is the heron that stretches its vast wings lazily; and the cow that creaks as it pushes one foot before another, munching; and the wild, swooping swallow; and the faint red in the sky, and the green when the red fades; the silence and the bell; the call of the man fetching cart-horses from the fields—all are mine.

"I cannot be divided, or kept apart. I was sent to school; I was sent to Switzerland to finish my education. I hate linoleum; I hate fir trees and mountains. Let me now fling myself on this flat ground under a pale sky where the clouds pace slowly. The cart grows gradually larger as it comes along the road. The sheep gather in the middle of the field. The birds gather in the middle of the road—they need not fly yet. The wood smoke rises. The starkness of the dawn is going out of it. Now the day stirs. Colour returns. The day waves yellow with all its crops. The earth hangs heavy beneath me.

"But who am I, who lean on this gate and watch my setter nose in a circle? I think sometimes (I am not twenty yet) I am not a woman, but the light that falls on this gate, on this ground. I am the seasons, I think sometimes, January, May, November; the mud, the mist, the dawn. I cannot be tossed about, or float gently, or mix with other people. Yet now leaning here, till the gate prints my arm, I feel the weight that has formed itself in my side. Something has formed, at school, in Switzerland, some hard thing. Not sighs and laughter; not circling and ingenious phrases; not Rhoda's strange communications when she looks past us, over our shoulders; nor Jinny's pirouetting, all of a piece, limbs and body. What I give is fell. I cannot float gently, mixing with other people. I like best the stare of shepherds met in the road; the stare of gipsy women beside a cart in a ditch suckling their children as I shall suckle my children. For soon in the hot mid-day when the bees hum round the hollyhocks my lover will come. He will stand under the cedar tree. To his one word I shall answer my one word. What has formed in me I shall give him. I shall have children; I shall have maids in aprons; men with pitchforks; a kitchen where they bring the ailing lambs to warm in baskets, where the hams hang and the onions glisten. I shall be like my mother, silent in a blue apron locking up the cupboards.

"Now I am hungry. I will call my setter. I think of crusts and bread and butter and white plates in a sunny room. I will go back across the fields. I will walk along this grass path with strong, even strides, now swerving to avoid the puddle, now leaping lightly to a clump. Beads of wet form on my rough skirt; my shoes become supple and dark. The stiffness has gone from the day; it is shaded with grey, green and umber. The birds no longer settle on the high road.

"I return, like a cat or fox returning, whose fur is grey with rime, whose pads are hardened by the coarse earth. I push through the cabbages, making their leaves squeak and their drops spill. I sit waiting for my father's footsteps as he shuffles down the passage pinching some herb between his fingers. I pour out cup after cup while the unopened flowers hold themselves erect on the table among the pots of jam, the loaves and the butter. We are silent.

"I go then to the cupboard, and take the damp bags of rich sultanas; I lift the heavy flour on to the clean scrubbed kitchen table. I knead; I stretch; I pull, plunging my hands in the warm inwards of the dough. I let the cold water stream fanwise through my fingers. The fire roars; the flies buzz in a circle. All my currants and rices, the silver bags and the blue bags, are locked again in the cupboard. The meat is stood in the oven; the bread rises in a soft dome under the clean towel. I walk in the afternoon down to the river. All the world is breeding. The flies are going from grass to grass. The flowers are thick with pollen. The swans ride the stream in order. The clouds warm now, sun-spotted, sweep over the hills, leaving gold in the water, and gold on the necks of the swans. Pushing one foot before the other, the cows munch their way across the field. I feel through the grass for the white-domed mushroom; and break its stalk and pick the purple orchid that grows beside it and lay the orchid by the mushroom with the earth at its root, and so home to make the kettle boil for my father among the just reddened roses on the tea-table.

"But evening comes and the lamps are lit. And when evening comes and the lamps are lit they make a yellow fire in the ivy. I sit with my sewing by the table. I think of Jinny; of Rhoda; and hear the rattle of wheels on the pavement as the farm horses plod home; I hear traffic roaring in the evening wind. I look at the quivering leaves in the dark garden and think, 'They dance in London. Jinny kisses Louis.'"

"How strange," said Jinny, "that people should sleep, that people should put out the lights and go upstairs. They have taken off their dresses, they have put on white night-gowns. There are no lights in any of these houses. There is a line of chimney-pots against the sky; and a street lamp or two burning, as lamps burn when nobody needs them. The only people in the streets are poor people hurrying. There is no one coming or going in this street; the day is over. A few policemen stand at the corners. Yet night is beginning. I feel myself shining in the dark. Silk is on my knee. My silk legs rub smoothly together. The stones of a neck-lace lie cold on my throat. My feet feel the pinch of shoes. I sit bolt upright so that my hair may not touch the back of the seat. I am arrayed, I am prepared. This is the momentary pause; the dark moment. The fiddlers have lifted their bows.

"Now the car slides to a stop. A strip of pavement is lighted. The door is opening and shutting. People are arriving; they do not speak; they hasten in. There is the swishing sound of cloaks falling in the hall. This is the prelude, this is the beginning. I glance, I peep, I powder. All is exact, prepared. My hair is swept in one curve. My lips are precisely red. I am ready now to join men and women on the stairs, my peers. I pass them, exposed to their gaze, as they are to mine. Like lightning we look but do not soften or show signs of recognition. Our bodies communicate. This is my calling. This is my world. All is decided and ready; the servants, standing here, and again here, take my name, my fresh, my unknown name, and toss it before me. I enter.

"Here are gilt chairs in the empty, the expectant rooms, and flowers, stiller, statelier, than flowers that grow, spread green, spread white, against the walls. And on one small table is one bound book. This is what I have dreamt; this is what I have foretold. I am native here. I tread naturally on thick carpets. I slide easily on smooth-polished floors. I now begin to unfurl, in this scent, in this radiance, as a fern when its curled leaves unfurl. I stop. I take stock of this world. I look among the groups of unknown people. Among the lustrous green, pink, pearl-grey women stand upright the bodies of men. They are black and white; they are grooved beneath their clothes with deep rills. I feel again the reflection in the window of the tunnel; it moves. The black-and-white figures of unknown men look at me as I lean forward; as I turn aside to look at a picture, they turn too. Their hands go fluttering to their ties. They touch their waistcoats, their pocket-handkerchiefs. They are very young. They are anxious to make a good impression. I feel a thousand capacities spring up in me. I am arch, gay, languid, melancholy by turns. I am rooted, but I flow. All gold, flowing that way, I say to this one, 'Come.' Rippling black, I say to that one, 'No.' One breaks off from his station under the glass cabinet. He approaches. He makes towards me. This is the most exciting moment I have ever known. I flutter. I ripple. I stream like a plant in the river, flowing this way, flowing that way, but rooted, so that he may come to me. 'Come,' I say, 'come.' Pale, with dark hair the one who is coming is melancholy, romantic. And I am arch and fluent and capricious; for he is melancholy, he is romantic. He is here; he stands at my side.

"Now with a little jerk, like a limpet broken from a rock, I am broken off: I fall with him; I am carried off. We yield to this slow flood. We go in and out of this hesitating music. Rocks break the current of the dance; it jars, it shivers. In and out, we are swept now into this large figure; it holds us together; we cannot step outside its sinuous, its hesitating, its abrupt, its perfectly encircling walls. Our bodies, his hard, mine flowing, are pressed together within its body; it holds us together; and then lengthening out, in smooth, in sinuous folds, rolls us between it, on and on. Suddenly the music breaks. My blood runs on but my body stands still. The room reels past my eyes. It stops.

"Come then, let us wander whirling to the gilt chairs. The body is stronger than I thought. I am dizzier than I supposed. I do not care for anything in the world. I do not care for anybody save this man whose name I do not know. Are we not acceptable, moon? Are we not lovely sitting together here, I in my satin; he in black and white? My peers may look at me now. I look straight back at you, men and women. I am one of you. This is my world. Now I take this thin-stemmed glass and sip. Wine has a drastic, an astringent taste. I cannot help wincing as I drink. Scent and flowers, radiance and heat, are distilled here to a fiery, to a yellow liquid. Just behind my shoulder-blades some dry thing, wide-eyed, gently closes, gradually lulls itself to sleep. This is rapture; this is relief. The bar at the back of my throat lowers itself. Words crowd and cluster and push forth one on top of another. It does not matter which. They jostle and mount on each other's shoulders. The single and the solitary mate, tumble and become many. It does not matter what I say.

Crowding, like a fluttering bird, one sentence crosses the empty space between us. It settles on his lips. I fill my glass again. I drink. The veils drop between us. I am admitted to the warmth and privacy of another soul. We are together, high up, on some Alpine pass. He stands melancholy on the crest of the road. I stoop. I pick a blue flower and fix it, standing on tiptoe to reach him, in his coat. There! That is my moment of ecstasy. Now it is over.

"Now slackness and indifference invade us. Other people brush past. We have lost consciousness of our bodies uniting under the table. I also like fair-haired men with blue eyes. The door opens. The door goes on opening. Now I think, next time it opens the whole of my life will be changed. Who comes? But it is only a servant, bringing glasses. That is an old man—I should be a child with him. That is a great lady—with her I should dissemble. There are girls of my own age, for whom I feel the drawn swords of an honourable antagonism. For these are my peers. I am a native of this world. Here is my risk, here is my adventure. The door opens. Oh, come, I say to this one, rippling gold from head to heels. 'Come,' and he comes towards me."

"I shall edge behind them," said Rhoda, "as if I saw some one I know. But I know no one. I shall twitch the curtain and look at the moon. Draughts of oblivion shall quench my agitation. The door opens; the tiger leaps. The door opens; terror rushes in; terror upon terror, pursuing me. Let me visit furtively the treasures I have laid apart. Pools lie on the other side of the world reflecting marble columns. The swallow dips her wing in dark pools. But here the door opens and people come; they come towards me. Throwing faint smiles to mask their cruelty, their indifference, they seize me. The swallow dips her wings; the moon rides through the blue seas alone. I must take his hand; I must answer. But what answer shall I give? I am thrust back to stand burning in this clumsy, this ill-fitting body, to receive the shafts of his indifference, and his scorn, I who long for marble columns and pools on the other side of the world where the swallow dips her wings.

"Night has wheeled a little further over the chimney-pots. I see out of the window over his shoulder some unembarrassed cat, not drowned in light, not trapped in silk, free to pause, to stretch, and to move again. I hate all details of the individual life. But I am fixed here to listen. An immense pressure is on me. I cannot move without dislodging the weight of centuries. A million arrows pierce me. Scorn and ridicule pierce me. I, who could beat my breast against the storm and let the hail choke me joyfully, am pinned down here; am exposed. The tiger leaps. Tongues with their whips are upon me. Mobile, incessant, they flicker over me. I must prevaricate and fence them off with lies. What amulet is there against this disaster? What face can I summon to lay cool upon this heat? I think of names on boxes; of mothers from whose wide knees skirts descend; of glades where the many-backed steep hills come down. Hide me, I cry, protect me, for I am the youngest, the most naked of you all. Jinny rides like a gull on the wave, dealing her looks adroitly here and there, saying this, saying that, with truth. But I lie; I prevaricate.

"Alone, I rock my basins; I am mistress of my fleet of ships. But here, twisting the tassels of this brocaded curtain in my hostess's window, I am broken into separate pieces; I am no longer one. What then is the knowledge that Jinny has as she dances; the assurance that Susan has as, stooping quietly beneath the lamplight, she draws the white cotton through the eye of her needle? They say, Yes; they say, No; they bring their fists down with a bang on the table. But I doubt; I tremble; I see the wild thorn tree shake its shadow in the desert.

"Now I will walk, as if I had an end in view, across the room, to the balcony under the awning. I see the sky, softly feathered with its sudden effulgence of moon. I also see the railings of the square, and two people without faces, leaning like statues against the sky. There is then a world immune from change. When I have passed through this drawing-room flickering with tongues that cut me like knives, making me stammer, making me lie, I find faces rid of features, robed in beauty. The lovers crouch under the plane tree. The policeman stands sentinel at the corner. A man passes. There is then a world immune from change. But I am not composed enough, standing on tiptoe on the verge of fire, still scorched by the hot breath, afraid of the door opening and the leap of the tiger, to make even one sentence. What I say is perpetually contradicted. Each time the door opens I am interrupted. I am not yet twenty-one. I am to be broken. I am to be derided all my life. I am to be cast up and down among these men and women, with their twitching faces, with their lying tongues, like a cork on a rough sea. Like a ribbon of weed I am flung far every time the door opens. The wave breaks. I am the foam that sweeps and fills the uttermost rims of the rocks with whiteness; I am also a girl, here in this room."

*T*HE SUN, *risen, no longer couched on a green mattress darting a fit-ful glance through watery jewels, bared its face and looked straight over the waves. They fell with a regular thud. They fell with the concussion of horses' hooves on the turf. Their spray rose like the tossing of lances and assegais over the riders' heads. They swept the beach with steel blue and diamond-tipped water. They drew in and out with the energy, the muscu-larity of an engine which sweeps its force out and in again. The sun fell on cornfields and woods. Rivers became blue, and many-plaited, lawns that sloped down to the water's edge became green as birds' feathers softly ruf-fling their plumes. The hills curved and controlled, seemed bound back by thongs, as a limb is laced by muscles; and the woods which bristled proudly on their flanks were like the curt, clipped mane on the neck of a horse.*

In the garden where the trees stood thick over flower-beds, ponds, and greenhouses the birds sang in the hot sunshine, each alone. One sang under the bedroom window; another on the topmost twig of the lilac bush; an-other on the edge of the wall. Each sang stridently, with passion, with ve-hemence, as if to let the song burst out of it, no matter if it shattered the song of another bird with harsh discord. Their round eyes bulged with brightness; their claws gripped the twig or rail. They sang exposed with-out shelter, to the air and the sun, beautiful in their new plumage, shell-veined or brightly mailed, here barred with soft blues, here splashed with gold, or striped with one bright feather. They sang as if the song were urged out of them by the pressure of the morning. They sang as if the edge of being were sharpened and must cut, must split the softness of the blue-green light, the dampness of the wet earth; the fumes and steams of the greasy kitchen vapour; the hot breath of mutton and beef; the richness of pastry and fruit; the damp shreds and peelings thrown from the kitchen bucket, from which a slow steam oozed on the rubbish heap. On all the sodden, the damp-spotted, the curled with wetness, they descended, dry-beaked, ruthless, abrupt. They swooped suddenly from the lilac bough or the fence. They spied a snail and tapped the shell against a stone. They tapped furi-ously, methodically, until the shell broke and something slimy oozed from the crack. They swept and soared sharply in flights high into the air, twit-

tering short, sharp notes, and perched in the upper branches of some tree, and looked down upon leaves and spires beneath, and the country white with blossom, flowing with grass, and the sea which beat like a drum that raises a regiment of plumed and turbaned soldiers. Now and again their songs ran together in swift scales like the interlacings of a mountain stream whose waters, meeting, foam and then mix, and hasten quicker and quicker down the same channel brushing the same broad leaves. But there is a rock; they sever.

The sun fell in sharp wedges inside the room. Whatever the light touched became dowered with a fanatical existence. A plate was like a white lake. A knife looked like a dagger of ice. Suddenly tumblers revealed themselves upheld by streaks of light. Tables and chairs rose to the surface as if they had been sunk under water and rose, filmed with red, orange, purple like the bloom on the skin of ripe fruit. The veins on the glaze of the china, the grain of the wood, the fibres of the matting became more and more finely engraved. Everything was without shadow. A jar was so green that the eye seemed sucked up through a funnel by its intensity and stuck to it like a limpet. Then shapes took on mass and edge. Here was the boss of a chair; here the bulk of a cupboard. And as the light increased, flocks of shadow were driven before it and conglomerated and hung in many-pleated folds in the background.

"HOW FAIR, how strange," said Bernard, "glittering, many-pointed and many-domed London lies before me under mist. Guarded by gasometers, by factory chimneys, she lies sleeping as we approach. She folds the ant-heap to her breast. All cries, all clamour are softly enveloped in silence. Not Rome herself looks more majestic. But we are aimed at her. Already her maternal somnolence is uneasy. Ridges fledged with houses rise from the mist. Factories, cathedrals, glass domes, institutions and theatres erect themselves. The early train from the north is hurled at her like a missile. We draw a curtain as we pass. Blank expectant faces stare at us as we rattle and flash through stations. Men clutch their newspapers a little tighter, as our wind sweeps them, envisaging death. But we roar on. We are about to explode in the flanks of the city like a shell in the side of some ponderous, maternal, majestic animal. She hums and murmurs; she awaits us.

"Meanwhile as I stand looking from the train window, I feel strangely, persuasively, that because of my great happiness (being engaged to be married), I am become part of this speed, this missile, hurled at the city. I am numbed to tolerance and acquiescence. My dear sir, I could say, why do you fidget, taking down your suitcase and pressing into it the cap that you have worn all night? Nothing we can do will avail. Over us all broods a splendid unanimity. We are enlarged and solemnised and brushed into uniformity as with the grey wing of some enormous goose (it is a fine, but colourless morning) because we have only one desire—to arrive at the station. I do not want the train to stop with a thud. I do not want the connection which has bound us together sitting opposite each other all night long to be broken. I do not want to feel that hate and rivalry have resumed their sway; and different desires. Our community in the rushing train sitting together with only one wish to arrive at Euston was very welcome. But behold! It is over. We have attained our desire. We have drawn up at the platform. Hurry and confusion and the wish to be first through the gate into the lift assert themselves. But I do not wish to be first through the gate, to assume the burden of individual life. I, who have been since Monday, when she accepted me, charged in every nerve with a sense of identity, who could not see a tooth-brush in a glass without saying, '*My* toothbrush,' now wish to unclasp my hands and let fall my possessions, and merely stand here in the street, taking no part, watching the omnibuses, without desire; without envy; with what would be boundless curiosity about human destiny if there were any longer an edge to my mind. But it has none. I have arrived; am accepted. I ask nothing.

"Having dropped off satisfied like a child from the breast, I am at liberty now to sink down, deep, into what passes, this omnipresent, general life. (How much, let me note, depends upon trousers; the intelligent head is entirely handicapped by shabby trousers.) One observes curious hesitations at the door of the lift. This way, that way, the other? Then individuality asserts itself. They are off. They are all impelled by some necessity. Some miserable affair of keeping an appointment, of buying a hat, severs these beautiful human beings once so united. For myself, I have no aim. I have no ambition. I will let myself be carried on by the general impulse. The surface of my mind slips along like a pale-grey stream reflecting what passes. I cannot remember my past, my nose, or the colour of my eyes, or what my general opinion of myself is. Only in moments of emergency, at a crossing, at a kerb, the wish to preserve my body springs out and seizes me and stops me, here, before this omnibus. We insist, it seems, on living. Then again, indifference descends. The roar of the traffic, the passage of undifferentiated faces, this way and that way, drugs me into dreams; rubs the features from faces. People might walk through me. And, what is this moment of time, this particular day in which I have found myself caught?

The growl of traffic might be any uproar—forest trees or the roar of wild beasts. Time has whizzed back an inch or two on its reel; our short progress has been cancelled. I think also that our bodies are in truth naked. We are only lightly covered with buttoned cloth; and beneath these pavements are shells, bones and silence.

"It is, however, true that my dreaming, my tentative advance like one carried beneath the surface of a stream, is interrupted, torn, pricked and plucked at by sensations, spontaneous and ir-relevant, of curiosity, greed, desire, irresponsible as in sleep. (I covet that bag—etc.) No, but I wish to go under; to visit the profound depths; once in a while to exercise my prerogative not always to act, but to explore; to hear vague, ancestral sounds of boughs creaking, of mammoths, to indulge impossible desires to embrace the whole world with the arms of understanding, impossible to those who act. Am I not, as I walk, trembling with strange oscillations and vibrations of sympathy, which, un-moored as I am from a private being, bid me embrace these en-grossed flocks; these starers and trippers; these errand-boys and furtive and fugitive girls who, ignoring their doom, look in at shop-windows? But I am aware of our ephemeral passage.

"It is, however, true that I cannot deny a sense that life for me is now mysteriously prolonged. Is it that I may have chil-dren, may cast a fling of seed wider, beyond this generation, this doom-encircled population, shuffling each other in endless com-petition along the street? My daughters shall come here, in other summers; my sons shall turn new fields. Hence we are not rain-drops, soon dried by the wind; we make gardens blow and forests roar; we come up differently, for ever and ever. This then serves to explain my confidence, my central stability, otherwise so monstrously absurd as I breast the stream of this crowded thor-oughfare, making always a passage for myself between people's bodies, taking advantage of safe moments to cross. It is not vanity; for I am emptied of ambition; I do not remember my special gifts, or idiosyncrasy, or the marks I bear on my person, eyes, nose or mouth. I am not, at this moment, myself.

"Yet behold, it returns. One cannot extinguish that persistent smell. It steals in through some crack in the structure — one's identity. I am not part of the street—no, I observe the street. One splits off, therefore. For instance, up that back street a girl stands waiting; for whom? A romantic story. On the wall of that shop is fixed a small crane, and for what reason, I ask, was that crane fixed there? and invent a purple lady swelling, circumambient, hauled from a barouche landau by a perspiring husband sometime in the sixties. A grotesque story. That is, I am a natural coiner of words, a blower of bubbles through one thing and another. And striking off these observations spontaneously I elaborate myself; differentiate myself and listening to the voice that says as I stroll past, 'Look! Take note of that!' I conceive myself called upon to provide, some winter's night, a meaning for all my observations—a line that runs from one to another, a summing up that completes. But soliloquies in back streets soon pall. I need an audience. That is my downfall. That always ruffles the edge of the final statement and prevents it from forming. I cannot seat myself in some sordid eating-house and order the same glass day after day and imbue myself entirely in one fluid—this life. I make my phrase and run off with it to some furnished room where it will be lit by dozens of candles. I need eyes on me to draw out these frills and furbelows. To be myself (I note) I need the illumination of other people's eyes, and therefore cannot be entirely sure what is my self. The authentics, like Louis, like Rhoda, exist most completely in solitude. They resent illumination, reduplication. They toss their pictures, once painted, face downward on the field. On Louis's words the ice is packed thick. His words issue pressed, condensed, enduring.

"I wish then after this somnolence to sparkle, many-faceted under the light of my friends' faces. I have been traversing the sunless territory of non-identity. A strange land. I have heard in my moment of appeasement, in my moment of obliterating satisfaction, the sigh, as it goes in, comes out, of the tide that draws beyond this circle of bright light, this drumming of insensate fury. I have had one moment of enormous peace. This is perhaps happiness. Now I am drawn back by pricking sensations; by curiosity, greed (I am hungry) and the irresistible desire to be myself. I think of people to whom I could say things; Louis; Neville; Susan; Jinny and Rhoda. With them I am many-sided. They retrieve me from darkness. We shall meet tonight, thank Heaven. Thank Heaven, I need not be alone. We shall dine together. We shall say good-bye to Percival, who goes to India. The hour is still distant but I feel already those harbingers, those outriders, figures of one's friends in absence. I see Louis, stone-carved, sculpturesque; Neville, scissor-cutting, exact; Susan with eyes like lumps of crystal; Jinny dancing like a flame, febrile, hot, over dry earth; and Rhoda the nymph of the fountain always wet. These are fantastic pictures—these are figments, these visions of friends in absence, grotesque, dropsical, vanishing at the first touch of the toe of a real boot. Yet they drum me alive. They brush off these vapours. I begin to be impatient of solitude—to feel its draperies hang sweltering, unwholesome about me. Oh, to toss them off and be active! Anybody will do. I am not fastidious. The crossing-sweeper will do; the postman; the waiter in this French restaurant; better still the genial proprietor, whose geniality seems reserved for oneself. He mixes the salad with his own hands for some privileged guest. Which is the privileged guest, I ask, and why? And what is he saying to the lady in ear-rings, is she a friend or a customer? I feel at once, as I sit down at a table, the delicious jostle of confusion, of uncertainty, of possibility, of speculation. Images breed instantly. I am embarrassed by my own fertility. I could describe every chair, table, luncher here copiously, freely. My mind hums hither and thither with its veil of words for everything. To speak, about wine even to the waiter, is to bring about an explosion. Up goes the rocket. Its golden grain falls, fertilising, upon the rich soil of my imagination. The entirely unexpected nature of this explosion—that is the joy of intercourse. I, mixed with an unknown Italian waiter—what am I? There is no stability in this world. Who is to say what meaning there is in anything? Who is to foretell the flight of a word? It is a balloon that sails over tree-tops. To speak of knowledge is futile. All is experiment and adventure. We are for ever mixing ourselves with unknown quantities. What is to come? I know not. But, as I put down my glass I remember; I am engaged to be married. I am to dine with my friends tonight. I am Bernard."

"It is now five minutes to eight," said Neville. "I have come early. I have taken my place at the table ten minutes before the time in order to taste every moment of anticipation; to see the door open and to say, 'Is it Percival? No; it is not Percival.' There is a morbid pleasure in saying, 'No, it is not Percival.' I have seen the door open and shut twenty times already; each time the suspense sharpens. This is the place to which he is coming. This is the table at which he will sit. Here, incredible as it seems, will be his actual body. This table, these chairs, this metal vase with its three red flowers are about to undergo an extraordinary transformation. Already the room, with its swing-doors, its tables heaped with fruit, with cold joints, wears the wavering, unreal appearance of a place where one waits expecting something to happen. Things quiver as if not yet in being. The blankness of the white table-cloth glares. The hostility, the indifference of other people dining here is oppressive. We look at each other; see that we do not know each other, stare, and go off. Such looks are lashes. I feel the whole cruelty and indifference of the world in them. If he should not come I could not bear it. I should go. Yet somebody must be seeing him now. He must be in some cab; he must be passing some shop. And every moment he seems to pump into this room this prickly light, this intensity of being so that things have lost their normal uses—this knife-blade is only a flash of light, not a thing to cut with. The normal is abolished.

"The door opens, but he does not come. That is Louis hesitating there. That is his strange mixture of assurance and timidity. He looks at himself in the looking-glass as he comes in; he touches his hair; he is dissatisfied with his appearance. He says, 'I am a Duke—the last of an ancient race.' He is acrid, suspicious, domineering, difficult (I am comparing him with Percival). At the same time he is formidable, for there is laughter in his eyes. He has seen me. Here he is."

"There is Susan," said Louis. "She does not see us. She has not dressed, because she despises the futility of London. She stands for a moment at the swing-door, looking about her like a creature dazed by the light of a lamp. Now she moves. She has the stealthy yet assured movements (even among tables and chairs) of a wild beast. She seems to find her way by instinct in and out among these little tables, touching no one, disregarding waiters, yet comes straight to our table in the corner. When she sees us (Neville, and myself) her face assumes a certainty which is alarming, as if she had what she wanted. To be loved by Susan would be to be impaled by a bird's sharp beak, to be nailed to a barnyard door. Yet there are moments when I could wish to be speared by a beak, to be nailed to a barnyard door, positively, once and for all.

"Rhoda comes now, from nowhere, having slipped in while we were not looking. She must have made a tortuous course, taking cover now behind a waiter, now behind some ornamental pillar, so as to put off as long as possible the shock of recognition, so as to be secure for one more moment to rock her petals in her basin. We wake her. We torture her. She dreads us, she despises us, yet comes cringing to our sides because for all our cruelty there is always some name, some face which sheds a radiance, which lights up her pavements and makes it possible for her to replenish her dreams."

"The door opens, the door goes on opening," said Neville, "yet he does not come."

"There is Jinny," said Susan. "She stands in the door. Everything seems stayed. The waiter stops. The diners at the table by the door look. She seems to centre everything; round her tables, lines of doors, windows, ceilings, ray themselves, like rays round the star in the middle of a smashed window-pane. She brings things to a point, to order. Now she sees us, and moves, and all the rays ripple and flow and waver over us, bringing in new tides of sensation. We change. Louis puts his hand to his tie. Neville, who sits waiting with agonised intensity, nervously straightens the forks in front of him. Rhoda sees her with surprise, as if on some far horizon a fire blazed. And I, though I pile my mind with damp grass, with wet fields, with the sound of rain on the roof and the gusts of wind that batter at the house in winter and so protect my soul against her, feel her derision steal round me, feel her laughter curl its tongues of fire round me and light up unsparingly my shabby dress, my square-tipped finger-nails, which I at once hide under the table-cloth."

"He has not come," said Neville. "The door opens and he does not come. That is Bernard. As he pulls off his coat he shows, of course, the blue shirt under his arm-pits. And then, unlike the rest of us, he comes in without pushing open a door, without knowing that he comes into a room full of strangers. He does not look in the glass. His hair is untidy, but he does not know it. He has no perception that we differ, or that this table is his goal. He hesitates on his way here. Who is that? he asks himself, as he half knows a woman in an opera cloak. He half knows everybody; he knows nobody (I compare him with Percival). But now, perceiving us, he waves a benevolent salute; he bears down with such benignity, with such love of mankind (crossed with humour at the futility of 'loving mankind'), that, if it were not for Percival, who turns all this to vapour, one would feel, as the others already feel: Now is our festival; now we are together. But without Percival there is no solidity. We are silhouettes, hollow phantoms moving mistily without a background."

"The swing-door goes on opening," said Rhoda. "Strangers keep on coming, people we shall never see again, people who brush us disagreeably with their familiarity, their indifference, and the sense of a world continuing without us. We cannot sink down, we cannot forget our faces. Even I who have no face, who make no difference when I come in (Susan and Jinny change bodies and faces), flutter unattached, without anchorage anywhere, unconsolidated, incapable of composing any blankness or continuity or wall against which these bodies move. It is because of Neville and his misery. The sharp breath of his misery scatters my being. Nothing can settle; nothing can subside. Every time the door opens he looks fixedly at the table—he dare not raise his eyes—then looks for one second and says, 'He has not come.' But here he is."

"Now," said Neville, "my tree flowers. My heart rises. All oppression is relieved. All impediment is removed. The reign of chaos is over. He has imposed order. Knives cut again."

"Here is Percival," said Jinny. "He has not dressed."

"Here is Percival," said Bernard, "smoothing his hair, not from vanity (he does not look in the glass), but to propitiate the god of decency. He is conventional; he is a hero. The little boys trooped after him across the playing-fields. They blew their noses as he blew his nose, but unsuccessfully, for he is Percival. Now, when he is about to leave us, to go to India, all these trifles come together. He is a hero. Oh, yes, that is not to be denied, and when he takes his seat by Susan, whom he loves, the occasion is crowned. We who yelped like jackals biting at each other's heels now assume the sober and confident air of soldiers in the presence of their captain. We who have been separated by our youth (the oldest is not yet twenty-five), who have sung like eager birds each his own song and tapped with the remorseless and savage egotism of the young our own snail-shell till it cracked (I am engaged), or perched solitary outside some bedroom window and sang of love, of fame and other single experiences so dear to the callow bird with a yellow tuft on its beak, now come nearer; and shuffling closer on our perch in this restaurant where everybody's interests are at variance, and the incessant passage of traffic chafes us with distractions, and the door opening perpetually its glass cage solicits us with myriad temptations and offers insults and wounds to our confidence — sitting together now we love each other and believe in our own endurance."

"Now let us issue from the darkness of solitude," said Louis.

"Now let us say, brutally and directly, what is in our minds," said Neville. "Our isolation, our preparation, is over. The furtive days of secrecy and hiding, the revelations on staircases, moments of terror and ecstasy."

"Old Mrs. Constable lifted her sponge and warmth poured over us," said Bernard. "We became clothed in this changing, this feeling garment of flesh."

"The boot boy made love to the scullery-maid in the kitchen garden," said Susan, "among the blown-out washing."

"The breath of the wind was like a tiger panting," said Rhoda.

"The man lay livid with his throat cut in the gutter," said Neville. "And going upstairs I could not raise my foot against the immitigable apple-tree with its silver leaves held stiff!"

"The leaf danced in the hedge without any one to blow it," said Jinny.

"In the sun-baked corner," said Louis, "the petals swam on depths of green."

"At Elvedon the gardeners swept and swept with their great brooms, and the woman sat at a table writing," said Bernard.

"From these close-furled balls of string we draw now every filament," said Louis, "remembering, when we meet."

"And then," said Bernard, "the cab came to the door, and, pressing our new bowler hats tightly over our eyes to hide our unmanly tears, we drove through streets in which even the housemaids looked at us, and our names painted in white letters on our boxes proclaimed to all the world that we were going to school with the regulation number of socks and drawers, on which our mothers for some nights previously had stitched our initials, in our boxes. A second severance from the body of our mother."

"And Miss Lambert, Miss Cutting, and Miss Bard," said Jinny, "monumental ladies, white-ruffed, stone-coloured, enigmatic, with amethyst rings moving like virginal tapers, dim glowworms over the pages of French, geography and arithmetic, presided; and there were maps, green-baize boards, and rows of shoes on a shelf."

"Bells rang punctually," said Susan, "maids scuffled and giggled. There was a drawing in of chairs and a drawing out of chairs on the linoleum. But from one attic there was a blue view, a distant view of a field unstained by the corruption of this regimented, unreal existence."

"Down from our heads veils fell," said Rhoda. "We clasped the flowers with their green leaves rustling in garlands."

"We changed, we became unrecognisable," said Louis. "Exposed to all these different lights, what we had in us (for we are all so different) came intermittently, in violent patches, spaced by blank voids, to the surface as if some acid had dropped un-equally on the plate. I was this, Neville that, Rhoda different again, and Bernard too."

"Then canoes slipped through palely tinted yellow branches," said Neville, "and Bernard, advancing in his casual way against breadths of green, against houses of very ancient foundation, tumbled in a heap on the ground beside me. In an access of emotion—winds are not more raving, nor lightning more sud-den—I took my poem, I flung my poem, I slammed the door behind me."

"I, however," said Louis, "losing sight of you, sat in my of-fice and tore the date from the calendar, and announced to the world of ship-brokers, corn-chandlers and actuaries that Friday the tenth, or Tuesday the eighteenth, had dawned on the city of London."

"Then," said Jinny, "Rhoda and I, exposed in bright dresses, with a few precious stones nestling on a cold ring round our throats, bowed, shook hands and took a sandwich from a plate with a smile."

"The tiger leapt, and the swallow dipped her wings in dark pools on the other side of the world," said Rhoda.

"But here and now we are together," said Bernard. "We have come together, at a particular time, to this particular spot. We are drawn into this communion by some deep, some com-mon emotion. Shall we call it, conveniently, 'love'? Shall we say 'love of Percival' because Percival is going to India?

"No, that is too small, too particular a name. We cannot at-tach the width and spread of our feelings to so small a mark. We have come together (from the North, from the South, from Susan's farm, from Louis's house of business) to make one thing, not enduring—for what endures?—but seen by many eyes simultaneously. There is a red carnation in that vase. A single flower as we sat here waiting, but now a seven-sided flower, many-petalled, red, puce, purple-shaded, stiff with silver-tinted leaves—a whole flower to which every eye brings its own contribution."

"After the capricious fires, the abysmal dulness of youth," said Neville, "the light falls upon real objects now. Here are knives and forks. The world is displayed, and we too, so that we can talk."

"We differ, it may be too profoundly," said Louis, "for explanation. But let us attempt it. I smoothed my hair when I came in, hoping to look like the rest of you. But I cannot, for I am not single and entire as you are. I have lived a thousand lives already. Every day I unbury—I dig up. I find relics of myself in the sand that women made thousands of years ago, when I heard songs by the Nile and the chained beast stamping. What you see beside you, this man, this Louis, is only the cinders and refuse of something once splendid. I was an Arab prince; behold my free gestures. I was a great poet in the time of Elizabeth. I was a Duke at the court of Louis the Fourteenth. I am very vain, very confident; I have an immeasurable desire that women should sigh in sympathy. I have eaten no lunch today in order that Susan may think me cadaverous and that Jinny may extend to me the exquisite balm of her sympathy. But while I admire Susan and Percival, I hate the others, because it is for them that I do these antics, smoothing my hair, concealing my accent. I am the little ape who chatters over a nut, and you are the dowdy women with shiny bags of stale buns; I am also the caged tiger, and you are the keepers with red-hot bars. That is, I am fiercer and stronger than you are, yet the apparition that appears above ground after ages of non-entity will be spent in terror lest you should laugh at me, in veerings with the wind against the soot storms, in efforts to make a steel ring of clear poetry that shall connect the gulls and the women with bad teeth, the church spire and the bobbing billycock hats as I see them when I take my luncheon and prop my poet—is it Lucretius?—against a cruet and the gravy-splashed bill of fare."

"But you will never hate me," said Jinny. "You will never see me, even across a room full of gilt chairs and ambassadors, without coming to me across the room to seek my sympathy. When I came in just now everything stood still in a pattern. Waiters stopped, diners raised their forks and held them. I had the air of being prepared for what would happen. When I sat down you put your hands to your ties, you hid them under the table. But I hide nothing. I am prepared. Every time the door opens I cry 'More!' But my imagination is the bodies. I can imagine nothing beyond the circle cast by my body. My body goes before me, like a lantern down a dark lane, bringing one thing after another out of darkness into a ring of light. I dazzle you; I make you believe that this is all."

"But when you stand in the door," said Neville, "you inflict stillness, demanding admiration, and that is a great impediment to the freedom of intercourse. You stand in the door making us notice you. But none of you saw me approach. I came early; I came quickly and directly, *here,* to sit for the person whom I love. My life has a rapidity that yours lack. I am like a hound on the scent. I hunt from dawn to dusk. Nothing, not the pursuit of perfection through the sand, nor fame, nor money has meaning for me. I shall have riches; I shall have fame. But I shall never have what I want, for I lack bodily grace and the courage that comes with it. The swiftness of my mind is too strong for my body. I fail before I reach the end and fall in a heap, damp, perhaps disgusting. I excite pity in the crises of life, not love. Therefore I suffer horribly. But I do not suffer, as Louis does, to make myself a spectacle. I have too fine a sense of fact to allow myself these juggleries, these pretences. I see everything—except one thing—with complete clarity. That is my saving. That is what gives my suffering an unceasing excitement. That is what makes me dictate, even when I am silent. And since I am, in one respect, deluded, since the person is always changing, though not the desire, and I do not know in the morning by whom I shall sit at night, I am never stagnant; I rise from my worst disasters, I turn, I change. Pebbles bounce off the mail of my muscular, my extended body. In this pursuit I shall grow old."

"If I could believe," said Rhoda, "that I should grow old in pursuit and change, I should be rid of my fear: nothing persists. One moment does not lead to another. The door opens and the tiger leaps. You did not see me come. I circled round the chairs to avoid the horror of the spring. I am afraid of you all. I am afraid of the shock of sensation that leaps upon me, because I cannot deal with it as you do—I cannot make one moment merge in the next. To me they are all violent, all separate; and if I fall under the shock of the leap of the moment you will be on me, tearing me to pieces. I have no end in view. I do not know how to run minute to minute and hour to hour, solving them by some natural force until they make the whole and indivisible mass that you call life. Because you have an end in view—one person, is it, to sit beside, an idea is it, your beauty is it? I do not know—your days and hours pass like the boughs of forest trees and the smooth green of forest rides to a hound running on the scent. But there is no single scent, no single body for me to follow. And I have no face. I am like the foam that races over the beach or the moonlight that falls arrowlike here on a tin can, here on a spike of the mailed sea holly, or a bone or a half-eaten boat. I am whirled down caverns, and flap like paper against endless corridors, and must press my hand against the wall to draw myself back.

"But since I wish above all things to have lodgment, I pretend, as I go upstairs lagging behind Jinny and Susan, to have an end in view. I pull on my stockings as I see them pull on theirs. I wait for you to speak and then speak like you. I am drawn here across London to a particular spot, to a particular place, not to see you or you or you, but to light my fire at the general blaze of you who live wholly, indivisibly and without caring in the moment."

"When I came into the room tonight," said Susan, "I stopped, I peered about like an animal with its eyes near to the ground. The smell of carpets and furniture and scent disgusts me. I like to walk through the wet fields alone, or to stop at a gate and watch my setter nose in a circle, and to ask, Where is the hare? I like to be with people who twist herbs, and spit into the fire and shuffle down long passages in slippers like my father. The only sayings I understand are cries of love, hate, rage and pain. This talking is undressing an old woman whose dress had seemed to be part of her, but now, as we talk, she turns pinkish underneath, and has wrinkled thighs and sagging breasts. When you are silent you are again beautiful. I shall never have anything but natural happiness. It will almost content me. I shall go to bed tired. I shall lie like a field bearing crops in rotation; in the summer heat will dance over me; in the winter I shall be cracked with the cold. But heat and cold will follow each other naturally without my willing or unwilling. My children will carry me on; their teething, their crying, their going to school and coming back will be like the waves of the sea under me. No day will be without its movement. I shall be lifted higher than any of you on the backs of the seasons. I shall possess more than Jinny, more than Rhoda, by the time I die. But on the other hand, where you are various and dimple a million times to the ideas and laughter of others, I shall be sullen, storm-tinted and all one purple. I shall be debased and hide-bound by the bestial and beautiful passion of maternity. I shall push the fortunes of my children unscrupulously. I shall hate those who see their faults. I shall lie basely to help them. I shall let them wall me away from you, from you and from you. Also, I am torn with jealousy. I hate Jinny because she shows me that my hands are red, my nails bitten. I love with such ferocity that it kills me when the object of my love shows by a phrase that he can escape. He escapes, and I am left clutching at a string that slips in and out among the leaves on the tree-tops. I do not understand phrases."

"Had I been born," said Bernard, "not knowing that one word follows another I might have been, who knows, perhaps anything. As it is, finding sequences everywhere, I cannot bear the pressure of solitude. When I cannot see words curling like rings of smoke round me I am in darkness—I am nothing. When I am alone I fall into lethargy, and say to myself dismally as I poke the cinders through the bars of the grate, Mrs. Moffat will come. She will come and sweep it all up. When Louis is alone he sees with astonishing intensity, and will write some words that may outlast us all. Rhoda loves to be alone. She fears us because we shatter the sense of being which is so extreme in solitude—see how she grasps her fork—her weapon against us. But I only come into existence when the plumber, or the horse-dealers, or whoever it may be, says something which sets me alight. Then how lovely the smoke of my phrase is, rising and falling, flaunting and falling, upon red lobsters and yellow fruit, wreathing them into one beauty. But observe how meretricious the phrase is—made up of what evasions and old lies. Thus my character is in part made of the stimulus which other people provide, and is not mine, as yours are. There is some fatal streak, some wandering and irregular vein of silver, weakening it. Hence the fact that used to enrage Neville at school, that I left him. I went with the boasting boys with little caps and badges, driving off in big brakes—there are some here tonight, dining together, correctly dressed before they go off in perfect concord to the music hall; I loved them. For they bring me into existence as certainly as you do. Hence, too, when I am leaving you and the train is going, you feel that it is not the train that is

going, but I, Bernard, who does not care, who does not feel,
who has no ticket, and has lost perhaps his purse. Susan, staring at the string that slips in and out among the leaves of the
beech trees, cries: 'He is gone! He has escaped me!' For there is
nothing to lay hold of. I am made and remade continually. Different people draw different words from me.

"Thus there is not one person but fifty people whom I
want to sit beside tonight. But I am the only one of you who
is at home here without taking liberties. I am not gross; I am
not a snob. If I lie open to the pressure of society I often succeed with the dexterity of my tongue in putting something
difficult into the currency. See my little toys, twisted out of
nothing in a second, how they entertain. I am no hoarder—I
shall leave only a cupboard of old clothes when I die—and I
am almost indifferent to the minor vanities of life which cause
Louis so much torture. But I have sacrificed much. Veined as I
am with iron, with silver and streaks of common mud, I cannot contract into the firm fist which those clench who do not
depend upon stimulus. I am incapable of the denials, the hero-
isms of Louis and Rhoda. I shall never succeed, even in talk, in
making a perfect phrase. But I shall have contributed more to
the passing moment than any of you; I shall go into more rooms,
more different rooms, than any of you. But because there is
something that comes from outside and not from within I shall
be forgotten; when my voice is silent you will not remember
me, save as the echo of a voice that once wreathed the fruit into
phrases."

"Look," said Rhoda; "listen. Look how the light becomes
richer, second by second, and bloom and ripeness lie everywhere; and our eyes, as they range round this room with all its
tables, seem to push through curtains of colour, red, orange,
umber and queer ambiguous tints, which yield like veils and
close behind them, and one thing melts into another."

"Yes," said Jinny, "our senses have widened. Membranes, webs of nerve that lay white and limp, have filled and spread themselves and float round us like filaments, making the air tangible and catching in them far-away sounds unheard before."

"The roar of London," said Louis, "is round us. Motor-cars, vans, omnibuses pass and repass continuously. All are merged in one turning wheel of single sound. All separate sounds— wheels, bells, the cries of drunkards, of merrymakers—are churned into one sound, steel blue, circular. Then a siren hoots. At that shores slip away, chimneys flatten themselves, the ship makes for the open sea."

"Percival is going," said Neville. "We sit here, surrounded, lit up, many coloured; all things—hands, curtains, knives and forks, other people dining—run into each other. We are walled in here. But India lies outside."

"I see India," said Bernard. "I see the low, long shore; I see the tortuous lanes of stamped mud that lead in and out among ramshackle pagodas; I see the gilt and crenellated buildings which have an air of fragility and decay as if they were temporarily run up buildings in some Oriental exhibition. I see a pair of bullocks who drag a low cart along the sun-baked road. The cart sways incompetently from side to side. Now one wheel sticks in the rut, and at once innumerable natives in loin-cloths swarm round it, chattering excitedly. But they do nothing. Time seems endless, ambition vain. Over all broods a sense of the uselessness of human exertion. There are strange sour smells. An old man in a ditch continues to chew betel and to contemplate his navel. But now, behold, Percival advances; Percival rides a flea-bitten mare, and wears a sun-helmet. By applying the standards of the West, by using the violent language that is natural to him, the bullock-cart is righted in less than five minutes. The Oriental problem is solved. He rides on; the multitude cluster round him, regarding him as if he were—what indeed he is—a God."

"Unknown, with or without a secret, it does not matter," said Rhoda, "he is like a stone fallen into a pond round which minnows swarm. Like minnows, we who had been shooting this way, that way, all shot round him when he came. Like minnows, conscious of the presence of a great stone, we undulate and eddy contentedly. Comfort steals over us. Gold runs in our blood. One, two; one, two; the heart beats in serenity, in confidence, in some trance of well-being, in some rapture of benignity; and look—the outermost parts of the earth—pale shadows on the utmost horizon, India for instance, rise into our purview. The world that had been shrivelled, rounds itself; remote provinces are fetched up out of darkness; we see muddy roads, twisted jungle, swarms of men, and the vulture that feeds on some bloated carcass as within our scope, part of our proud and splendid province, since Percival, riding alone on a flea-bitten mare, advances down a solitary path, has his camp pitched among desolate trees, and sits alone, looking at the enormous mountains."

"It is Percival," said Louis, "sitting silent as he sat among the tickling grasses when the breeze parted the clouds and they formed again, who makes us aware that these attempts to say, 'I am this, I am that,' which we make, coming together, like separated parts of one body and soul, are false. Something has been left out from fear. Something has been altered, from vanity. We have tried to accentuate differences. From the desire to be separate we have laid stress upon our faults, and what is particular to us. But there is a chain whirling round, round, in a steel-blue circle beneath."

"It is hate, it is love," said Susan. "That is the furious coal-black stream that makes us dizzy if we look down into it. We stand on a ledge here, but if we look down we turn giddy."

"It is love," said Jinny, "it is hate, such as Susan feels for me because I kissed Louis once in the garden; because equipped as I am, I make her think when I come in, 'My hands are red,' and hide them. But our hatred is almost indistinguishable from our love."

"Yet these roaring waters," said Neville, "upon which we build our crazy platforms are more stable than the wild, the weak and inconsequent cries that we utter when, trying to speak, we rise; when we reason and jerk out these false sayings, 'I am this; I am that!' Speech is false.

"But I eat. I gradually lose all knowledge of particulars as I eat. I am becoming weighed down with food. These delicious mouthfuls of roast duck, fitly piled with vegetables, following each other in exquisite rotation of warmth, weight, sweet and bitter, past my palate, down my gullet, into my stomach, have stabilised my body. I feel quiet, gravity, control. All is solid now. Instinctively my palate now requires and anticipates sweetness and lightness, something sugared and evanescent; and cool wine, fitting glove-like over those finer nerves that seem to tremble from the roof of my mouth and make it spread (as I drink) into a domed cavern, green with vine leaves, musk-scented, purple with grapes. Now I can look steadily into the mill-race that foams beneath. By what particular name are we to call it? Let Rhoda speak, whose face I see reflected mistily in the looking-glass opposite; Rhoda whom I interrupted when she rocked her petals in a brown basin, asking for the pocket-knife that Bernard had stolen. Love is not a whirlpool to her. She is not giddy when she looks down. She looks far away over our heads, beyond India."

"Yes, between your shoulders, over your heads, to a land-scape," said Rhoda, "to a hollow where the many-backed steep hills come down like birds' wings folded. There, on the short, firm turf, are bushes, dark leaved, and against their darkness I see a shape, white, but not of stone, moving, perhaps alive. But it is not you, it is not you, it is not you; not Percival, Susan, Jinny, Neville or Louis. When the white arm rests upon the knee it is a triangle; now it is upright—a column; now a fountain, falling. It makes no sign, it does not beckon, it does not see us. Behind it roars the sea. It is beyond our reach. Yet there I venture. There I go to replenish my emptiness, to stretch my nights and fill them fuller and fuller with dreams. And for a second even now, even here, I reach my object and say, 'Wander no more. All else is trial and make-believe. Here is the end.' But these pilgrimages, these moments of departure, start always in your presence, from this table, these lights, from Percival and Susan, here and now. Always I see the grove over your heads, between your shoulders, or from a window when I have crossed the room at a party and stand looking down into the street."

"But his slippers?" said Neville. "And his voice downstairs in the hall? And catching sight of him when he does not see one? One waits and he does not come. It gets later and later. He has forgotten. He is with some one else. He is faithless, his love meant nothing. Oh, then the agony—then the intolerable despair! And then the door opens. He is here."

"Rippling gold, I say to him, 'Come,'" said Jinny. "And he comes; he crosses the room to where I sit, with my dress like a veil billowing round me on the gilt chair. Our hands touch, our bodies burst into fire. The chair, the cup, the table—nothing remains unlit. All quivers, all kindles, all burns clear."

("Look, Rhoda," said Louis, "they have become nocturnal, rapt. Their eyes are like moth's wings moving so quickly that they do not seem to move at all."

"Horns and trumpets," said Rhoda, "ring out. Leaves unfold; the stags blares in the thicket. There is a dancing and a drumming, like the dancing and the drumming of naked men with assegais."

"Like the dance of savages," said Louis, "round the camp fire. They are savage; they are ruthless. They dance in a circle, flapping bladders. The flames leap over their painted faces, over the leopard skins and the bleeding limbs which they have torn from the living body."

"The flames of the festival rise high," said Rhoda. "The great procession passes, flinging green boughs and flowering branches. Their horns spill blue smoke; their skins are dappled red and yellow in the torchlight. They throw violets. They deck the beloved with garlands and with laurel leaves, there on the ring of turf where the steep-backed hills come down. The procession passes. And while it passes, Louis, we are aware of downfalling, we forebode decay. The shadow slants. We who are conspirators, withdrawn together to lean over some cold urn, note how the purple flame flows downwards."

"Death is woven in with the violets," said Louis. "Death and again death.")

"How proudly we sit here," said Jinny, "we who are not yet twenty-five! Outside the trees flower; outside the women linger; outside the cabs swerve and sweep. Emerged from the tentative ways, the obscurities and dazzle of youth, we look straight in front of us, ready for what may come (the door opens, the door keeps on opening). All is real; all is firm without shadow or illusion. Beauty rides our brows. There is mine, there is Susan's. Our flesh is firm and cool. Our differences are clear-cut as the shadows of rocks in full sunlight. Beside us lie crisp rolls, yellow-glazed and hard; the table-cloth is white, our hands lie half curled, ready to contract. Days and days are to come; winter days, summer days; we have scarcely broken into our hoard. Now the fruit is swollen beneath the leaf. The room is golden, and I say to him, 'Come.'"

"He has red ears," said Louis, "and the smell of meat hangs down in a damp net while the city clerks take snacks at the lunch bar."

"With infinite time before us," said Neville, "we ask what shall we do? Shall we loiter down Bond Street, looking here and there, and buying perhaps a fountain-pen because it is green, or asking how much is the ring with the blue stone? Or shall we sit indoors and watch the coals turn crimson? Shall we stretch our hands for books and read here a passage and there a passage? Shall we shout with laughter for no reason? Shall we push through flowering meadows and make daisy chains? Shall we find out when the next train starts for the Hebrides and engage a reserved compartment? All is to come."

"For you," said Bernard, "but yesterday I walked bang into a pillar-box. Yesterday I became engaged."

"How strange," said Susan, "the little heaps of sugar look by the side of our plates. Also the mottled peelings of pears, and the plush rims to the looking-glasses. I had not seen them before. Everything is now set; everything is fixed. Bernard is engaged. Something irrevocable has happened. A circle has been cast on the waters; a chain is imposed. We shall never flow freely again."

"For one moment only," said Louis. "Before the chain breaks, before disorder returns, see us fixed, see us displayed, see us held in a vice.

"But now the circle breaks. Now the current flows. Now we rush faster than before. Now passions that lay in wait down there in the dark weeds which grow at the bottom rise and pound us with their waves. Pain and jealousy, envy and desire, and something deeper than they are, stronger than love and more subterranean. The voice of action speaks. Listen, Rhoda (for we are conspirators, with our hands on the cold urn), to the casual, quick, exciting voice of action, of hounds running on the scent. They speak now without troubling to finish their sentences. They talk a little language such as lovers use. An imperious brute possesses them. The nerves thrill in their thighs. Their hearts pound and churn in their sides. Susan screws her pocket-handkerchief. Jinny's eyes dance with fire."

"They are immune," said Rhoda, "from picking fingers and searching eyes. How easily they turn and glance; what poses they take of energy and pride! What life shines in Jinny's eyes; how fell, how entire Susan's glance is, searching for insects at the roots! Their hair shines lustrous. Their eyes burn like the eyes of animals brushing through leaves on the scent of the prey. The circle is destroyed. We are thrown asunder."

"But soon, too soon," said Bernard, "this egotistic exultation fails. Too soon the moment of ravenous identity is over, and the appetite for happiness, and happiness, and still more happiness is glutted. The stone is sunk; the moment is over. Round me there spreads a wide margin of indifference. Now open in my eyes a thousand eyes of curiosity. Any one now is at liberty to murder Bernard, who is engaged to be married, so long as they leave untouched this margin of unknown territory, this forest of the unknown world. Why, I ask (whispering discreetly), do women dine alone together there? Who are they? And what has brought them on this particular evening to this particular spot? The youth in the corner, judging from the nervous way in which he puts his hand from time to time to the back of his head, is from the country. He is suppliant, and so anxious to respond suitably to the kindness of his father's friend, his host, that he can scarcely enjoy now what he will enjoy very much at about half-past eleven tomorrow morning. I have also seen that lady powder her nose three times in the midst of an absorbing conversation—about love perhaps, about the unhappiness of their dearest friend perhaps. 'Ah, but the state of my nose!' she thinks, and out comes her powder-puff, obliterating in its passage all the most fervent feelings of the human heart. There remains, however, the insoluble problem of the solitary man with the eyeglass; of the elderly lady drinking champagne alone. Who and what are these unknown people? I ask. I could make a dozen stories of what he said, of what she said—I can see a dozen pictures. But what are stories? Toys I twist, bubbles I blow, one ring passing through another. And sometimes I begin to doubt if there are stories. What is my story? What is Rhoda's? What is Neville's? There are facts, as, for example: 'The handsome young man in the grey suit, whose reserve contrasted so strangely with the loquacity of the others, now brushed the crumbs from his waistcoat and, with a characteristic gesture at once commanding and benign, made a sign to the waiter, who came instantly and returned a moment later with the bill discreetly folded upon a plate.' That is the truth; that is a fact, but beyond it all is darkness and conjecture."

"Now once more," said Louis, "as we are about to part, having paid our bill, the circle in our blood, broken so often, so sharply, for we are so different, closes in a ring. Something is made. Yes, as we rise and fidget, a little nervously, we pray, holding in our hands this common feeling, 'Do not move, do not let the swing-door cut to pieces the thing that we have made, that globes itself here, among these lights, these peelings, this litter of bread crumbs and people passing. Do not move, do not go. Hold it for ever.'"

"Let us hold it for one moment," said Jinny; "love, hatred, by whatever name we call it, this globe whose walls are made of Percival, of youth and beauty, and something so deep sunk within us that we shall perhaps never make this moment out of one man again."

"Forests and far countries on the other side of the world," said Rhoda, "are in it; seas and jungles; the howlings of jackals and moonlight falling upon some high peak where the eagle soars."

"Happiness is in it," said Neville, "and the quiet of ordinary things. A table, a chair, a book with a paper-knife stuck between the pages. And the petal falling from the rose, and the light flickering as we sit silent, or, perhaps, bethinking us of some trifle, suddenly speak."

"Week-days are in it," said Susan, "Monday, Tuesday, Wednesday; the horses going up to the fields, and the horses returning; the rooks rising and falling, and catching the elm-trees in their net, whether it is April, whether it is November."

"What is to come is in it," said Bernard. "That is the last drop and the brightest that we let fall like some supernal quicksilver into the swelling and splendid moment created by us from Percival. What is to come? I ask, brushing the crumbs from my waistcoat, what is outside? We have proved, sitting eating, sitting talking, that we can add to the treasury of moments. We are not slaves bound to suffer incessantly unrecorded petty blows on our bent backs. We are not sheep either, following a master. We are creators. We too have made something that will join the innumerable congregations of past time. We too, as we put on our hats and push open the door, stride not into chaos, but into a world that our own force can subjugate and make part of the illumined and everlasting road.

"Look, Percival, while they fetch the taxi, at the prospect which you are so soon to lose. The street is hard and burnished with the churning of innumerable wheels. The yellow canopy of our tremendous energy hangs like a burning cloth above our heads. Theatres, music halls and lamps in private houses make that light."

"Peaked clouds," said Rhoda, "voyage over a sky dark like polished whalebone."

"Now the agony begins; now the horror has seized me with its fangs," said Neville. "Now the cab comes; now Percival goes. What can we do to keep him? How bridge the distance between us? How fan the fire so that it blazes for ever? How signal to all time to come that we, who stand in the street, in the lamplight, loved Percival? Now Percival is gone."

*T*HE SUN *had risen to its full height. It was no longer half seen and guessed at, from hints and gleams, as if a girl couched on her green-sea mattress tired her brows with water-globed jewels that sent lances of opal-tinted light falling and flashing in the uncertain air like the flanks of a dolphin leaping, or the flash of a falling blade. Now the sun burnt uncompromising, undeniable. It struck upon the hard sand, and the rocks became furnaces of red heat; it searched each pool and caught the minnow hiding in the cranny, and showed the rusty cartwheel, the white bone, or the boot without laces stuck, black as iron, in the sand. It gave to everything its exact measure of colour; to the sandhills their innumerable glitter, to the wild grasses their glancing green; or it fell upon the arid waste of the desert, here wind-scourged into furrows, here swept into desolate cairns, here sprinkled with stunted dark-green jungle-trees. It lit up the smooth gilt mosque, the frail pink-and-white card houses of the southern village, and the long-breasted, white-haired women who knelt in the river bed beating wrinkled cloths upon stones. Steamers thudding slowly over the sea were caught in the level stare of the sun, and it beat through the yellow awnings upon passengers who dozed or paced the deck, shading their eyes to look for the land, while day after day, compressed in its oily throbbing sides, the ship bore them on monotonously over the waters.*

The sun beat on the crowded pinnacles of southern hills and glared into deep, stony river beds where the water was shrunk beneath the high slung bridge so that washerwomen kneeling on hot stones could scarcely wet their linen; and lean mules went picking their way among the chattering grey stones with panniers slung across their narrow shoulders. At midday the heat of the sun made the hills grey as if shaved and singed in an explosion, while, further north, in cloudier and rainier countries, hills smoothed into slabs as with the back of a spade had a light in them as if a warder, deep within, went from chamber to chamber carrying a green lamp. Through atoms of grey-blue air the sun struck at English fields and lit up marshes and pools, a white gull on a stake, the slow sail of shadows over blunt-headed woods and young corn and flowing hayfields. It beat on the orchard wall, and every pit and grain of the brick was silver pointed, purple, fiery as if soft to touch, as if touched it must melt into hot-baked grains of dust. The currants hung against the wall in ripples and cascades of polished red; plums swelled out their leaves, and all the blades of the grass were run together in one fluent green blaze. The trees' shadow was sunk to a dark pool at the root. Light descending in floods dissolved the separate foliation into one green mound.

The birds sang passionate songs addressed to one ear only and then stopped. Bubbling and chuckling they carried little bits of straw and twig to the dark knots in the higher branches of the trees. Gilt and purpled they perched in the garden, where cones of laburnum and purple shook down gold and lilac, for now at midday the garden was all blossom and profusion and even the tunnels under the plants were green and purple and tawny as the sun beat through the red petal, or the broad yellow petal, or was barred by some thickly furred green stalk.

The sun struck straight upon the house, making the white walls glare between the dark windows. Their panes, woven thickly with green branches, held circles of impenetrable darkness. Sharp-edged wedges of light lay upon the window-sill and showed inside the room plates with blue rings, cups with curved handles, the bulge of a great bowl, the criss-cross pattern in the rug, and the formidable corners and lines of cabinets and bookcases. Behind their conglomeration hung a zone of shadow in which might be a further shape to be disencumbered of shadow or still denser depths of darkness.

The waves broke and spread their waters swiftly over the shore. One after another they massed themselves and fell; the spray tossed itself back with the energy of their fall. The waves were steeped deep-blue save for a pattern of diamond-pointed light on their backs which rippled as the backs of great horses ripple with muscles as they move. The waves fell; withdrew and fell again, like the thud of a great beast stamping.

"HE IS DEAD," said Neville. "He fell. His horse tripped. He was thrown. The sails of the world have swung round and caught me on the head. All is over. The lights of the world have gone out. There stands the tree which I cannot pass.

"Oh, to crumple this telegram in my fingers—to let the light of the world flood back—to say this has not happened! But why turn one's head hither and thither? This is the truth. This is the fact. His horse stumbled; he was thrown. The flashing trees and white rails went up in a shower. There was a surge; a drumming in his ears. Then the blow; the world crashed; he breathed heavily. He died where he fell.

"Barns and summer days in the country, rooms where we sat—all now lies in the unreal world which is gone. My past is cut from me. They came running. They carried him to some pavilion, men in riding-boots, men in sun helmets; among unknown men he died. Loneliness and silence often surrounded him. He often left me. And then, returning, 'See where he comes!' I said.

"Women shuffle past the window as if there were no gulf cut in the street; no tree with stiff leaves which we cannot pass. We deserve then to be tripped by molehills. We are infinitely abject, shuffling past with our eyes shut. But why should I submit? Why try to lift my foot and mount the stair? This is where I stand; here, holding the telegram. The past summer days and rooms where we sat stream away like burnt paper with red eyes in it. Why meet and resume? Why talk and eat and make up other combinations with other people? From this moment I am solitary. No one will know me now. I have three letters, 'I am about to play quoits with a colonel, so no more,' thus he ends our friendship, shouldering his way through the crowd with a wave of his hand. This farce is worth no more formal celebration. Yet if some one had but said: 'Wait'; had pulled the strap three holes tighter—he would have done justice for fifty years, and sat in Court and ridden alone at the head of troops and denounced some monstrous tyranny, and come back to us.

"Now I say there is a grinning, there is a subterfuge. There is something sneering behind our backs. That boy almost lost his footing as he leapt on the bus. Percival fell; was killed; is buried, and I watch people passing; holding tight to the rails of omnibuses; determined to save their lives.

"I will not lift my foot to climb the stair. I will stand for one moment beneath the immitigable tree, alone with the man whose throat is cut, while downstairs the cook shoves in and out the dampers. I will not climb the stair. We are doomed, all of us. Women shuffle past with shopping-bags. People keep on passing. Yet you shall not destroy me. For this moment, this one moment, we are together. I press you to me. Come, pain, feed on me. Bury your fangs in my flesh. Tear me asunder. I sob, I sob."

"Such is the incomprehensible combination," said Bernard, "such is the complexity of things, that as I descend the staircase I do not know which is sorrow, which joy. My son is born; Percival is dead. I am upheld by pillars, shored up on either side by stark emotions; but which is sorrow, which is joy? I ask, and do not know, only that I need silence, and to be alone and to go out, and to save one hour to consider what has happened to my world, what death has done to my world.

"This then is the world that Percival sees no longer. Let me look. The butcher delivers meat next door; two old men stumble along the pavement; sparrows alight. The machine then works; I note the rhythm, the throb, but as a thing in which I have no part, since he sees it no longer. (He lies pale and bandaged in some room.) Now then is my chance to find out what is of great importance, and I must be careful, and tell no lies. About him my feeling was: he sat there in the centre. Now I go to that spot no longer. The place is empty.

"Oh, yes, I can assure you, men in felt-hats and women carrying baskets—you have lost something that would have been very valuable to you. You have lost a leader, whom you would have followed; and one of you has lost happiness and children. He is dead who would have given you that. He lies on a camp-bed, bandaged, in some hot Indian hospital while coolies squatted on the floor agitate those fans—I forget how they call them. But this is important; 'You are well out of it,' I said, while the doves descended over the roofs and my son was born, as if it were a fact. I remember, as a boy, his curious air of detachment. And I go on to say (my eyes fill with tears and then are dry), 'But this is better than one had dared to hope.' I say, addressing what is abstract, facing me eyeless at the end of the avenue, in the sky, 'Is this the utmost you can do?' 'Then we have triumphed. You have done your utmost,' I say, addressing that blank and brutal face (for he was twenty-five and should have lived to be eighty) without avail. I am not going to lie down and weep away a life of care. (An entry to be made in my pocket-book; contempt for those who inflict meaningless death.) Further, this is important; that I should be able to place him in trifling and ridiculous situations, so that he may not feel himself absurd, perched on a great horse. I must be able to say, 'Percival, a ridiculous name.' At the same time let me tell you, men and women, hurrying to the tube station, you would have had to respect him. You would have had to form up and follow behind him. How strange to oar one's way through crowds seeing life through hollow eyes, burning eyes.

"Yet already signals begin, beckonings, attempts to lure me back. Curiosity is knocked out only for a short time. One cannot live outside the machine for more perhaps than half an hour. Bodies, I note, already begin to look ordinary; but what is behind them differs—the perspective. Behind that newspaper placard is the hospital; the long room with black men pulling ropes; and then they bury him. Yet since it says a famous actress has been divorced, I ask instantly Which? Yet I cannot take out my penny; I cannot buy a paper; I cannot suffer interruption yet.

"I ask, if I shall never see you again and fix my eyes on that solidity, what form will our communication take? You have gone across the court, further and further, drawing finer and finer the thread between us. But you exist somewhere. Something of you remains. A judge. That is, if I discover a new vein in myself I shall submit it to you privately. I shall ask, 'What is your verdict?' You shall remain the arbiter. But for how long? Things will become too difficult to explain: there will be new things; already my son. I am now at the zenith of an experience. It will decline. Already I no longer cry with conviction, 'What luck!' Exaltation, the flight of doves descending, is over. Chaos, detail, return. I am no longer amazed by names written over shop-windows. I do not feel Why hurry? Why catch trains? The sequence returns; one thing leads to another—the usual order.

"Yes, but I still resent the usual order. I will not let myself be made yet to accept the sequence of things. I will walk; I will not change the rhythm of my mind by stopping, by looking; I will walk. I will go up these steps into the gallery and submit myself to the influence of minds like mine outside the sequence. There is little time left to answer the question; my powers flag; I become torpid. Here are pictures. Here are cold madonnas among their pillars. Let them lay to rest the incessant activity of the mind's eye, the bandaged head, the men with ropes, so that I may find something unvisual beneath. Here are gardens; and Venus among her flowers; here are saints and blue madonnas. Mercifully these pictures make no reference; they do not nudge; they do not point. Thus they expand my consciousness of him and bring him back to me differently. I remember his beauty. 'Look, where he comes,' I said.

"Lines and colours almost persuade me that I too can be heroic, I, who make phrases so easily, am so soon seduced, love what comes next, and cannot clench my fist, but vacillate weakly making phrases according to my circumstances. Now, through my own infirmity I recover what he was to me: my opposite. Being naturally truthful, he did not see the point of these exaggerations, and was borne on by a natural sense of the fitting, was indeed a great master of the art of living so that he seems to have lived long, and to have spread calm round him, indifference one might almost say, certainly to his own advancement, save that he had also great compassion. A child playing—a summer evening—doors will open and shut, will keep opening and shutting, through which I see sights that make me weep. For they cannot be imparted. Hence our loneliness; hence our desolation. I turn to that spot in my mind and find it empty. My own infirmities oppress me. There is no longer him to oppose them.

"Behold then, the blue madonna streaked with tears. This is my funeral service. We have no ceremonies, only private dirges and no conclusions, only violent sensations, each separate. Nothing that has been said meets our case. We sit in the Italian room at the National Gallery picking up fragments. I doubt that Titian ever felt this rat gnaw. Painters live lives of methodical absorption, adding stroke to stroke. They are not like poets—scapegoats; they are not chained to the rock. Hence the silence, the sublimity. Yet that crimson must have burnt in Titian's gizzard. No doubt he rose with the great arms holding the cornucopia, and fell, in that descent. But the silence weighs on me— the perpetual solicitation of the eye. The pressure is intermittent and muffled. I distinguish too little and too vaguely. The bell is pressed and I do not ring or give out irrelevant clamours all jangled. I am titillated inordinately by some splendour; the ruffled crimson against the green lining; the march of pillars; the orange light behind the black, pricked ears of the olive trees. Arrows of sensation strike from my spine, but without order.

"Yet something is added to my interpretation. Something lies deeply buried. For one moment I thought to grasp it. But bury it, bury it; let it breed, hidden in the depths of my mind some day to fructify. After a long lifetime, loosely, in a moment of revelation, I may lay hands on it, but now the idea breaks in my hand. Ideas break a thousand times for once that they globe themselves entire. They break; they fall over me 'Line and colours they survive, therefore . . .'

"I am yawning. I am glutted with sensations. I am exhausted with the strain and the long, long time—twenty-five minutes, half an hour—that I have held myself alone outside the machine. I grow numb; I grow stiff. How shall I break up this numbness which discredits my sympathetic heart? There are others suffering—multitudes of people suffering. Neville suffers. He loved Percival. But I can no longer endure extremities; I want some one with whom to laugh, with whom to yawn, with whom to remember how he scratched his head; some one he was at ease with and liked (not Susan, whom he loved but Jinny rather). In her room also I could do penance. I could ask, Did he tell you how I refused him when he asked me to go to Hampton Court that day? Those are the thoughts that will wake me leaping in anguish in the middle of the night—the crimes for which one would do penance in all the markets of the world bareheaded; that one did not go to Hampton Court that day.

"But now I want life round me, and books and little ornaments, and the usual sounds of tradesmen calling on which to pillow my head after this exhaustion, and shut my eyes after this revelation. I will go straight then down the stairs, and hail the first taxi and drive to Jinny."

"There is the puddle," said Rhoda, "and I cannot cross it. I hear the rush of the great grindstone within an inch of my head.

Its wind roars in my face. All palpable forms of life have failed me. Unless I can stretch and touch something hard, I shall be blown down the eternal corridors for ever. What then can I touch? What brick, what stone? and so draw myself across the enormous gulf into my body safely?

"Now the shadow has fallen and the purple light slants downwards. The figure that was robed in beauty is now clothed in ruin. The figure that stood in the grove where the steep backed hills come down falls in ruin, as I told them when they said they loved his voice on the stair, and his old shoes and moments of being together.

"Now I will walk down Oxford Street envisaging a world rent by lightning; I will look at oaks cracked asunder and red where the flowering branch has fallen. I will go to Oxford Street and buy stockings for a party. I will do the usual things under the lightning flash. On the bare ground I will pick violets and bind them together and offer them to Percival, something given him by me. Look now at what Percival has given me. Look at the street now that Percival is dead. The houses are lightly founded to be puffed over by a breath of air. Reckless and random the cars race and roar and hunt us to death like bloodhounds. I am alone in a hostile world. The human face is hideous. This is to my liking. I want publicity and violence and to be dashed like a stone on the rocks. I like factory chimneys and cranes and lorries. I like the passing of face and face and face, deformed, indifferent. I am sick of prettiness; I am sick of privacy. I ride rough waters and shall sink with no one to save me.

"Percival, by his death, has made me this present, has revealed this terror, has left me to undergo this humiliation— faces and faces, served out like soup-plates by scullions; coarse, greedy, casual; looking in at shop-windows with pendent parcels; ogling, brushing, destroying everything, leaving even our love impure, now touched by their dirty fingers.

"Here is the shop where they sell stockings. And I could believe that beauty is once more set flowing. Its whisper comes down these aisles, through these laces, breathing among baskets of coloured ribbons. There are then warm hollows grooved in the heart of the uproar; alcoves of silence where we can shelter under the wing of beauty from truth which I desire. Pain is suspended as a girl silently slides open a drawer. And then, she speaks; her voice wakes me. I shoot to the bottom among the weeds and see envy, jealousy, hatred and spite scuttle like crabs over the sand as she speaks. These are our companions. I will pay my bill and take my parcel.

"This is Oxford Street. Here are hate, jealousy, hurry, and indifference frothed into the wild semblance of life. These are our companions. Consider the friends with whom we sit and eat. I think of Louis, reading the sporting column of an evening newspaper, afraid of ridicule; a snob. He says, looking at the people passing, he will shepherd us if we will follow. If we submit he will reduce us to order. Thus he will smooth out the death of Percival to his satisfaction, looking fixedly over the cruet, past the houses at the sky. Bernard, meanwhile, flops red-eyed into some arm-chair. He will have out his notebook; under D, he will enter 'Phrases to be used on the deaths of friends.' Jinny, pirouetting across the room, will perch on the arm of his chair and ask, 'Did he love me?' 'More than he loved Susan?' Susan, engaged to her farmer in the country, will stand for a second with the telegram before her, holding a plate; and then, with a kick of her heel, slam to the oven door. Neville, after staring at the window through his tears will see through his tears, and ask, 'Who passes the window?'—'What lovely boy?' This is my tribute to Percival; withered violets, blackened violets.

"Where shall I go then? To some museum, where they keep rings under glass cases, where there are cabinets, and the dresses that queens have worn? Or shall I go to Hampton Court and

look at the red walls and courtyards and the seemliness of
herded yew trees making black pyramids symmetrically on the
grass among flowers? There shall I recover beauty, and impose
order upon my raked, my dishevelled soul? But what can one
make in loneliness? Alone I should stand on the empty grass
and say, Rooks fly; somebody passes with a bag; there is a gardener with a wheelbarrow. I should stand in a queue and smell
sweat, and scent as horrible as sweat; and be hung with other
people like a joint of meat among other joints of meat.

"Here is a hall where one pays money and goes in, where
one hears music among somnolent people who have come here
after lunch on a hot afternoon. We have eaten beef and pudding
enough to live for a week without tasting food. Therefore we
cluster like maggots on the back of something that will carry us
on. Decorous, portly—we have white hair waved under our
hats; slim shoes; little bags; clean-shaven cheeks; here and there
a military moustache, not a speck of dust has been allowed to
settle anywhere on our broadcloth. Swaying and opening pro-
grammes, with a few words of greeting to friends, we settle
down, like walruses stranded on rocks, like heavy bodies incapable of waddling to the sea, hoping for a wave to lift us, but
we are too heavy, and too much dry shingle lies between us and
the sea. We lie gorged with food, torpid in the heat. Then,
swollen but contained in slippery satin, the sea-green woman
comes to our rescue. She sucks in her lips, assumes an air of intensity, inflates herself and hurls herself precisely at the right
moment as if she saw an apple and her voice was the arrow into
the note, 'Ah!'

"An axe has split a tree to the core; the core is warm; sound
quivers within the bark. 'Ah,' cried a woman to her lover, leaning from her window in Venice, 'Ah, Ah!' she cried, and again
she cries 'Ah!' She has provided us with a cry. But only a cry.
And what is a cry? Then the beetle-shaped men come with their

violins; wait; count; nod; down come their bows. And there is ripple and laughter like the dance of olive trees and their myriad-tongued grey leaves when a seafarer, biting a twig between his lips where the many-backed steep hills come down, leaps on shore.

"'Like' and 'like' and 'like'—but what is the thing that lies beneath the semblance of the thing? Now that lightning has gashed the tree and the flowering branch has fallen and Percival, by his death, has made me this gift, let me see the thing. There is a square; there is an oblong. The players take the square and place it upon the oblong. They place it very accurately; they make a perfect dwelling-place. Very little is left outside. The structure is now visible; what is inchoate is here stated; we are not so various or so mean; we have made oblongs and stood them upon squares. This is our triumph; this is our consolation.

"The sweetness of this content overflowing runs down the walls of my mind, and liberates understanding. Wander no more, I say; this is the end. The oblong has been set upon the square; the spiral is on top. We have been hauled over the shingle, down to the sea. The players come again. But they are mopping their faces. They are no longer so spruce or so debonair. I will go. I will set aside this afternoon. I will make a pilgrimage. I will go to Greenwich. I will fling myself fearlessly into trams, into omnibuses. As we lurch down Regent Street, and I am flung upon this woman, upon this man, I am not injured, I am not outraged by the collision. A square stands upon an oblong. Here are mean streets where chaffering goes on in street markets, and every sort of iron rod, bolt and screw is laid out, and people swarm off the pavement, pinching raw meat with thick fingers. The structure is visible. We have made a dwelling-place.

"These then are the flowers that grow among the rough grasses of the field which the cows trample, wind-bitten, almost deformed, without fruit or blossom. These are what I bring, torn up by the roots from the pavement of Oxford Street, my penny bunch, my penny bunch of violets. Now from the window of the tram I see masts among chimneys; there is the river; there are ships that sail to India. I will walk by the river. I will pace this embankment, where an old man reads a newspaper in a glass shelter. I will pace this terrace and watch the ships bowling down the tide. A woman walks on deck, with a dog barking round her. Her skirts are blown; her hair is blown; they are going out to sea; they are leaving us; they are vanishing this summer evening. Now I will relinquish; now I will let loose. Now I will at last free the checked, the jerked back desire to be spent, to be consumed. We will gallop together over desert hills where the swallow dips her wings in dark pools and the pillars stand entire. Into the wave that dashes upon the shore, into the wave that flings its white foam to the uttermost corners of the earth I throw my violets, my offering to Percival."

*T*HE SUN *no longer stood in the middle of the sky. Its light slanted, falling obliquely. Here it caught on the edge of a cloud and burnt it into a slice of light, a blazing island on which no foot could rest. Then another cloud was caught in the light and another and another, so that the waves beneath were arrow-struck with fiery feathered darts that shot erratically across the quivering blue.*

The topmost leaves of the tree were crisped in the sun. They rustled stiffly in the random breeze. The birds sat still save that they flicked their heads sharply from side to side. Now they paused in their song as if glutted with sound, as if the fullness of midday had gorged them. The dragonfly poised motionless over a reed then shot its blue stitch further through the air. The far hum in the distance seemed made of the broken tremor of fine wings dancing up and down on the horizon. The river water held the reeds now fixed as if glass had hardened round them; and then the glass wavered and the reeds swept low. Pondering, sunken headed the cattle stood in the fields and cumbrously moved one foot and then another. In the bucket near the house the tap stopped dripping, as if the bucket were full, and then the tap dripped one, two, three separate drops in succession.

The windows showed erratically spots of burning fire, the elbow of one branch, and then some tranquil space of pure clarity. The blind hung red at the window's edge and within the room daggers of light fell upon chairs and tables making cracks across their lacquer and polish. The green pot bulged enormously, with its white window elongated in its side. Light driving darkness before it spilt itself profusely upon the corners and bosses; and yet heaped up darkness in mounds of unmoulded shape.

The waves massed themselves, curved their backs and crashed. Up spurted stones and shingle. They swept round the rocks, and the spray, leaping high, spattered the walls of a cave that had been dry before, and left pools inland, where some fish, stranded, lashed its tail as the wave drew back.

"I HAVE SIGNED my name," said Louis, "already twenty times. I, and again I, and again I. Clear, firm, unequivocal, there it stands, my name. Clear-cut and unequivocal am I too. Yet a vast inheritance of experience is packed in me. I have lived thousands of years. I am like a worm that has eaten its way through the wood of a very old oak beam. But now I am compact; now I am gathered together this fine morning.

"The sun shines from a clear sky. But twelve o'clock brings neither rain nor sunshine. It is the hour when Miss Johnson brings me my letters in a wire tray. Upon these white sheets I indent my name. The whisper of leaves, water running down gutters, green depths flecked with dahlias or zinnias; I, now a duke, now Plato, companion of Socrates; the tramp of dark men and yellow men migrating east, west, north and south; the eternal procession, women going with attaché cases down the Strand as they went once with pitchers to the Nile; all the furled and close-packed leaves of my many-folded life are now summed in my name; incised cleanly and barely on the sheet. Now a full-grown man; now upright standing in sun or rain, I must drop heavy as a hatchet and cut the oak with my sheer weight, for if I deviate, glancing this way, or that way, I shall fall like snow and be wasted.

"I am half in love with the typewriter and the telephone. With letters and cables and brief but courteous commands on the telephone to Paris, Berlin, New York I have fused my many lives into one; I have helped by my assiduity and decision to score those lines on the map there by which the different parts of the world are laced together. I love punctually at ten to come into my room; I love the purple glow of the dark mahogany; I love the table and its sharp edge; and the smooth-running drawers. I love the telephone with its lip stretched to my whisper, and the date on the wall; and the engagement book. Mr. Prentice at four; Mr. Eyres sharp at four-thirty.

"I like to be asked to come to Mr. Burchard's private room and report on our commitments to China. I hope to inherit an arm-chair and a Turkey carpet. My shoulder is to the wheel; I roll the dark before me, spreading commerce where there was chaos in the far parts of the world. If I press on, from chaos making order, I shall find myself where Chatham stood, and Pitt, Burke, and Sir Robert Peel. Thus I expunge certain stains, and erase old defilements; the woman who gave me a flag from the top of the Christmas tree; my accent; beatings and other tortures; the boasting boys; my father, a banker at Brisbane.

"I have read my poet in an eating-house, and, stirring my coffee, listened to the clerks making bets at the little tables, watched the women hesitating at the counter. I said that nothing should be irrelevant, like a piece of brown paper dropped casually on the floor. I said their journeys should have an end in view; they should earn their two pound ten a week at the command of an august master; some hand, some robe, should fold us about in the evening. When I have healed these fractures and comprehended these monstrosities so that they need neither excuse nor apology which both waste our strength, I shall give back to the street and the eating-shop what they lost when they fell on these hard times and broke on these stony beaches. I shall assemble a few words and forge round us a hammered ring of beaten steel.

"But now I have not a moment to spare. There is no respite here, no shadow made of quivering leaves, or alcove to which one can retreat from the sun, to sit, with a lover, in the cool of the evening. The weight of the world is on our shoulders; its vision is through our eyès; if we blink or look aside, or turn back to finger what Plato said or remember Napoleon and his conquests, we inflict on the world the injury of some obliquity. This is life; Mr. Prentice at four; Mr. Eyres at four-thirty. I like to hear the soft rush of the lift and the thud with which it stops on my landing and the heavy male tread of responsible feet down the corridors. So by dint of our united exertions we send ships to the remotest parts of the globe; replete with lavatories and gymnasiums. The weight of the world is on our shoulders. This is life. If I press on, I shall inherit a chair and a rug; a place in Surrey with glass houses, and some rare conifer, melon, or flowering tree which other merchants will envy.

"Yet I still keep my attic room. There I open the usual little book; there I watch the rain glisten on the tiles till they shine like a policeman's waterproof; there I see the broken windows in poor people's houses; the lean cats; some slattern squinting in a cracked looking-glass as she arranges her face for the street corner; there Rhoda sometimes comes. For we are lovers.

"Percival has died; (he died in Egypt; he died in Greece; all deaths are one death). Susan has children; Neville mounts rapidly to the conspicuous heights. Life passes. The clouds change perpetually over our houses. I do this, do that, and again do this and then that. Meeting and parting, we assemble different forms, make different patterns. But if I do not nail these impressions to the board and out of the many men in me make one; exist here and now and not in streaks and patches, like scattered snow wreaths on far mountains; and ask Miss Johnson as I pass through the office about the movies and take my cup of tea and accept also my favourite biscuit, then I shall fall like snow and be wasted.

"Yet when six o'clock comes and I touch my hat to the commissionaire, being always too effusive in ceremony since I desire so much to be accepted; and struggle, leaning against the wind, buttoned up, with my jaws blue and my eyes running water, I wish that a little typist would cuddle on my knees; I think that my favourite dish is liver and bacon; and so am apt to wander to the river, to the narrow streets where there are frequent public-houses, and the shadows of ships passing at the end of the street, and women fighting. But I say to myself, recovering my sanity, Mr. Prentice at four; Mr. Eyres at four-thirty. The hatchet must fall on the block; the oak must be cleft to the centre. The weight of the world is on my shoulders. Here is the pen and the paper; on the letters in the wire basket I sign my name, I, I, and again I."

"Summer comes, and winter," said Susan. "The seasons pass. The pear fills itself and drops from the tree. The dead leaf rests on its edge. But steam has obscured the window. I sit by the fire watching the kettle boil. I see the pear tree through the streaked steam on the window-pane.

"Sleep, sleep, I croon, whether it is summer or winter, May or November. Sleep I sing—I, who am unmelodious and hear no music save rustic music when a dog barks, a bell tinkles, or wheels crunch upon the gravel. I sing my song by the fire like an old shell murmuring on the beach. Sleep, sleep, I say, warning off with my voice all who rattle milk-cans, fire at rooks, shoot rabbits, or in any way bring the shock of destruction near this wicker cradle, laden with soft limbs, curled under a pink coverlet.

"I have lost my indifference, my blank eyes, my pear-shaped eyes that saw to the root. I am no longer January, May or any other season, but am all spun to a fine thread round the cradle, wrapping in a cocoon made of my own blood the delicate limbs of my baby. Sleep, I say, and feel within me uprush some wilder, darker violence, so that I would fell down with one blow any intruder, any snatcher, who should break into this room and wake the sleeper.

"I pad about the house all day long in apron and slippers, like my mother who died of cancer. Whether it is summer, whether it is winter, I no longer know by the moor grass, and the heath flower; only by the steam on the window-pane, or the frost on the window-pane. When the lark peels high his ring of sound and it falls through the air like an apple paring, I stoop; I feed my baby. I, who used to walk through beech woods noting the jay's feather turning blue as it falls, past the shepherd and the tramp, who stared at the woman squatted beside a tilted cart in a ditch, go from room to room with a duster. Sleep, I say, desiring sleep to fall like a blanket of down and cover these weak limbs; demanding that life shall sheathe its claws and gird its lightning and pass by, making of my own body a hollow, a warm shelter for my child to sleep in. Sleep, I say, sleep. Or I go to the window, I look at the rook's high nest; and the pear tree. 'His eyes will see when mine are shut,' I think. 'I shall go mixed with them beyond my body and shall see India. He will come home, bringing me trophies to be laid at my feet. He will increase my possessions.'

"But I never rise at dawn and see the purple drops in the cabbage leaves; the red drops in the roses. I do not watch the setter nose in a circle, or lie at night watching the leaves hide the stars and the stars move and the leaves hang still. The butcher calls; the milk has to be stood under a shade lest it should sour.

"Sleep, I say, sleep, as the kettle boils and its breath comes thicker and thicker issuing in one jet from the spout. So life fills my veins. So life pours through my limbs. So I am driven forward, till I could cry, as I move from dawn to dusk opening and shutting, 'No more. I am glutted with natural happiness.' Yet more will come, more children; more cradles, more baskets in the kitchen and hams ripening; and onions glistening; and more beds of lettuce and potatoes. I am blown like a leaf by the gale; now brushing the wet grass, now whirled up. I am glutted with natural happiness; and wish sometimes that the fullness would pass from me and the weight of the sleeping house rise, when we sit reading, and I stay the thread at the eye of my needle. The lamp kindles a fire in the dark pane. A fire burns in the heart of the ivy. I see a lit-up street in the evergreens. I hear traffic in the brush of the wind down the lane, and broken voices, and laughter, and Jinny, who cries as the door opens, 'Come, Come!'

"But no sound breaks the silence of our house, where the fields sigh close to the door. The wind washes through the elm trees; a moth hits the lamp; a cow lows; a crack of sound starts in the rafter, and I push my thread through the needle and murmur, 'Sleep.'"

"Now is the moment," said Jinny. "Now we have met, and have come together. Now let us talk, let us tell stories. Who is he? Who is she? I am infinitely curious and do not know what is to come. If you, whom I meet for the first time, were to say to me, 'The coach starts at four from Piccadilly,' I would not stay to fling a few necessaries in a bandbox, but would come at once.

"Let us sit here under the cut flowers, on the sofa by the picture. Let us decorate our Christmas tree with facts and again with facts. People are so soon gone; let us catch them. That man there, by the cabinet; he lives, you say, surrounded by china pots. Break one and you shatter a thousand pounds. And he loved a girl in Rome and she left him. Hence the pots, old junk found in lodging-houses or dug from the desert sands. And since beauty must be broken daily to remain beautiful, and he is static, his life stagnates in a china sea. It is strange though; for once as a young man, he sat on damp ground and drank rum with soldiers.

"One must be quick and add facts deftly, like toys to a tree, fixing them with a twist of the fingers. He stoops, how he stoops, even over an azalea. He stoops over the old woman even, because she wears diamonds in her ears, and, bundling about her estate in a pony carriage, directs who is to be helped, what tree felled, and who turned out tomorrow. (I have lived my life I must tell you all these years and I am now past thirty, perilously, like a mountain goat leaping from crag to crag; I do not settle long anywhere; I do not attach myself to one person in particular; but you will find that if I raise my arm, some figure at once breaks off and will come.) And that man is a judge; and that man is a millionaire, and that man, with the eyeglass, shot his governess through the heart with an arrow when he was ten years old. Afterwards he rode through deserts with dispatches, took part in revolutions and now collects materials for a history of his mother's family, long settled in Norfolk. That little man with a blue chin has a right hand that is withered. But why? We do not know. That woman, you whisper discreetly, with the pearl pagodas hanging from her ears, was the pure flame who lit the life of one of our statesmen; now since his death she sees ghosts, tells fortunes, and has adopted a coffee-coloured youth whom she calls the Messiah. That man with the drooping moustache, like a cavalry officer, lived a life of the utmost debauchery (it is all in some memoir) until one day he met a stranger in a train who converted him between Edinburgh and Carlisle by reading the Bible.

"Thus, in a few seconds, deftly, adroitly, we decipher the hieroglyphs written on other people's faces. Here, in this room, are the abraded and battered shells cast on the shore. The door goes on opening. The room fills and fills with knowledge, anguish, many kinds of ambition, much indifference, some despair. Between us, you say, we could build cathedrals, dictate policies, condemn men to death, and administer the affairs of several public offices. The common fund of experience is very deep. We have between us scores of children of both sexes, whom we are educating, going to see at school with the measles, and bringing up to inherit our houses. In one way or another we make this day, this Friday, some by going to the Law Courts; others to the city; others to the nursery; others by marching and forming fours. A million hands stitch, raise hods with bricks. The activity is endless. And tomorrow it begins again; tomorrow we make Saturday. Some take train for France; others ship for India. Some will never come into this room again. One may die tonight. Another will beget a child. From us every sort of

building, policy, venture, picture, poem, child, factory, will
spring. Life comes; life goes; we make life. So you say.

"But we who live in the body see with the body's imagination things in outline. I see rocks in bright sunshine. I cannot
take these facts into some cave and, shading my eyes, grade their
yellows, blues, umbers into one substance. I cannot remain seated
for long. I must jump up and go. The coach may start from Piccadilly. I drop all these facts — diamonds, withered hands, china
pots and the rest of it, as a monkey drops nuts from its naked
paws. I cannot tell you if life is this or that. I am going to push
out into the heterogeneous crowd. I am going to be buffeted; to
be flung up, and flung down, among men, like a ship on the sea.

"For now my body, my companion, which is always sending its signals, the rough black 'No,' the golden 'Come' in rapid
running arrows of sensation, beckons. Some one moves. Did I
raise my arm? Did I look? Did my yellow scarf with the strawberry spots float and signal? He has broken from the wall. He
follows. I am pursued through the forest. All is rapt, all is nocturnal and the parrots go screaming through the branches. All
my senses stand erect. Now I feel the roughness of the fibre of
the curtain through which I push; now I feel the cold iron rail-
ing and its blistered paint beneath my palm. Now the cool tide
of darkness breaks its waters over me. We are out of doors.
Night opens; night traversed by wandering moths; night hiding
lovers roaming to adventure. I smell roses; I smell violets; I see
red and blue just hidden. Now gravel is under my shoes; now
grass. Up reel the tall backs of houses guilty with lights. All London is uneasy with flashing lights. Now let us sing our love
song — Come, come, come. Now my gold signal is like a dragon-
fly flying taut. Jug, jug, jug, I sing like the nightingale whose
melody is crowded in the too narrow passage of her throat.
Now I hear crash and rending of boughs and the crack of
antlers as if the beasts of the forest were all hunting, all rearing

high and plunging down among the thorns. One has pierced me. One is driven deep within me. And velvet flowers and leaves whose coolness has been stood in water wash me round, and sheathe me, embalming me."

"Why, look," said Neville, "at the clock ticking on the mantelpiece? Time passes, yes. And we grow old. But to sit with you, alone with you, here in London, in this firelit room, you there, I here, is all. The world ransacked to its uttermost ends, and all its heights stripped and gathered of their flowers holds no more. Look at the firelight running up and down the gold thread in the curtain. The fruit it circles droops heavy. It falls on the toe of your boot, it gives your face a red rim—I think it is the firelight and not your face; I think those are books against the wall, and that a curtain, and that perhaps an arm-chair. But when you come everything changes. The cups and saucers changed when you came in this morning. There can be no doubt, I thought, pushing aside the newspaper, that our mean lives, unsightly as they are, put on splendour and have meaning only under the eyes of love.

"I rose. I had done my breakfast. There was the whole day before us, and as it was fine, tender, non-committal, we walked through the Park to the Embankment, along the Strand to St. Paul's, then to the shop where I bought an umbrella, always talking, and now and then stopping to look. But can this last? I said to myself, by a lion in Trafalgar Square, by the lion seen once and for ever;—so I revisit my past life, scene by scene, there is an elm tree, and there lies Percival. For ever and ever, I swore. Then darted in the usual doubt. I clutched your hand. You left me. The descent into the Tube was like death. We were cut up, we were dissevered by all those faces and the hollow wind that seemed to roar down there over desert boulders. I sat staring in my own room. By five I knew that you were faithless. I snatched the telephone and the buzz, buzz, buzz of its stupid voice in your empty room battered my heart down, when the door opened and there you stood. That was the most perfect of our meetings. But these meetings, these partings, finally destroy us.

"Now this room seems to me central, something scooped out of the eternal night. Outside lines twist and intersect, but round us, wrapping us about. Here we are centred. Here we can be silent, or speak without raising our voices. Did you notice that and then that? we say. He said that, meaning. . . . She hesitated, and I believe suspected. Anyhow, I heard voices, a sob on the stair late at night. It is the end of their relationship. Thus we spin round us infinitely fine filaments and construct a system. Plato and Shakespeare are included, also quite obscure people, people of no importance whatsoever. I hate men who wear crucifixes on the left side of their waistcoats. I hate ceremonies and lamentations and the sad figure of Christ trembling beside another trembling and sad figure. Also the pomp and the indifference and the emphasis, always on the wrong place, of people holding forth under chandeliers in full evening dress, wearing stars and decorations. Some spray in a hedge, though, or a sunset over a flat winter field, or again the way some old woman sits, arms akimbo, in an omnibus with a basket—those we point at for the other to look at. It is so vast an alleviation to be able to point for another to look at. And then not to talk. To follow the dark paths of the mind and enter the past, to visit books, to brush aside their branches and break off some fruit. And you take it and marvel, as I take the careless movements of your body and marvel at its ease, its power—how you fling open windows and are dexterous with your hands. For alas! my mind is a little impeded, it soon tires; I fall damp, perhaps disgusting, at the goal.

"Alas! I could not ride about India in a sun-helmet and return to a bungalow. I cannot tumble, as you do, like half-naked boys on the deck of a ship, squirting each other with hose-pipes. I want this fire, I want this chair. I want some one to sit beside after the day's pursuit and all its anguish, after its listenings, and its waitings, and its suspicions. After quarrelling and reconciliation I need privacy—to be alone with you, to set this hubbub in order. For I am as neat as a cat in my habits. We must oppose the waste and deformity of the world, its crowds eddying round and round disgorged and trampling. One must slip paper-knives, even, exactly through the pages of novels, and tie up packets of letters neatly with green silk, and brush up the cinders with a hearth broom. Everything must be done to rebuke the horror of deformity. Let us read writers of Roman severity and virtue; let us seek perfection through the sand. Yes, but I love to slip the virtue and severity of the noble Romans under the grey light of your eyes, and dancing grasses and summer breezes and the laughter and shouts of boys at play—of naked cabin-boys squirting each other with hose-pipes on the decks of ships. Hence I am not a disinterested seeker, like Louis, after perfection through the sand. Colours always stain the page; clouds pass over it. And the poem, I think, is only your voice speaking. Alcibiades, Ajax, Hector and Percival are also you. They loved riding, they risked their lives wantonly, they were not great readers either. But you are not Ajax or Percival. They did not wrinkle their noses and scratch their foreheads with your precise gesture. You are you. That is what consoles me for the lack of many things—I am ugly, I am weak—and the depravity of the world, and the flight of youth and Percival's death, and bitterness and rancour and envies innumerable.

"But if one day you do not come after breakfast, if one day I see you in some looking-glass perhaps looking after another, if the telephone buzzes and buzzes in your empty room, I shall then, after unspeakable anguish, I shall then—for there is no end to the folly of the human heart—seek another, find another, you. Meanwhile, let us abolish the ticking of time's clock with one blow. Come closer."

*T*HE SUN *had now sunk lower in the sky. The islands of cloud had gained in density and drew themselves across the sun so that the rocks went suddenly black, and the trembling sea holly lost its blue and turned silver, and shadows were blown like grey cloths over the sea. The waves no longer visited the further pools or reached the dotted black line which lay irregularly marked upon the beach. The sand was pearl white, smoothed and shining.*

Birds swooped and circled high up in the air. Some raced in the furrows of the wind and turned and sliced through them as if they were one body cut into a thousand shreds. Birds fell like a net descending on the tree-tops. Here one bird taking its way alone made wing for the marsh and sat solitary on a white stake, opening its wings and shutting them.

Some petals had fallen in the garden. They lay shell-shaped on the earth. The dead leaf no longer stood upon its edge, but had been blown, now running, now pausing, against some stalk. Through all the flowers the same wave of light passed in a sudden flaunt and flash as if a fin cut the green glass of a lake. Now and again some level and masterly blast blew the multitudinous leaves up and down and then, as the wind flagged, each blade regained its identity. The flowers, burning their bright discs in the sun, flung aside the sunlight as the wind tossed them, and then some heads too heavy to rise again drooped slightly.

The afternoon sun warmed the fields, poured blue into the shadows and reddened the corn. A deep varnish was laid like a lacquer over the fields. A cart, a horse, a flock of rooks—whatever moved in it was rolled round in gold. If a cow moved a leg it stirred ripples of red gold, and its horns seemed lined with light. Sprays of flaxen-haired corn lay on the hedges, brushed from the shaggy carts that came up from the meadows short legged and primeval looking. The round-headed clouds never dwindled as they bowled along, but kept every atom of their rotundity. Now, as they passed, they caught a whole village in the fling of their net and, passing, let it fly free again. Far away on the horizon, among the million grains of blue grey dust, burnt one pane, or stood the single line of one steeple or one tree.

The red curtains and the white blinds blew in and out, flapping against the edge of the window, and the light which entered by flaps and breadths unequally had in it some brown tinge, and some abandonment as it blew through the blowing curtains in gusts. Here it browned a cabinet, there reddened a chair, here it made the window waver in the side of the green jar.

All for a moment wavered and bent in uncertainty and ambiguity, as if a great moth sailing through the room had shadowed the immense solidity of chairs and tables with floating wings.

"AND TIME," said Bernard, "lets fall its drop. The drop that has formed on the roof of the soul falls. On the roof of my mind time, forming, lets fall its drop. Last week, as I stood shaving, the drop fell. I, standing with my razor in my hand, became suddenly aware of the merely habitual nature of my action (this is the drop forming) and congratulated my hands, ironically, for keeping at it. Shave, shave, shave, I said. Go on shaving. The drop fell. All through the day's work, at intervals, my mind went to an empty place, saying, 'What is lost? What is over?' And 'Over and done with,' I muttered, 'over and done with,' solacing myself with words. People noticed the vacuity of my face and the aimlessness of my conversation. The last words of my sentence tailed away. And as I buttoned on my coat to go home I said more dramatically, 'I have lost my youth.'

"It is curious how, at every crisis, some phrase which does not fit insists upon coming to the rescue — the penalty of living in an old civilisation with a notebook. This drop falling has nothing to do with losing my youth. This drop falling is time tapering to a point. Time, which is a sunny pasture covered with a dancing light, time, which is widespread as a field at midday, becomes pendent. Time tapers to a point. As a drop falls from a glass heavy with some sediment, time falls. These are the true cycles, these are the true events. Then as if all the luminosity of the atmosphere were withdrawn I see to the bare bottom. I see what habit covers. I lie sluggish in bed for days. I dine out and gape like a codfish. I do not trouble to finish my sentences, and my actions, usually so uncertain, acquire a mechanical precision. On this occasion, passing an office, I went in and bought, with all the composure of a mechanical figure, a ticket for Rome.

"Now I sit on a stone seat in these gardens surveying the eternal city, and the little man who was shaving in London five days ago looks already like a heap of old clothes. London has also crumbled. London consists of fallen factories and a few gasometers. At the same time I am not involved in this pageantry. I see the violet-sashed priests and the picturesque nursemaids; I notice externals only. I sit here like a convalescent, like a very simple man who knows only words of one syllable. 'The sun is hot,' I say. 'The wind is cold.' I feel myself carried round like an insect on top of the earth and could swear that, sitting here, I feel its hardness, its turning movement. I have no desire to go the opposite way from the earth. Could I prolong this sense another six inches I have a foreboding that I should touch some queer territory. But I have a very limited proboscis. I never wish to prolong these states of detachment; I dislike them; I also despise them. I do not wish to be a man who sits for fifty years on the same spot thinking of his navel. I wish to be harnessed to a cart, a vegetable-cart that rattles over the cobbles.

"The truth is that I am not one of those who find their satisfaction in one person, or in infinity. The private room bores me, also the sky. My being only glitters when all its facets are exposed to many people. Let them fail and I am full of holes, dwindling like burnt paper. Oh, Mrs. Moffat, Mrs. Moffat, I say, come and sweep it all up. Things have dropped from me. I have outlived certain desires; I have lost friends, some by death—Percival—others through sheer inability to cross the street. I am not so gifted as at one time seemed likely. Certain things lie beyond my scope. I shall never understand the harder problems of philosophy. Rome is the limit of my travelling. As I drop asleep at night it strikes me sometimes with a pang that I shall never see savages in Tahiti spearing fish by the light of a blazing cresset, or a lion spring in the jungle, or a naked man eating raw flesh. Nor shall I learn Russian or read the Vedas. I shall never again walk bang into the pillar-box. (But still a few stars fall through my night, beautifully, from the violence of that concussion.) But as I think, truth has come nearer. For many years I crooned complacently, 'My children . . . my wife . . . my house . . . my dog.' As I let

myself in with my latch-key I would go through that familiar ritual and wrap myself in those warm coverings. Now that lovely
veil has fallen. I do not want possessions now. (Note: an Italian
washerwoman stands on the same rung of physical refinement
as the daughter of an English duke.)

"But let me consider. The drop falls; another stage has been
reached. Stage upon stage. And why should there be an end of
stages? and where do they lead? To what conclusion? For they
come wearing robes of solemnity. In these dilemmas the devout
consult those violet-sashed and sensual-looking gentry who are
trooping past me. But for ourselves, we resent teachers. Let a
man get up and say, 'Behold, this is the truth,' and instantly I
perceive a sandy cat filching a piece of fish in the background.
Look, you have forgotten the cat, I say. So Neville, at school,
in the dim chapel, raged at the sight of the doctor's crucifix. I,
who am always distracted, whether by a cat or by a bee buzzing
round the bouquet that Lady Hampden keeps so diligently
pressed to her nose, at once make up a story and so obliterate
the angles of the crucifix. I have made up thousands of stories;
I have filled innumerable notebooks with phrases to be used
when I have found the true story, the one story to which all
these phrases refer. But I have never yet found that story. And
I begin to ask, Are there stories?

"Look now from this terrace at the swarming population
beneath. Look at the general activity and clamour. That man is
in difficulties with his mule. Half a dozen good-natured loafers
offer their services. Others pass by without looking. They have
as many interests as there are threads in a skein. Look at the
sweep of the sky, bowled over by round white clouds. Imagine
the leagues of level land and the aqueducts and the broken
Roman pavement and the tombstones in the Campagna, and
beyond the Campagna, the sea, then again more land, then the
sea. I could break off any detail in all that prospect—say the

mule-cart—and describe it with the greatest ease. But why describe a man in trouble with his mule? Again, I could invent stories about that girl coming up the steps. 'She met him under the dark archway. . . . "It is over," he said, turning from the cage where the china parrot hangs.' Or simply, 'That was all.' But why impose my arbitrary design? Why stress this and shape that and twist up little figures like the toys men sell in trays in the street? Why select this, out of all that,—one detail?

"Here am I shedding one of my life-skins, and all they will say is, 'Bernard is spending ten days in Rome.' Here am I marching up and down this terrace alone, unoriented. But observe how dots and dashes are beginning, as I walk, to run themselves into continuous lines, how things are losing the bald, the separate identity that they had as I walked up those steps. The great red pot is now a reddish streak in a wave of yellowish green. The world is beginning to move past me like the banks of a hedge when the train starts, like the waves of the sea when a steamer moves. I am moving too, am becoming involved in the general sequence when one thing follows another and it seems inevitable that the tree should come, then the telegraph-pole, then the break in the hedge. And as I move, surrounded, included and taking part, the usual phrases begin to bubble up, and I wish to free these bubbles from the trap-door in my head, and direct my steps therefore towards that man, the back of whose head is half familiar to me. We were together at school. We shall undoubtedly meet. We shall certainly lunch together. We shall talk. But wait, one moment wait.

"These moments of escape are not to be despised. They come too seldom. Tahiti becomes possible. Leaning over this parapet I see far out a waste of water. A fin turns. This bare visual impression is unattached to any line of reason, it springs up as one might see the fin of a porpoise on the horizon. Visual impressions often communicate thus briefly statements that we shall in time to come uncover and coax into words. I note under F., therefore, 'Fin in a waste of waters.' I, who am perpetually making notes in the margin of my mind for some final statement, make this mark, waiting for some winter's evening.

"Now I shall go and lunch somewhere, I shall hold my glass up, I shall look through the wine, I shall observe with more than my usual detachment, and when a pretty woman enters the restaurant and comes down the room between the tables I shall say to myself, Look where she comes against a waste of waters. A meaningless observation, but to me, solemn, slate-coloured, with a fatal sound of ruining worlds and waters falling to destruction.

"So, Bernard (I recall you, you the usual partner in my enterprises), let us begin this new chapter, and observe the formation of this new, this unknown, strange, altogether unidentified and terrifying experience — the new drop — which is about to shape itself. Larpent is that man's name."

"In this hot afternoon," said Susan, "here in this garden, here in this field where I walk with my son, I have reached the summit of my desires. The hinge of the gate is rusty; he heaves it open. The violent passions of childhood, my tears in the garden when Jinny kissed Louis, my rage in the schoolroom, which smelt of pine, my loneliness in foreign places, when the mules came clattering in on their pointed hoofs and the Italian women chattered at the fountain, shawled, with carnations twisted in their hair, are rewarded by security, possession, familiarity. I have had peaceful, productive years. I possess all I see. I have grown trees from the seed. I have made ponds in which goldfish hide under the broad-leaved lilies. I have netted over strawberry beds and lettuce beds, and stitched the pears and the plums into white bags to keep them safe from the wasps. I have seen my sons and daughters, once netted over like fruit in their cots, break the meshes and walk with me, taller than I am, casting shadows on the grass.

"I am fenced in, planted here like one of my own trees. I say, 'My son,' I say, 'My daughter,' and even the ironmonger looking up from his counter strewn with nails, paint and wire-fencing respects the shabby car at the door with its butterfly nets, pads and bee-hives. We hang mistletoe over the clock at Christmas, weigh our blackberries and mushrooms, count out jam-pots, and stand year by year to be measured against the shutter in the drawing-room window. I also make wreaths of white flowers, twisting silver-leaved plants among them for the dead, attaching my card with sorrow for the dead shepherd, with sympathy for the wife of the dead carter; and sit by the beds of dying women, who murmur their last terrors, who clutch my hand; frequenting rooms intolerable except to one born as I was and early acquainted with the farmyard and the dung-heap and the hens straying in and out, and the mother with two rooms and growing children. I have seen the windows run with heat, I have smelt the sink.

"I ask now, standing with my scissors among my flowers, Where can the shadow enter? What shock can loosen my laboriously gathered, relentlessly pressed-down life? Yet sometimes I am sick of natural happiness, and fruit growing, and children scattering the house with oars, guns, skulls, books won for prizes and other trophies. I am sick of the body, I am sick of my own craft, industry and cunning, of the unscrupulous ways of the mother who protects, who collects under her jealous eyes at one long table her own children, always her own.

"It is when spring comes, cold, showery, with sudden yellow flowers—then as I look at the meat under the blue shade and press the heavy silver bags of tea, of sultanas, I remember how the sun rose, and the swallows skimmed the grass, and phrases that Bernard made when we were children, and the leaves shook over us, many-folded, very light, breaking the blue of the sky, scattering wandering lights upon the skeleton roots of the beech trees where I sat, sobbing. The pigeon rose. I jumped up and ran after the words that trailed like the dangling string from an air ball, up and up, from branch to branch escaping. Then like a cracked bowl the fixity of my morning broke, and putting down the bags of flour I thought, Life stands round me like a glass round the imprisoned reed.

"I hold scissors and snip off hollyhocks, who went to Elvedon and trod on rotten oak-apples, and saw the lady writing and the gardeners with their great brooms. We ran back panting lest we should be shot and nailed like stoats to the wall. Now I measure, I preserve. At night I sit in the arm-chair and stretch my arm for my sewing; and hear my husband snore; and look up when the light from a passing car dazzles the windows and feel the waves of my life tossed, broken, round me who am rooted; and hear cries, and see others' lives eddying like straws round the piers of a bridge while I push my needle in and out and draw my thread through the calico.

"I think sometimes of Percival who loved me. He rode and fell in India. I think sometimes of Rhoda. Uneasy cries wake me at dead of night. But for the most part I walk content with my sons. I cut the dead petals from hollyhocks. Rather squat, grey before my time, but with clear eyes, pear-shaped eyes, I pace my fields."

"Here I stand," said Jinny, "in the Tube station where everything that is desirable meets—Piccadilly South Side, Piccadilly North Side, Regent Street and the Haymarket. I stand for a moment under the pavement in the heart of London. Innumerable wheels rush and feet press just over my head. The great avenues of civilisation meet here and strike this way and that. I am in the heart of life. But look—there is my body in that looking glass.

How solitary, how shrunk, how aged! I am no longer young. I am no longer part of the procession. Millions descend those stairs in a terrible descent. Great wheels churn inexorably urging them downwards. Millions have died. Percival died. I still move. I still live. But who will come if I signal?

"Little animal that I am, sucking my flanks in and out with fear, I stand here, palpitating, trembling. But I will not be afraid. I will bring the whip down on my flanks. I am not a whimpering little animal making for the shadow. It was only for a moment, catching sight of myself before I had time to prepare myself as I always prepare myself for the sight of myself, that I quailed. It is true; I am not young—I shall soon raise my arm in vain and my scarf will fall to my side without having signalled. I shall not hear the sudden sigh in the night and feel through the dark some one coming. There will be no reflections in window-panes in dark tunnels. I shall look into faces, and I shall see them seek some other face. I admit, for one moment the soundless flight of upright bodies down the moving stairs like the pinioned and terrible descent of some army of the dead downwards and the churning of the great engines remorselessly forwarding us, all of us, onwards made me cower and run for shelter.

"But now I swear, making deliberately in front of the glass those slight preparations that equip me, I will not be afraid. Think of the superb omnibuses, red and yellow, stopping and starting, punctually in order. Think of the powerful and beautiful cars that now slow to a foot's pace and now shoot forward; think of men, think of women, equipped, prepared, driving onward. This is the triumphant procession; this is the army of victory with banners and brass eagles and heads crowned with laurel-leaves won in battle. They are better than savages in loincloths, and women whose hair is dank, whose long breasts sag, with children tugging at their long breasts. These broad thoroughfares—Piccadilly South, Piccadilly North, Regent Street and the Haymarket—are sanded paths of victory driven through the jungle. I too, with my little patent-leather shoes, my handkerchief that is but a film of gauze, my reddened lips and my finely pencilled eyebrows march to victory with the band.

"Look how they show off clothes here even under ground in a perpetual radiance. They will not let the earth even lie wormy and sodden. There are gauzes and silks illumined in glass cases and underclothes trimmed with a million close stitches of fine embroidery. Crimson, green, violet, they are dyed all colours. Think how they organise, roll out, smooth, dip in dyes, and drive tunnels blasting the rock. Lifts rise and fall; trains stop, trains start as regularly as the waves of the sea. This is what has my adhesion. I am a native of this world, I follow its banners. How could I run for shelter when they are so magnificently adventurous, daring, curious, too, and strong enough in the midst of effort to pause and scrawl with a free hand a joke upon the wall? Therefore I will powder my face and redden my lips. I will make the angle of my eyebrows sharper than usual. I will rise to the surface, standing erect with the others in Piccadilly Circus. I will sign with a sharp gesture to a cab whose driver will signify by some indescribable alacrity his understanding of my signals. For I still excite eagerness. I still feel the bowing of men in the street like the silent stoop of the corn when the light wind blows, ruffling it red.

"I will drive to my own house. I will fill the vases with lavish, with luxurious, with extravagant flowers nodding in great bunches. I will place one chair there, another here. I will put ready cigarettes, glasses and some gaily covered new unread book in case Bernard comes, or Neville or Louis. But perhaps it will not be Bernard, Neville or Louis, but somebody new, somebody unknown, somebody I passed on a staircase and, just turning as we passed, I murmured, 'Come.' He will come this afternoon; somebody I do not know, somebody new. Let the silent army of the dead descend. I march forward."

"I no longer need a room now," said Neville, "or walls and firelight. I am no longer young. I pass Jinny's house without envy, and smile at the young man who arranges his tie a little nervously on the door-step. Let the dapper young man ring the bell; let him find her. I shall find her if I want her, if not, I pass on. The old corrosion has lost its bite — envy, intrigue and bitterness have been washed out. We have lost our glory too. When we were young we sat anywhere, on bare benches in draughty halls with the doors always banging. We tumbled about half naked like boys on the deck of a ship squirting each other with hose-pipes. Now I could swear that I like people pouring profusely out of the Tube when the day's work is done, unanimous, indiscriminate, uncounted. I have picked my own fruit. I look dispassionately.

"After all, we are not responsible. We are not judges. We are not called upon to torture our fellows with thumbscrews and irons; we are not called upon to mount pulpits and lecture them on pale Sunday afternoons. It is better to look at a rose, or to read Shakespeare as I read him here in Shaftesbury Avenue. Here's the fool, here's the villain, here in a car comes Cleopatra, burning on her barge. Here are figures of the damned too, noseless men by the police-court wall, standing with their feet in fire, howling. This is poetry if we do not write it. They act their parts infallibly, and almost before they open their lips I know what they are going to say, and wait the divine moment when they speak the word that must have been written. If it were only for the sake of the play, I could walk Shaftesbury Avenue for ever.

"Then coming from the street, entering some room, there are people talking, or hardly troubling to talk. He says, she says, somebody else says things have been said so often that one word is now enough to lift a whole weight. Argument, laughter, old grievances—they fall through the air, thickening it. I take a book and read half a page of anything. They have not mended the spout of the teapot yet. The child dances, dressed in her mother's clothes.

"But then Rhoda, or it may be Louis, some fasting and anguished spirit, passes through and out again. They want a plot, do they? They want a reason? It is not enough for them, this ordinary scene. It is not enough to wait for the thing to be said as if it were written; to see the sentence lay its dab of clay precisely on the right place, making character; to perceive, suddenly, some group in outline against the sky. Yet if they want violence, I have seen death and murder and suicide all in one room. One comes in, one goes out. There are sobs on the staircase. I have heard threads broken and knots tied and the quiet stitching of white cambric going on and on on the knees of a woman. Why ask, like Louis, for a reason, or fly like Rhoda to some far grove and part the leaves of the laurels and look for statues? They say that one must beat one's wings against the storm in the belief that beyond this welter the sun shines; the sun falls sheer into pools that are fledged with willows. (Here it is November; the poor hold out matchboxes in wind-bitten fingers.) They say truth is to be found there entire, and virtue, that shuffles along here, down blind alleys, is to be had there perfect. Rhoda flies with her neck outstretched and blind fanatic eyes, past us. Louis, now so opulent, goes to his attic window among the blistered roofs and gazes where she has vanished, but must sit down in his office among the typewriters and the telephone and work it all out for our instruction, for our regeneration, and the reform of an unborn world.

"But now in this room, which I enter without knocking, things are said as if they had been written. I go to the bookcase. If I choose, I read half a page of anything. I need not speak. But I listen. I am marvellously on the alert. Certainly, one cannot read this poem without effort. The page is often corrupt and mud-stained, and torn and stuck together with faded leaves, with scraps of verbena or geranium. To read this poem one must have myriad eyes, like one of those lamps that turn on slabs of racing water at midnight in the Atlantic, when perhaps only a spray of seaweed pricks the surface, or suddenly the waves gape and up shoulders a monster. One must put aside antipathies and jealousies and not interrupt. One must have patience and infinite care and let the light sound, whether of spiders' delicate feet on a leaf or the chuckle of water in some irrelevant drainpipe, unfold too. Nothing is to be rejected in fear or horror. The poet who has written this page (what I read with people talking) has withdrawn. There are no commas or semicolons. The lines do not run in convenient lengths. Much is sheer nonsense. One must be sceptical, but throw caution to the winds and when the door opens accept absolutely. Also sometimes weep; also cut away ruthlessly with a slice of the blade soot, bark, hard accretions of all sorts. And so (while they talk) let down one's net deeper and deeper and gently draw in and bring to the surface what he said and she said and make poetry.

"Now I have listened to them talking. They have gone now. I am alone. I could be content to watch the fire burn for ever, like a dome, like a furnace; now some spike of wood takes the look of a scaffold, or pit, or happy valley; now it is a serpent curled crimson with white scales. The fruit on the curtain swells beneath the parrot's beak. Cheep, cheep, creaks the fire, like the cheep of insects in the middle of a forest. Cheep, cheep, it clicks while out there the branches thrash the air, and now, like a volley of shot, a tree falls. These are the sounds of a London night. Then I hear the one sound I wait for. Up and up it comes, approaches, hesitates, stops at my door. I cry, 'Come in. Sit by me. Sit on the edge of the chair.' Swept away by the old hallucination, I cry, 'Come closer, closer.'"

"I come back from the office," said Louis. "I hang my coat here, place my stick there—I like to fancy that Richelieu walked with such a cane. Thus I divest myself of my authority. I have been sitting at the right hand of a director at a varnished table. The maps of our successful undertakings confront us on the wall. We have laced the world together with our ships. The globe is strung with our lines. I am immensely respectable. All the young ladies in the office acknowledge my entrance. I can dine where I like now, and without vanity may suppose that I shall soon acquire a house in Surrey, two cars, a conservatory and some rare species of melon. But I still return, I still come back to my attic, hang up my hat and resume in solitude that curious attempt which I have made since I brought down my fist on my master's grained oak door. I open a little book. I read one poem. One poem is enough.

O western wind . . .

O western wind, you are at enmity with my mahogany table and spats, and also, alas, with the vulgarity of my mistress, the little actress, who has never been able to speak English correctly—

O western wind, when wilt thou blow . . .

Rhoda, with her intense abstraction, with her unseeing eyes the colour of snail's flesh, does not destroy you, western wind, whether she comes at midnight when the stars blaze or at the most prosaic hour of midday. She stands at the window and looks at the chimney pots and the broken windows in the houses of poor people—

O western wind, when wilt thou blow . . .

"My task, my burden, has always been greater than other
people's. A pyramid has been set on my shoulders. I have tried
to do a colossal labour. I have driven a violent, an unruly, a vi-
cious team. With my Australian accent I have sat in eating shops
and tried to make the clerks accept me, yet never forgotten my
solemn and severe convictions and the discrepancies and inco-
herences that must be resolved. As a boy I dreamt of the Nile,
was reluctant to awake, yet brought down my fist on the grained
oak door. It would have been happier to have been born without a destiny, like Susan, like Percival, whom I most admire.

> O western wind, when wilt thou blow,
>   That the small rain down can rain?

"Life has been a terrible affair for me. I am like some vast
sucker, some glutinous, some adhesive, some insatiable mouth.
I have tried to draw from the living flesh the stone lodged at
the centre. I have known little natural happiness, though I
chose my mistress in order that, with her cockney accent, she
might make me feel at my ease. But she only tumbled the floor
with dirty under linen, and the charwoman and the shop boys
called after me a dozen times a day, mocking my prim and supercilious gait.

> O western wind, when wilt thou blow,
>   That the small rain down can rain?

"What has my destiny been, the sharp-pointed pyramid that
has pressed on my ribs all these years? That I remember the Nile
and the women carrying pitchers on their heads; that I feel myself woven in and out of the long summers and winters that

have made the corn flow and have frozen the streams. I am not
a single and passing being. My life is not a moment's bright
spark like that on the surface of a diamond. I go beneath ground
torturously, as if a warder carried a lamp from cell to cell. My
destiny has been that I remember and must weave together,
must plait into one cable the many threads, the thin, the thick,
the broken, the enduring of our long history, of our tumultuous
and varied day. There is always more to be understood; a discord to be listened for; a falsity to be reprimanded. Broken and
soot-stained are these roofs with their chimney cowls, their
loose slates, their slinking cats and attic windows. I pick my way
over broken glass, among blistered tiles, and see only vile and
famished faces.

"Let us suppose that I make reason of it all—one poem on
a page, and then die. I can assure you it will not be unwillingly.
Percival died. Rhoda left me. But I shall live to be gaunt and
sere, to tap my way, much respected, with my gold-headed cane
along the pavements of the city. Perhaps I shall never die, shall
never attain even that continuity and permanence—

> O western wind, when wilt thou blow,
> That the small rain down can rain?

"Percival was flowering with green leaves and was laid in the
earth with all his branches still sighing in the summer wind.
Rhoda, with whom I shared silence when the others spoke, she
who hung back and turned aside when the herd assembled and
galloped with orderly, sleek backs over the rich pastures, has
gone now like the desert heat. When the sun blisters the roofs
of the city I think of her; when the dry leaves patter to the
ground; when the old men come with pointed sticks and pierce
little bits of paper as we pierced her—

O western wind, when wilt thou blow,
That the small rain down can rain?
Christ! that my love were in my arms,
And I in my bed again!

I return now to my book; I return now to my attempt."

"Life, how I have dreaded you," said Rhoda, "oh, human beings, how I have hated you! How you have nudged, how you have interrupted, how hideous you have looked in Oxford Street, how squalid sitting opposite each other staring in the Tube! Now as I climb this mountain, from the top of which I shall see Africa, my mind is printed with brown-paper parcels and your faces. I have been stained by you and corrupted. You smelt so unpleasant, too, lining up outside doors to buy tickets. All were dressed in indeterminate shades of grey and brown, never even a blue feather pinned to a hat. None had the courage to be one thing rather than another. What dissolution of the soul you demanded in order to get through one day, what lies, bowings, scrapings, fluency and servility! How you chained me to one spot, one hour, one chair, and sat yourselves down opposite! How you snatched from me the white spaces that lie between hour and hour and rolled them into dirty pellets and tossed them into the wastepaper basket with your greasy paws. Yet those were my life.

"But I yielded. Sneers and yawns were covered with my hand. I did not go out into the street and break a bottle in the gutter as a sign of rage. Trembling with ardour, I pretended that I was not surprised. What you did, I did. If Susan and Jinny pulled up their stockings like that, I pulled mine up like that also. So terrible was life that I held up shade after shade. Look at life through this, look at life through that; let there be rose leaves, let there be vine leaves—I covered the whole street, Oxford

Street, Piccadilly Circus, with the blaze and ripple of my mind, with vine leaves and rose leaves. There were boxes, too, standing in the passage when the school broke up. I stole secretly to read the labels and dream of names and faces. Harrogate, perhaps, Edinburgh, perhaps, was ruffled with golden glory where some girl whose name I forget stood on the pavement. But it was the name only. I left Louis; I feared embraces. With fleeces, with vestments I have tried to cover the blue-black blade. I implored day to break into night. I have longed to see the cupboard dwindle, to feel the bed soften, to float suspended, to perceive lengthened trees, lengthened faces, a green bank on a moor and two figures in distress saying good-bye. I flung words in fans like those the sower throws over the ploughed fields when the earth is bare. I desired always to stretch the night and fill it fuller and fuller with dreams.

"Then in some hall I parted the boughs of music and saw the house we have made; the square stood upon the oblong. 'The house which contains us all,' I said, lurching against people's shoulders in an omnibus after Percival died; yet I went to Greenwich. Walking on the embankment, I prayed that I might thunder for ever on the verge of the world where there is no vegetation, but here and there a marble pillar. I threw my bunch into the spreading wave. I said, 'Consume me, carry me to the furthest limit.' The wave has broken; the bunch is withered. I seldom think of Percival now.

"Now I climb this Spanish hill; and I will suppose that this mule back is my bed and that I lie dying. There is only a thin sheet between me now and the infinite depths. The lumps in the mattress soften beneath me. We stumble up—we stumble on. My path has been up and up, towards some solitary tree with a pool beside it on the very top. I have sliced the waters of beauty in the evening when the hills close themselves like birds' wings folded. I have picked sometimes a red carnation, and wisps of hay. I have sunk alone on the turf and fingered some old bone and thought: When the wind stoops to brush this height, may there be nothing found but a pinch of dust.

"The mule stumbles up and on. The ridge of the hill rises like mist, but from the top I shall see Africa. Now the bed gives under me. The sheets spotted with yellow holes let me fall through. The good woman with a face like a white horse at the end of the bed makes a valedictory movement and turns to go. Who then comes with me? Flowers only, the cowbind and the moonlight coloured may. Gathering them loosely in a sheaf I made of them a garland and gave them—Oh, to whom? We launch out now over the precipice. Beneath us lie the lights of the herring fleet. The cliffs vanish. Rippling small, rippling grey, innumerable waves spread beneath us. I touch nothing. I see nothing. We may sink and settle on the waves. The sea will drum in my ears. The white petals will be darkened with sea water. They will float for a moment and then sink. Rolling me over the waves will shoulder me under. Everything falls in a tremendous shower, dissolving me.

"Yet that tree has bristling branches; that is the hard line of a cottage roof. Those bladder shapes painted red and yellow are faces. Putting my foot to the ground I step gingerly and press my hand against the hard door of a Spanish inn."

*T*HE SUN *was sinking. The hard stone of the day was cracked and light poured through its splinters. Red and gold shot through the waves, in rapid running arrows, feathered with darkness. Erratically rays of light flashed and wandered, like signals from sunken islands, or darts shot through laurel groves by shameless, laughing boys. But the waves, as they neared the shore, were robbed of light, and fell in one long concussion, like a wall falling, a wall of grey stone, unpierced by any chink of light.*

A breeze rose; a shiver ran through the leaves; and thus stirred they lost their brown density and became grey or white as the tree shifted its mass, winked and lost its domed uniformity. The hawk poised on the topmost branch flicked its eyelids and rose and sailed and soared far away. The wild plover cried in the marshes, evading circling, and crying further off in loneliness. The smoke of trains and chimneys was stretched and torn and became part of the fleecy canopy that hung over the sea and the fields.

Now the corn was cut. Now only a brisk stubble was left of all its flowing and waving. Slowly a great owl launched itself from the elm tree and swung and rose, as if on a line that dipped, to the height of the cedar. On the hills the slow shadows now broadened, now shrank, as they passed over. The pool on the top of the moor lay blank. No furry face looked there, or hoof splashed, or hot muzzle seethed in the water. A bird, perched on an ash-coloured twig, sipped a beakful of cold water. There was no sound of cropping, and no sound of wheels, but only the sudden roar of the wind letting its sails fill and brushing the tops of the grasses. One bone lay rain-pocked and sun-bleached till it shone like a twig that the sea has polished. The tree, that had burnt foxy red in spring and in midsummer, bent pliant leaves to the south wind, was now black as iron, and as bare.

The land was so distant that no shining roof or glittering window could be any longer seen. The tremendous weight of the shadowed earth had engulfed such frail fetters, such snail-shell encumbrances. Now there was only the liquid shadow of the cloud, the buffeting of the rain, a single darting spear of sunshine, or the sudden bruise of the rainstorm. Solitary trees marked distant hills like obelisks.

The evening sun, whose heat had gone out of it and whose burning spot of intensity had been diffused, made chairs and tables mellower and inlaid them with lozenges of brown and yellow. Lined with shadows their weight seemed more ponderous as if colour, tilted, had run to one side. Here lay knife, fork and glass, but lengthened, swollen, and made portentous. Rimmed in a gold circle the looking-glass held the scene immobile as if everlasting in its eye.

Meanwhile the shadows lengthened on the beach; the blackness deepened. The iron black boot became a pool of deep blue. The rocks lost their hardness. The water that stood round the old boat was dark as if mussels had been steeped in it. The foam had turned livid and left here and there a white gleam of pearl on the misty sand.

"HAMPTON COURT," said Bernard. "Hampton Court. This is our meeting-place. Behold the red chimneys, the square battlements of Hampton Court. The tone of my voice as I say 'Hampton Court' proves that I am middle-aged. Ten years, fifteen years ago, I should have said 'Hampton Court?' with interrogation—what will it be like? Will there be lakes, mazes? Or with anticipation, What is going to happen to me here? Whom shall I meet? Now, Hampton Court—Hampton Court—the words beat a gong in the space which I have so laboriously cleared with half a dozen telephone messages and post cards, give off ring after ring of sound, booming, sonorous: and pictures rise—summer afternoons, boats, old ladies holding their skirts up, one urn in winter, some daffodils in March—these all float to the top of the waters that now lie deep on every scene.

"There at the door by the Inn, our meeting-place, they are already standing—Susan, Louis, Rhoda, Jinny and Neville. They have come together already. In a moment, when I have joined them, another arrangement will form, another pattern. What now runs to waste, forming scenes profusely, will be checked, stated. I am reluctant to suffer that compulsion. Already at fifty yards' distance I feel the order of my being changed. The tug of the magnet of their society tells upon me. I come nearer. They do not see me. Now Rhoda sees me, but she pretends, with her horror of the shock of meeting, that I am a stranger. Now Neville turns. Suddenly, raising my hand, saluting Neville I cry, 'I too have pressed flowers between the pages of Shakespeare's sonnets,' and am churned up. My little boat bobs unsteadily upon the chopped and tossing waves. There is no panacea (let me note) against the shock of meeting.

"It is uncomfortable too, joining ragged edges, raw edges; only gradually, as we shuffle and trample into the Inn, taking coats and hats off, does meeting become agreeable. Now we assemble in the long, bare dining-room that overlooks some park, some green space still fantastically lit by the setting sun so that there is a gold bar between the trees, and sit ourselves down."

"Now sitting side by side," said Neville, "at this narrow table, now before the first emotion is worn smooth, what do we feel? Honestly now, openly and directly as befits old friends meeting with difficulty, what do we feel on meeting? Sorrow. The door will not open; he will not come. And we are laden. Being now all of us middle-aged, loads are on us. Let us put down our loads. What have you made of life, we ask, and I? You, Bernard; you, Susan; you, Jinny; and Rhoda and Louis? The lists have been posted on the doors. Before we break these rolls, and help ourselves to fish and salad, I feel in my private pocket and find my credentials—what I carry to prove my superiority. I have passed. I have papers in my private pocket that prove it. But your eyes, Susan, full of turnips and cornfields, disturb me. These papers in my private pocket—the clamour that proves that I have passed—make a faint sound like that of a man clapping in an empty field to scare away rooks. Now it has died down altogether, under Susan's stare (the clapping, the reverberation that I have made), and I hear only the wind sweeping over the ploughed land and some bird singing—perhaps some intoxicated lark. Has the waiter heard of me, or those furtive everlasting couples, now loitering, now holding back and looking at the trees which are not yet dark enough to shelter their prostrate bodies? No; the sound of clapping has failed.

"What then remains, when I cannot pull out my papers and make you believe by reading aloud my credentials that I have passed? What remains is what Susan brings to light under the acid of her green eyes, her crystal, pear-shaped eyes. There is always somebody, when we come together, and the edges of meeting are still sharp, who refuses to be submerged; whose identity therefore one wishes to make crouch beneath one's own. For me now, it is Susan. I talk to impress Susan. Listen to me, Susan.

"When some one comes in at breakfast, even the embroidered fruit on my curtain swells so that parrots can peck it; one can break it off between one's thumb and finger. The thin, skimmed milk of early morning turns opal, blue, rose. At that hour your husband—the man who slapped his gaiters, pointing with his whip at the barren cow—grumbles. You say nothing. You see nothing. Custom blinds your eyes. At that hour your relationship is mute, null, dun-coloured. Mine at that hour is warm and various. There is no repetition for me. Each day is dangerous. Smooth on the surface, we are all bone beneath like snakes coiling. Suppose we read the *Times;* suppose we argue. It is an experience. Suppose it is winter. The snow falling loads down the roof and seals us together in a red cave. The pipes have burst. We stand a yellow tin bath in the middle of the room. We rush helter-skelter for basins. Look there—it has burst again over the bookcase. We shout with laughter at the sight of ruin. Let solidity be destroyed. Let us have no possessions. Or is it summer? We may wander to a lake and watch Chinese geese waddling flat-footed to the water's edge, or see a bone—like a city church with young green trembling before it. (I choose at random; I choose the obvious.) Each sight is an arabesque scrawled suddenly to illustrate some hazard and marvel of intimacy. The snow, the burst pipe, the tin bath, the Chinese goose—these are signs swung high aloft upon which, looking back, I read the character of each love; how each was different.

"You meanwhile—for I want to diminish your hostility, your green eyes fixed on mine, and your shabby dress, your rough hands, and all the other emblems of your maternal splendour—have stuck like a limpet to the same rock. Yet it is true, I do not want to hurt you; only to refresh and furbish up my belief in myself that failed at your entry. Change is no longer possible. We are committed. Before, when we met in a restaurant in London with Percival, all simmered and shook; we could have been anything. We have chosen now, or sometimes it seems the choice was made for us—a pair of tongs pinched us between the shoulders. I chose. I took the print of life not outwardly, but inwardly upon the raw, the white, the unprotected fibre. I am clouded and bruised with the print of minds and faces and things so subtle that they have smell, colour, texture, substance, but no name. I am merely 'Neville' to you, who see the narrow limits of my life and the line it cannot pass. But to myself I am immeasurable; a net whose fibres pass imperceptibly beneath the world. My net is almost indistinguishable from that which it surrounds. It lifts whales—huge leviathans and white jellies, what is amorphous and wandering; I detect, I perceive. Beneath my eyes opens—a book; I see to the bottom; the heart—I see to the depths. I know what loves are trembling into fire; how jealousy shoots its green flashes hither and thither; how intricately love crosses love; love makes knots; love brutally tears them apart. I have been knotted; I have been torn apart.

"But there was another glory once, when we watched for the door to open, and Percival came; when we flung ourselves unattached on the edge of a hard bench in a public room."

"There was the beech wood," said Susan, "Elvedon, and the gilt hands of the clock sparkling among the trees. The pigeons broke the leaves. The changing travelling lights wandered over me. They escaped me. Yet look, Neville, whom I discredit in order to be myself, at my hand on the table. Look at the gradations of healthy colour here on the knuckles, here on the palm. My body has been used daily, rightly, like a tool by a good workman, all over. The blade is clean, sharp, worn in the centre. (We battle together like beasts fighting in a field, like stags making their horns clash.) Seen through your pale and yielding flesh, even apples and bunches of fruit must have a filmed look as if they stood under glass. Lying deep in a chair with one person, one person only, but one person who changes, you see one inch of flesh only; its nerves, fibres, the sullen or quick flow of blood on it; but nothing entire. You do not see a house in a garden; a horse in a field; a town laid out, as you bend like an old woman straining her eyes over her darning. But I have seen life in blocks, substantial, huge; its battlements and towers, factories and gasometers; a dwelling place made from time immemorial after an hereditary pattern. These things remain square, prominent, undissolved in my mind. I am not sinuous or suave; I sit among you abrading your softness with my hardness, quenching the silver-grey flickering moth-wing quiver of words with the green spurt of my clear eyes.

"Now we have clashed our antlers. This is the necessary prelude; the salute of old friends."

"The gold has faded between the trees," said Rhoda, "and a slice of green lies behind them, elongated like the blade of a knife seen in dreams, or some tapering island on which nobody sets foot. Now the cars begin to wink and flicker, coming down the avenue. Lovers can draw into the darkness now; the boles of the trees are swollen, are obscene with lovers."

"It was different once," said Bernard. "Once we could break the current as we chose. How many telephone calls, how many post cards, are now needed to cut this hole through which we come together, united, at Hampton Court? How swift life runs from January to December! We are all swept on by the torrent of things grown so familiar that they cast no shade; we make no comparisons; think scarcely ever of I or of you; and in this unconsciousness attain the utmost freedom from friction and part the weeds that grow over the mouths of sunken channels. We have to leap like fish, high in the air, in order to catch the train from Waterloo. And however high we leap we fall back again into the stream. I shall never now take ship for the South Sea Islands. A journey to Rome is the limit of my travelling. I have sons and daughters. I am wedged into my place in the puzzle.

"But it is only my body—this elderly man here whom you call Bernard—that is fixed irrevocably—so I desire to believe. I think more disinterestedly than I could when I was young and must dig furiously like a child rummaging in a bran-pie to discover my self. 'Look, what is this? And this? Is this going to be a fine present? Is that all?' and so on. Now I know what the parcels hold; and do not care much. I throw my mind out in the air as a man throws seeds in great fan-flights, falling through the purple sunset, falling on the pressed and shining ploughland which is bare.

"A phrase. An imperfect phrase. And what are phrases? They have left me very little to lay on the table, beside Susan's hand; to take from my pocket, with Neville's credentials. I am not an authority on law, or medicine, or finance. I am wrapped round with phrases, like damp straw; I glow, phosphorescent. And each of you feels when I speak, 'I am lit up. I am glowing.' The little boys used to feel, 'That's a good one, that's a good one,' as the phrases bubbled up from my lips under the elm trees in the playing-fields. They too bubbled up; they also escaped with my phrases. But I pine in solitude. Solitude is my undoing.

"I pass from house to house like the friars in the Middle Ages who cozened the wives and girls with beads and ballads. I am a traveller, a pedlar, paying for my lodging with a ballad; I am an indiscriminate, an easily pleased guest; often putting up in the best room in a four-poster; then lying in a barn on a haystack. I don't mind the fleas and find no fault with silk either. I am very tolerant. I am not a moralist. I have too great a sense of the shortness of life and its temptations to rule red lines. Yet I am not so indiscriminate as you think, judging me—as you judge me—from my fluency. I have a little dagger of contempt and severity hidden up my sleeve. But I am apt to be deflected. I make stories. I twist up toys out of anything. A girl sits at a cottage door; she is waiting; for whom? Seduced, or not seduced?

The headmaster sees the hole in the carpet. He sighs. His wife, drawing her fingers through the waves of her still abundant hair reflects—et cetera. Waves of hands, hesitations at street corners, some one dropping a cigarette into the gutter—all are stories. But which is the true story? That I do not know. Hence I keep my phrases hung like clothes in a cupboard, waiting for some one to wear them. Thus waiting, thus speculating, making this note and then another I do not cling to life. I shall be brushed like a bee from a sunflower. My philosophy, always accumulating, welling up moment by moment, runs like quicksilver a dozen ways at once. But Louis, wild-eyed but severe, in his attic, in his office, has formed unalterable conclusions upon the true nature of what is to be known."

"It breaks," said Louis, "the thread I try to spin; your laughter breaks it, your indifference, also your beauty. Jinny broke the thread when she kissed me in the garden years ago. The boasting boys mocked me at school for my Australian accent and broke it. 'This is the meaning,' I say; and then start with a pang—vanity. 'Listen,' I say, 'to the nightingale, who sings among the trampling feet; the conquests and migrations. Believe—' and then am twitched asunder. Over broken tiles and splinters of glass I pick my way. Different lights fall, making the ordinary leopard-spotted and strange. This moment of reconciliation, when we meet together united, this evening moment, with its wine and shaking leaves, and youth coming up from the river in white flannels, carrying cushions, is to me black with the shadows of dungeons and the tortures and infamies practised by man upon man. So imperfect are my senses that they never blot out with one purple the serious charge that my reason adds and adds against us, even as we sit here. What is the solution, I ask myself, and the bridge? How can I reduce these dazzling, these dancing apparitions to one line capable of linking all in one? So

I ponder; and you meanwhile observe maliciously my pursed lips, my sallow cheeks and my invariable frown.

"But I beg you also to notice my cane and my waistcoat. I have inherited a desk of solid mahogany in a room hung with maps. Our steamers have won an enviable reputation for their cabins replete with luxury. We supply swimming-baths and gymnasiums. I wear a white waistcoat now and consult a little book before I make an engagement.

"This is the arch and ironical manner in which I hope to distract you from my shivering, my tender, and infinitely young and unprotected soul. For I am always the youngest; the most naïvely surprised; the one who runs in advance in apprehension and sympathy with discomfort or ridicule—should there be a smut on a nose, or a button undone. I suffer for all humiliations. Yet I am also ruthless, marmoreal. I do not see how you can say that it is fortunate to have lived. Your little excitements, your childish transports, when a kettle boils, when the soft air lifts Jinny's spotted scarf and it floats weblike, are to me like silk streamers thrown in the eyes of the charging bull. I condemn you. Yet my heart yearns towards you. I would go with you through the fires of death. Yet am happiest alone. I luxuriate in gold and purple vestments. Yet I prefer a view over chimney-pots; cats scraping their mangy sides upon blistered chimney-stacks; broken windows; and the hoarse clangour of bells from the steeple of some brick chapel."

"I see what is before me," said Jinny. "This scarf, these wine-coloured spots. This glass. This mustard pot. This flower. I like what one touches, what one tastes. I like rain when it has turned to snow and become palpable. And being rash, and much more courageous than you are, I do not temper my beauty with meanness lest it should scorch me. I gulp it down entire. It is made of flesh; it is made of stuff. My imagination is the body's. Its visions are not fine spun and white with purity like Louis's. I do not like your lean cats and your blistered chimney-pots. The scrannel beauties of your roof-tops repel me. Men and women, in uniforms, wigs and gowns, bowler hats and tennis shirts beautifully open at the neck, the infinite variety of women's dresses (I note all clothes always) delight me. I eddy with them, in and out, in and out, into rooms, into halls, here, there, everywhere, wherever they go. This man lifts the hoof of a horse. This man shoves in and out the drawers of his private collection. I am never alone. I am attended by a regiment of my fellows. My mother must have followed the drum, my father the sea. I am like a little dog that trots down the road after the reg-imental band, but stops to snuff a tree-trunk, to sniff some brown stain, and suddenly careers across the street after some mongrel cur and then holds one paw up while it sniffs an en-trancing whiff of meat from the butcher's shop. My traffics have led me into strange places. Men, how many, have broken from the wall and come to me. I have only to hold my hand up. Straight as a dart they have come to the place of assignation— perhaps a chair on a balcony, perhaps a shop at a street corner. The torments, the divisions of your lives have been solved for me night after night, sometimes only by the touch of a finger under the table-cloth as we sat dining—so fluid has my body become, forming even at the touch of a finger into one full drop, which fills itself, which quivers, which flashes, which falls in ecstasy.

"I have sat before a looking-glass as you sit writing, adding up figures at desks. So, before the looking-glass in the temple of my bedroom, I have judged my nose, and my chin; my lips that open too wide and show too much gum. I have looked. I have noted. I have chosen what yellow or white, what shine or dull-ness, what loop or straightness suits. I am volatile for one, rigid for another, angular as an icicle in silver, or voluptuous as a candle flame in gold. I have run violently like a whip flung out to the extreme end of my tether. His shirt front, there in the corner, has been white; then purple; smoke and flame have wrapped us about; after a furious conflagration—yet we scarcely raised our voices, sitting on the hearth-rug, as we murmured all the secrets of our hearts as into shells so that nobody might hear in the sleeping-house, but I heard the cook stir once, and once we thought the ticking of the clock was a footfall—we have sunk to ashes, leaving no relics, no unburnt bones, no wisps of hair to be kept in lockets such as your intimacies leave behind them. Now I turn grey; now I turn gaunt; but I look at my face at mid-day sitting in front of the looking-glass in broad daylight, and note precisely my nose, my chin, my lips that open too wide and show too much gum. But I am not afraid."

"There were lamp-posts," said Rhoda, "and trees that had not yet shed their leaves on the way from the station. The leaves might have hidden me still. But I did not hide behind them. I walked straight up to you instead of circling round to avoid the shock of sensation as I used. But it is only that I have taught my body to do a certain trick. Inwardly I am not taught; I fear, I hate, I love, I envy and despise you, but I never join you happily. Coming up from the station refusing to accept the shadow of the trees and the pillar-boxes, I perceived, from your coats and umbrellas, even at a distance, how you stand embedded in a substance made of repeated moments run together; are committed, have an attitude, with children, authority, fame, love, society; where I have nothing. I have no face.

"Here in this dining-room you see the antlers and the tumblers; the salt-cellars; the yellow stains on the table-cloth. 'Waiter!' says Bernard. 'Bread!' says Susan. And the waiter comes; he brings bread. But I see the side of a cup like a mountain and only parts of antlers, and the brightness on the side of that jug like a crack in darkness with wonder and terror. Your voices sound like trees creaking in a forest. So with your faces and their prominences and hollows. How beautiful, standing at a distance immobile at midnight against the railings of some square! Behind you is a white crescent of foam, and fishermen on the verge of the world are drawing in nets and casting them. A wind ruffles the topmost leaves of primeval trees. (Yet here we sit at Hampton Court.) Parrots shrieking break the intense stillness of the jungle. (Here the trams start.) The swallow dips her wings in midnight pools. (Here we talk.) That is the circumference that I try to grasp as we sit together. Thus I must undergo the penance of Hampton Court at seven-thirty precisely.

"But since these rolls of bread and wine bottles are needed by me, and your faces with their hollows and prominences are beautiful, and the table-cloth and its yellow stains, far from being allowed to spread in wider and wider circles of understanding that may at last (so I dream, falling off the edge of the earth at night when my bed floats suspended) embrace the entire world, I must go through the antics of the individual. I must start when you pluck at me with your children, your poems, your chilblains or whatever it is that you do and suffer. But I am not deluded. After all these callings hither and thither, these pluckings and searchings, I shall fall alone through this thin sheet into gulfs of fire. And you will not help me. More cruel than the old torturers you will let me fall, and will tear me to pieces when I am fallen. Yet there are moments when the walls of the mind grow thin; when nothing is unabsorbed, and I could fancy that we might blow so vast a bubble that the sun might set and rise in it and we might take the blue of midday and the black of midnight and be cast off and escape from here and now."

"Drop upon drop," said Bernard, "silence falls. It forms on the roof of the mind and falls into pools beneath. For ever alone, alone, alone,—hear silence fall and sweep its rings to the farthest edges. Gorged and replete, solid with middle-aged content, I, whom loneliness destroys, let silence fall, drop by drop.

"But now silence falling pits my face, wastes my nose like a snowman stood out in a yard in the rain. As silence falls I am dissolved utterly and become featureless and scarcely to be distinguished from another. It does not matter. What matters? We have dined well. The fish, the veal cutlets, the wine have blunted the sharp tooth of egotism. Anxiety is at rest. The vainest of us, Louis perhaps, does not care what people think. Neville's tortures are at rest. Let others prosper—that is what he thinks. Susan hears the breathing of all her children safe asleep. Sleep, sleep, she murmurs. Rhoda has rocked her ships to shore. Whether they have foundered, whether they have anchored, she cares no longer. We are ready to consider any suggestion that the world may offer quite impartially. I reflect now that the earth is only a pebble flicked off accidentally from the face of the sun and that there is no life anywhere in the abysses of space."

"In this silence," said Susan, "it seems as if no leaf would ever fall, or bird fly."

"As if the miracle had happened," said Jinny, "and life were stayed here and now."

"And," said Rhoda, "we had no more to live."

"But listen," said Louis, "to the world moving through abysses of infinite space. It roars; the lighted strip of history is past and our Kings and Queens; we are gone; our civilisation; the Nile; and all life. Our separate drops are dissolved; we are extinct, lost in the abysses of time, in the darkness."

"Silence falls; silence falls," said Bernard. "But now listen, tick, tick; hoot, hoot; the world has hailed us back to it. I heard for one moment the howling winds of darkness as we passed beyond life. Then tick, tick (the clock); then hoot, hoot (the cars). We are landed; we are on shore; we are sitting, six of us, at a table. It is the memory of my nose that recalls me. I rise; 'Fight,' I cry, 'fight!' remembering the shape of my own nose and strike with this spoon upon this table pugnaciously."

"Oppose ourselves to this illimitable chaos," said Neville, "this formless imbecility. Making love to a nursemaid behind a tree, that soldier is more admirable than all the stars. Yet sometimes one trembling star comes in the clear sky and makes me think the world beautiful and we maggots deforming even the trees with our lust."

("Yet, Louis," said Rhoda, "how short a time silence lasts. Already they are beginning to smooth their napkins by the side of their plates. 'Who comes?' says Jinny; and Neville sighs, remembering that Percival comes no more. Jinny has taken out her looking-glass. Surveying her face like an artist, she draws a powder-puff down her nose, and after one moment of deliberation, has given precisely that red to the lips that the lips need. Susan, who feels scorn and fear at the sight of these preparations, fastens the top button of her coat, and unfastens it. What is she making ready for? For something, but something different."

"They are saying to themselves," said Louis, "'it is time. I am still vigorous,' they are saying, 'My face shall be cut against the black of infinite space.' They do not finish their sentences. 'It is time,' they keep saying. 'The gardens will be shut.' And going with them, Rhoda, swept into their current, we shall perhaps drop a little behind."

"Like conspirators who have something to whisper," said Rhoda.)

"It is true, and I know for a fact," said Bernard, "as we walk down this avenue, that a King, riding, fell over a molehill here. But how strange it seems to set against the whirling abysses of infinite space a little figure with a golden teapot on his head.

Soon one recovers a belief in figures: but not at once in what
they put on their heads. Our English past—one inch of light.
Then people put teapots on their heads and say, 'I am a King!'
No, I try to recover, as we walk, the sense of time, but with that
streaming darkness in my eyes I have lost my grip. This Palace
seems light as a cloud set for a moment on the sky. It is a trick
of the mind—to put Kings on their thrones, one following another, with crowns on their heads. And we ourselves, walking
six abreast, what do we oppose, with this random flicker of light
in us that we call brain and feeling, how can we do battle against
this flood; what has permanence? Our lives too stream away,
down the unlighted avenues, past the strip of time, unidentified.
Once Neville threw a poem at my head. Feeling a sudden conviction of immortality I said, 'I too know what Shakespeare
knew.' But that has gone."

"Unreasonably, ridiculously," said Neville, "as we walk, time
comes back. A dog does it, prancing. The machine works. Age
makes hoary that gateway. Three hundred years now seem more
than a moment vanished against that dog. King William mounts
his horse wearing a wig, and the court ladies sweep the turf with
their embroidered panniers. I am beginning to be convinced, as
we walk, that the fate of Europe is of immense importance, and,
ridiculous as it still seems, that all depends upon the battle of
Blenheim. Yes; I declare, as we pass through this gateway, it is
the present moment; I am become a subject of King George."

"While we advance down this avenue," said Louis, "I leaning slightly upon Jinny, Bernard arm-in-arm with Neville, and
Susan with her hand in mine, it is difficult not to weep, calling
ourselves little children, praying that God may keep us safe
while we sleep. It is sweet to sing together, clasping hands, afraid
of the dark, while Miss Curry plays the harmonium."

"The iron gates have rolled back," said Jinny. "Time's fangs have ceased their devouring. We have triumphed over the abysses of space, with rouge, with powder, with flimsy pocket-handkerchiefs."

"I grasp, I hold fast," said Susan. "I hold firmly to this hand, any one's, with love, with hatred; it does not matter which."

"The still mood, the disembodied mood is on us," said Rhoda, "and we enjoy this momentary alleviation (it is not often that one has no anxiety) when the walls of the mind become transparent. Wren's palace, like the quartet played to the dry and stranded people in the stalls, makes an oblong. A square is stood upon the oblong and we say, 'This is our dwelling-place. The structure is now visible. Very little is left outside.'"

"The flower," said Bernard, "the red carnation that stood in the vase on the table of the restaurant when we dined together with Percival is become a six-sided flower; made of six lives."

"A mysterious illumination," said Louis, "visible against those yew trees."

"Built up with much pain, many strokes," said Jinny.

"Marriage, death, travel, friendship," said Bernard; "town, and country; children and all that; a many-sided substance cut out of this dark; a many-faceted flower. Let us stop for a moment; let us behold what we have made. Let it blaze against the yew trees. One life. There. It is over. Gone out."

"Now they vanish," said Louis. "Susan with Bernard. Neville with Jinny. You and I, Rhoda, stop for a moment by this stone urn. What song shall we hear now that these couples have sought the groves and Jinny, pointing with her gloved hand, pretends to notice the water-lilies, and Susan, who has always loved Bernard, says to him, 'My ruined life, my wasted life.' And Neville, taking Jinny's little hand, with the cherry-coloured finger-nails, by the lake by the moonlit water, cries, 'Love, love,' and she answers, imitating the bird, 'Love, love?' What song do we hear?"

"They vanish, towards the lake," said Rhoda. "They slink away over the grass furtively, yet with assurance as if they asked of our pity their ancient privilege—not to be disturbed. The tide in the soul, tipped, flows that way; they cannot help deserting us. The dark has closed over their bodies. What song do we hear, the owl's, the nightingale's, the wren's? The steamer hoots; the light on the electric rails flashes; the trees gravely bow and bend. The flare hangs over London. Here is an old woman, quietly returning, and a man, a late fisherman comes down the terrace with his rod. Not a sound, not a movement must escape us."

"A bird flies homeward," said Louis. "Evening opens her eyes and gives one quick glance among the bushes before she sleeps. How shall we put it together, the confused and composite message, that they send back to us, and not they only, but many dead, boys and girls, grown men and women, who have wandered here, under one king or another?"

"A weight has dropped into the night," said Rhoda, "dragging it down. Every tree is big with a shadow that is not the shadow of the tree behind it. We hear a drumming on the roofs of a fasting city when the Turks are hungry and uncertain tempered. We hear them crying with sharp, stag-like barks, 'Open, open.' Listen to the trams squealing and to the flashes from the electric rails. We hear the beech trees and the birch trees raise their branches as if the bride had let her silken nightdress fall and come to the doorway saying, 'Open, open.'"

"All seems alive," said Louis. "I cannot hear death anywhere tonight. Stupidity, on that man's face, age, on that woman's, would be strong enough, one would think, to resist the incantation, and bring in death. But where is death tonight? All the crudity, odds and ends, this and that, have been crushed like glass splinters into the blue, the red-fringed tide, which, drawing into the shore, fertile with innumerable fish, breaks at our feet."

"If we could mount together, if we could perceive from a sufficient height," said Rhoda, "if we could remain untouched without any support—but you, disturbed by faint clapping sounds of praise and laughter, and I, resenting compromise and right and wrong on human lips, trust only in solitude and the violence of death and thus are divided."

"For ever," said Louis, "divided. We have sacrificed the embrace among the ferns, and love, love, love by the lake, standing, like conspirators who have drawn apart to share some secret, by the urn. But now look, as we stand here, a ripple breaks on the horizon. The net is raised higher and higher. It comes to the top of the water. The water is broken by silver, by quivering little fish. Now leaping, now lashing, they are laid on shore. Life tumbles its catch upon the grass. There are figures coming towards us. Are they men or are they women? They still wear the ambiguous draperies of the flowing tide in which they have been immersed."

"Now," said Rhoda, "as they pass that tree, they regain their natural size. They are only men, only women. Wonder and awe change as they put off the draperies of the flowing tide. Pity returns, as they emerge into the moonlight, like the relics of an army, our representatives, going every night (here or in Greece) to battle, and coming back every night with their wounds, their ravaged faces. Now light falls on them again. They have faces. They become Susan and Bernard, Jinny and Neville, people we know. Now what a shrinkage takes place! Now what a shrivelling, what an humiliation! The old shivers run through me, hatred and terror, as I feel myself grappled to one spot by these hooks they cast on us; these greetings, recognitions, pluckings of the finger and searchings of the eyes. Yet they have only to speak, and their first words, with the remembered tone and the perpetual deviation from what one expects and their hands moving and making a thousand past days rise again in the darkness, shake my purpose."

"Something flickers and dances," said Louis. "Illusion returns as they approach down the avenue. Rippling and questioning begin. What do I think of you—what do you think of me? Who are you? Who am I?—that quivers again its uneasy air over us, and the pulse quickens and the eye brightens and all the insanity of personal existence without which life would fall flat and die, begins again. They are on us. The southern sun flickers over this urn; we push off in to the tide of the violent and cruel sea. Lord help us to act our parts as we greet them returning— Susan and Bernard, Neville and Jinny."

"We have destroyed something by our presence," said Bernard, "a world perhaps."

"Yet we scarcely breathe," said Neville, "spent as we are. We are in that passive and exhausted frame of mind when we only wish to rejoin the body of our mother from whom we have been severed. All else is distasteful, forced and fatiguing. Jinny's yellow scarf is moth-coloured in this light; Susan's eyes are quenched. We are scarcely to be distinguished from the river. One cigarette end is the only point of emphasis among us. And sadness tinges our content, that we should have left you, torn the fabric; yielded to the desire to press out, alone, some bitterer, some blacker juice, which was sweet too. But now we are worn out."

"After our fire," said Jinny, "there is nothing left to put in lockets."

"Still I gape," said Susan, "like a young bird, unsatisfied, for something that has escaped me."

"Let us stay for a moment," said Bernard, "before we go. Let us pace the terrace by the river almost alone. It is nearly bedtime. People have gone home. Now how comforting it is to watch the lights coming out in the bedrooms of small shopkeepers on the other side of the river. There is one—there is another. What do you think their takings have been today? Only just enough to pay for the rent, for light and food and the children's clothing. But just enough. What a sense of the tolerableness of life the lights in the bedrooms of small shopkeepers give us! Saturday comes, and there is just enough to pay perhaps for seats at the Pictures. Perhaps before they put out the light they go into the little garden and look at the giant rabbit couched in its wooden hut. That is the rabbit they will have for Sunday dinner. Then they put out the light. Then they sleep. And for thousands of people sleep is nothing but warmth and silence and one moment's sport with some fantastic dream. I have posted my letter, the green-grocer thinks, to the Sunday newspaper. Suppose I win five hundred pounds in the football competition? And we shall kill the rabbit. Life is pleasant. Life is good. I have posted the letter. We shall kill the rabbit. And he sleeps.

"That goes on. Listen. There is a sound like the knocking of railway trucks in a siding. That is the happy concatenation of one event following another in our lives. Knock, knock, knock. Must, must, must. Must go, must sleep, must wake, must get up—sober, merciful word which we pretend to revile, which we press tight to our hearts, without which we should be undone. How we worship that sound like the knocking together of trucks in a siding!

"Now far off down the river I hear the chorus; the song of the boasting boys, who are coming back in large charabancs from a day's outing on the decks of crowded steamers. Still they are singing as they used to sing, across the court, on winters' nights, or with the windows open in summer, getting drunk, breaking the furniture, wearing little striped caps, all turning their heads the same way as the brake rounded the corner; and I wished to be with them.

"What with the chorus, and the spinning water and the just perceptible murmur of the breeze we are slipping away. Little bits of ourselves are crumbling. There! Something very important fell then. I cannot keep myself together. I shall sleep. But we must go; must catch our train; must walk back to the station—must, must, must. We are only bodies jogging along side by side. I exist only in the soles of my feet and in the tired muscles of my thighs. We have been walking for hours it seems. But where? I cannot remember. I am like a log slipping smoothly over some waterfall. I am not a judge. I am not called upon to give my opinion. Houses and trees are all the same in this grey light. Is that a post? Is that a woman walking? Here is the station, and if the train were to cut me in two, I should come together on the further side, being one, being indivisible. But what is odd is that I still clasp the return half of my ticket to Waterloo firmly between the fingers of my right hand, even now, even sleeping."

*N*OW THE *sun had sunk. Sky and sea were indistinguishable. The waves breaking spread their white fans far out over the shore, sent white shadows into the recesses of sonorous caves and then rolled back sighing over the shingle.*

The tree shook its branches and a scattering of leaves fell to the ground. There they settled with perfect composure on the precise spot where they would await dissolution. Black and grey were shot into the garden from the broken vessel that had once held red light. Dark shadows blackened the tunnels between the stalks. The thrush was silent and the worm sucked itself back into its narrow hole. Now and again a whitened and hollow straw was blown from an old nest and fell into the dark grasses among the rotten apples. The light had faded from the toolhouse wall and the adder's skin hung from the nail empty. All colours in the room had overflown their banks. The precise brush stroke was swollen and lopsided; cupboards and chairs melted their brown masses into one huge obscurity. The height from floor to ceiling was hung with vast curtains of darkness. The looking-glass was pale as the mouth of a cave shadowed by hanging creepers.

The substance had gone from the solidity of the hills. Travelling lights drove a plumy wedge among unseen and sunken roads, but no lights opened among the folded wings of the hills, and there was no sound save the cry of a bird seeking some lonelier tree. At the cliff's edge there was an equal murmur of air that had been brushed through forests, of water that had been cooled in a thousand glassy hollows of mid-ocean.

As if there were waves of darkness in the air, darkness moved on, covering houses, hills, trees, as waves of water wash round the sides of some sunken ship. Darkness washed down streets eddying round single figures, engulfing them; blotting out couples clasped under the showery darkness of elm trees in full summer foliage. Darkness rolled its waves along grassy rides and over the wrinkled skin of the turf, enveloping the solitary thorn tree and the empty snail shells at its foot. Mounting higher, darkness blew along the bare upland slopes, and met the fretted and abraded pinnacles of the mountain where the snow lodges for ever on the hard rock even when the valleys are full of running streams and yellow vine leaves, and girls, sitting on verandahs, look up at the snow, shading their faces with their fans. Them, too, darkness covered.

"Now to sum up," said Bernard. "Now to explain to you the meaning of my life. Since we do not know each other (though I met you once I think on board a ship going to Africa) we can talk freely. The illusion is upon me that something adheres for a moment, has roundness, weight, depth, is completed. This, for the moment, seems to be my life. If it were possible, I would hand it you entire. I would break it off as one breaks off a bunch of grapes. I would say, 'Take it. This is my life.'

"But unfortunately, what I see (this globe, full of figures) you do not see. You see me, sitting at a table opposite you, a rather heavy, elderly man, grey at the temples. You see me take my napkin and unfold it. You see me pour myself out a glass of wine. And you see behind me the door opening, and people passing. But in order to make you understand, to give you my life, I must tell you a story—and there are so many, and so many—stories of childhood, stories of school, love, marriage, death, and so on; and none of them are true. Yet like children we tell each other stories, and to decorate them we make up these ridiculous, flamboyant, beautiful phrases. How tired I am of stories, how tired I am of phrases that come down beautifully with all their feet on the ground! Also, how I distrust neat designs of life that are drawn upon half sheets of note-paper. I begin to long for some little language such as lovers use, broken words, inarticulate words, like the shuffling of feet on the pavement. I begin to seek some design more in accordance with those moments of humiliation and triumph that come now and then undeniably. Lying in a ditch on a stormy day, when it has been raining, then enormous clouds come marching over the sky, tattered clouds, wisps of cloud. What delights me then is the confusion, the height, the indifference and the fury. Great clouds always changing, and movement; something sulphurous and sinister, bowled up, helter-skelter; towering, trailing, broken off, lost, and I forgotten, minute, in a ditch. Of story, of design I do not see a trace then.

"But meanwhile, while we eat, let us turn over these scenes as children turn over the pages of a picture-book and the nurse says, pointing: 'That's a cow. That's a boat.' Let us turn over the pages, and I will add, for your amusement, a comment in the margin.

"In the beginning, there was the nursery, with windows opening on to a garden, and beyond that the sea. I saw something brighten—no doubt the brass handle of a cupboard. Then Mrs. Constable raised the sponge above her head, squeezed it, and out shot, right, left, all down the spine, arrows of sensation. And so, as long as we draw breath, for the rest of time, if we knock against a chair, a table, or a woman, we are pierced with arrows of sensation—if we walk in a garden, if we drink this wine. Sometimes indeed, when I pass a cottage with a light in the window where a child has been born, I could implore them not to squeeze the sponge over that new body. Then, there was the garden and the canopy of the currant leaves which seemed to enclose everything; flowers, burning like sparks upon the depths of green; a rat wreathing with maggots under a rhubarb leaf; the fly going buzz, buzz, buzz upon the nursery ceiling, and plates upon plates of innocent bread and butter. All these things happen in one second and last for ever. Faces loom. Dashing round the corner, 'Hullo,' one says, 'there's Jinny. That's Neville. That's Louis in grey flannel with a snake belt. That's Rhoda.' She had a basin in which she sailed petals of white flowers. It was Susan who cried, that day when I was in the tool-house with Neville; and I felt my indifference melt. Neville did not melt. 'Therefore,' I said, 'I am myself, not Neville,' a wonderful discovery. Susan cried and I followed her. Her wet pocket-handkerchief, and the sight of her little back heaving up and down like a pump-handle, sobbing for what was denied her, screwed my nerves up. 'This is not to be borne,' I said, as I sat beside her on the roots that were hard as skeletons. I then first became aware of the presence of those enemies who change, but are always there; the forces we fight against. To let oneself be carried on passively is unthinkable. 'That's your course, world,' one says, 'mine is this.' 'So let's explore,' I cried, and jumped up, and ran downhill with Susan and saw the stableboy clattering about the yard in great boots. Down below, through the depths of the leaves, the gardeners swept the lawns with great brooms. The lady sat writing. Transfixed, stopped dead, I thought, 'I cannot interfere with a single stroke of those brooms. They sweep and they sweep. Nor with the fixity of that woman writing.' It is strange that one cannot stop gardeners sweeping nor dislodge a woman. There they have remained all my life. It is as if one had woken in Stonehenge surrounded by a circle of great stones, these enemies, these presences. Then a wood-pigeon flew out of the trees. And being in love for the first time, I made a phrase—a poem about a wood-pigeon—a single phrase, for a hole had been knocked in my mind, one of those sudden transparences through which one sees everything. Then more bread and butter and more flies droning round the nursery ceiling on which quivered islands of light, ruffled, opalescent, while the pointed fingers of the lustre dripped blue pools on the corner of the mantelpiece. Day after day as we sat at tea we observed these sights.

"But we were all different. The wax—the virginal wax that coats the spine melted in different patches for each of us. The growl of the boot-boy making love to the tweeny among the gooseberry bushes; the clothes blown out hard on the line; the dead man in the gutter; the apple tree, stark in the moonlight; the rat swarming with maggots; the lustre dripping blue—our white wax was streaked and stained by each of these differently. Louis was disgusted by the nature of human flesh; Rhoda by our cruelty; Susan could not share; Neville wanted order; Jinny love; and so on. We suffered terribly as we became separate bodies.

"Yet I was preserved from these excesses and have survived many of my friends, am a little stout, grey, rubbed on the thorax as it were, because it is the panorama of life, seen not from the roof, but from the third story window that delights me, not what one woman says to one man, even if that man is myself. How could I be bullied at school therefore? How could they make things hot for me? There was the Doctor lurching into chapel, as if he trod a battleship in a gale of wind, shouting out his commands through a megaphone, since people in authority always become melodramatic—I did not hate him like Neville, or revere him like Louis. I took notes as we sat together in chapel. There were pillars, shadows, memorial brasses, boys scuffling and swopping stamps behind Prayer Books; the sound of a rusty pump; the Doctor booming, about immortality and quitting ourselves like men; and Percival scratching his thigh. I made notes for stories; drew portraits in the margin of my pocketbook and thus became still more separate. Here are one or two of the figures I saw.

"Percival sat staring straight ahead of him that day in chapel. He also had a way of flicking his hand to the back of his neck. His movements were always remarkable. We all flicked our hands to the backs of our heads—unsuccessfully. He had the kind of beauty which defends itself from any caress. As he was not in the least precocious, he read whatever was written up for our edification without any comment, and thought with that magnificent equanimity (Latin words come naturally) that was to preserve him from so many meannesses and humiliations, that Lucy's flaxen pigtails and pink cheeks were the height of female beauty. Thus preserved, his taste later was of extreme fineness. But there should be music, some wild carol. Through the window should come a hunting-song from some rapid

unapprehended life—a sound that shouts among the hills and
dies away. What is startling, what is unexpected, what we cannot
account for, what turns symmetry to nonsense—that comes
suddenly to my mind, thinking of him. The little apparatus of
observation is unhinged. Pillars go down; the Doctor floats off;
some sudden exaltation possesses me. He was thrown, riding in
a race, and when I came along Shaftesbury Avenue tonight,
those insignificant and scarcely formulated faces that bubble up
out of the doors of the Tube, and many obscure Indians, and
people dying of famine and disease, and women who have been
cheated, and whipped dogs and crying children—all these
seemed to me bereft. He would have done justice. He would
have protected. About the age of forty he would have shocked
the authorities. No lullaby has ever occurred to me capable of
singing him to rest.

"But let me dip again and bring up in my spoon another of
these minute objects which we call optimistically, 'characters of
our friends'—Louis. He sat staring at the preacher. His being
seemed conglobulated in his brow, his lips were pressed; his eyes
were fixed, but suddenly they flashed with laughter. Also he suffered from chilblains, the penalty of an imperfect circulation.
Unhappy, unfriended, in exile he would sometimes, in moments
of confidence, describe how the surf swept over the beaches of
his home. The remorseless eye of youth fixed itself upon his
swollen joints. Yes, but we were also quick to perceive how cutting, how apt, how severe he was, how naturally, when we lay
under the elm trees pretending to watch cricket, we waited his
approval, seldom given. His ascendancy was resented, as Percival's was adored. Prim, suspicious, lifting his feet like a crane,
there was yet a legend that he had smashed a door with his naked
fist. But his peak was too bare, too stony for that kind of mist to
cling to it. He was without those simple attachments by which
one is connected with another. He remained aloof; enigmatic; a

scholar capable of that inspired accuracy which has something formidable about it. My phrases (how to describe the moon) did not meet with his approval. On the other hand, he envied me to the point of desperation for being at my ease with servants. Not that the sense of his own deserts failed him. That was commensurate with his respect for discipline. Hence his success, finally. His life, though, was not happy. But look—his eye turns white as he lies in the palm of my hand. Suddenly the sense of what people are leaves one. I return him to the pool where he will acquire lustre.

"Neville next—lying on his back staring up at the summer sky. He floated among us like a piece of thistle-down, indolently haunting the sunny corner of the playing-field, not listening, yet not remote. It was through him that I have nosed round without ever precisely touching the Latin classics and have also derived some of those persistent habits of thought which make us irredeemably lopsided—for instance about crucifixes, that they are the mark of the devil. Our half-loves and half-hates and ambiguities on these points were to him indefensible treacheries. The swaying and sonorous Doctor, whom I made to sit swinging his braces over a gas-fire, was to him nothing but an instrument of the inquisition. So he turned with a passion that made up for his indolence upon Catullus, Horace, Lucretius, lying lazily dormant, yes, but regardant, noticing, with rapture, cricketers, while with a mind like the tongue of an ant-eater, rapid, dexterous, glutinous, he searched out every curl and twist of those Roman sentences, and sought out one person, always one person to sit beside.

"And the long skirts of the masters' wives would come swishing by, mountainous, menacing; and our hands would fly to our caps. And immense dullness would descend unbroken, monotonous. Nothing, nothing, nothing broke with its fin that leaden waste of waters. Nothing would happen to lift that weight of intolerable boredom. The terms went on. We grew; we changed; for, of course, we are animals. We are not always aware by any means; we breathe, eat, sleep automatically. We exist not only separately but in undifferentiated blobs of matter. With one scoop a whole brakeful of boys is swept up and goes cricketing, footballing. An army marches across Europe. We assemble in parks and halls and sedulously oppose any renegade (Neville, Louis, Rhoda), who sets up a separate existence. And I am so made, that, while I hear one or two distinct melodies, such as Louis sings, or Neville, I am also drawn irresistibly to the sound of the chorus chanting its old, chanting its almost wordless, almost senseless song that comes across courts at night; which we hear now booming round us as cars and omnibuses take people to theatres. (Listen; the cars rush past this restaurant; now and then, down the river, a siren hoots, as a steamer makes for the sea.) If a bagman offers me snuff in a train I accept. I like the copious, shapeless, warm, not so very clever, but extremely easy and rather coarse aspect of things; the talk of men in clubs and public-houses, of miners half naked in drawers — the forthright, perfectly unassuming, and without end in view except dinner, love, money and getting along tolerably; that which is without great hopes, ideals, or anything of that kind; what is unassuming except to make a tolerably good job of it. I like all that. So I joined them, when Neville sulked or Louis, as I quite agree sublimely, turned on his heel.

"Thus, not equally by any means or with order, but in great streaks my waxen waistcoat melted, here one drop, there another. Now through this transparency became visible those wondrous pastures, at first so moon-white, radiant, where no foot has been; meadows of the rose, the crocus, of the rock and the snake too; of the spotted and swart; the embarrassing, the binding and tripping up. One leaps out of bed, throws up the window; with what a whirr the birds rise! You know that sudden

rush of wings, that exclamation, carol, and confusion; the riot
and babble of voices; and all the drops are sparkling, trembling,
as if the garden were a splintered mosaic, vanishing, twinkling,
not yet formed into one whole; and a bird sings close to the window. I heard those songs. I followed those phantoms. I saw
Joans, Dorothys, Miriams, I forget their names, passing down avenues, stopping on the crest of bridges to look down into the
river. And from among them rise one or two distinct figures,
birds who sang with the rapt egotism of youth by the window;
broke their snails on stones, dipped their beaks in sticky, viscous
matter; hard, avid, remorseless; Jinny, Susan, Rhoda. They had
been educated on the east coast or on the south coast. They had
grown long pigtails and acquired the look of startled foals, which
is the mark of adolescence.

"Jinny was the first to come sidling up to the gate to eat
sugar. She nipped it off the palms of one's hands very cleverly,
but her ears were laid back as if she might bite. Rhoda was
wild—Rhoda one never could catch. She was both frightened
and clumsy. It was Susan who first became wholly woman, purely
feminine. It was she who dropped on my face those scalding
tears which are terrible, beautiful; both, neither. She was born
to be the adored of poets, since poets require safety; some one
who sits sewing, who says, 'I hate, I love,' who is neither comfortable nor prosperous, but has some quality in accordance
with the high but unemphatic beauty of pure style which those
who create poetry so particularly admire. Her father trailed
from room to room and down flagged corridors in his flapping
dressing-gown and worn slippers. On still nights a wall of water
fell with a roar a mile off. The ancient dog could scarcely heave
himself up on to his chair. And some witless servant could be
heard laughing at the top of the house as she whirred the wheel
of the sewing-machine round and round.

"That I observed even in the midst of my anguish when,

twisting her pocket-handkerchief, Susan cried, 'I hate; I love.' 'A worthless servant,' I observed, 'laughs upstairs in the attic,' and that little piece of dramatisation shows how incompletely we are merged in our own experiences. On the outskirts of every agony sits some observant fellow who points; who whispers as he whispered to me that summer morning in the house where the corn comes up to the window, 'The willow grows on the turf by the river. The gardeners sweep with great brooms and the lady sits writing.' Thus he directed me to that which is beyond and outside our own predicament; to that which is symbolic, and thus perhaps permanent, if there is any permanence in our sleeping, eating, breathing, so animal, so spiritual and tumultuous lives.

"The willow tree grew by the river. I sat on the smooth turf with Neville, with Larpent, with Baker, Romsey, Hughes, Percival and Jinny. Through its fine plumes specked with little pricked ears of green in spring, of orange in autumn, I saw boats; buildings; I saw hurrying, decrepit women. I buried match after match in the turf decidedly to mark this or that stage in the process of understanding (it might be philosophy; science; it might be myself) while the fringe of my intelligence floating unattached caught those distant sensations which after a time the mind draws in and works upon; the chime of bells; general murmurs; vanishing figures; one girl on a bicycle who, as she rode, seemed to lift the corner of a curtain concealing the populous undifferentiated chaos of life which surged behind the outlines of my friends and the willow tree.

"The tree alone resisted our eternal flux. For I changed and changed; was Hamlet, was Shelley, was the hero, whose name I now forget, of a novel by Dostoevsky; was for a whole term, incredibly, Napoleon; but was Byron chiefly. For many weeks at a time it was my part to stride into rooms and fling gloves and

coat on the back of chairs, scowling slightly. I was always going
to the bookcase for another sip of the divine specific. Therefore, I let fly my tremendous battery of phrases upon somebody
quite inappropriate—a girl now married, now buried; every
book, every window-seat was littered with the sheets of my unfinished letters to the woman who made me Byron. For it is difficult to finish a letter in somebody else's style. I arrived all in a
lather at her house; exchanged tokens but did not marry her
being no doubt unripe for that intensity.

"Here again there should be music. Not that wild hunting-
song, Percival's music; but a painful, guttural, visceral, also soar-
ing, lark-like, pealing song to replace these flagging, foolish
transcripts—how much too deliberate! how much too reason-
able!—which attempt to describe the flying moment of first
love. A purple slide is slipped over the day. Look at a room before she comes and after. Look at the innocents outside pursuing their way. They neither see nor hear; yet on they go. Moving
oneself in this radiant yet gummy atmosphere, how conscious
one is of every movement—something adheres, something
sticks to one's hands, taking up a newspaper even. Then there is
the being eviscerated—drawn out, spun like a spider's web and
twisted in agony round a thorn. Then a thunder-clap of complete indifference; the light blown out; then the return of measureless irresponsible joy; certain fields seem to glow green for
ever, and innocent landscapes appear as if in the light of the first
dawn—one patch of green, for example, up at Hampstead; and
all faces are lit up, all conspire in a hush of tender joy; and then
the mystic sense of completion and then that rasping, dog-fish
skin-like roughness—those black arrows of shivering sensation,
when she misses the post, when she does not come. Out rush
a bristle of horned suspicions, horror, horror, horror—but what
is the use of painfully elaborating these consecutive sentences

when what one needs is nothing consecutive but a bark, a groan? And years later to see a middle-aged woman in a restaurant taking off her cloak.

"But to return. Let us again pretend that life is a solid substance, shaped like a globe, which we turn about in our fingers. Let us pretend that we can make out a plain and logical story, so that when one matter is despatched—love for instance—we go on, in an orderly manner, to the next. I was saying there was a willow tree. Its shower of falling branches, its creased and crooked bark had the effect of what remains outside our illusions yet cannot stay them, is changed by them for the moment, yet shows through stable, still, and with a sternness that our lives lack. Hence the comment it makes; the standard it supplies, and the reason why, as we flow and change, it seems to measure. Neville, for example, sat with me on the turf. But can anything be as clear as all that, I would say, following his gaze, through the branches, to a punt on the river, and a young man eating bananas from a paper bag? The scene was cut out with such intensity and so permeated with the quality of his vision that for a moment I could see it too; the punt, the bananas, the young man, through the branches of the willow tree. Then it faded.

"Rhoda came wandering vaguely. She would take advantage of any scholar in a blowing gown, or donkey rolling the turf with slippered feet to hide behind. What fear wavered and hid itself and blew to a flame in the depths of her grey, her startled, her dreaming eyes? Cruel and vindictive as we are, we are not bad to that extent. We have our fundamental goodness surely or to talk as I talk freely to some one I hardly know would be impossible—we should cease. The willow as she saw it grew on the verge of a grey desert where no bird sang. The leaves shrivelled as she looked at them, tossed in agony as she passed them. The trams and omnibuses roared hoarse in the street, ran over rocks and sped foaming away. Perhaps one pillar, sunlit, stood

in her desert by a pool where wild beasts come down stealthily
to drink.

"Then Jinny came. She flashed her fire over the tree. She
was like a crinkled poppy, febrile, thirsty with the desire to drink
dry dust. Darting, angular, not in the least impulsive, she came
prepared. So little flames zig-zag over the cracks in the dry
earth. She made the willows dance, but not with illusion; for she
saw nothing that was not there. It was a tree; there was the river;
it was afternoon; here we were; I in my serge suit; she in green.
There was no past, no future; merely the moment in its ring of
light, and our bodies; and the inevitable climax, the ecstasy.

"Louis, when he let himself down on the grass, cautiously
spreading (I do not exaggerate) a mackintosh square, made one
acknowledge his presence. It was formidable. I had the intelligence to salute his integrity; his research with bony fingers
wrapped in rags because of chilblains for some diamond of in-
dissoluble veracity. I buried boxes of burnt matches in holes in
the turf at his feet. His grim and caustic tongue reproved my
indolence. He fascinated me with his sordid imagination. His
heroes wore bowler-hats and talked about selling pianos for
tenners. Through his landscape the tram squealed; the factory
poured its acrid fumes. He haunted mean streets and towns
where women lay drunk, naked, on counterpanes on Christmas
day. His words falling from a shot tower hit the water and up
it spurted. He found one word, one only for the moon. Then
he got up and went; we all got up; we all went. But I, pausing,
looked at the tree, and as I looked in autumn at the fiery and
yellow branches, some sediment formed; I formed; a drop fell;
I fell—that is from some completed experience I had emerged.

"I rose and walked away—I, I, I; not Byron, Shelley, Dostoevsky, but I, Bernard. I even repeated my own name once or
twice. I went, swinging my stick, into a shop, and bought—not
that I love music—a picture of Beethoven in a silver frame. Not

that I love music, but because the whole of life, its masters, its
adventurers then appeared in long ranks of magnificent human
beings behind me; and I was the inheritor; I, the continuer; I,
the person miraculously appointed to carry it on. So, swinging
my stick, with my eyes filmed, not with pride, but with humility
rather, I walked down the street. The first whirr of wings had
gone up, the carol, the exclamation; and now one enters; one
goes into the house, the dry, uncompromising, inhabited house,
the place with all its traditions, its objects, its accumulations of
rubbish, and treasures displayed upon tables. I visited the family tailor, who remembered my uncle. People turned up in great
quantities, not cut out, like the first faces (Neville, Louis, Jinny,
Susan, Rhoda), but confused, featureless, or changed their features so fast that they seemed to have none. And blushing yet
scornful, in the oddest condition of raw rapture and scepticism,
I took the blow; the mixed sensations; the complex and disturb-
ing and utterly unprepared-for impacts of life all over, in all
places at the same time. How upsetting! How humiliating never
to be sure what to say next, and those painful silences, glaring
as dry deserts, with every pebble apparent; and then to say what
one ought not to have said, and then to be conscious of a ramrod of incorruptible sincerity which one would willingly exchange for a shower of smooth pence, but could not, there at
that party, where Jinny sat quite at her ease, rayed out on a gilt
chair.

"Then says some lady with an impressive gesture, 'Come
with me.' She leads one into a private alcove and admits one to
the honour of her intimacy. Surnames change to Christian
names; Christian names to nicknames. What is to be done about
India, Ireland or Morocco? Old gentlemen answer the question
standing decorated under chandeliers. One finds oneself sur-
prisingly supplied with information. Outside the undifferentiated forces roar; inside we are very private, very explicit, have a

sense indeed, that it is here, in this little room, that we make whatever day of the week it may be. Friday or Saturday. A shell forms upon the soft soul, nacreous, shiny, upon which sensations tap their beaks in vain. On me it formed earlier than on most. Soon I could carve my pear when other people had done dessert. I could bring my sentence to a close in a hush of complete silence. It is at that season too that perfection has a lure. One can learn Spanish, one thinks, by tying a string to the right toe and waking early. One fills up the little compartments of one's engagement book with dinner at eight; luncheon at one-thirty. One has shirts, socks, ties laid out on one's bed.

"But it is a mistake, this extreme precision, this orderly and military progress; a convenience, a lie. There is always deep below it, even when we arrive punctually at the appointed time with our white waistcoats and polite formalities, a rushing stream of broken dreams, nursery rhymes, street cries, half-finished sentences and sights—elm trees, willow trees, gardeners sweeping, women writing—that rise and sink even as we hand a lady down to dinner. While one straightens the fork so precisely on the table-cloth, a thousand faces mop and mow. There is nothing one can fish up in a spoon; nothing one can call an event. Yet it is alive too and deep, this stream. Immersed in it I would stop between one mouthful and the next, and look intently at a vase, perhaps with one red flower, while a reason struck me, a sudden revelation. Or I would say, walking along the Strand, 'That's the phrase I want,' as some beautiful, fabulous phantom bird, fish or cloud with fiery edges swam up to enclose once and for all some notion haunting me, after which on I trotted taking stock with renewed delight of ties and things in shop-windows.

"The crystal, the globe of life as one calls it, far from being hard and cold to the touch, has walls of thinnest air. If I press them all will burst. Whatever sentence I extract whole and entire from this cauldron is only a string of six little fish that let themselves be caught while a million others leap and sizzle, making the cauldron bubble like boiling silver, and slip through my fingers. Faces recur, faces and faces—they press their beauty to the walls of my bubble—Neville, Susan, Louis, Jinny, Rhoda and a thousand others. How impossible to order them rightly; to detach one separately, or to give the effect of the whole—again like music. What a symphony, with its concord and its discord and its tunes on top and its complicated bass beneath, then grew up! Each played his own tune, fiddle, flute, trumpet, drum or whatever the instrument might be. With Neville, 'Let's discuss Hamlet.' With Louis, science. With Jinny, love. Then suddenly, in a moment of exasperation, off to Cumberland with a quiet man for a whole week in an inn, with the rain running down the window-panes and nothing but mutton and mutton and again mutton for dinner. Yet that week remains a solid stone in the welter of unrecorded sensation. It was then we played dominoes; then we quarrelled about tough mutton. Then we walked on the fell. And a little girl, peeping round the door, gave me that letter, written on blue paper, in which I learnt that the girl who had made me Byron was to marry a squire. A man in gaiters, a man with a whip, a man who made speeches about fat oxen at dinner—I exclaimed derisively and looked at the racing clouds, and felt my own failure; my desire to be free; to escape; to be bound; to make an end; to continue; to be Louis; to be myself; and walked out in my mackintosh alone, and felt grumpy under the eternal hills and not in the least sublime; and came home and blamed the meat and packed and so back again to the welter; to the torture.

"Nevertheless, life is pleasant, life is tolerable. Tuesday follows Monday; then comes Wednesday. The mind grows rings; the identity becomes robust; pain is absorbed in growth. Opening and shutting, shutting and opening, with increasing hum and sturdiness, the haste and fever of youth are drawn into service until the whole being seems to expand in and out like the main-spring of a clock. How fast the stream flows from January to December! We are swept on by the torrent of things grown so familiar that they cast no shadow. We float, we float. . . .

"However, since one must leap (to tell you this story) I leap, here, at this point, and alight now upon some perfectly commonplace object—say the poker and tongs, as I saw them sometime later, after that lady who had made me Byron had married, under the light of one whom I will call the third Miss Jones. She is the girl who wears a certain dress expecting one at dinner, who picks a certain rose, who makes one feel 'Steady, steady, this is a matter of some importance,' as one shaves. Then one asks, 'How does she behave to children?' One observes that she is a little clumsy with her umbrella; but minded when the mole was caught in the trap; and finally, would not make the loaf at breakfast (I was thinking of the interminable breakfasts of married life as I shaved) altogether prosaic—it would not sur-prise one sitting opposite this girl to see a dragon-fly perched on the loaf at breakfast. Also she inspired me with a desire to rise in the world; also she made me look with curiosity at the hitherto repulsive faces of new-born babies. And the little fierce beat—tick-tack, tick-tack—of the pulse of one's mind took on a more majestic rhythm. I roamed down Oxford Street. We are the continuers, we are the inheritors, I said, thinking of my sons and daughters; and if the feeling is so grandiose as to be absurd and one conceals it by jumping on to a bus or buying the eve-ning paper, it is still a curious element in the ardour with which one laces up one's boots, with which one now addresses old friends committed to different careers. Louis, the attic dweller; Rhoda, the nymph of the fountain always wet, both contra-dicted what was then so positive to me; both gave the other side

of what seemed to me so evident (that we marry, that we do-
mesticate); for which I loved them, pitied them, and also deeply
envied them their different lot.

"Once I had a biographer, dead long since, but if he still
followed my footsteps with his old flattering intensity he would
here say, 'About this time Bernard married and bought a
house.... His friends observed in him a growing tendency to
domesticity.... The birth of children made it highly desirable
that he should augment his income.' That is the biographic style,
and it does to tack together torn bits of stuff, stuff with raw
edges. After all, one cannot find fault with the biographic style
if one begins letters 'Dear Sir,' ends them 'yours faithfully'; one
cannot despise these phrases laid like Roman roads across the
tumult of our lives, since they compel us to walk in step like
civilised people with the slow and measured tread of policemen
though one may be humming any nonsense under one's breath
at the same time—'Hark, hark, the dogs do bark,' 'Come away,
come away, death,' 'Let me not to the marriage of true minds,'
and so on. 'He attained some success in his profession.... He
inherited a small sum of money from an uncle'—that is how the
biographer continues and if one wears trousers and hitches
them up with braces, one has to say that though it is tempting
now and then to go blackberrying; tempting to play ducks and
drakes with all these phrases. But one has to say that.

"I became, I mean, a certain kind of man, scoring my path
across life as one treads a path across the fields. My boots became worn a little on the left side. When I came in, certain re-
arrangements took place. 'Here's Bernard!' How differently
different people say that! There are many rooms—many
Bernards. There was the charming, but weak; the strong, but
supercilious; the brilliant, but remorseless; the very good fellow,
but, I make no doubt, the awful bore; the sympathetic, but cold;

the shabby, but—go into the next room—the foppish, worldly, and too well dressed. What I was to myself was different; was none of these. I am inclined to pin myself down most firmly there before the loaf at breakfast with my wife, who being now entirely my wife and not at all the girl who wore when she hoped to meet me a certain rose, gave me that feeling of exist-ing in the midst of unconsciousness such as the tree-frog must have couched on the right shade of green leaf. 'Pass' . . . I would say. 'Milk' . . . she might answer, or 'Mary's coming' . . .—simple words for those who have inherited the spoils of all the ages but not as said then, day after day, in the full tide of life, when one feels complete, entire, at breakfast. Muscles, nerves, intestines, blood-vessels, all that makes the coil and spring of our being, the unconscious hum of the engine, as well as the dart and flicker of the tongue, functioned superbly. Opening, shutting; shutting, opening; eating, drinking; sometimes speaking—the whole mechanism seemed to expand, to contract, like the main-spring of a clock. Toast and butter, coffee and bacon, the *Times* and letters—suddenly the telephone rang with urgency and I rose deliberately and went to the telephone. I took up the black mouth. I marked the ease with which my mind adjusted itself to assimilate the message—it might be (one has these fancies) to assume command of the British Empire; I observed my com-posure; I remarked with what magnificent vitality the atoms of my attention dispersed, swarmed round the interruption, assim-ilated the message, adapted themselves to a new state of affairs and had created, by the time I put back the receiver, a richer, a stronger, a more complicated world in which I was called upon to act my part and had no doubt whatever that I could do it. Clapping my hat on my head, I strode into a world inhabited by vast numbers of men who had also clapped their hats on their heads, and as we jostled and encountered in trains and tubes we exchanged the knowing wink of competitors and comrades braced with a thousand snares and dodges to achieve the same end—to earn our livings.

"Life is pleasant. Life is good. The mere process of life is satisfactory. Take the ordinary man in good health. He likes eating and sleeping. He likes the snuff of fresh air and walking at a brisk pace down the Strand. Or in the country there's a cock crowing on a gate; there's a foal galloping round a field. Something always has to be done next. Tuesday follows Monday; Wednesday Tuesday. Each spreads the same ripple of well-being, repeats the same curve of rhythm; covers fresh sand with a chill or ebbs a little slackly without. So the being grows rings; identity becomes robust. What was fiery and furtive like a fling of grain cast into the air and blown hither and thither by wild gusts of life from every quarter is now methodical and orderly and flung with a purpose—so it seems.

"Lord, how pleasant! Lord, how good! How tolerable is the life of little shopkeepers, I would say, as the train drew through the suburbs and one saw lights in bedroom windows. Active, energetic as a swarm of ants, I said, as I stood at the window and watched workers, bag in hand, stream into town. What hardness, what energy and violence of limb, I thought, seeing men in white drawers scouring after a football on a patch of snow in January. Now being grumpy about some small matter—it might be the meat—it seemed luxurious to disturb with a little ripple the enormous stability, whose quiver, for our child was about to be born, increased its joy, of our married life. I snapped at dinner. I spoke unreasonably as if, being a millionaire, I could throw away five shillings; or, being a perfect steeple-jack, stumbled over a footstool on purpose. Going up to bed we settled our quarrel on the stairs, and standing by the window looking at a sky clear like the inside of a blue stone, 'Heaven be praised,' I said, 'we need not whip this prose into poetry. The little language is enough.' For the space of the prospect and its clarity seemed to offer no impediment whatsoever, but to allow our lives to spread out and out beyond all bristling of roofs and chimneys to the flawless verge.

"Into this crashed death—Percival's. 'Which is happiness?' I said (our child had been born), 'which pain?' referring to the two sides of my body, as I came downstairs, making a purely physical statement. Also I made note of the state of the house; the curtain blowing; the cook singing; the wardrobe showing through the half-opened door. I said, 'Give him (myself) another moment's respite,' as I went downstairs. 'Now in this drawing-room he is going to suffer. There is no escape.' But for pain words are lacking. There should be cries, cracks, fissures, whiteness passing over chintz covers, interference with the sense of time, of space; the sense also of extreme fixity in passing objects; and sounds very remote and then very close; flesh being gashed and blood spurting, a joint suddenly twisted—beneath all of which appears something very important, yet remote, to be just held in solitude. So I went out. I saw the first morning he would never see—the sparrows were like toys dangled from a string by a child. To see things without attachment, from the outside, and to realise their beauty in itself—how strange! And then the sense that a burden has been removed; pretence and make-believe and unreality are gone, and lightness has come with a kind of transparency, making oneself invisible and things seen through as one walks—how strange. 'And now what other discovery will there be?' I said, and in order to hold it tight ignored newspaper placards and went and looked at pictures. Madonnas and pillars, arches and orange trees, still as on the first day of creation, but acquainted with grief, there they hung, and I gazed at them. 'Here,' I said, 'we are together without interruption.' This freedom, this immunity, seemed then a conquest, and stirred in me such exaltation that I sometimes go

there, even now, to bring back exaltation and Percival. But it did
not last. What torments one is the horrible activity of the mind's
eye—how he fell, how he looked, where they carried him; men
in loin-cloths, pulling ropes; the bandages and the mud. Then
comes the terrible pounce of memory, not to be foretold, not
to be warded off—that I did not go with him to Hampton
Court. That claw scratched; that fang tore; I did not go. In spite
of his impatiently protesting that it did not matter; why interrupt, why spoil our moment of uninterrupted community?—
Still, I repeated sullenly, I did not go, and so, driven out of the
sanctuary by these officious devils, went to Jinny because she
had a room; a room with little tables, with little ornaments scattered on little tables. There I confessed, with tears—I had not
gone to Hampton Court. And she, remembering other things,
to me trifles but torturing to her, showed me how life withers
when there are things we cannot share. Soon, too, a maid came
in with a note and as she turned to answer it and I felt my own
curiosity to know what she was writing and to whom, I saw the
first leaf fall on his grave. I saw us push beyond this moment,
and leave it behind us for ever. And then sitting side by side on
the sofa we remembered inevitably what had been said by others; 'the lily of the day is fairer far in May'; we compared Percival to a lily—Percival whom I wanted to lose his hair, to shock
the authorities, to grow old with me; he was already covered
with lilies.

"So the sincerity of the moment passed; so it became sym-
bolical; and that I could not stand. Let us commit any blas-
phemy of laughter and criticism rather than exude this lily-sweet
glue; and cover him with phrases, I cried. Therefore I broke off,
and Jinny, who was without future, or speculation, but respected
the moment with complete integrity, gave her body a flick with
the whip, powdered her face (for which I loved her), and waved

to me as she stood on the doorstep, pressing her hand to her hair so that the wind might not disorder it, a gesture for which I honoured her, as if it confirmed our determination—not to let lilies grow.

"I observed with disillusioned clarity the despicable nonentity of the street; its porches; its window curtains; the drab clothes, the cupidity and complacency of shopping women; and old men taking the air in comforters; the caution of people crossing; the universal determination to go on living, when really, fools and gulls that you are, I said, any slate may fly from a roof, any car may swerve, for there is neither rhyme nor reason when a drunk man staggers about with a club in his hand—that is all. I was like one admitted behind the scenes: like one shown how the effects are produced. I returned, however, to my own snug home and was warned by the parlourmaid to creep upstairs in my stockings. The child was asleep. I went to my room.

"Was there no sword, nothing with which to batter down these walls, this protection, this begetting of children and living behind curtains, and becoming daily more involved and committed, with books and pictures? Better burn one's life out like Louis, desiring perfection; or like Rhoda leave us, flying past us, to the desert; or choose one out of millions and one only like Neville; better be like Susan and love and hate the heat of the sun or the frost-bitten grass; or be like Jinny, honest, an animal. All had their rapture; their common feeling with death; something that stood them in stead. Thus I visited each of my friends in turn, trying with fumbling fingers to prise open their locked caskets. I went from one to the other holding my sorrow—no, not my sorrow but the incomprehensible nature of this our life for their inspection. Some people go to priests; others to poetry; I to my friends, I to my own heart, I to seek among phrases and fragments something unbroken—I to whom there is not beauty enough in moon or tree; to whom the touch of one person with another is all, yet who cannot grasp even that, who am so imperfect, so weak, so unspeakably lonely. There I sat.

"Should this be the end of the story? a kind of sigh? a last ripple of the wave? A trickle of water in some gutter where, burbling, it dies away? Let me touch the table — so — and thus recover my sense of the moment. A sideboard covered with cruets; a basket full of rolls; a plate of bananas — these are comfortable sights. But if there are no stories, what end can there be, or what beginning? Life is not susceptible perhaps to the treatment we give it when we try to tell it. Sitting up late at night it seems strange not to have more control. Pigeon-holes are not then very useful. It is strange how force ebbs away and away into some dry creek. Sitting alone, it seems we are spent; our waters can only just surround feebly that spike of sea-holly; we cannot reach that further pebble so as to wet it. It is over, we are ended. But wait — I sat all night waiting — an impulse again runs through us; we rise, we toss back a mane of white spray; we pound on the shore; we are not to be confined. That is, I shaved and washed; did not wake my wife, and had breakfast; put on my hat, and went out to earn my living. After Monday, Tuesday comes.

"Yet some doubt remained, some note of interrogation. I was surprised, opening a door, to find people thus occupied; I hesitated, taking a cup of tea, whether one said milk or sugar. And the light of the stars falling, as it falls now, on my hand after travelling for millions upon millions of years — I could get a cold shock from that for a moment — not more, my imagination is too feeble. But some doubt remained. A shadow flitted through my mind like moths' wings among chairs and tables in a room in the evening. When, for example, I went to Lincolnshire that summer to see Susan and she advanced towards me across the garden with the lazy movement of a half-filled sail,

with the swaying movement of a woman with child, I thought,
'It goes on; but why?' We sat in the garden; the farm carts came
up dripping with hay; there was the usual country gabble of
rooks and doves; fruit was netted and covered over; the gardener dug. Bees boomed down the purple tunnels of flowers;
bees embedded themselves on the golden shields of sunflowers.
Little twigs were blown across the grass. How rhythmical, and
half conscious and like something wrapped in mist it was; but
to me hateful, like a net folding one's limbs in its meshes,
cramping. She who had refused Percival lent herself to this, to
this covering over.

"Sitting down on a bank to wait for my train I thought then
how we surrender, how we submit to the stupidity of nature.
Woods covered in thick green leafage lay in front of me. And
by some flick of a scent or a sound on a nerve, the old image—
the gardeners sweeping, the lady writing—returned. I saw the
figures beneath the beech trees at Elvedon. The gardeners swept;
the lady at the table sat writing. But I now made the contribution of maturity to childhood's intuitions—satiety and doom;
the sense of what is unescapable in our lot; death; the knowledge of limitations; how life is more obdurate than one had
thought it. Then, when I was a child, the presence of an enemy
had asserted itself; the need for opposition had stung me. I had
jumped up and cried, 'Let's explore.' The horror of the situation
was ended.

"Now what situation was there to end? Dullness and doom.
And what to explore? The leaves and the wood concealed nothing. If a bird rose I should no longer make a poem—I should
repeat what I had said before. Thus if I had a stick with which
to point to indentations in the curve of being, this is the lowest;
here it coils useless on the mud where no tide comes—here,
where I sat with my back to a hedge, and my hat over my eyes,
while the sheep advanced remorselessly in that wooden way of

theirs, step by step on stiff, pointed legs. But if you hold a blunt blade to a grindstone long enough, something spurts—a jagged edge of fire; so held to lack of reason, aimlessness, the usual, all massed together, out spurted in one flame hatred, contempt. I took my mind, my being, the old dejected, almost inanimate object and lashed it about among these odds and ends, sticks and straws, detestable little bits of wreckage, flotsam and jetsam, floating on the oily surface. I jumped up, I said, 'Fight.' 'Fight,' I repeated. It is the effort and the struggle, it is the perpetual warfare, it is the shattering and piecing together—this is the daily battle, defeat or victory, the absorbing pursuit. The trees, scattered, put on order; the thick green of the leaves thinned itself to a dancing light. I netted them under with a sudden phrase. I retrieved them from formlessness with words.

"The train came in. Lengthening down the platform, the train came to a stop. I caught my train. And so back to London in the evening. How satisfactory, the atmosphere of common sense and tobacco; old women clambering into the third-class carriage with their baskets; the sucking at pipes; the good nights and see you tomorrows of friends parting at wayside stations, and then the lights of London—not the flaring ecstasy of youth, not that tattered violet banner, but still the lights of London all the same; hard, electric lights, high up in offices; street lamps laced along dry pavements; flares roaring above street markets. I like all this when I have dispatched the enemy for a moment.

"Also I like to find the pageant of existence roaring, in a theatre for instance. The clay-coloured, earthy nondescript animal of the field here erects himself and with infinite ingenuity and effort puts up a fight against the green woods and green fields and sheep advancing with measured tread, munching. And, of course, windows in the long grey streets were lit up; strips of carpet cut the pavement; there were swept and garnished rooms, fire, food, wine, talk. Men with withered hands, women with pearl pagodas hanging from their ears came in and went out. I saw old men's faces carved into wrinkles and sneers by the work of the world; beauty cherished so that it seemed newly sprung even in age; and youth so apt for pleasure that pleasure, one thought, must exist; it seemed that grass-lands must roll for it; and the sea be chopped up into little waves; and the woods rustle with bright-coloured birds for youth, for youth expectant. There one met Jinny and Hal, Tom, and Betty; there we had our jokes and shared our secrets; and never parted in the doorway without arranging to meet again in some other room as the occasion, as the time of the year, suggested. Life is pleasant; life is good; after Monday comes Tuesday, and Wednesday follows Tuesday.

"Yes, but after a time with a difference. It may be that something in the look of the room one night, in the arrangement of the chairs, suggests it. It seems comfortable to sink down on a sofa in a corner, to look, to listen. Then it happens that two figures standing with their backs to the window appear against the branches of a spreading tree. With a shock of emotion one feels, 'There are figures without features robed in beauty, doomed yet eternal.' In the pause that follows, while the ripples spread, the girl to whom one should be talking says to herself, 'He is old.' But she is wrong. It is not age; it is that a drop has fallen; another drop. Time has given the arrangement another shake. Out we creep from the arch of the currant leaves, out into a wider world. The true order of things—this is our perpetual illusion—is now apparent. Thus in a moment, in a drawing-room, our life adjusts itself to the majestic march of day across the sky.

"It was for this reason that instead of pulling on my patent-leather shoes and finding a tolerable tie, I sought Neville. I sought my oldest friend, who had known me when I was Byron; when I was Meredith's young man, and also that hero in a book by Dostoevsky whose name I have forgotten. I found him alone, reading. A perfectly neat table; a curtain pulled methodically straight; a paper-knife dividing a French volume—nobody, I thought, ever changes the attitude in which we saw them first, or the clothes. Here he has sat in this chair, in these clothes, ever since we first met. Here was freedom; here was intimacy; the firelight broke off some round apple on the curtain. There we talked; sat talking; sauntered down that avenue, the avenue which runs under the trees, under the thick-leaved murmuring trees, the trees that hung with fruit, which we have trodden so often together, so that now the turf is bare round some of those trees, round certain plays and poems, certain favourites of ours—the turf is trodden bare by our incessant unmethodical pacing. If I have to wait, I read; if I wake in the night, I feel along the shelf for a book. Swelling perpetually augmented, there is a vast accumulation of unrecorded matter in my head. Now and then I break off a lump, Shakespeare it may be, it may be some old woman called Peck; and say to myself, smoking a cigarette in bed, 'That's Shakespeare. That's Peck'—with a certainty of recognition and a shock of knowledge which is endlessly delightful, though not to be imparted. So we shared our Pecks, our Shakespeares; compared each other's versions; allowed each other's insight to set our own Peck or Shakespeare in a better light; and then sank into one of those silences which are now and again broken by a few words, as if a fin rose in the wastes of silence; and then the fin, the thought, sinks back into the depths spreading round it a little ripple of satisfaction, content.

"Yes, but suddenly one hears a clock tick. We who had been immersed in this world became aware of another. It is painful. It was Neville who changed our time. He who had been thinking with the unlimited time of the mind, which stretches in a flash from Shakespeare to ourselves, poked the fire and began to live by that other clock which marks the approach of a particular person. The wide and dignified sweep of his mind contracted. He became on the alert. I could feel him listening to sounds in the street. I noted how he touched a cushion. From the myriads of mankind and all time past he had chosen one person, one moment in particular. A sound was heard in the hall. What he was saying wavered in the air like an uneasy flame. I watched him disentangle one footstep from other footsteps; wait for some particular mark of identification and glance with the swiftness of a snake at the handle of the door. (Hence the astonishing acuteness of his perceptions; he has been trained always by one person.) So concentrated a passion shot out others like foreign matter from a still, sparkling fluid. I became aware of my own vague and cloudy nature full of sediment, full of doubt, full of phrases and notes to be made in pocket-books. The folds of the curtain became still, statuesque; the paper-weight on the table hardened; the threads on the curtain sparkled; everything became definite, external, a scene in which I had no part. I rose, therefore; I left him.

"Heavens! how they caught me as I left the room, the fangs of that old pain! the desire for some one not there. For whom? I did not know at first; then remembered Percival. I had not thought of him for months. Now to laugh with him, to laugh with him at Neville—that was what I wanted, to walk off arm-in-arm together laughing. But he was not there. The place was empty.

"It is strange how the dead leap out on us at street corners, or in dreams.

"This fitful gust blowing so sharp and cold upon me sent me that night across London to visit other friends, Rhoda and Louis, desiring company, certainty, contact. I wondered, as I mounted the stairs, what was their relationship? What did they say alone? I figured her awkward with the tea-kettle. She gazed over the slate roofs—the nymph of the fountain always wet, obsessed with visions, dreaming. She parted the curtain to look at the night. 'Away!' she said. 'The moor is dark beneath the moon' (I rang, I waited). Louis perhaps poured out milk in a saucer for the cat; Louis, whose bony hands shut like the sides of a dock closing themselves with a slow anguish of effort upon an enormous tumult of waters, who knew what has been said by the Egyptian, the Indian, by men with high cheek-bones and solitaries in hair shirts. I knocked: I waited; there was no answer. I tramped down the stone stairs again. Our friends—how distant, how mute, how seldom visited and little known. And I, too, am dim to my friends and unknown; a phantom, sometimes seen, often not. Life is a dream surely. Our flame, the will-o'-the-wisp that dances in a few eyes is soon to be blown out and all will fade. I recalled my friends. I thought of Susan. She had bought fields; cucumbers and tomatoes ripened in her hot-houses. The vine that had been killed by last year's frost was putting out a leaf or two. She walked heavily with her sons across her meadows. She went about the land attended by men in gaiters, pointing with her stick at a roof, at hedges, at walls fallen into disrepair. The pigeons followed her, waddling, for the grain that she let fall from her capable, earthy fingers. 'But I no longer rise at dawn,' she said. Then Jinny—entertaining, no doubt, some new young man. They reached the crisis of the usual conversation. The room would be darkened; chairs arranged. For she still sought the moment. Without illusions, hard and clear as crystal, she rode at the day with her breast bared. She let its spikes pierce her. When the lock whitened on her forehead she twisted it fearlessly among the rest. So when they come to bury her nothing will be out of order. Bits of ribbons will be found curled up. But still the door opens. Who is coming in? she asks, and rises to meet him, prepared, as on those first spring nights when the tree under the big London houses where respectable citizens were going soberly to bed scarcely sheltered her love; and the squeak of trams mixed with

her cry of delight and the rippling of leaves had to shade her lan-
guor, her delicious lassitude as she sank down cooled by all the
sweetness of nature satisfied. Our friends, how seldom visited,
how little known—it is true; and yet, when I meet an unknown
person, and try to break off, here at this table, what I call 'my
life,' it is not one life that I look back upon; I am not one person; I am many people; I do not altogether know who I am—
Jinny, Susan, Neville, Rhoda, or Louis: or how to distinguish my
life from theirs.

"So I thought that night in early autumn when we came together and dined once more at Hampton Court. Our discomfort
was at first considerable, for each by that time was committed to
a statement, and the other person coming along the road to the
meeting-place dressed like this or that, with a stick or without
seemed to contradict it. I saw Jinny look at Susan's earthy fingers
and then hide her own; I, considering Neville, so neat and exact,
felt the nebulosity of my own life blurred with all these phrases.
He then boasted, because he was ashamed of one room and one
person and his own success. Louis and Rhoda, the conspirators,
the spies at table, who take notes, felt, 'After all, Bernard can
make the waiter fetch us rolls—a contact denied us.' We saw for
a moment laid out among us the body of the complete human
being whom we have failed to be, but at the same time, cannot
forget. All that we might have been we saw; all that we had
missed, and we grudged for a moment the other's claim, as children when the cake is cut, the one cake, the only cake, watch
their slice diminishing.

"However, we had our bottle of wine, and under that seduction lost our enmity, and stopped comparing. And, half-way
through dinner, we felt enlarge itself round us the huge blackness of what is outside us, of what we are not. The wind, the
rush of wheels became the roar of time, and we rushed—
where? And who were we? We were extinguished for a moment,

went out like sparks in burnt paper and the blackness roared. Past time, past history we went. For me this lasts but one second. It is ended by my own pugnacity. I strike the table with a spoon. If I could measure things with compasses I would, but since my only measure is a phrase, I make phrases—I forget what, on this occasion. We became six people at a table in Hampton Court. We rose and walked together down the avenue. In the thin, the unreal twilight, fitfully like the echo of voices laughing down some alley, geniality returned to me and flesh. Against the gateway, against some cedar tree I saw blaze bright, Neville, Jinny, Rhoda, Louis, Susan and myself, our life, our identity. Still King William seemed an unreal monarch and his crown mere tinsel. But we—against the brick, against the branches, we six, out of how many million millions, for one moment out of what measureless abundance of past time and time to come, burnt there triumphant. The moment was all; the moment was enough. And then Neville, Jinny, Susan and I as a wave breaks, burst asunder, surrendered—to the next leaf, to the precise bird, to a child with a hoop, to a prancing dog, to the warmth that is hoarded in woods after a hot day, to the lights twisted like white ribbon on rippled waters. We drew apart; we were consumed in the darkness of the trees leaving Rhoda and Louis to stand on the terrace by the urn.

"When we returned from that immersion—how sweet, how deep!—and came to the surface and saw the conspirators still standing there it was with some compunction. We had lost what they had kept. We interrupted. But we were tired, and whether it had been good or bad, accomplished or left undone, the dusky veil was falling upon our endeavours; the lights were sinking as we paused for a moment upon the terrace that overlooks the river. The steamers were landing their trippers on the bank; there was a distant cheering, the sound of singing, as if people waved their hats and joined in some last song. The sound of the chorus came across the water and I felt leap up that old impulse, which has moved me all my life, to be thrown up and down on the roar of other people's voices, singing the same song; to be tossed up and down on the roar of almost senseless merriment, sentiment, triumph, desire. But not now. No! I could not collect myself; I could not distinguish myself; I could not help letting fall the things that had made me a minute ago eager, amused, jealous, vigilant and hosts of other things into the water. I could not recover myself from that endless throwing away, dissipation, flooding forth without our willing it and rushing soundlessly away out there under the arches of the bridge, round some clump of trees or an island, out where sea-birds sit on stakes, over the roughened water to become waves in the sea—I could not recover myself from that dissipation. So we parted.

"Was this then, this streaming away mixed with Susan, Jinny, Neville, Rhoda, Louis, a sort of death? A new assembly of elements? Some hint of what was to come? The note was scribbled, the book shut, for I am an intermittent student. I do not say my lessons by any means at the stated hour. Later, walking down Fleet Street at the rush hour, I recalled that moment; I continued it. 'Must I for ever,' I said, 'beat my spoon on the tablecloth? Shall I not, too, consent?' The omnibuses were clogged; one came up behind another and stopped with a click, like a link added to a stone chain. People passed.

"Multitudinous, carrying attaché-cases, dodging with incredible celerity in and out, they went past like a river in spate. They went past roaring like a train in a tunnel. Seizing my chance I crossed; dived down a dark passage and entered the shop where they cut my hair. I leant my head back and was swathed in a sheet. Looking-glasses confronted me in which I could see my pinioned body and people passing; stopping, looking, and going on indifferent. The hairdresser began to move his scissors to and fro. I felt myself powerless to stop the oscillations of the cold steel. So we are cut and laid in swathes, I said; so we lie side by side on the damp meadows, withered branches and flowering. We have no more to expose ourselves on the bare hedges to the wind and snow; no more to carry ourselves erect when the gale sweeps, to bear our burden upheld; or stay, unmurmuring, on those pallid noondays when the bird creeps close to the bough and the damp whitens the leaf. We are cut, we are fallen. We are become part of that unfeeling universe that sleeps when we are at our quickest and burns red when we lie asleep. We have renounced our station and lie now flat, withered and how soon forgotten! Upon which I saw an expression in the tail of the eye of the hairdresser as if something interested him in the street.

"What interested the hairdresser? What did the hairdresser see in the street? It is thus that I am recalled. (For I am no mystic; something always plucks at me — curiosity, envy, admiration, interest in hairdressers and the like bring me to the surface.) While he brushed the fluff from my coat I took pains to assure myself of his identity and then, swinging my stick, I went into the Strand, and evoked to serve as opposite to myself the figure of Rhoda always so furtive, always with fear in her eyes, always seeking some pillar in the desert, to find which she had gone; she had killed herself. 'Wait,' I said, putting my arm in imagination (thus we consort with our friends) through her arm. 'Wait until these omnibuses have gone by. Do not cross so dangerously. These men are your brothers.' In persuading her I was also persuading my own soul. For this is not one life; nor do I always know if I am man or woman, Bernard or Neville, Louis, Susan, Jinny or Rhoda — so strange is the contact of one with another.

"Swinging my stick, with my hair newly cut and the nape of my neck tingling, I went past all those trays of penny toys imported from Germany that men hold out in the street by St. Paul's — St. Paul's, the brooding hen with spread wings from

whose shelter run omnibuses and streams of men and women
at the rush hour. I thought how Louis would mount those steps
in his neat suit with his cane in his hand and his angular, rather
detached gait. With his Australian accent ('My father, a banker
at Brisbane') he would come, I thought, with greater respect to
these old ceremonies than I do, who have heard the same lul-
labies for a thousand years. I am always impressed, as I enter, by
the rubbed noses; the polished brasses; the flapping and the
chanting, while one boy's voice wails round the dome like some
lost and wandering dove. The recumbency and the peace of the
dead impress me—warriors at rest under their old banners.
Then I scoff at the floridity and absurdity of some scrolloping
tomb; and the trumpets and the victories and the coats of arms
and the certainty, so sonorously repeated, of resurrection, of
eternal life. My wandering and inquisitive eye then shows me an
awe-stricken child; a shuffling pensioner; or the obeisances of
tired shop-girls burdened with heaven knows what strife in their
poor thin breasts come to solace themselves in the rush hour. I
stray and look and wonder and sometimes, rather furtively, try
to rise on the shaft of somebody else's prayer into the dome,
out, beyond, wherever they go. But then like the lost and wailing dove, I find myself failing, fluttering, descending and perch-
ing upon some curious gargoyle, some battered nose or absurd
tombstone, with humour, with wonder, and so again watch the
sightseers with their Baedekers shuffling past, while the boy's
voice soars in the dome and the organ now and then indulges
in a moment of elephantine triumph. How then, I asked, would
Louis roof us all in? How would he confine us, make us one,
with his red ink, with his very fine nib? The voice petered out
in the dome, wailing.

"So into the street again, swinging my stick, looking at wire
trays in stationers' shop-windows, at baskets of fruit grown in
the colonies, murmuring Pillicock sat on Pillicock's hill, or Hark,

hark, the dogs do bark, or The World's great age begins anew, or Come away, come away, death—mingling nonsense and poetry, floating in the stream. Something always has to be done next. Tuesday follows Monday; Wednesday, Tuesday. Each spreads the same ripple. The being grows rings, like a tree. Like a tree, leaves fall.

"For one day as I leant over a gate that led into a field, the rhythm stopped: the rhymes and the hummings, the nonsense and the poetry. A space was cleared in my mind. I saw through the thick leaves of habit. Leaning over the gate I regretted so much litter, so much unaccomplishment and separation, for one cannot cross London to see a friend, life being so full of engagements; nor take ship to India and see a naked man spearing fish in blue water. I said life had been imperfect, an unfinished phrase. It had been impossible for me, taking snuff as I do from any bagman met in a train, to keep coherency—that sense of the generations, of women carrying red pitchers to the Nile, of the nightingale who sings among conquests and migrations. It had been too vast an undertaking, I said, and how can I go on lifting my foot perpetually to climb the stair? I addressed my self as one would speak to a companion with whom one is voyaging to the North Pole.

"I spoke to that self who had been with me in many tremendous adventures; the faithful man who sits over the fire when everybody has gone to bed, stirring the cinders with a poker; the man who has been so mysteriously and with sudden accretions of being built up, in a beech wood, sitting by a willow tree on a bank, leaning over a parapet at Hampton Court; the man who has collected himself in moments of emergency and banged his spoon on the table, saying, 'I will not consent.'

"This self now as I leant over the gate looking down over fields rolling in waves of colour beneath me made no answer. He threw up no opposition. He attempted no phrase. His fist did not form. I waited. I listened. Nothing came, nothing. I cried then with a sudden conviction of complete desertion, Now there is nothing. No fin breaks the waste of this immeasurable sea. Life has destroyed me. No echo comes when I speak, no varied words. This is more truly death than the death of friends, than the death of youth. I am the swathed figure in the hairdresser's shop taking up only so much space.

"The scene beneath me withered. It was like the eclipse when the sun went out and left the earth, flourishing in full summer foliage, withered, brittle, false. Also I saw on a winding road in a dust dance the groups we had made, how they came together, how they ate together, how they met in this room or that. I saw my own indefatigable busyness—how I had rushed from one to the other, fetched and carried, travelled and returned, joined this group and that, here kissed, here withdrawn; always kept hard at it by some extraordinary purpose with my nose to the ground like a dog on the scent; with an occasional toss of the head, an occasional cry of amazement, despair and then back again with my nose to the scent. What a litter—what a confusion; with here birth, here death; succulence and sweetness; effort and anguish; and myself always running hither and thither. Now it was done with. I had no more appetites to glut; no more stings in me with which to poison people; no more sharp teeth and clutching hands or desire to feel the pear and the grape and the sun beating down from the orchard wall.

"The woods had vanished; the earth was a waste of shadow. No sound broke the silence of the wintry landscape. No cock crowed; no smoke rose; no train moved. A man without a self, I said. A heavy body leaning on a gate. A dead man. With dispassionate despair, with entire disillusionment I surveyed the dust dance; my life, my friends' lives, and those fabulous presences, men with brooms, women writing, the willow tree by the river—clouds and phantoms made of dust too, of dust that changed, as clouds lose and gain and take gold or red and lose their summits and billow this way and that, mutable, vain. I, carrying a notebook, making phrases, had recorded merely changes; a shadow, I had been sedulous to take note of shadows. How can I proceed now, I said, without a self, weightless and visionless, through a world weightless, without illusion?

"The heaviness of my despondency thrust open the gate I leant on and pushed me, an elderly man, a heavy man with grey hair, through the colourless field, the empty field. No more to hear echoes, no more to see phantoms, to conjure up no opposition, but to walk always unshadowed making no impress upon the dead earth. If even there had been sheep munching, pushing one foot after another, or a bird, or a man driving a spade into the earth, had there been a bramble to trip me, or a ditch, damp with soaked leaves, into which to fall—but no, the melancholy path led along the level, to more wintriness, and pallor and the equal and uninteresting view of the same landscape.

"How then does light return to the world after the eclipse of the sun? Miraculously. Frailly. In thin stripes. It hangs like a glass cage. It is a hoop to be fractured by a tiny jar. There is a spark there. Next moment a flush of dun. Then a vapour as if earth were breathing in and out, once, twice, for the first time. Then under the dullness some one walks with a green light. Then off twists a white wraith. The woods throb blue and green, and gradually the fields drink in red, gold, brown. Suddenly a river snatches a blue light. The earth absorbs colour like a sponge, slowly drinking water. It puts on weight; rounds itself; hangs pendent; settles and swings beneath our feet.

"So the landscape returned to me; so I saw the fields rolling in waves of colour beneath me, but now with this difference; I saw but was not seen. I walked unshadowed; I came unheralded. From me had dropped the old cloak, the old response; the hollowed hand that beats back sounds. Thin, as a ghost, leaving no trace where I trod, perceiving merely, I walked alone in a new world, never trodden; brushing new flowers, unable to speak save in a child's words of one syllable; without shelter from phrases—I who have made so many; unattended, I who have always gone with my kind; solitary I who have always had some one to share the empty grate, or the cupboard with its hanging loop of gold.

"But how describe the world seen without a self? There are no words. Blue, red—even they distract, even they hide with thickness instead of letting the light through. How describe or say anything in articulate words again?—save that it fades, save that it undergoes a gradual transformation, becomes, even in the course of one short walk, habitual—this scene also. Blindness returns as one moves and one leaf repeats another. Loveliness returns as one looks with all its train of phantom phrases. One breathes in and out substantial breath; down in the valley the train draws across the fields lop-eared with smoke.

"But for a moment I had sat on the turf somewhere high above the flow of the sea and the sounds of the woods, had seen the house, the garden, and the waves breaking. The old nurse who turns the pages of the picture-book had stopped and had said, 'Look. This is the truth.'

"So I was thinking as I came along Shaftesbury Avenue tonight. I was thinking of that page in the picture-book. And when I met you in the place where one goes to hang up one's coat I said to myself, 'It does not matter whom I meet. All this little affair of "being" is over. Who this is I do not know; nor care; we will dine together.' So I hung up my coat, tapped you on the shoulder, and said, 'Sit with me.'

"Now the meal is finished; we are surrounded by peelings and bread-crumbs. I have tried to break off this bunch and hand it you; but whether there is substance or truth in it I do not know. Nor do I know exactly where we are. What city does that stretch of sky look down upon? Is it Paris, is it London where we sit or some southern city of pink-washed houses lying under cypresses, under high mountains, where eagles soar? I do not at this moment feel certain.

"I begin now to forget; I begin to doubt the fixity of tables, the reality of here and now, to tap my knuckles smartly upon the edges of apparently solid objects and say, 'Are you hard?' I have seen so many different things, have made so many different sentences. I have lost in the process of eating and drinking and rubbing my eyes along surfaces that thin, hard shell which cases the soul, which, in youth, shuts one in—hence the fierceness, and the tap, tap, tap of the remorseless beaks of the young. And now I ask, 'Who am I?' I have been talking of Bernard, Neville, Jinny, Susan, Rhoda and Louis. Am I all of them? Am I one and distinct? I do not know. We sat here together. But now Percival is dead, and Rhoda is dead; we are divided; we are not here. Yet I cannot find any obstacle separating us. There is no division between me and them. As I talked I felt, 'I am you.' This difference we make so much of, this identity we so feverishly cherish, was overcome. Yes, ever since old Mrs. Constable lifted her sponge and pouring warm water over me covered me with flesh I have been sensitive, percipient. Here on my brow is the blow I got when Percival fell. Here on the nape of my neck is the kiss Jinny gave Louis. My eyes fill with Susan's tears. I see far away, quivering like a gold thread, the pillar Rhoda saw, and feel the rush of the wind of her flight when she leapt.

"Thus when I come to shape here at this table between my hands the story of my life and set it before you as a complete thing, I have to recall things gone far, gone deep, sunk into this life or that and become part of it; dreams, too, things surrounding me, and the inmates, those old half-articulate ghosts who keep up their hauntings by day and night; who turn over in their sleep, who utter their confused cries, who put out their phantom fingers and clutch at me as I try to escape—shadows of people one might have been; unborn selves. There is the old brute, too, the savage, the hairy man who dabbles his fingers in ropes of entrails; and gobbles and belches; whose speech is guttural, visceral—well, he is here. He squats in me. Tonight he has been feasted on quails, salad, and sweetbread. He now holds a glass of fine old brandy in his paw. He brindles, purrs and shoots warm thrills all down my spine as I sip. It is true, he washes his hands before dinner, but they are still hairy. He buttons on trousers and waistcoats, but they contain the same organs. He jibs if I keep him waiting for dinner. He mops and mows perpetually pointing with his half-idiot gestures of greed and covetousness at what he desires. I assure you, I have great difficulty sometimes in controlling him. That man, the hairy, the ape-like, has contributed his part to my life. He has given a greener glow to green things, has held his torch with its red flames, its thick and smarting smoke, behind every leaf. He has lit up the cool garden even. He has brandished his torch in murky by-streets where girls suddenly seem to shine with a red and intoxicating translucency. Oh, he has tossed his torch high! He has led me wild dances!

"But no more. Now tonight, my body rises tier upon tier like some cool temple whose floor is strewn with carpets and murmurs rise and the altars stand smoking; but up above, here in my serene head, comes only fine gusts of melody, waves of incense, while the lost dove wails, and the banners tremble above tombs, and the dark airs of midnight shake trees outside the open windows. When I look down from this transcendency, how beautiful are even the crumbled relics of bread! What shapely spirals the peelings of pears make—how thin, and mottled like some sea-bird's egg. Even the forks laid straight side by side appear lucid, logical, exact; and the horns of the rolls which we have left are glazed, yellow-plated, hard. I could worship my hand even, with its fan of bones laced by blue mysterious veins and its astonishing look of aptness, suppleness and ability to curl softly or suddenly crush—its infinite sensibility.

"Immeasurably receptive, holding everything, trembling with fullness, yet clear, contained—so my being seems, now that desire urges it no more out and away; now that curiosity no longer dyes it a thousand colours. It lies deep, tideless, immune, now that he is dead, the man I called 'Bernard,' the man who kept a book in his pocket in which he made notes—phrases for the moon, notes of features; how people looked, turned, dropped their cigarette ends; under B, butterfly powder, under D, ways of naming death. But now let the door open, the glass door that is for ever turning on its hinges. Let a woman come, let a young man in evening-dress with a moustache sit down; is there anything that they can tell me? No! I know all that, too. And if she suddenly gets up and goes, 'My dear,' I say, 'you no longer make me look after you.' The shock of the falling wave which has sounded all my life, which woke me so that I saw the gold loop on the cupboard, no longer makes quiver what I hold.

"So now, taking upon me the mystery of things, I could go like a spy without leaving this place, without stirring from my chair. I can visit the remote verges of the desert lands where the savage sits by the camp-fire. Day rises; the girl lifts the watery fire-hearted jewels to her brow; the sun levels his beams straight at the sleeping house; the waves deepen their bars; they fling themselves on shore; back blows the spray; sweeping their waters they surround the boat and the sea-holly. The birds sing in chorus; deep tunnels run between the stalks of flowers; the house is whitened; the sleeper stretches; gradually all is astir. Light floods the room and drives shadow beyond shadow to where they hang in folds inscrutable. What does the central shadow hold? Something? Nothing? I do not know.

"Oh, but there is your face. I catch your eye. I, who had been thinking myself so vast, a temple, a church, a whole universe, unconfined and capable of being everywhere on the verge of things and here too, am now nothing but what you see — an elderly man, rather heavy, grey above the ears, who (I see myself in the glass) leans one elbow on the table, and holds in his left hand a glass of old brandy. That is the blow you have dealt me. I have walked bang into the pillar-box. I reel from side to side. I put my hands to my head. My hat is off — I have dropped my stick. I have made an awful ass of myself and am justly laughed at by any passer-by.

"Lord, how unutterably disgusting life is! What dirty tricks it plays us, one moment free; the next, this. Here we are among the breadcrumbs and the stained napkins again. That knife is already congealing with grease. Disorder, sordidity and corruption surround us. We have been taking into our mouths the bodies of dead birds. It is with these greasy crumbs, slobbered over napkins, and little corpses that we have to build. Always it begins again; always there is the enemy; eyes meeting ours; fingers twitching ours; the effort waiting. Call the waiter. Pay the bill. We must pull ourselves up out of our chairs. We must find our coats. We must go. Must, must, must — detestable word. Once more, I who had thought myself immune, who had said, 'Now I am rid of all that,' find that the wave has tumbled me over, head over heels, scattering my possessions, leaving me to collect, to assemble, to heap together, summon my forces, rise and confront the enemy.

"It is strange that we who are capable of so much suffering, should inflict so much suffering. Strange that the face of a person, whom I scarcely know save that I think we met once on the gangway of a ship bound for Africa — a mere adumbration of eyes, cheeks, nostrils — should have power to inflict this insult. You look, eat, smile, are bored, pleased, annoyed — that is all I know. Yet this shadow which has sat by me for an hour or two, this mask from which peep two eyes, has power to drive me back, to pinion me down among all those other faces, to shut me in a hot room; to send me dashing like a moth from candle to candle.

"But wait. While they add up the bill behind the screen wait one moment. Now that I have reviled you for the blow that sent me staggering among peelings and crumblings and old scraps of meat, I will record in words of one syllable how also under your gaze with that compulsion on me I begin to perceive this, that and the other. The clock ticks; the woman sneezes; the waiter comes—there is a gradual coming together, running into one, acceleration and unification. Listen: a whistle sounds, wheels rush, the door creaks on its hinges. I regain the sense of the complexity and the reality and the struggle, for which I thank you. And with some pity, some envy and much good will, take your hand and bid you good night.

"Heaven be praised for solitude! I am alone now. That almost unknown person has gone, to catch some train, to take some cab, to go to some place or person whom I do not know. The face looking at me has gone. The pressure is removed. Here are empty coffee-cups. Here are chairs turned but nobody sits on them. Here are empty tables and nobody any more coming to dine at them tonight.

"Let me now raise my song of glory. Heaven be praised for solitude. Let me be alone. Let me cast and throw away this veil of being, this cloud that changes with the least breath, night and day, and all night and all day. While I sat here I have been changing. I have watched the sky change. I have seen clouds cover the stars, then free the stars, then cover the stars again. Now I look at their changing no more. Now no one sees me and I change no more. Heaven be praised for solitude that has removed the pressure of the eye, the solicitation of the body, and all need of lies and phrases.

"My book, stuffed with phrases, has dropped to the floor. It lies under the table to be swept up by the charwoman when she comes wearily at dawn looking for scraps of paper, old tram tickets, and here and there a note screwed into a ball and left with the litter to be swept up. What is the phrase for the moon? And the phrase for love? By what name are we to call death? I do not know. I need a little language such as lovers use, words of one syllable such as children speak when they come into the room and find their mother sewing and pick up some scrap of bright wool, a feather, or a shred of chintz. I need a howl; a cry. When the storm crosses the marsh and sweeps over me where I lie in the ditch unregarded I need no words. Nothing neat. Nothing that comes down with all its feet on the floor. None of those resonances and lovely echoes that break and chime from nerve to nerve in our breasts making wild music, false phrases. I have done with phrases.

"How much better is silence; the coffee-cup, the table. How much better to sit by myself like the solitary sea-bird that opens its wings on the stake. Let me sit here for ever with bare things, this coffee-cup, this knife, this fork, things in themselves, myself being myself. Do not come and worry me with your hints that it is time to shut the shop and be gone. I would willingly give all my money that you should not disturb me but will let me sit on and on, silent, alone.

"But now the head waiter, who has finished his own meal, appears and frowns; he takes his muffler from his pocket and ostentatiously makes ready to go. They must go; must put up the shutters, most fold the tablecloths, and give one brush with a wet mop under the tables.

"Curse you then. However beat and done with it all I am, I must haul myself up, and find the particular coat that belongs to me; must push my arms into the sleeves; must muffle myself up against the night air and be off. I, I, I, tired as I am, spent as I am, and almost worn out with all this rubbing of my nose along the surfaces of things, even I, an elderly man who is getting rather heavy and dislikes exertion must take myself off and catch some last train.

"Again I see before me the usual street. The canopy of civilisation is burnt out. The sky is dark as polished whale-bone. But there is a kindling in the sky whether of lamplight or of dawn. There is a stir of some sort—sparrows on plane trees somewhere chirping. There is a sense of the break of day. I will not call it dawn. What is dawn in the city to an elderly man standing in the street looking up rather dizzily at the sky? Dawn is some sort of whitening of the sky; some sort of renewal. Another day; another Friday; another twentieth of March, January, or September. Another general awakening. The stars draw back and are extinguished. The bars deepen themselves between the waves. The film of mist thickens on the fields. A redness gathers on the roses, even on the pale rose that hangs by the bedroom window. A bird chirps. Cottagers light their early candles. Yes, this is the eternal renewal, the incessant rise and fall and fall and rise again.

"And in me too the wave rises. It swells; it arches its back. I am aware once more of a new desire, something rising beneath me like the proud horse whose rider first spurs and then pulls him back. What enemy do we now perceive advancing against us, you whom I ride now, as we stand pawing this stretch of pavement? It is death. Death is the enemy. It is death against whom I ride with my spear couched and my hair flying back like a young man's, like Percival's, when he galloped in India. I strike spurs into my horse. Against you I will fling myself, unvanquished and unyielding, O Death!"

The waves broke on the shore.

THE END

These notes refer to two other annotated editions of *The Waves*, published in England: *The Waves*, edited and with an introduction by Gillian Beer (Oxford: The World's Classics/Oxford University Press, 1992) ("Beer"); and *The Waves*, edited by James M. Haule and Philip H. Smith, Jr. (Oxford: Blackwell/Shakespeare Head, 1993) ("Haule and Smith"). Details of other works referred to are in the list of works cited, which follows the introduction, or in the suggestions for further reading.

The sun had not yet risen. The sea was indistinguishable from the sky . . .
   [3]   Compare with Genesis 1:1–2 (King James Version): "In the beginning God created the heaven and the earth / And the earth was without form, and void; and darkness was upon the face of the deep." For Woolf's use of creation myths, see the introduction, pages xli, xliii, li, lix. Beer suggests that Woolf also may have been influenced by *Light Arising: Thoughts on the Central Radiance* (Cambridge: W. Heffer, 1908), a meditative tract written by her Quaker aunt, Caroline Emelia Stephen. In the first draft of this novel, the unnamed female narrator claims authorship of her own creation myth: "I am telling myself the story of the world from the beginning. I am not concerned with the single life, but with lives together" (*The Waves: The Two Holograph Drafts* 6).

wave [3]   Woolf's use of waves as a metaphor structuring the whole novel alludes especially to the complicated interplay among images of waves, the passage of time, and the arc of human life in Shakespeare's Sonnet 60. Here is the octave of this sonnet:

> Like as the waves make towards the pebbled shore,
> So do our minutes hasten to their end,
> Each changing place with that which goes before;
> In sequent toil all forwards do contend.
> Nativity, once in the main of light,
> Crawls to maturity, wherewith being crowned
> Crooked eclipses 'gainst his glory fight,
> And time that gave doth now his gift confound.

or as if the arm of a woman couched beneath the horizon . . . Then she raised . . . [3]   A characteristic use of simile that becomes an extended metaphor. The woman carrying a lamp is unusual in the Western literary tradition because this personification of the sun is female.

The blind stirred slightly [3]   In "A Sketch of the Past," Woolf wrote, "If life has a base that it stands upon, if it is a bowl that one fills and fills and fills — then my bowl without a doubt stands upon this memory. It is of lying half asleep, half awake, in bed in the nursery at St Ives. It is of hearing the waves breaking, one, two, one, two, and sending a splash of water over the beach; and then breaking, one, two, one, two, behind a yellow blind. It is of hearing the blind draw its little acorn across the floor as the wind blew the blind out. It is of lying and hearing this splash and seeing this light, and feeling, it is almost impossible that I should be here; of feeling the purest ecstasy I can conceive" (64–65).

"I see a ring" . . . "I hear something stamping" . . . [4]   The six characters, here young children in elementary school, are introduced with present-tense "speeches" reporting on immediate sense impressions. Despite the simplicity of the observations, the

senses of sight or sound, and the figures of speech—Bernard's ring, Neville's globe, Louis's "great beast's foot"—all in some respects indicate individual qualities of the speakers. Human life in *The Waves* begins with statements about the outside world. See the introduction, pages xliv–xlviii, for a discussion of the ways the six people who speak are represented.

Louis's "something stamping" and "beast's foot" are phrases in a motif that characterizes this speaker, who is associated with tradition, especially ancient history, and the impulse to pull together the disparate facts of the past.

Jinny [4]   Virginia Woolf's childhood nickname. See the introduction, pages xliv–lv, for a discussion of the characters and their sources.

Mrs. Constable [5]   The children's caregiver.

Biddy [5]   The cook at the school.

harlequins [6]   Brightly dressed clowns.

I am the stalk. [6]   Beer suggests that in hiding, Louis metamorphoses into a reed the way Daphne, in Ovid's *Metamorphoses,* turned into a tree.

My body is a stalk. . . . A drop oozes . . . [7]   A suggestion that Louis is masturbating to console and calm himself. Jinny's kiss is a violation of this privacy, prompting his extreme response: "All is shattered."

I love . . . and I hate. [9]   Susan's focused, obdurate personality is expressed in these lines, translations of Catullus's poem "Odi et amo"—"I hate and I love." In translation, the entire poem reads, "I hate and I love. Why I do so, perhaps you ask. I know not, but I feel it, and am in torment."

to which moths come [9]   "The Moths" was Woolf's original title for

The Waves, inspired by a letter written by her sister, Vanessa Bell, linking moths to the maternal and sexual instincts; see the introduction, pages liii–liv.

Elvedon [9]   Bernard reports that he saw this name on a signpost (10). He may seize upon it for his story because it combines "Elf" and "Eden." In "A Sketch of the Past," Woolf mentions a similar instance of imaginative childhood naming, a wood near the family's summer house in St. Ives that the Stephen children called Fairyland ("Sketch" 134). Virginia and her sister, Vanessa, spent part of a 1906 summer holiday in Suffolk, close to a house called Elveden (note the slightly different spelling). This house was presented to the Maharajah Duleep Singh by the British government as compensation for the annexation of the Punjab, and thus constitutes one of the subtle reminders of British imperial activities running through the text (Briggs 247).

The lady sits between the two long windows, writing. [10]   In the first draft of the novel, the two children see a lady writing a letter: "writing to her lover or sailor son" (*Holograph Drafts* 16). Haule and Smith associate her with Mrs. Ramsay, "that woman sitting there, writing under a rock" (Haule and Smith 196), and Mark Hussey notes that another "lady writing" is Betty Flanders at the opening of *Jacob's Room.* But many critics see the writer figured in Bernard's embedded story as an image of the woman novelist, most obviously Woolf herself (see, for instance, DiBattista 159–60, Briggs 247).

stoats [10]   Ermine, especially when their coats are brown. Like jays, they are nailed to barn doors or sides to frighten away other would-be predators.

Sweet Alice [11]   Sweet alyssum, a small herb with four-petaled white flowers.

One sails alone. That is my ship. [11]   Beer notes that while Woolf was finishing the composition of *The Waves,* she wrote of seeing a crashed plane in which three men were killed: "But we went on, reminding me of that epitaph in the Greek anthology: when I sank, the other ships sailed on" (January 26, 1931, *Diary* 4: 7).

islands where the parrots chatter . . . [11]   Rhoda's fantasy of these islands, apparently in the South Seas, is one of her motifs and reflects a preoccupation among Europeans of the late nineteenth and early twentieth centuries. Other motifs, such as the large white pillars and white figures, suggest a Greek setting.

baize [12]   A thick feltlike cloth, often used on pool tables.

conjugate the verb [12]   In Latin, a language at this time still the mark of the "educated classes" who attended what the British call public (and Americans call private) schools. Latin was an effective class demarcation because it was part of the examination for the top administrative class of the British Civil Service until the end of World War II.

My father is a banker in Brisbane [12]   Louis has two reasons for his insecurity. First, his father is a banker, a businessman who earns money rather than a gentleman—he notes, "Bernard and Neville are the sons of gentlemen"—who "has" money, through land and/or other investments. Second, he is from Brisbane, Australia, then a British colony originally settled by convicts, and is thus considered inferior to natives of the mother country, England. Like T. S. Eliot, on whom he is modeled to some degree, Louis has an identifiable accent, although Eliot's accent was American rather than Australian.

Bernard softly lisping Latin [12]   In the approved British (as opposed to Continental) pronunciation of Latin, the "v" is always pronounced as "w," producing more of an Elmer Fudd effect than a lisp (e.g., the greeting *salve* is pronounced sal-way). On the European continent, Latin pronunciation tends to follow the pronunciation of contemporary Italian.

fulvous [13]   Tawny colored.

southernwood [14]   A bushy, fragrant shrub.

censers [14]   Vessels in which incense is burned; in religious services and processions, they are often on the end of a long chain and are swung to disperse the aroma.

Queen Alexandra [15]   Wife of Edward VII, King of England from 1901 to 1910.

an apple tree netted under [15]   Farmers still put nets over fruit trees to keep off birds and larger insects.

'death among the apple trees' for ever . . . [15]   Neville's experience draws on two early memories that Woolf recounts in "A Sketch of the Past." The first involved "some people called Valpy" who had stayed for a while at the family's summer home in St. Ives, on the Cornish coast. (The St. Ives house was the setting for Woolf's most autobiographical novel, *To the Lighthouse.*) Woolf wrote, "We were waiting at dinner one night, when somehow I overheard my father or my mother say that Mr. Valpy had killed himself. The next thing I remember is being in the garden at night and walking on the path by the apple tree. It seemed to me that the apple tree was connected with the horror of Mr. Valpy's suicide. I could not pass it. I stood there looking at the grey-green creases of the bark—it was a moonlit night—in a trance of horror. I seemed to be dragged down, hopelessly, into some pit of absolute despair from which I could not escape. My body seemed paralysed" ("Sketch" 71).

The second association of death with trees shares fewer details with Neville's experience but was even more traumatic for the young Virginia Stephen, originating in the period right after her older half sister Stella died: "I always see when I think of the months that followed her death a leafless bush, a skeleton bush, in the dark of a summer's night. . . . And the tree outside in the August summer half light was giving me . . . a symbol . . . of our sterile agony; was summing it all up" ("Sketch" 140–41).

calling ourselves little children [17]   The fourth verse of the popular hymn "Now the Day Is Over" begins, "Grant to little children / Visions bright of Thee" (*Hymns Ancient and Modern* 346; cited in Beer).

I sink, I fall [18]   Rhoda's cry seems to signal a hypnic jerk, a common physical phenomenon in which, just upon losing consciousness, the body twitches awake with an acute sensation of falling. Throughout *The Waves,* Rhoda is associated with the poetry of Percy Bysshe Shelley. In Shelley's *Epipsychidion,* the poetic speaker laments his inability to use language in the paradoxical effort to rise above language:

> Woe is me!
> The winged words on which my soul would pierce
> Into the height of Love's rare Universe,
> Are chains of lead round its flight of fire—
> I pant, I sink, I tremble, I expire! (lines 587–91)

In a similar moment of impassioned self-description in one of Shelley's most famous poems, "Ode to the West Wind," the poetic speaker implores:

> Oh! lift me as a wave, a leaf, a cloud!
> I fall upon the thorns of life! I bleed! (lines 55–56)

sea-holly [19]   A plant with prickly leaves and thistle-like blue flowers, which grows by the seashore.

stoneless fruit [19]   Fruit without a pit.

knucklebones [20]   An ancient game, combining elements of dice and jacks, originally played with the knucklebones of a sheep.

the sonorous hexameters of Virgil; of Lucretius; and . . . the loves of Catullus [21]   Hexameters are six-foot poetic lines. Dactylic hexameters, with each foot having three syllables and a strong-weak-weak stress, are the most common form for Greek and Latin epic poetry. Vergilius Maro, called Virgil (70–19 B.C.), is most famous for his epic poem the *Aeneid,* which deals with the aftermath of the Trojan War and the founding of Rome. Lucretius (ca. 95–55 B.C.) wrote *De rerum natura,* or *On the Nature of Things,* an early scientific work. Love poems by Catullus (ca. 82–57 B.C.) were translated by Meredith, Byron, and Tennyson, three English poets named in *The Waves.* Study of these Latin authors would have been introduced in this public (i.e., private) school for young men and continued at Oxford and Cambridge. Virginia Woolf's own brothers went to the Clifton School in Bristol, which, like most such schools, until recently was dominated by Latin and Greek learning (Haule and Smith 197, Beer 250).

at the rocks [22]   The English edition reads "at the rooks." As rooks are birds, this makes better sense.

serge [22]   A durable fabric, usually wool, often used for uniforms.

Union Jack [23]   The British flag, combining the cross of Saint George, patron saint of England since 1270, the cross of Saint Andrew, patron saint of Scotland, and the cross of Saint Patrick, patron saint of Ireland. Being given this symbol of the mother country is especially humiliating to the colonial Louis.

memorial brasses [23]   Brass plaques on the walls and floors of the chapel commemorating dead students, faculty, or donors.

a white road shadowed by fig trees where boys sprawl in the dust—naked boys [24]   Neville here articulates an image of classical and pagan rather than Christian culture, a Greek or Italian landscape celebrating the body and especially male homoeroticism. Woolf visited Greece in 1906 with a group that included her brother Thoby Stephen, an extremely handsome young man who was the center of a group of admirers at Cambridge University and one source for the character Percival.

Percival [24]   Percival is a major character in many versions of the Arthur legend, notably Sir Thomas Malory's *Le Morte d'Arthur* (ca. 1469) and Alfred, Lord Tennyson's *Idylls of the King* (1859–85), where he is the virginal knight who succeeds in finding the Holy Grail, the cup that Christ drank from at the Last Supper and that received Christ's blood from the cross when he was speared in his side. Virginia Woolf was most evidently familiar with the version of the Percival story in Richard Wagner's opera *Parsifal,* which she saw twice within one week in 1909 at the Bayreuth Wagner Festival. In her review for the London *Times,* she described the opera as formally innovative, thwarting conventional expectations about plot and emphasis: "One feels vaguely for a crisis that never comes, for, accustomed as one is to find the explanation of a drama in the love of a man and woman, or in battle, one is bewildered by a music that continues with the utmost calm and intensity independently of them." She is acute about the overdetermined meaning of the Grail in Wagner's treatment: "Somehow Wagner has conveyed the desire of the Knights for the Grail in such a way that the intense emotion of human beings is combined with the unearthly nature of the things they seek. It tears, as we hear it, as though its wings were sharply edged." And she commends the "astonishing power" of the music to combine the very personal and the universal: "Its statements have all the majesty of a generalisation, and yet contain our private emotions" (*Essays* 1: 289, 291). She seems to have been after some of the same effects in *The Waves*.

In *Parsifal,* the innocent hero is a "holy fool" whose quest, associated with the Grail, can heal an ailing king. The story is basically the same as the ground story of T. S. Eliot's *The Waste Land,* which Woolf knew intimately, both because she was very close to Eliot during the period when he was writing it and because with Leonard Woolf she hand set the type for the Hogarth Press's 1923 edition.

minced the dance of the white butterflies . . . I shall enter my phrases. [24] The Stephen children caught and collected butterflies during the summer, especially in St. Ives, the seaside town in Cornwall that the first chapter of *The Waves* evokes. Bernard's habit of "phrase making" was to some extent Woolf's own, although her phrases occur in diary entries and letters, not a single, alphabetized notebook. In a letter of June 1908, for example, she described a landscape that particularly affected her and added, "This is what Adrian calls 'phrase making'" (*Letters* 1: 335). In "A Sketch of the Past," she wrote about a vision of flower and flower bed as a whole, and added, "It was a thought I put away as being likely to be very useful to me later" (71).

the Duke's birthday [25]   The Duke of York was Edward VII's second son, later George V, king from 1910 to 1936. He was born June 3, 1865.

cricket . . . pads . . . batsmen [25]   Cricket is a bat-and-ball game played with a flat willow paddle and a hard leather ball. It continues to be popular in Britain and its former colonies. When batting, a player wears long, heavy leg pads to protect shins and knees.

his slovenly accents [25]   Louis may be referring to Percival's pronunciation of Latin or to the distinctive speech mannerisms of the British aristocracy, which include dropping the -g in -ing words (fishin' and shootin') and using "ain't." In *The Voyage Out,* Woolf wrote sharply observant dialogue full of these mannerisms for the character Mrs. Wilfred Flushing.

winkles [25]   Also called periwinkles. A very small shellfish, one of several kinds that during the nineteenth and early twentieth centuries were sold ready-cooked from carts.

'Like a camel,' . . . 'a vulture' [26]   Neville's critical characterization of Bernard echoes the famous conversation in *Hamlet,* act 3, scene 2, where Polonius too readily agrees with Hamlet that a cloud is "like" any image Hamlet proposes:

HAMLET Do you see yonder cloud that's almost in shape of a camel?
POLONIUS By th' mass, and 'tis: like a camel, indeed.
HAMLET Methinks it is like a weasel.
POLONIUS It is backed like a weasel.
HAMLET Or like a whale.
POLONIUS Very like a whale.

midsummer [27]   In England the school year begins in September and ends in July.

We listen to missionaries from China. We drive off in brakes . . . [28]   A brake (also spelled *break*) is a large, open carriage. Although in the late nineteenth and early twentieth centuries only a small minority of upper- and upper-middle-class girls were sent to (expensive, fashionable) boarding schools like this one, apparently in East Anglia, their education was not substantively different from the education of the majority of girls who were taught at home. The religious and cultural experiences described here, along with sports like tennis, were intended to prepare women to bring up children, preside over tea tables, make intelligent conversation, and serve as companions to educated men in the various activities of private life.

stile [28]   An arrangement of steps allowing people, but not animals, to pass over a fence or wall.

the ugly, the encaustic tiles [28]   Encaustic tiles have colored patterns burned into them. *Encaustic* incorporates the word *caustic,* meaning something that burns or corrodes, so Susan's use of the technical name suggests further that the ugliness of the tiles actively damages perceivers.

fell [28]   Fierce, ruthless, destructive.

distempered [29]   Painted with a thin, often streaky, non-oil-based paint.

skirting [29]   Narrow board running along the base of an interior wall.

I often die pierced with arrows [30]   Rhoda imagines for herself the martyrdom suffered by Saint Sebastian (d. ca. A.D. 293), pictured in numerous paintings as a beautiful young man covered with bleeding wounds. By the late nineteenth century, Saint Sebastian had become an important symbol of homosexual passion within the Aesthetic movement. Because Virginia Woolf was close to T. S. Eliot during the writing of *The Waste Land* as well as because she set type for the British published version, she probably knew Eliot's homoerotic poem "The Love Song of St. Sebastian," deleted by Ezra Pound from the original *Waste Land* manuscript.

Scarborough [30]   Seaside town in North Yorkshire.

I hate looking-glasses which show me my real face [30]   In an important incident in "A Sketch of the Past," Woolf describes "the looking-glass shame" that "has lasted all my life," associated with her younger half brother's hands feeling under her clothes and underwear and a dream in which "I was looking in a glass when a horrible face—the face of an animal—suddenly showed over my shoulder" (68, 69).

sixpence [30]   A six-penny coin (similar in value to the U.S. nickel), in use in England from 1551 to 1967.

her vinous, her amethystine ring [31]   *Vinous* means "like wine," and *amethystine* refers to the purple or violet precious stone called amethyst, so that both adjectives describe the color of the stone in the headmistress Miss Lambert's ring. In putting these two Latinate words together, however, Woolf exploits secondary meanings: Whereas wine intoxicates, amethystine is a stone that in antiquity was supposed to prevent intoxication. The contradictory properties attach to Miss Lambert, who has a profound effect on Rhoda in this paragraph, making things become "luminous" but also associated with the softening and melting of her adolescent body. In "Sketch" Woolf refers to the opal ring on her mother's finger pointing at the text during lessons (117).

Smith's father made a century at Lords [32]   As a cricket batsman, Smith's father scored one hundred runs at Lord's Cricket Ground, St. John's Wood, London—home of the Marylebone Cricket Club, the England and Wales Cricket Board, and the International Cricket Council.

Pope, Dryden [33]   Alexander Pope, 1688–1744, and John Dryden, 1631–1700, English poets, dramatists, and critics, greatly admired by Woolf's close friend Lytton Strachey, a prototype of Neville. Beer suggests that because Dryden and Pope are technically brilliant, the implication is that Neville can imitate technique but cannot represent sincere feeling.

sock suspenders [34]   Also called sock garters. An elastic band fitting around the upper calf and supporting one or more clips, to hold up men's socks.

with my hand on the grained oak panel of Mr. Wickham's door [36] Louis's formative school experience visiting the office of the headmaster echoes the moment in a novel Woolf very much admired, James Joyce's *A Portrait of the Artist as a Young Man* (1916), when the young Stephen Dedalus goes to the room of the rector of Clongowes College (New York: Knopf, 1991: 55).

Richelieu, or the Duke of St. Simon . . . the King himself [36]   Armand Jean du Plessis, Cardinal Richelieu (1585–1642), was the chief minister to the French king Louis XIII. Louis de Rouvroy, the Duke of Saint-Simon (1675–1755), was an army officer, public official, and author of *Mémoires* of life under kings Louis XIV and Louis XV.

Virgil's companion, and Plato's [37]   Famous mentors, as well as poet and philosopher, respectively. In Dante Alighieri's *The Divine Comedy* (written 1306–21), Virgil (see the note to page 21) is a major character who guides the poet's persona through Hell, Purgatory, and Heaven. Plato's most important student was Aristotle. Like Louis, here, Virginia read Plato's dialogues when young; in her case, the *Republic* at the age of sixteen.

gaiters [37]   A covering of leather or cloth for the leg from knee to ankle.

moor [37]   Open, uncultivated land, usually high hills.

Russian Empress's veil . . . Imperial crown . . . hostile mob [39]   Although readers in 1931 might have been reminded of the Empress Alexandra Fyodorovna (1872–1918), who, during the 1917 revolution, was consort to the hated Russian emperor Nicholas II, Rhoda appears to be acting out her fantasy much earlier, at around the turn of the twentieth century. The Russian empress she is more likely to be invoking here is Catherine II (reigned 1762–96), known as Catherine the Great, who expanded the Russian empire and reinforced landowners' authority over their serfs.

green cowbind ... may .... Oh! to whom? [39–40]   Cowbind is a regional name for white bryony, a poisonous, vinelike plant with white blossoms that turn to red berries. It grows in leaves and hedges in southern and central England. May is mayflower, a name applied to cowslip or other spring-blooming wildflowers. Rhoda's monologue quotes from Percy Bysshe Shelley's 1822 poem "The Question," especially the third stanza:

> And in the warm hedge grew lush eglantine,
> Green cowbind and the moonlight-coloured may,
> And cherry-blossoms, and white cups, whose wine
> Was the bright dew, yet drained not by the day;
> And wild roses, and ivy serpentine,
> With its dark buds and leaves, wandering astray;
> And flowers azure, black, and streaked with gold,
> Fairer than any wakened eyes behold.

Having assembled the bouquet, the speaker asks "the question" in the closing lines:

> I hastened to the spot whence I had come,
> That I might there present it!—Oh! to whom?

I faint, I fail. [40]   This part of Rhoda's monologue echoes Shelley's "The Indian Serenade" (1822), which begins, "I arise from dreams of thee" and concludes:

> O lift me from the grass!
>   I die! I faint! I fail!
> Let thy love in kisses rain
>   On my lips and eyelids pale.

My cheek is cold and white, alas!
My heart beats loud and fast:
O press it to thine own again,
Where it will break at last!

Horace, Tennyson ... Keats and Matthew Arnold [40]   When they graduated, students who excelled at various academic subjects received as prizes books by various approved authors, with a handwritten message from the headmaster on the title page. The Latin poet Horace (Quintus Horatius Flaccus, ca. 65–17 B.C.), the Victorian poet Alfred, Lord Tennyson (1809–1892), the Romantic poet John Keats (1795–1821), and the Victorian poet and essayist Matthew Arnold (1822–1888) would have been recommended reading for students.

'quit ourselves like men' [40]   *Quit* here has the archaic meaning of to do one's part, bear oneself in a certain way. The biblical injunction has become a cliché, especially in formal ceremonies. Ironically, in its first biblical use, it is spoken by a Philistine leader beginning a battle against the Hebrews: "Be strong, and quit yourselves like men, O ye Philistines . . ." (I Samuel 4:9). A version of the phrase recurs in Paul's First Epistle to the Corinthians: "Watch ye, stand fast in the faith, quit you like men, be strong" (16:13).

Times [41]   The London *Times* newspaper.

billycock hat [42]   A round, low-crowned, soft hat.

elate [42]   Elated.

carbolic smell [43]   Carbolic acid, made from heavy coal oils, was a powerful disinfectant. In diluted form it was widely used in the nineteenth and early twentieth centuries as an institutional cleaning fluid.

matchboard [43]   A board with a tongue cut along one edge and a groove along the other edge, to fit with other boards: often a cheap form of planking for interior walls or floors.

gorse bushes [43]   Common name for several kinds of prickly, yellow-flowered shrub growing wild.

pitch-pine [44]   Common name for several kinds of pine tree with very resinous wood.

I came to the puddle. I could not cross it. Identity failed me. [45]   In "A Sketch of the Past," Woolf described her own childhood experience from the winter of 1894: "Again those moments of being. . . . There was the moment of the puddle in the path; when for no reason I could discover, everything suddenly became unreal; I was suspended; I could not step across the puddle; I tried to touch something . . . the whole world became unreal" (78; second ellipsis in original).

sudden as the springs of a tiger [45]   Rhoda's figure for "life" echoes in its disruptive force the tiger in T. S. Eliot's "Gerontion," who breaks into the seductions of "history": "The tiger springs in the new year. Us he devours" (line 48).

Oxford or Cambridge, to Edinburgh, Rome, Paris, Berlin [46]   European cities with famous, historic universities.

cockneys and clerks [47]   Native Londoners, usually those born "within sound of Bow [Church] Bells" in London's East End; thus by the mid-nineteenth century, working-class Londoners with a distinctive accent. As office staff performing routine jobs, clerks were the lowest rung of white-collar employees.

My book will certainly run to many volumes . . . [48]   Desmond Mac-Carthy, the Bloomsbury editor and critic who was one inspiration for the character of Bernard, spoke for years of writing a novel—or novels. Woolf wrote to Lytton Strachey in 1912 that MacCarthy planned to write "the story of [John] Donne's life. As the greater part of the history of England is somehow coming in, the book will be apoplectic." She went on to report on how prolific MacCarthy thought he would be: "'One volume and a half every year' he says—What'll the half volumes be d'you think?" (November 16, 1912, *Letters* 2: 12). Despite his friends' admiration of his storytelling abilities, MacCarthy, like Bernard, never managed to complete a novel.

stopped with gold [48]   Filled.

breasting the world with half-finished phrases [50]   *Breast* here has the archaic sense of applying or opposing oneself to. The most conventional use is probably "breasting the waves."

Sophocles and Euripides . . . with a high-minded wife, one of those University women [50]   Sophocles (ca. 496–406 B.C.) and Euripides (ca. 484–406 B.C.) were two of the three most famous Greek tragic dramatists (the third was Aeschylus, ca. 525–456 B.C.). Neville self-critically projects for himself the life not of a famous poet, but of a classical scholar at a major university. He plays on the idea of classical Greek as a "dead language," as well as on the fact that these poets died long ago, when he imagines feasting on the brains of these playwrights like a larva that feasts upon decaying matter. When he goes on to imagine himself with "a high-minded wife, one of those University women," he seems to be suggesting that an intellectual and stereotypically sexually repressed woman would make a suitable marriage of convenience with him, as he has made clear that he is homosexual.

finick [50]   To be concerned over unnecessary details or to affect airs.

gasometers [50]   Tanks in which natural gas is stored.

lovelily [52]   Beer suggests that Woolf alludes to Byron's "The Bride of Abydos," canto 1, stanza 3: "So lovelily the morning shone."

assegais [53]   Hardwood spears with iron points, used by the Bantu of southern Africa.

bran pie [54]   Originally a tub full of dry bran with gifts hidden in it; more recently, a container full of small gifts that children or guests reach into.

Who am I thinking of? Byron of course. [56]   In imitating the popular image of George Gordon, Lord Byron (1788–1824), Bernard picks up attitudes and phrases from several of Byron's poems. Haule and Smith note that the speaker of *Don Juan* gives us the general outlines of the character Bernard is playing: "I cannot stop to alter words once written" (canto 9, stanza 77); that the phrase "hot haste" occurs in *Childe Harold's Pilgrimage* (canto 3, stanza 25); and that "the hot, molten effect, the lava flow of sentence into sentence that I need" owes something to *The Giaour* speaker's description of his blood, which "was like the lava flood / That boils in Ætna's breast of flame" (canto 1, lines 1102–3).

Restover, King's Laughton, Station Langley [56]   Bernard has mixed together several English place-names in this fantasy of visiting "the girl with whom he is passionately in love" (55). Restover seems to be the name of the house. There is no village of King's Laughton, with Langley as the nearest train station, but there is a King's Langley in Hertfordshire and a Laughton in East Sussex, fairly near Rodmell, where the Woolfs lived.

A hunter's hoof on the writing-table [56]   Quentin Bell's biography tells of how on New Year's Eve 1906, Virginia and other family members stayed with Clive Bell's family in a house full of hunting and sporting trophies, including "an inkpot fashioned out of the hoof of a favorite hunter. The animal's name and the date of its death were inscribed upon a silver cartouche. She often adverted to that inkpot in later life: never, in her experience, had there been an inkpot like it; it seemed a note of the entire house" (Bell, *Virginia Woolf*, Vol. 1: 113 [New York: Harcourt, Brace and Company, 1972]) (Haule and Smith).

'Mrs. Moffat will come and sweep it all up—' [58]   One of Bernard's refrains (see also pages 96 and 135). Mrs. Moffat, cleaning woman for Bernard's college residence hall, becomes a recurring symbol for Bernard's privilege to make messes without having to deal with the consequences.

And so to bed. [58]   Samuel Pepys (1633–1703) often ended his diary entries with this phrase.

In a world which contains the present moment . . . why discriminate? [58] Haule and Smith suggest that Neville's meditation draws on Walter Pater's "Conclusion" to *The Renaissance* (3rd ed. 1888), which advocates that one should attend to particularities of sensation rather than generalize: "Not to discriminate every moment some passionate attitude in those about us, and in the very brilliancy of their gifts some tragic dividing on their ways, is, on this short day of frost and sun, to sleep before evening" (London and New York: Oxford University Press, 1986: 152).

Far away a bell tolls, but not for death. [58]   Echoes John Donne's Meditation 17: "Any man's death diminishes me, because I am involved in mankind; and therefore never send to know for whom the bell tolls; it tolls for thee."

cruets [58]   Small containers used at the table to hold vinegar or sauces.

oleographs [58]   Prints made to resemble oil paintings.

'the fountains of the pendent trees' [58] Neville seems to be quoting his own poem.

Gray's Elegy [60] Thomas Gray, "Elegy Written in a Country Churchyard" (1750).

Tolstoi's . . . Byron's . . . Meredith's young man [62] Beer suggests that Bernard may have been identifying with Levin in *Anna Karenina*, Byron's Childe Harold, and George Meredith's Richard Feverel (in *The Ordeal of Richard Feverel*, 1859).

ridiculous in Piccadilly [62] Neville plays with alliteration and assonance in this phrase, as well as with the uncharacteristic image of himself as bedraggled poet wandering one of the most fashionable streets in London.

some run with the beagles [64] A hunt for foxes or hares, conducted on foot rather than on horseback.

go to India [65] To serve in some part of the colonial government or military, a common career for ruling-class men.

I shall fail . . . imperfect phrases littered with sand [65] A prophetic utterance, both for Bernard and for Desmond MacCarthy (see the introduction, page l–li).

Worcester sauce [66] i.e., Worcestershire sauce, a spicy liquid, used in working-class restaurants to add flavor to bland food.

a tenner [66] A ten-pound note.

guillemots [67] Common black-and-white seabirds, members of the auk family.

Homburg hats and all the plumed and variegated head-dresses of women [68] Men's homburgs are stiff felt hats with a creased crown and a brim with the edge sharply turned up all the way around.

Women's hats decorated with the feathers of rare birds were fashionable during the first two decades of the twentieth century. A 1920 Plumage Bill, debated in Parliament, attributed the near-extinction of these birds to women's vanity, a point Woolf contested in an article in the *Woman's Leader,* where she pointed out that women were not the ones shooting the birds or making a profit from their death (*Essays* 3: 241–45).

with each stopping [68]   The English edition has "with earth stopping," which makes better sense.

I have yet heard rumours of wars; and the nightingale [68]   Louis's meditation touches on prominent themes of world history and Western literature. For instance, the first observation echoes the Gospel of Matthew 24:6: "You will hear of wars and rumors of wars," while the nightingale figures in the myth of Philomela and, more recently for Louis's poetic tradition, in Keats's "Ode to a Nightingale" (1819) and in T. S. Eliot's "Sweeney Among the Nightingales" (1920) and *The Waste Land* (1922).

tea-urn . . . eternity [68–69]   Beer points out a "lexical twist" here: The rearrangement of syllables makes a working-class serving-piece into a symbol of poetic timelessness.

The door opens; the tiger leaps. [75]   See the note to page 45.

A million arrows pierce me. [76]   See the note to page 30.

people without faces [77]   The paintings of Virginia Woolf's sister, Vanessa Bell, including a famous portrait of Virginia herself, frequently depict faceless people.

How fair, how strange [80]   Bernard's description of London alludes at several points to Wordsworth's 1802 sonnet "Upon Westminster Bridge."

Euston [80]   Railway station in north-central London.

barouche landau [83]   Horse-drawn carriage with a collapsible top.

frills and furbelows [83]   Set phrase for fancy or ostentatious ornaments. A furbelow is a gathered or pleated border of a skirt or petticoat, a flounce.

I see Louis, stone-carved . . . and Rhoda the nymph of the fountain always wet [84]   Bernard's aphoristic descriptions of his friends catch some, but not all, of the characteristics revealed by the individual speeches. He appears to compare Rhoda with Arethusa, a nymph who was pursued by the river god Alpheus and saved when Diana changed her into a fountain.

dropsical [84]   Swollen.

I who have no face [88]   See the note to page 77.

I am not single and entire as you are. I have lived a thousand lives already. [92]   In his 1919 essay "Tradition and the Individual Talent," T. S. Eliot wrote, "The historical sense compels a man to write not merely with his own generation in his bones, but with a feeling that the whole of the literature of Europe from Homer and within it the whole of the literature of his own country has a simultaneous existence and composes a simultaneous order" (*Selected Essays, 1917–1932* [New York: Harcourt, Brace and Company, 1932], 4).

the women with bad teeth, the church spire and the bobbing billycock hats [92] Eliot's 1922 poem *The Waste Land* contains a woman with bad teeth (lines 144–46), London churches (lines 67, 264), and moving crowds (lines 56, 62).

debased . . . by . . . maternity. [95]   See the introduction, pages liii–liv.

Thus my character . . . as yours are [96]   In 1919 Woolf wrote about her friend Desmond MacCarthy, "It goes without saying that he is not an heroic character. He finds pleasure too pleasant, cushions too soft, dallying too seductive, & then, as I sometimes feel now, he has ceased to be ambitious. His 'great work' (it may be philosophy or biography now, & is certainly to be begun, after a series of long walks, this very spring) only appears, I believe, in that hour between tea & dinner, when so many things appear not merely possible but achieved." But she added, "Yet it is true, & no one can deny it, that he has the floating elements of something brilliant, beautiful—some book of stories, reflections, studies, scattered about in him, for they show themselves indisputably in his talk" (February 18, 1919; *Diary* 1: 241).

buildings in some Oriental exhibition [98] In an article on the 1924 British Empire Exhibition, "Thunder at Wembley," Woolf satirizes the pretensions of empire by showing the forces of nature destroying models of buildings in the colonies: "Pagodas are dissolving in dust. Ferro-concrete is fallible. Colonies are perishing and dispersing in spray of inconceivable beauty and terror which some malignant power illuminates. Ash and violet are the colours of its decay" (*Essays* 3: 413).

betel [98] The nut of the betel or areca palm tree in south and central Asia. When chewed, it releases a mild central nervous system stimulant called arecoline.

The Oriental problem is solved. [98] Bernard's speech satirizes British imperial assumptions, although it can be debated whether Bernard himself is being satiric or whether Woolf satirizes Bernard's reverent attitude. Leonard Woolf's memories of being a colonial administrator in Ceylon (recorded in his 1961 memoir *Growing* and 1913 novel *The Village in the Jungle*), as well as E. M. Forster's 1924 novel *A Passage to India,* suggest the critical stance of Virginia Woolf and her Bloomsbury companions toward British imperialism. See the introduction, pages lviii–lxi.

When the white arm rests upon the knee it is a triangle . . . [100–1]　Like many of Rhoda's cherished images, this one seems vaguely Greek in its landscape as well as its evocation of monumental statuary. The abstracted human figures of Rhoda's fantasies bear some resemblance to paintings by Vanessa Bell, such as the stylized nudes of *Bather's Screen* (1913).

The flames of the festival rise high . . . *The great procession passes* [102]　Virginia Woolf was a student and friend of the anthropologist Jane Harrison, who described such ancient rituals in her *Prolegomena to the Study of Greek Religion* (1903). Woolf also had read Sir James Frazier's classic anthropological study of ritual sacrifice, *The Golden Bough* (1922).

We who are conspirators . . . *some cold urn* [102]　Rhoda places herself and Louis outside the "festival" celebrated by the others because of their broader sense that the moment tends always toward death. The image of the "cold urn," picked up later at a second gathering at Hampton Court (168), suggests the "Cold Pastoral" of the Grecian urn in Keats's famous ode (1819), which similarly depicts a ritual sacrifice.

the Hebrides [103]　Islands off the west coast of Scotland, setting for *To the Lighthouse.*

pillar-box [103]　A public mailbox shaped like a pillar.

cairns [107]　Rough mounds of stones used as monuments.

The lights of the world have gone out. [109]　Neville's phrase anticipates the famous observation of Lord Grey, the British foreign secretary, on the eve of World War I: "The lamps are going out all over Europe; we shall not see them lit again in our lifetime." As Mark Hussey has shown, the allusion occurs near the beginning of the "Time Passes" section of *To the Lighthouse* (annotated by Hussey 2005: 229–30). Lord Grey's comment seems ironically to refer to John 8:12, where Jesus says, "I am the light of the world." Both here and in *To the Lighthouse,* Woolf may also be alluding to Holman Hunt's famous painting *The Light of the World*; in the autobiographical essay "22 Hyde Park Gate," she describes her half brother George taking her to the artist's studio, where a copy was on display (176; see also Emily Dalgarno, *Virginia Woolf and the Visible World* [New York: Cambridge University Press, 2001], 112).

quoits [109]   A lawn or pub game in which rings are thrown over upright stakes.

and weep away a life of care [111]   Shelley's "Stanzas Written in Dejection Near Naples" (published 1824) contains the lines:

I could lie down like a tired child,
And weep away the life of care
Which I have born and yet must bear. (lines 30–32)

I will go up these steps into the gallery [112]   The National Gallery, in London's Trafalgar Square.

the blue madonna streaked with tears . . . Titian [113]   The tears here appear to be Bernard's, not part of the painting. The Madonna could be Titian's *The Virgin and Child with Saints,* which shows the Virgin Mary in her traditional blue gown. According to Haule and Smith, in 1930 the paintings by Titian (ca. 1480–1576) would have been in room VII, one of five Italian Rooms.

chained to the rock [113]   Like Prometheus, who was punished for giving fire to human beings by being chained to a boulder and having an eagle eat his liver.

Hampton Court [114]   Former royal palace with extensive gardens, located southwest of London on the River Thames. (See the note to page 168.)

Oxford Street [115]   Major shopping street in London, bordering on Bloomsbury. In the 1931 essay "Oxford Street Tide," Woolf noted, "The garishness and gaudiness of the great rolling ribbon of Oxford Street has its fascination," and called it "a breeding ground, a forcing house of sensation" (*Selected Essays, Volume 2: The Crowded Dance of Modern Life,* edited by Rachel Bowlby [London: Penguin, 1993], 112, 114). At this moment, however, Rhoda finds the crowds, colors, and noise brutalizing and humiliating.

I will pick violets and bind them together and offer them to Percival [115] Shelley's poem "The Question" (see the note to pages 39–40) mentions "pied wind-flowers and violets." The initially erotic question, "Oh! to whom?" is answered ironically here. Rhoda will present her flowers to Percival but only when, and because, he is dead. On page 116 she continues, "This is my tribute to Percival; withered violets, blackened violets."

To some museum . . . [116]   The Victoria and Albert Museum, on the Cromwell Road in South Kensington, which specializes in the decorative arts of Great Britain.

Here is a hall . . . [117]   Wigmore Hall, about two blocks north of Oxford Street.

'Like' and 'like' and 'like'— but what is the thing that lies beneath the semblance of the thing? [118]   In "A Sketch of the Past," Woolf wrote about "shocks," which were her most privileged moments of awareness, as "a revelation of some order . . . a token of some real thing behind appearances." To get at what Rhoda here calls "the thing that lies beneath the semblance of the thing," Woolf used the materials of art, in her case literature: "It is only by putting it into words that I make it whole; this wholeness means that it has lost its power to hurt me" ("Sketch" 72). After beginning a simile to her usual Greek landscape, Rhoda abandons her habitual iconography and uses visual, geometric language to

embody her revelation: "There is a square; there is an oblong. The players take the square and place it upon the oblong. They place it very accurately; they make a perfect dwelling-place" (118). Rhoda's geometrical figures, suggestive of cubist painting and other aesthetic attempts at rigorous abstraction, constitute a modernist dirge at the center of the novel.

Greenwich [118]   East of central London on the south bank of the River Thames, home of the Royal Observatory. Moving in the direction of the sea, Rhoda will walk to the embankment and "throw" into the Thames "my violets, my offering to Percival" (119).

Regent Street [118]   Rhoda's bus turns at the busy corner of Oxford Street known as Oxford Circus and goes south on Regent Street, with its upscale shops, past Piccadilly Circus to the small "mean streets" leading to the Thames wharfs.

shingle [120]   Small rounded pebbles on a seashore.

I have signed my name . . . already twenty times. I, and again I, and again I. [121]   Louis appears to be in international business; T. S. Eliot worked in the international division of Lloyds Bank. The repetition of Louis's "clear-cut and unequivocal" "I" recalls Woolf's skewering of hypermasculine contemporary writers in *A Room of One's Own* (annotated by Gubar 98).

Strand [121]   A major London thoroughfare linking Fleet Street to Trafalgar Square.

I am half in love with the typewriter and the telephone. [121]   An ironic play on Keats's famous line in "Ode to a Nightingale" (line 52): "I have been half in love with easeful Death."

Turkey carpet [122]   A Turkish or more generally Middle or Far Eastern carpet.

where Chatham stood, and Pitt, Burke, and Sir Robert Peel [122]   All
were members of Parliament; two—William Pitt the Younger
(1759–1806) and Sir Robert Peel (1788–1850)—were prime min-
isters. William Pitt the Elder, first Earl of Chatham (1708–1778),
was instrumental in making Great Britain into an imperial power,
while Edmund Burke (1729–1797) was an important conservative political theorist. Like Louis, all these men helped expand
the British empire.

feel within me uprush some wilder, darker violence [124]   Susan embodies the maternal instinct that Vanessa Bell urged her sister
to write about, "one of the worst of the passions, animal and remorseless" (*Selected Letters of Vanessa Bell*, May 3, 1927: 315). See
the introduction, page liv.

the city [127]   The City of London is the oldest part of London and
its financial center.

Jug, jug, jug, I sing like the nightingale [128]   From the Elizabethans onward, British poets have represented the song of the nightingale
as "jug jug." In Ovid's *Metamorphoses,* the nightingale is Philomela,
whose beautiful voice has its origins in rape and mutilation. In
"Poetry, Fiction and the Future," posthumously retitled "The
Narrow Bridge of Art," Woolf wrote about the "modern poet"
who embodies "some mocking spirit which sneers at beauty for
being beautiful," turning "the looking glass and show[ing] us that
the other side of her cheek is pitted and deformed"; this poet
"talks of the nightingale who sings 'jug jug' to dirty ears" (*Granite and Rainbow* 16). It was her friend T. S. Eliot who wrote that
line, incorporating the Philomela myth into *The Waste Land*:

> . . . yet there the nightingale
> Filled all the desert with inviolable voice
> And still she cried, and still the world pursues,
> "Jug Jug" to dirty ears. (lines 100–103)

Jinny's "Jug, jug" prompts a pursuit with "crash and rending of boughs and the crack of antlers," but the imagery is erotic and pleasurable when she says, "One has pierced me. One is driven deep within me."

St. Paul's [129]   In the "Abbeys and Cathedrals" segment of a six-part article "The London Scene," Woolf wrote, "St. Paul's dominates London. It swells like a great grey bubble from a distance; it looms over us, huge and menacing, as we approach" (*Selected Essays, Volume 2: The Crowded Dance of Modern Life*, edited by Rachel Bowlby [London: Penguin, 1993], 122).

a lion in Trafalgar Square [129]   There are stone lions at the base of Nelson's column, the extremely tall plinth that dominates Trafalgar Square in the heart of London.

bungalow [130]   Originally an Indian one-story dwelling.

Alcibiades, Ajax, Hector and Percival [131]   Neville compares his new lover to the Athenian general Alcibiades, disciple and beloved of Socrates; to Ajax, the Achaean hero of the Trojan War; to Hector, the most courageous of the Trojan warriors; and to the beloved, dead Percival.

as if a fin cut the green glass of a lake [132]   See the introduction, page xlix.

Sprays of flaxen-haired corn [132]   In England, *corn* is grain, usually wheat, rye, or barley.

as if a great moth [133]   "The Moths" was Woolf's original title for *The Waves*. See introduction pages liii–liv.

proboscis [135]   Long, flexible trunk or snout—of a moth, for instance. Bernard speaks of his limited curiosity, his curtailed tendency to poke into things.

thinking of his navel [135]   A popular Western orientalist belief was that Buddhist or Hindu mystics turned away from involvement in the world, preferring instead to concentrate on their own navels.

the Vedas [135]   Ancient Hindu sacred writings.

For many years I crooned complacently, 'My children . . . my wife . . .' [135]   Compare to Susan's maternal singing, page 124.

Are there stories? [136]   Bernard here begins to question the mode of narrative connection and causality that has governed his mode of living.

But why describe a man in trouble with his mule? [137]   A case in point for the question, "Are there stories?" An earlier version of this story was offered (on some level ironically) as a microcosm of British colonial rule—see Bernard's story of Percival and the "Oriental problem," page 98, and the introduction, pages lix–lx.

the general sequence when one thing follows another . . . the usual phrases begin to bubble up [137]   In invoking the "general sequence," to be described by "the usual phrases," Bernard seems to name a level of experience that Woolf in "A Sketch of the Past" described as "non-being," a semiconscious "cotton wool" of everyday, habitual living (70, 71).

I see far out a waste of water. A fin turns. [137]   See introduction page xlix.

wreaths of white flowers . . . and sit by the beds of dying women [139]   In these respects, as in others, Susan resembles Virginia Woolf's mother, Julia Stephen, who volunteered to nurse the dying.

Piccadilly South Side, Piccadilly North Side, Regent Street and the Haymarket [140]   Beer observes that the same sign still stands in the central hall of the Piccadilly Underground station.

Cleopatra, burning on her barge. Here are figures of the damned too [143]
Neville sees members of the London crowd as recurring human
types—as did Eliot in *The Waste Land,* when he took the speech
of Enobarbus in Shakespeare's *Antony and Cleopatra* alluded to
here (act 2, scene 2, lines 198–99) for the opening of the "Game
of Chess" section: "The Chair she sat in, like a burnished
throne" (line 77). Neville's "figures of the damned" seem to be
from Dante's *Inferno,* which Virginia Woolf was reading nightly
in 1930, while writing *The Waves.*

some fasting and anguished spirit [144]   Neville compares Rhoda and
Louis to religious ascetics who torture themselves in pursuit of
revelation. Farther down the page he describes Rhoda "with her
neck outstretched and blind fanatic eyes."

O western wind [146–49]   An anonymous medieval lyric, ca. 1500.
Beer notes that it was the first poem in a 1924 collection, *The
Week-End Book,* and that Woolf followed the punctuation of this
anthology, although she modernized the spellings. "O western
wind" is also the first example of lyric poetry in "How Should
One Read a Book?" where it elicits the comment, "The impact
of poetry is so hard and direct that for the moment there is no
other sensation except that of the poem itself" (*The Second Common Reader* 1932 [San Diego: Harcourt, 1986], 265).

I shall see Africa [149]   Rhoda is in the south of Spain, climbing a
hill that will allow her to see over the Mediterranean. In the
pages that follow, she anticipates her eventual death, although
this section ends with her going to an inn for the night.

obelisks [152]   Tapering pillars set up as landmarks or monuments.

Hampton Court [154]   See the note to page 114.

I have seen life in blocks, substantial, huge [158]   Susan's monumental
imagery here echoes Rhoda's dirge for Percival, page 118.

scrannel [162]   Lean, thin, meager. Milton's "Lycidas" (1637) describes the shepherds' "scrannel pipes of wretched straw," adding a connotation of harsh, unmelodious sound.

earth is only a pebble flicked off accidentally from the face of the sun [165] Haule and Smith note that in her diary entry for December 18, 1930, a period when she was trying to arrive at a final shape for *The Waves,* Woolf mentioned a gathering where people engaged in "talk about the riddle of the universe (Jeans' book) whether it will be known; not by us. . . ." And then in midsentence she suddenly announces, "found out suddenly about rhythm in prose" (*Diary* 3: 337). The book referred to is the physicist Sir James Jeans's *The Mysterious Universe* (1930), a study that begins, "We believe . . . that some two thousand million years ago this rare event took place, and that a second star, wandering blindly through space, happened to come within hailing distance of the sun . . . threw off small fragments of itself, much as the crest of a wave throws off spray. These small fragments have been circulating around their parent sun ever since. They are the planets . . ." (Jeans 1–2). The idea of solar "waves" throwing up tiny fragments and thus producing the earth added another dimension of human insignificance to the structural metaphor of Woolf's novel in process.

'Fight,' I cry, 'fight!' [166]   In her diary entry for October 11, 1929, Woolf wrote, "And no one knows how I suffer, walking up this street, engaged with my anguish, as I was after Thoby died— alone; fighting something alone. . . . On the whole, I do not much mind; because what I like is to flash and dash from side to side, goaded on by what I call reality. If I never felt these extraordinarily pervasive strains—of unrest or rest or happiness or discomfort—I should float down into acquiescence. Here is something to fight; and when I wake early I say to myself Fight, fight" (*Diary* 3: 260).

("Yet, Louis," said Rhoda, "how short a time silence lasts. . . .") [166]   This whole passage within parentheses, of Rhoda's and Louis's alternating addresses, functions as dialogue rather than monologue or soliloquy, in that Rhoda addresses Louis and Louis appears to respond. The communication highlights the sense in which they are, as they claim, "conspirators," etymologically those who breathe together. Hampton Court was also the site of a conspiracy against King Charles I in 1647.

a King, riding, fell over a molehill here [166]   William III of Orange suffered this accident in 1702 and died of the injuries three days later. In Woolf's second draft of *The Waves,* Percival, too, dies when "his horse stumbled over a molehill" (*Two Holograph Drafts* 560 and 617).

how can we do battle against this flood; what has permanence? [167]   One of the central questions of this novel, and one of the ways in which the oceanic imagery is most effective. In the midst of writing *The Waves,* Woolf asked in a diary entry, "Now is life very solid or very shifting? I am haunted by the two contradictions. This has gone on for ever; will last for ever; goes down to the bottom of the world—this moment I stand on. Also it is transitory, flying, diaphanous. I shall pass like a cloud on the waves" (January 4, 1929, *Diary* 3: 218).

battle of Blenheim [167]   Fought August 13, 1704, this battle, resulting in the defeat of Louis XIV, arguably did change "the fate of Europe," curtailing French imperialism and giving the British their first major victory on the Continent in almost three hundred years.

King George [167]   George V, who reigned from 1910 to 1936. In the 1924 essay "Character in Fiction," Woolf called writers of her own generation "Georgians," another indication that the six speakers of *The Waves* are contemporaries of the Bloomsbury Group.

The iron gates have rolled back [167]   Andrew Marvell, "To His Coy Mistress" (1681), lines 43–44: "And tear our pleasures with rough strife / Through the iron gates of life." Beer also locates iron gates in Dante's *Inferno.*

Wren's palace [168]   The original Tudor palace of Hampton Court was built for Henry VIII, but William of Orange commissioned the famous architect Sir Christopher Wren (1632–1723) to convert it to the Baroque style, using red brick with white stone accents and Portland stone embellishments. The improvements began in 1689 and were completed in 1700. At the same time, George Landon and Henry Wise designed and planted elaborate gardens, including a famous hedge maze.

like the quartet . . . makes an oblong [168]   Rhoda seems to allude here to the concert she attended after hearing of Percival's death (118), but she heard a vocal performance, not a string quartet. Woolf herself conceived the form of the final chapter, however, "while listening to a Beethoven quartet" (*Diary* 3: 339). Like the published version, the second draft of the novel has a female singer, but she is specifically singing "mocking" music by Mozart. In the published version, the female singer, "swollen but contained in slippery satin," delivers a wordless "Ah!" prompting Rhoda's meditation on (nonlinguistic, nonrepresentational) squares and oblongs.

a six-sided flower [168]   At the farewell dinner for Percival, the assembled friends contributed to "a seven-sided flower, manypetalled" (91–92).

by this stone urn [168]   See the note to page 102. Rhoda and Louis stand together as the others go off in heterosexual pairs, to "embrace among the ferns" or sing "love, love, love by the lake" (170).

drumming on the roofs of a fasting city ... [169]   The sounds that Rhoda
reports hearing here are similar in geographical scope to the images in the three of the interludes (53, 79, 107). Like Louis, however, Rhoda perceives an event that is historically as well as
geographically distant, the siege of Byzantine Constantinople by
the Ottoman Turks in 1453. The fall of Constantinople marked
the end of the Roman Empire.

sum up [176]   In this section, Bernard takes over the role of narrator, imposing coherence by providing a single point of view for
the retelling of the lives of his friends and himself.

we can talk freely [176]   Bernard speaks to an unidentified man
whom he met on a voyage. Woolf had originally imagined the
last section as a "gigantic conversation" (*Diary* 3: 285).

In the beginning, there was the nursery [177]   John 1:1 (King James
Version): "In the beginning was the Word, and the Word
was with God, and the Word was God." Just as the Gospel
of John tells a new version of the tale of origins found in
Genesis (see the note to page 3), Bernard provides a slightly
different account of origins in his retelling of the story of *The
Waves*.

Stonehenge [178]   Forty-five-hundred-year-old circle of immense
standing stones, some with lintels—stone crosspieces bridging
two stones—on Salisbury Plain in Wiltshire.

the boot-boy ... the tweeny [178]   Lower-rank servants in a Victorian
household. A boot-boy cleans boots; a tweeny is a "between-
maid" who serves other servants.

Shaftesbury Avenue [180]   Major London thoroughfare and home
of many theaters, running from New Oxford Street on the edge
of Bloomsbury to Piccadilly Circus.

chilblains [180]   Painful or itchy swelling of the skin caused by exposure to cold and poor circulation.

nothing broke with its fin that leaden waste of waters [181]   See introduction page xlix.

An army marches across Europe. [182]   A reference to the massive recruitments of World War I, when men as "undifferentiated blobs of matter" were destroyed en masse. Woolf presented a grim satire of this perception in *Jacob's Room,* pages 166–67.

bagman [182]   Traveling salesman.

some witless servant could be heard laughing at the top of the house [183]   In a scene in Charlotte Brontë's *Jane Eyre,* which Woolf discusses in *A Room of One's Own* (annotated by Gubar 68), Jane's meditation on the limits placed on her because she is a woman is interrupted by "Grace Poole's laugh" from the attic—in reality, the laugh of Mr. Rochester's imprisoned, mad wife, Bertha.

Dostoevsky [184]   Woolf greatly admired the Russian novelist Fyodor Mikhaylovich Dostoyevsky (1821–1881) and even learned enough Russian with her Russian friend S. S. Koteliansky to be co-translator of two chapters left out of the English translation of *The Possessed.* See *Stavrogin's Confession* and *The Plan of the Life of a Great Sinner* (Richmond, UK: Hogarth Press, 1922). In 1912, in the middle of reading *Crime and Punishment,* she wrote to Lytton Strachey, "It is directly obvious that he [Dostoyevsky] is the greatest writer ever born" (*Letters* 2: 5). In a 1925 essay "The Russian Point of View," she describes some of Dostoyevsky's techniques in constructing a novel that may have helped her conceive the method of *The Waves*: "But where are we? Surely it is the part of a novelist to inform us whether we are in an hotel, a flat, or hired lodging. Nobody thinks of explaining. We are souls, tortured, unhappy souls, whose only business it is to talk, to reveal, to confess, to draw up at whatever rending of flesh and nerve those crabbed sins which crawl on the sand at the bottom of us. But, as we listen, our confusion slowly settles. A rope is flung to us; we catch hold of a soliloquy; holding on by the skin of our teeth, we are rushed through the water; feverishly, wildly, we rush on and on, now submerged, now in a moment of vision understanding more than we have ever understood before, and receiving such revelations as we are wont to get only from the press of life at its fullest" (*Essays* 4: 186).

Then there is the being eviscerated . . . twisted in agony round a thorn [185] Woolf used a version of this violent image presenting the humiliation and pain of rejection in *Mrs. Dalloway*, when Elizabeth Dalloway leaves Miss Kilman, "and went off, drawing out, so Miss Kilman felt, the very entrails in her body, stretching them as she crossed the room, and then, with a final twist, bowing her head very politely, she went" (annotated by Scott 129).

Hampstead [185]   Hampstead Heath, a large open park in northern London.

punt [186]   A long, narrow, flat-bottomed boat propelled with a pole.

where no bird sang. The leaves shrivelled [186]   Keats's 1820 poem "La Belle Dame Sans Merci" opens:

> O what can ail thee, knight-at-arms,
> Alone and palely loitering?
> The sedge has wither'd from the lake,
> And no birds sing.

mackintosh square [187]   Square piece of a waterproof cloth made by gluing two layers of fabric together with India rubber.

He fascinated me with his sordid imagination. [187]   Woolf was intimately acquainted with T. S. Eliot's sordid imagination in poems like "Rhapsody on a Windy Night" and "Sweeney Erect."

falling from a shot tower hit the water and up it spurted [187]   A shot tower is a high, round tower from which molten lead is dropped into cold water, making small shot for shotguns.

What is to be done about India, Ireland or Morocco? [188]   Potential international trouble spots during the period in which *The Waves* was written.

A shell forms . . . tap their beaks in vain [189]   Bernard's "summing up" begins to assimilate images from the third-person-narrated interludes, for example, see pages 52–53 and 78.

a rushing stream . . . sentences and sights— [189]   In "Letter to a Young Poet" (1932), this undercurrent is "at the floor of your mind." Woolf calls this "instinct of rhythm" "the most profound and primitive of instincts" (221).

'Hark, hark, the dogs do bark' . . . and so on [192]   A whole collection of singable lyrics from the history of Western poetry, beginning with an old nursery rhyme of uncertain origin:

> Hark! Hark! The dogs do bark,
> The beggars are coming to town.
> Some in rags,
> And some in tags,
> And some in velvet gowns.

The dirge "Come away, come away, death," is sung by the clown Feste in Shakespeare's *Twelfth Night,* act 2, scene 4, and begins,

> Come away, come away death,
> And in sad cypress let me be laid.
> Fly away, fly away breath,
> I am slain by a fair cruel maid.

"Let me not to the marriage of true minds" is one of Shakespeare's most famous sonnets, Number 116.

ducks and drakes [192]   A game of skipping flat stones across water.

'the lily of the day is fairer far in May' [196]   This famous line (slightly misquoted), regarded by Jinny and Bernard as inadequate to Percival, comes from Ben Jonson's 1640 "Ode to the Immortal Memory and Friendship of that noble pair, Sir Lucius Cary and Sir H. Morison." This first stanza was widely anthologized as "The Noble Nature":

> It is not growing like a tree
> In bulk, doth make man better be;
> Or standing long an oak, three hundred year,
> To fall a log at last, dry, bald, and sere:
>   A lily of a day
>   Is fairer far in May,
> Although it fall and die that night;
> It was the plant and flower of Light.
> In small proportions we just beauties see;
> And in short measures, life may perfect be.

and love and hate the heat of the sun [197]   Bernard combines Susan's Catullan motif "Odi et amo" (see the note to page 9) with the song from Shakespeare's *Cymbeline* that echoes through Woolf's *Mrs. Dalloway*:

> Fear no more the heat o' th' sun,
> Nor the furious winter's rages.
> Thou thy worldly task hast done,
> Home art gone and ta'en thy wages.
> Golden lads and girls all must,
> As chimney-sweepers, come to dust. (*Cymbeline,* act 4, scene 2)

But if there are no stories . . . when we try to tell it [198]   One of Woolf's own central concerns, which led to her giving radically different treatments to "life" in her own fiction—especially *The Waves*. In the 1919 essay "Modern Novels," she called life "the semi-transparent envelope, or luminous halo, surrounding us from the beginning of consciousness to the end," and suggested that conventional modes of constructing stories could not "convey this incessantly varying spirit with whatever stress or sudden deviation it may display" (*Essays* 3: 33).

our waters can only just . . . we pound on the shore [198]   Identifying human beings with behaviors and descriptions of waves, Bernard here uses more of the language of the italicized intervals.

'Fight.' 'Fight' . . . I netted them under with a sudden phrase. I retrieved them from formlessness with words. [200]   See the notes to pages 15 and 166. In "A Sketch of the Past," Woolf describes this rescue work in more violent terms. The threatening formlessness of reality intrudes as "these sudden shocks," but she comments, "After the first surprise, I always feel instantly that they are particularly valuable" because "a shock is at once in my case followed by a desire to explain it. . . . it is or will become a revelation of some order; it is a token of some real thing behind appearances; and I make it real by putting it into words" (*Moments of Being* 72).

'Away!' she said. 'The moor is dark . . .' [204]   From Shelley's "Stanzas—1814," later anthologized as "Remorse." The first stanza is:

Away! the moor is dark beneath the moon,
Rapid clouds have drunk the last pale beam of even:
Away! the gathering winds will call the darkness soon,
And profoundest midnight shroud the serene lights of heaven.
Pause not! the time is past! Every voice cries, 'Away!'
Tempt not with one last tear thy friend's ungentle mood:
Thy lover's eye, so glazed and cold, dares not entreat thy stay:
Duty and dereliction guide thee back to solitude.

Fleet Street [207]   Another major London thoroughfare, running from the Strand to Ludgate Circus and linking the City to the Borough of Westminster, it was traditionally an area of newspapers and journalists.

scrolloping [209]   Woolf seems to have coined this word, which she uses to suggest a kind of clumsy, absurd ostentatiousness, either in people—as in "she detests the scrolloping honours of the great" (*Diary* 1: 232)—or, as here, in ornamentation. The *Oxford English Dictionary* suggests the word is a combination of *scroll* and *lollop*.

Baedekers [209]   Famous series of travel guidebooks published by the German firm founded by Karl Baedeker (1801–1859).

Pillicock sat on Pillicock's hill, or Hark, hark, the dogs do bark, or The World's great age begins anew, or Come away, come away, death [209–10] "Pillicock sat on Pillicock Hill" is chanted by Edgar, pretending to be a madman, in Shakespeare's *King Lear,* act 3, scene 4. For "Hark, hark" and "Come away," see the note to page 192. "The world's great age begins anew" is the first line of a chorus from act 2 of Shelley's 1822 "lyrical drama" *Hellas.* Beer observes that all these quotations "have to do with the overturning of established order and the fleetingness of life and death" (260).

It was like the eclipse [211]   With Leonard and other friends and family members, Woolf witnessed a total eclipse of the sun—the first in England in more than two hundred years—on June 30, 1927. Her diary entry describes the train journey to North Yorkshire, the drive to a high hill overlooking Richmond, and the abruptness of the event: "Suddenly the light went out. We had fallen. It was extinct. There was no colour. The earth was dead" (*Diary* 3: 143). Bernard's metaphoric eclipse, his experience as "a man without a self" draws directly from this description. On page 212, he begins to recover, asking, "How then does light return to the world after the eclipse of the sun?" and his description again is close to Woolf's diary entry: "As if a ball had rebounded, the cloud took colour on itself again, only a sparky aetherial colour & so the light came back. I had very strongly the feeling as the light . . . went out of some vast obeisance; something kneeling down, & low & suddenly raised up, when the colours came" (*Diary* 3: 143).

old nurse who turns the pages of the picture-book [213]   Mrs. Constable (the children's caregiver) becomes an allegorical figure who in Bernard's story shows Bernard "the truth" as a vision of woods, house, garden, and waves like the scene described especially in the first four italicized passages.

So now . . . I could go like a spy without leaving this place [216]   Bernard's meditation on mortality alludes to Shakespeare's *King Lear,* act 5, scene 3. After the broken king and his daughter Cordelia have been captured, Lear spins out a consolatory fantasy of the lives they will live out together in prison: they will "sing like birds i'th' cage" and

> . . . hear poor rogues
> Talk of court news, and we'll talk with them too —
> Who loses and who wins, who's in, who's out;
> And take upon 's the mystery of things
> As if we were God's spies; and we'll wear out
> In a walled prison packs and sects of great ones
> That ebb and flow by th' moon.

This moving passage is bitterly ironic in context because it occurs just before Cordelia is hanged.

Day rises; the girl lifts the watery fire-hearted jewels to her brow; the sun levels his beams straight at the sleeping house [216]   Another description from the interludes; see page 52.

I, I, I, tired as I am [219]   See the note to page 121.

Against you I will fling myself, unvanquished and unyielding, O Death! [220]
Woolf described writing this ending "having reeled across the
last ten pages with some moments of such intensity and intoxication that I seemed only to stumble after my own voice," and
added, "I have been sitting these 15 minutes in a state of glory,
and calm, and some tears, thinking of Thoby and if I could write
Julian Thoby Stephen 1881–1906 on the first page. I suppose
not" (*Diary* 4: 10). For the connection of Percival with Woolf's
dead older brother, Thoby, see the introduction, pages lvii–lviii.
The tone of the conclusion is ambivalent, however. Woolf's ear-
liest conception of this ending involved merging "all the inter-
jected passages into Bernard's final speech" and concluding
"with the words O solitude," rather than "O Death." She described how this device would work structurally and themati-
cally: "thus making him absorb all the scenes and having no
further break. This is also to show that the theme effort, effort
dominates; not the waves: and personality: and defiance" (*Diary*
3: 339). In having Bernard address Death rather than Solitude,
however, and in giving the waves the last word, she made more
ambiguous the question of whether effort dominates or whether
the waves—which she described earlier as "insensitive nature"
(*Diary* 3: 285)—necessarily triumph over mortal human en-
deavor. There is also an allusion here to the story of the British/
Viking king Canute, or Knud (991–1035), who tested the limits
of his authority by commanding the waves to stop coming in.
His feet got wet. And in Samuel Johnson's 1749 poem "The Vanity of Human Wishes," which Eliot edited and sent to the Woolfs
in 1930 (*Diary* 3: 324), the Persian leader Xerxes is offered as an
example of a tyrant who overreached his powers, demonstrating
his madness by trying to fight the waves: "Fresh Praise is try'd
till Madness fires his Mind, / The Waves he lashes, and enchains
the Wind" (lines 231–32).

Suggestions for Further Reading:
Virginia Woolf

Editions

The Complete Shorter Fiction. Edited by Susan Dick. 2nd ed. San Diego: Harcourt, 1989.

The Diary of Virginia Woolf. Edited by Anne Olivier Bell. 5 vols. New York: Harcourt, 1977–84.

The Essays of Virginia Woolf. Edited by Andrew McNeillie. 6 vols. [in progress]. San Diego: Harcourt Brace Jovanovich, 1986–.

The Letters of Virginia Woolf. Edited by Nigel Nicolson and Joanne Trautmann. 6 vols. New York: Harcourt Brace Jovanovich, 1975–80.

Moments of Being. Edited by Jeanne Schulkind. San Diego: Harcourt, 1985.

A Passionate Apprentice: The Early Journals, 1897–1909. Edited by Mitchell A. Leaska. San Diego: Harcourt, 1990.

Biographies and Reference Works

Briggs, Julia. *Virginia Woolf: An Inner Life*. San Diego: Harcourt, 2005.

Hussey, Mark. *Virginia Woolf A to Z: A Comprehensive Reference for Students, Teachers, and Common Readers to Her Life, Works, and Critical Reception*. New York: Facts on File, 1995.

Kirkpatrick, B. J., and Stuart N. Clarke. *A Bibliography of Virginia Woolf*. 4th ed. Oxford: Clarendon, 1997.

Lee, Hermione. *Virginia Woolf*. New York: Knopf, 1996.

Marder, Herbert. *The Measure of Life: Virginia Woolf's Last Years.* Ithaca, NY: Cornell University Press, 2000.

Poole, Roger. *The Unknown Virginia Woolf.* 4th ed. Cambridge: Cambridge University Press, 1995.

Reid, Panthea. *Art and Affection: A Life of Virginia Woolf.* New York: Oxford University Press, 1996.

General Criticism

Abel, Elizabeth. *Virginia Woolf and the Fictions of Psychoanalysis.* Chicago: University of Chicago Press, 1989.

Bazin, Nancy Topping. *Virginia Woolf and the Androgynous Vision.* New Brunswick, NJ: Rutgers University Press, 1973.

Beer, Gillian. *Virginia Woolf: The Common Ground.* Ann Arbor: University of Michigan Press, 1996.

Cuddy-Keane, Melba. *Virginia Woolf, the Intellectual, and the Public Sphere.* Cambridge: Cambridge University Press, 2003.

DiBattista, Maria. *Virginia Woolf's Major Novels: The Fables of Anon.* New Haven, CT: Yale University Press, 1980.

Fleishman, Avrom. *Virginia Woolf: A Critical Reading.* Baltimore: Johns Hopkins University Press, 1975.

Froula, Christine. *Virginia Woolf and the Bloomsbury Avant-Garde: War, Civilization, Modernity.* New York: Columbia University Press, 2005.

Guiguet, Jean. *Virginia Woolf and Her Works.* New York: Harcourt Brace Jovanovich, 1965.

Harper, Howard. *Between Language and Silence: The Novels of Virginia Woolf.* Baton Rouge: Louisiana State University Press, 1982.

Hussey, Mark. *The Singing of the Real World: The Philosophy of Virginia Woolf's Fiction.* Columbus: Ohio State University Press, 1986.

————, ed. *Virginia Woolf and War: Fiction, Reality and Myth.* Syracuse, NY: Syracuse University Press, 1991.

Majumdar, Robin, and Allen McLaurin, eds. *Virginia Woolf: The Critical Heritage.* Boston: Routledge, 1975.

Marcus, Jane. *Art and Anger: Reading Like a Woman.* Columbus: Ohio State University Press, 1988.

———, ed. *New Feminist Essays on Virginia Woolf.* Lincoln: University of Nebraska Press, 1981.

———, ed. *Virginia Woolf: A Feminist Slant.* Lincoln: University of Nebraska Press, 1983.

———, ed. *Virginia Woolf and Bloomsbury: A Centenary Celebration.* Bloomington: Indiana University Press, 1987.

———. *Virginia Woolf and the Languages of Patriarchy.* Bloomington: Indiana University Press, 1987.

McLaurin, Allen. *Virginia Woolf: The Echoes Enslaved.* Cambridge: Cambridge University Press, 1973.

McNees, Eleanor, ed. *Virginia Woolf: Critical Assessments.* 4 vols. New York: Routledge, 1994.

Minow-Pinkney, Makiko. *Virginia Woolf and the Problem of the Subject: Feminine Writing in the Major Novels.* New Brunswick, NJ: Rutgers University Press, 1987.

Phillips, Kathy J. *Virginia Woolf Against Empire.* Knoxville: University of Tennessee Press, 1994.

Roe, Sue, and Susan Sellers, eds. *The Cambridge Companion to Virginia Woolf.* Cambridge: Cambridge University Press, 2000.

Ruotolo, Lucio. *The Interrupted Moment: A View of Virginia Woolf's Novels.* Stanford, CA: Stanford University Press, 1986.

Silver, Brenda R. *Virginia Woolf Icon.* Chicago: University of Chicago Press, 1999.

Zwerdling, Alex. *Virginia Woolf and the Real World.* Berkeley: University of California Press, 1986.

Suggestions for Further Reading:
The Waves
(in addition to the works cited in the introduction)

Beer, Gillian. "The Body of the People in Virginia Woolf." In *Women Reading Women's Writing*. Edited by Sue Roe, 85–114. New York: St. Martin's, 1987.

Caramagno, Thomas C. "'I do not know altogether who I am': The Plurality of Intrasubjective Life in *The Waves*." In *The Flight of the Mind: Virginia Woolf's Art and Manic-Depressive Illness*, 270–95. Berkeley: University of California Press, 1992.

DiBattista, Maria. "*The Waves*: The Epic of 'Anon.'" In *Virginia Woolf's Major Novels: The Fables of Anon*, 146–89. New Haven, CT: Yale University Press, 1980.

Dick, Susan. "I Remembered, I Forgotten: Bernard's Final Soliloquy in *The Waves*." *Modern Language Studies* 13.3 (1983): 38–52.

Froula, Christine. "Another Nature: Abstract Form, Modern Physics, and the Garden of *The Waves*." In *Virginia Woolf and the Bloomsbury Avant-Garde: War, Civilization, Modernity*, 198–210. New York: Columbia University Press, 2005.

Katz, Tamar. "Modernism, Subjectivity, and Narrative Form: Abstraction in *The Waves*." *Narrative* 3.3 (1995): 232–51.

Lanser, Susan Sniader. "Fictions of Absence: Feminism, Modernism, Virginia Woolf." In *Fictions of Authority: Women Writers and Narrative Voice*, 102–19. Ithaca, NY: Cornell University Press, 1992.

Lee, Judith. "'This hideous shaping and moulding': War and *The Waves*." In *Virginia Woolf and War: Fiction, Reality, and Myth*. Edited by Mark Hussey, 180–202. Syracuse, NY: Syracuse University Press, 1991.

Levin, Gerald. "The Musical Style of *The Waves*." *Journal of Narrative Technique* 13.3 (1983): 164–71.

Marcus, Laura. "Writing Lives: *Orlando* and *The Waves*." In *Virginia Woolf*, 114–35. Plymouth, UK: Northcote House Publishers, 1997.

Medd, Jodie. "Re-Inverting Stephen Gordon: Rhoda Talks Back to Radclyffe Hall." In *Virginia Woolf and Her Influences: Selected Papers from the Seventh Annual Conference on Virginia Woolf*. Edited by Laura Davis, Jeanette McVicker, and Jeanne Dubino, 117–24. New York: Pace University Press, 1998.

Monson, Tamlyn. "A Trick of the Mind": Alterity, Ontology, and Representation in Virginia Woolf's *The Waves*." *Modern Fiction Studies* 50.1 (Spring 2004): 173–97.

Oxindine, Annette. "Rhoda Submerged: Lesbian Suicide in *The Waves*." In *Virginia Woolf: Lesbian Readings*. Edited by Eileen Barrett and Patricia Cramer, 203–21. New York: New York University Press, 1997.

Ruotolo, Lucio. "In Praise of Nothingness: *The Waves*." In *The Interrupted Moment: A View of Virginia Woolf's Novels*, 142–71. Stanford, CA: Stanford University Press, 1986.

Stewart, Jack F. "Spatial Form and Color in *The Waves*." *Twentieth Century Literature* 28.1 (Spring 1982): 86–107.

Virginia Woolf Annotated Editions

Top Woolf scholars provide valuable introductions, notes, suggestions for further reading, and critical analysis in this paperback series. Students reading these books will have the resources at hand to help them understand the text as well as the reasons and methods behind Woolf's writing.

Between the Acts
Annotated and with an introduction by Melba Cuddy-Keane
978-0-15-603473-9 • 0-15-603473-5

Jacob's Room
Annotated and with an introduction by Vara Neverow
978-0-15-603479-1 • 0-15-603479-4

Mrs. Dalloway
Annotated and with an introduction by Bonnie Kime Scott
978-0-15-603035-9 • 0-15-603035-7

Orlando: A Biography
Annotated and with an introduction by Maria DiBattista
978-0-15-603151-6 • 0-15-603151-5

A Room of One's Own
Annotated and with an introduction by Susan Gubar
978-0-15-603041-0 • 0-15-603041-1

Three Guineas
Annotated and with an introduction by Jane Marcus
978-0-15-603163-9 • 0-15-603163-9

To the Lighthouse
Annotated and with an introduction by Mark Hussey
978-0-15-603047-2 • 0-15-603047-0

The Waves
Annotated and with an introduction by Molly Hite
978-0-15-603157-8 • 0-15-603157-4

The Years
Annotated and with an introduction by Eleanor McNees
978-0-15-603485-2 • 0-15-603485-9

Each volume includes a preface by Mark Hussey, professor of English and women's and gender studies at Pace University, and editor of *Woolf Studies Annual*.

Harcourt | HARVEST BOOKS
www.HarcourtBooks.com